URRVENSKEYR MOUNTAIN

LAKE SKYLLIVRENG

ELDR

ISLAND OF ICHIL

SEA OF ICE

SILBER RIVER

VALLÉ DE LUMÉ

THE CHRYSÓS SEA

SÚNDRAILLE

LLORENYAE

D1053195

THE
BLOOD
SPELL

A Ravenspire Novel

C. J. REDWINE

Balzer + Bray
An *Imprint of* HarperCollins*Publishers*

Balzer + Bray is an imprint of HarperCollins Publishers.

The Blood Spell
Copyright © 2019 by C. J. Redwine
All rights reserved. Printed in the United States of America.
No part of this book may be used or reproduced in any manner whatsoever without
written permission except in the case of brief quotations embodied in critical articles
and reviews. For information address HarperCollins Children's Books, a division of
HarperCollins Publishers, 195 Broadway, New York, NY 10007.
www.epicreads.com

Library of Congress Control Number: 2018939831
ISBN 978-0-06-265301-7

Typography by Sarah Nichole Kaufman
19 20 21 22 23   PC/LSCH   10 9 8 7 6 5 4 3 2 1

First Edition

For Johanna and Isabella. May you always have the courage to be yourselves,
and may you know in the depths of your hearts that you are loved.

ONCE UPON A TIME . . .

THE WRAITH CREPT through the darkness of its forest prison, hunger gnawing at its bones. It was skeletal now, brushing against the thorn ferns and moss-covered tree bark with bony fingers that rattled in the breeze.

Once, its strength had been unrivaled. Its magic unmatched.

Until its sister had joined forces with others against it.

Now the wraith haunted the vast, damp darkness of its cage, a shadow bound by a spell it couldn't break no matter how hard it tried. The thought of vengeance was the meat and marrow of its dreams. It was the strength that bound its bones together and the breath that filled its lungs. Some days, memories of the ones who had trapped it blazed to life, leaving behind the scorched bitterness of shackled rage. But most days, it could feel only *hunger*.

As the gray-black light within the forest sank into the total darkness of yet another night, the wraith stalked the edges of the vast prison, hurling itself against the invisible spell that bound it here, feeling the magic spark, blister, and burn.

One day, it would break free. It would rush over the hills and move through the long stretches of farmland that stood between it and the city. It would find its sister and those who had helped her hunt it down, and it would destroy them all.

And then it would feed and feed and feed, and there would be no one left to stop it.

Hunger stabbed. The wraith dug its fingers into the closest tree trunk, gathered its magic, and shrieked, a long, razor-tipped wail that shivered through the air, sending birds screaming for the skies as the sound winged its way across the distance between the wraith and the city that sheltered its enemies.

The iron bells that hung along the road to warn people when a fae monster was near clanged wildly. The wraith lifted its face as their discordant, chaotic melody reached its ears, and smiled.

ONE

MORNINGS WERE A curse.

Bernadina "Blue" de la Cour yawned and blinked at the golden sunlight that bathed the streets of Falaise de la Mer, the capital city of Balavata. People bustled along the wide main roads that cut through the large city like swaths of ribbon, hurrying toward the open-air market that was held once a week in the heart of town. Others moved along the warren of side streets that curled away from the main roads and burrowed through each of the city's nine quarters.

Everyone seemed cheerful. Or if not cheerful, at least fully awake.

Blue didn't know what it took to wake at dawn and be cheerful about it, but whatever it was, she didn't have it.

"Isn't this a beautiful morning?" Papa asked as they moved through the iron arches that marked the entrance to the Gaillard quarter and headed for their alchemy shop. The arches were meant to weaken anyone with fae magic in their blood, but they'd never affected Blue. Maybe it was because the magic in her blood was harmless. Or maybe it was because the royal council was wrong about iron arches doing a single thing to protect the people from the kind of fae magic that *wasn't* harmless.

Blue shrugged away her thoughts and took a sip of the hot spiced chicory Papa had made for her before they'd left their farmhouse on the outskirts of the city. The drink tasted of bitter chicory root, sweet cream, and nutmeg, and it almost made up for the fact that the sea fog was still clinging to the edges of the city.

Nothing good came from getting out of bed before the sun had chased the fog away. Actually, nothing good came from getting out of bed before the noonday meal, but in seventeen years of trying, Blue had yet to convince Papa of that.

Papa slung an arm around her shoulder and laid his cheek against the pink headscarf Blue had hastily wrapped around her short black curls. "Almost awake?" he asked, laughter sparkling in his voice.

She grunted and took another sip as they reached the corner where he would turn left to open up the shop and she would turn right to join those moving toward the large square where the market was held.

"It's only one day a week that you have to get up at dawn," Papa said, his smile a wide slash of white against his light brown skin. "Need any help at the market today?"

Blue yawned again. "I'll be fine. Ana is meeting me there to help carry my purchases to the shop." She hefted the burlap sacks she'd tossed over her shoulder before leaving the farmhouse, though she knew as well as Papa that she'd carry most of them herself. Hiring little ten-year-old Ana, one of Falaise de la

Mer's many homeless, as a delivery girl had been more a decision of the heart than of practicality.

Papa nodded and reached for her nearly empty cup, the smile disappearing from his face. "Be careful. Don't let anyone catch you using your magic to check the goods before you buy them. Remember—"

"No one will believe I'm harmless, no matter what I say. I know." She finished his oft-repeated warning for him and leaned up to plant a kiss on his cheek. His skin was thinner now, sagging at the edges as strands of silvery gray worked their way into his close-cut black hair. There were laugh lines fanning out from his brown eyes, and sometimes when he thought she wasn't watching, he leaned heavily against the shop's counter at the end of the day as if being on his feet for hours on end was wearing on him.

He returned her kiss and then studied her face with a smile. "You remind me of your mother. She was always the most intriguing woman in any room. And she didn't like to take my warnings about her magic seriously either."

"I'll be careful. I promise."

She couldn't find herself in his face—she had her mother's dark brown skin and eyes, Grand-mère's pointed chin and sharp cheekbones, and the tiny stature of her mother's side of the family. In fact, the only proof Blue could find that she shared blood with her father, who was the son of a tall, dark-skinned man and a woman with the pale skin and smooth hair of her Morcantian ancestors, were the curls that lifted from Blue's scalp and framed her face.

But she didn't need to see herself in his face to feel every inch his daughter. They shared the same affection for the alchemy shop. The same passion for helping others. And the same love for a simple, uncomplicated life at their farmhouse, their garden, and the sea that bordered the cliff at the edge of their property.

Turning, Blue made her way toward the market. Falaise de la Mer was a busy port city that attracted people from Balavata and several of the surrounding kingdoms. But no matter how many moved into the city, the heart of Balavatan culture remained a celebration of food, artistry, and a fierce will to survive. Along the broad sides of buildings and homes, colorful pictures made from paint mixed with sand told the stories of Balavata—from the festivals to honor their folk heroes to the rise of the head families to the sea with its changing moods and constant bounty. The history of her kingdom surrounded Blue as she ducked through crowds, grumpily eyeing those who seemed wide awake and thrilled about it.

When she neared the eastern edge of the quarter, she cast a quick glance at the Gaillards' pale blue mansion. As one of the kingdom's nine head families, the Gaillards had coin to spare. Blue supposed they spent a fair amount of it on managing their quarter and the southern villages assigned to them—they answered to the queen for the safety, economy, and upkeep of their portion of the kingdom—but anyone who owned five carriages for a family of three could certainly afford to use some of their wealth to help the destitute who huddled in the city's back alleys, begging for food and taking jobs no one else wanted just to survive.

Blue had long since stopped hoping the head families would do right by those who needed them most. Instead, she'd taken matters into her own hands.

And today would be a test to see how close she was to succeeding.

Thrusting her hands into the inner pocket of her light summer cloak, she brushed her fingers against the cold chunks of pale yellow metal she'd created after staying late at the shop the night before. It had taken Blue far too long to realize that help for the children who slept in alleyways and foraged through trash in her quarter wasn't coming from the magistrate, the Gaillards, or even the queen. Once she'd accepted that if she wanted to solve the problem, she was going to have to do it herself, the answer had seemed obvious: she'd use her talent for alchemy to turn ordinary metal into gold.

Ten months later, after more failed experiments than Blue cared to count, she was close. Maybe even close enough to count it a success. She'd know soon enough, and once she could produce gold, she would buy a big home, hire tutors and provide fresh food, and gather up every child she could find so that they could finally do more than just survive.

She reached the northern edge of the quarter and followed a crowd through the gate that led to the market. The square was divided into twenty rows of stalls with small seating areas at the end of each for those who'd just purchased crisp gelleire fish or a platter of fried apple cakes, a Balavatan staple. The center of the square was dominated by a large raised stage, surrounded by benches. Some days traveling theatrical troupes put on shows or brokers auctioned off exotic creatures procured from far-off kingdoms. Other days, magistrates from each quarter brought a prisoner or two up on stage for public punishment, depending on their crime.

Blue looked toward the stage and winced as she entered the field. Nine flags—each with the crest of one of Balavata's head families—hung from the scaffolding. It was a magistrate day.

Last time, she'd accidentally seen a woman get whipped for the crime of stealing silver dishes from her employer. She'd rather not see anything like that again.

Turning away, Blue hurried down the ninth row of stalls toward one of her regular vendors, passing brightly patterned dresses with seashells embroidered along their hems, glittering beaded jewelry, freshly baked bread, and a stall featuring boots from the best cobbler in the city. There was another woman already talking with Maurice when Blue got to his stall, her voice rising as she debated something with the old merchant.

Ignoring them, Blue moved to the back of the stall to examine the crates of seeds, bark, roots, and dried berries that Maurice regularly procured from the fae isle of Llorenyae.

Casting a quick look over her shoulder to be sure no one was watching, Blue let her hands rest on a crate of yaeringlei seeds, feeling the gentle rush of the small magic she'd inherited from her mother tingle across her palms, seeking a connection with any natural thing—plant, animal, or mineral.

If they'd been harvested correctly, the large, pebble-size seeds would leap toward her magic, eager to be used. If the fruit that encased them had been forced from their bushes before they were ripe, the seeds would lie dormant, refusing her advances.

The crate's wood was rough, and bits of it curled toward Blue's hands as if eager to be used in her potions. She shot another look at Maurice and his customer, but they were engrossed in their discussion.

The seeds within the crate leaped for her hands, tapping against their wooden home like bits of hail against a window. Maurice's gaze jerked toward her, a frown digging into the sagging skin between his eyes. Blue stepped away from the crate and shoved her hands into her cloak pockets, a chill racing over her skin as the woman turned to face her, pale skin flushed with anger at Maurice.

She'd seen this woman a few times at the market or when Blue and Papa spent time at the castle, and Blue had no interest in catching her attention now. Dinah Chauveau, head of the Chauveau family, had a reputation for ruthlessly running her quarter and for making life miserable for anyone who tried to cheat her.

She also had a reputation for zealously punishing anyone caught violating the law against magic.

Swallowing hard, Blue gave Maurice and Dinah a wobbly smile and hurried toward a selection of jewels resting inside a locked glass case. Her breath felt too thin, her blood too thick as she turned her back to them and prayed they hadn't seen anything that could get her in trouble.

"We can resume our discussion of your failure to meet the terms of our contract once you get her out of here." Dinah's voice was cold and precise.

"What can I get for you today, Blue?" Maurice asked from beside her elbow. His brown face was folded in on itself, like a grape shriveling beneath the harsh summer sun, and his hands shook a bit with age, but his eyes were as shrewd as ever.

"Pink sapphire!" Blue's words were too loud, too rushed, and she folded her arms over her chest to give her hands something to do as magic tingled across her palms, reaching for the jewels that Maurice was pulling out of the case.

"I don't have pink today, but here's a blue and a white, and both are just as lovely," he said.

Blue shook her head. "I need pink for the potion I'm working on."

"I can get my hands on one soon enough and have it delivered, no extra fee."

"That's fine." Blue turned toward the crates and began rattling off the list of other items she needed, an itch between her shoulder blades where Dinah's gaze rested. Blue hadn't had a chance to check the rest of the ingredients she wanted to buy, but there was no way she could risk it now.

Maurice quickly wrapped up her purchases and loaded them into her burlap sacks. "Where's that young girl you use for deliveries and such?"

Blue frowned as she reached inside her cloak for the metal she hoped would pass as gold. "I'm not sure." Ana should've been here by now. She was usually very prompt, and she knew Blue needed help on market day.

"If you can't carry all these yourself, I'll deliver the rest later for a small fee." Maurice's eyes brightened, and Blue laughed.

"I've experienced your small fees before, Maurice. I can carry it all or find a child to help me."

Schooling her face into a mask of composure, Blue pulled out the chunks of pale yellow metal she'd created the night before. It was almost gold. And maybe almost would be good enough. She didn't want to cheat Maurice. She just wanted to test her experiment. And if anyone in the market could instantly spot a fake, it would be Maurice.

His eyes narrowed as she handed him the chunks of almost-gold. "Pretty pale for gold." He held it up to a bar of sunlight slanting in through the roof and turned it this way and that.

Blue flinched as Dinah took a step closer, her gaze on the metal as well.

Maurice brought the metal up to his mouth and bit gently. His brow folded into a frown. "Soft like gold, but the color's a little off. Where did you get this?"

Her face heated. "The shop."

It was as much of the truth as she was willing to give them. If anyone realized what she was doing, she and Papa would no longer be safe. Blue would bet everything they owned that one of the less scrupulous brokers who managed the illegal gambling dens throughout the city would be at their door within an hour with a plan to force Blue into working for him. And if a broker didn't get to her first, somebody else would.

Everyone in the kingdom would want a piece of the girl who'd figured out how to use alchemy to turn ordinary metal into gold.

Maurice's voice was rough. "Somebody cheated you, Miss Blue. This is a good imitation, but it isn't gold. Do you remember who paid with it?"

She shook her head and hurriedly grabbed a handful of coin out of her other pocket. Laying the coin out on Maurice's table, she took the almost gold out of his hand and pocketed it again.

"That's useless, Miss Blue," he said. "Unless you want to turn it over to the magistrate so they can hunt for the person who gave it to you."

"Oh, no. That's fine! I mean, obviously it's not fine, but I'm sure I can use it in one of my potions or something." Her voice was too bright, but she couldn't seem to change it. Gathering her bags from Maurice, she slung them over her shoulder, staggering a bit under their weight, and then bid a hasty farewell to Maurice, nodding respectfully to Dinah on her way out.

Scanning the crowd around her once more, Blue hurried to the end of the row. Where was Ana? Had she forgotten it was market day? Or had another, more lucrative job come up?

A tiny whisper of fear poisoned Blue's thoughts as she stopped to examine the crowd again.

Children went missing in Falaise de la Mer. Everyone knew it, though no one could really explain it. It was always the children whose parents were in prison or who'd died working dangerous jobs for one of Balavata's brokers. Children no one would really miss.

But Ana wasn't a girl no one would miss. She had a regular job with Blue at the Mortar & Pestle. She had friends. And to the best of Blue's knowledge, no one had gone missing from the Gaillard quarter for years. Besides, Ana had failed to show up twice before, and both times she'd returned after a few days, apologizing for leaving Blue on her own and explaining that she'd been hired for a cleaning job by one of the wealthier families of the city, who paid Ana twice what Blue could.

A shout broke through Blue's thoughts, and the crowd around her surged toward the stage, carrying her with it.

"The laws of our land have been broken. The queen wishes you to bear witness!" a man's voice boomed from the center of the stage. Blue dug her heels into the soft ground to avoid being pushed past the first row of benches as guards from each quarter brought prisoners onto the stage to have their crimes read aloud and their punishments delivered.

"Up first, we have Selina Bisset, who has been accused of breaking the law against using magic."

People around Blue murmured and shot fearful looks at the

stage, where a woman stood facing the crowd, her hands tied behind her back. Blue was too far away to see the expression on the woman's face, and she didn't want to.

"According to the law, no person shall use fae magic in any form." The man held a scroll in his hands, his eyes scraping over it as he read. "No magic may be used for healing, for spells, for altering the physical appearance of objects or people, for divining the future, or for affecting anything that lives on the land, the sea, or the air. It was the use of fae magic that turned the witch Marielle into a blood wraith who drank the blood of our children and terrorized the streets of Falaise de la Mer."

Actually, it was the misuse of fae magic that had created the blood wraith, but Blue knew no one was interested in the nuances. Not when most of them remembered the wraith haunting their streets, destroying lives in its unending quest for power. She took a few steps backward before running into a solid wall of bodies standing close behind her.

The crowd murmured louder, and Blue caught many of them saying the name *Marielle* like a curse.

The man onstage turned toward the woman. "You were seen using fae magic to transform rotten fruit into fresh in an attempt to deceive your customers. Do you deny the charge?"

Blue closed her eyes. There was no point in denying the charge. The magistrate wouldn't have brought the woman here if he didn't have at least three sworn witnesses. Blue's hands burned as if her own magic was reaching for the woman on the stage, and she clenched her fists and tried to take another step back.

Whatever the woman said in reply was lost as the crowd began chanting, "Death to witches!"

Not everyone who had fae magic was a witch, either, but that was another nuance no one who remembered the blood wraith wanted to discuss.

"According to the law of Balavata, under the blessing of our gracious queen, I hereby sentence you to death," the man shouted.

Blue's stomach lurched, and she turned and fought her way through the crowd as the guard next to the accused woman drew his sword from its sheath with a metallic hiss and plunged it through her chest.

TWO

BLUE ARRIVED AT the Mortar & Pestle shaken and queasy, the awful rasp of the guard's sword leaving its sheath ringing in her head. The shop floor was busy, and Papa had his hands full. Blue nodded to him as she made her way to the storeroom at the back of the shop.

The storeroom was a cozy space with floor-to-ceiling shelves against each wall, a long worktable in the center, a two-burner stove, a sink, and two chairs. A door at the back of the room led to the alley behind the shop. Blue set her purchases on the table and drew in a deep breath, taking comfort in the familiar scent of herbs, spices, and dried flowers that permeated the storeroom.

It had been wrong of the woman on the stage to magic decaying fruit into something that looked edible to others, but it hadn't been worth her life. If anyone saw how Blue harvested her ingredients, how she knew which items wanted to be combined into her potions, she'd find herself on the same stage faster than she could say, "I'm not a witch."

Before that thought could spiral into the cold fear that sometimes tore through Blue's dreams at night, turning them into nightmares, she threw herself into her work. The morning passed quickly. Blue packaged the shop's deliveries, sorted through her new supplies, shelved what she wasn't using for the day, and filled her worktable with everything she needed to make oils to treat beestings, powders to disinfect wounds, and tonics to combat everything from fatigue to insomnia. She then spent the next few hours moving from the table to the stove and back again, chopping, grinding, and steeping her ingredients. Letting her magic whisper to them in the solitude of her storeroom as she coaxed them to combine into the potions she wanted.

While her hands worked, she kept her thoughts away from the events on the stage by poking at her failed attempt to fully transmute lead into gold. Did she need to add more heat to speed up the molecules that bound the lead together? Build a better pressurized pot? There were still several rare minerals she could try adding. Or maybe the map to success was as simple as figuring out how to use her magic to coax the metal to do what she wanted.

What she wouldn't give for a magic wand, despite the danger of being caught with it. She could use it only when she was sure it was just Papa with her in the shop. That would be safe. Maybe if Grand-mère understood what was at stake, she'd finally relent and teach Blue how to use one. Or maybe Grand-mère's ability to briefly transfigure items into something different could be helpful.

Of course once Grand-mère's spell wore off and the merchants realized the gold had turned back into ordinary lead, Blue would be in the kind of trouble even her family's friendship with the queen couldn't fix. Besides, she wanted to do something to better the kingdom, not cheat merchants out of hard-earned coin.

"Lunch is here!" Papa sang as he entered the storeroom.

Blue looked up from a bubbling pot of fennel, scrub leaf, and ground cobalt, blinking in surprise at Papa, who stood in the doorway holding a bag from the Bronze Whale, their favorite pub. "It's lunchtime already?"

Papa smiled as he moved into the room. "Lost track of time again, eh?"

Blue rubbed her eyes and stretched her back. "I was focused on new ways to work the lead into gold tonight."

"Keep your voice down," Papa said, even though Blue hadn't spoken loudly. He cast an anxious glance over his shoulder, as if worried someone might have found a way inside their locked shop to overhear.

Blue's gaze followed his and landed on the pile of deliveries still sitting neatly on a shelf beside the door that led to the alley behind the shop. She frowned. "Ana didn't show up today."

"What time were you expecting her?" Papa set the bag down on Blue's worktable, sending a small puff of ground cobalt into the air. "And have you ever considered wiping down your table as you work?"

Blue tapped a finger to her lips and then winced at the sharp, unpleasant flavor of whatever residue was still on her hands. "She should've met me at the market. And I'll clean up when I'm done. It's a waste of time to stop and wipe things down every few minutes." She removed the bubbling mixture from the heat and set it on a rack to cool. Turning, she found Papa already cleaning the table. "I said I'd clean it when I'm done."

"I'm not eating in the middle of . . . whatever all this is." Papa gestured with his rag at the bits and pieces of the ingredients Blue had used throughout the morning. "Last time I did that, my tongue went numb for nearly an hour, and I had to wait on customers while sounding like I'd had a pint too many with my noon meal."

Blue grinned at the memory, and Papa flashed her a warm smile as he placed his cleaning rag neatly on the side of the storeroom's sink and rejoined her at the table. "I bought baked gelleire fish sandwiches and carrot soup."

"Sounds delicious. Thank you." Blue pulled a chair up to the table and accepted her lunch, but her gaze kept straying to the deliveries. She needed Ana to be reliable.

If she had been offered a quick job with better pay by one of the richer merchants in the quarter, she'd be back soon enough to resume her regular duties as the Mortar & Pestle's delivery girl, but until then, Blue had to find another way to get the orders to their customers.

Blue took a big bite of her sandwich, closing her eyes as she savored the flaky, buttery crust, the mild flavor of the fish, and the hint of heat from the sweet pepper sauce the Bronze Whale was known for.

"Will the princess be coming for her tutoring session today?" Papa asked as he pried the lids off small wooden cups of carrot soup, releasing the fragrance of ginger, brown sugar, and stewed carrots.

Blue nodded as she reached for her soup, earning a stern glance from Papa as he saw her hands.

"You want your tongue to go numb too?" he asked.

She hastily put her sandwich down and moved to the sink to wash while she thought about her upcoming time with Nessa and the pile of packages that still needed to be delivered. Usually, she and the princess spent several hours together while Blue taught her the basics of alchemy—a science for which Nessa had shown aptitude, and which the queen was happy to allow her to study while she focused on ruling the kingdom and grooming Nessa's older brother to take the throne. Today, however, Blue didn't have hours. She had deliveries that had to reach the shop's customers before the day's end. The shop did well enough, but it couldn't withstand losing regular customers over poor service.

Blue was going to have to check the street for any children hoping for a job, though she couldn't trust the shop's deliveries to someone she didn't know, so that narrowed down the possibilities. Maybe she'd do the deliveries herself. If she hurried through lunch, used the moss glider venom she'd just bought from Maurice to finish the queen's headache cream, and then cut the tutoring session short, she could—

"Stop thinking so hard and come eat while your food is still hot." There was a smile in Papa's voice.

Blue obeyed, smiling and nodding along to Papa's stories of the morning's customers. When lunch was finished, Papa began dusting shelves while Blue gathered the ingredients she needed for the queen's headache cream: beeswax, pressed almond oil, dried tryllis weed, essence of wintermint, and a few drops of the venom. She added a log to the stove and set a pot of water to boil on it and then placed a shallow pan over the bubbling liquid. The chunk of beeswax went into the shallow pan, where it immediately started to melt. When it was fully liquefied, she measured a thimble of almond oil, poured it into the wax, and reached for the wintermint, her lips pressed into a thin line.

It had been ten years since Blue had sat beside Mama's

damaged body in their root cellar, surrounded by spilled wintermint and the broken ladder that kept Blue trapped instead of running for help. Ten years since she'd watched Mama die, but the smell sometimes bothered her still.

The spicy sweetness of wintermint filled the air as Blue added a pinch of it to her mixture. A sprinkling of dried tryllis weed dotted the mixture with flecks of purple, and then Blue carefully added two drops of venom. Just enough to numb the queen's headaches without poisoning her. Blue had tried the dose on herself three times last week, just to be sure.

A knock sounded on the storeroom door. For an instant, Blue thought it might be Ana, late but still ready to do her job, but then a woman on the other side of the wall said firmly, "Open for the princess."

Papa set his dust cloth aside and obliged, smiling as he said, "Princess Nessa, how lovely to see you. Come right in."

Nessa threw herself into Papa's arms, giving him a fierce hug. One of the princess's guards stepped into the storeroom, stationing herself against the doorway that led to the shop floor, while the other two took up their posts in the alley outside. Papa returned Nessa's hug, patted her on the back a few times, and then let her go.

"I have to get back to the shop floor and open up for the afternoon customers." Papa's smile encompassed both girls. "When you have a break in your session, come see me. I brought fresh-baked cookies in with me today. Nutmeg wafers. Your favorite."

Nessa's face lit up, and Papa laughed as he left to reopen the store.

The twelve-year-old princess was already taller than Blue, though that was hardly an accomplishment given Blue's small stature. Nessa's body still held the gangly awkwardness of youth but was growing into the type of athletic gracefulness that her older brother, Kellan, may he fall off his horse, was known for. Today, the princess's hair was done up in intricate twists with strips of yellow ribbon woven throughout, and her yellow dress glowed against her brown skin like a beam of sunlight. Nessa's hands moved quickly, drawing together in fists at her chest and then pushing out toward Blue as she smiled, wide and joyful.

How are you?

"I'm good," Blue said, though it wasn't quite true. The deliveries were still waiting for someone to take them, and the memory of the woman sentenced to death on the stage lingered at the back of her thoughts like poison.

But it was impossible not to respond to Nessa's smile. Impossible to refuse her friendship, something Blue had learned years ago when the young princess decided she liked spending time with Blue more than she liked her tutors and their constant efforts to figure out why she could produce sound but couldn't move her mouth correctly to form words.

Nessa's hands moved again. *Excited! I have news.*

"What is it?" Blue's hands moved as well. She'd always thought it was polite to use Nessa's form of communicating as much as possible. Some of the signs were a language the scholars in Akram had developed for citizens who were deaf or had speech difficulties. Some of them were Nessa-specific signs that the princess had come up with on her own.

Nessa raised her hands as if placing a crown on her head and then lowered them to gently bang her fists twice against her chest. *Kellan.*

Blue's lip curled.

Coming home from school today. His carriage arrives soon.

"How . . . nice." Blue turned to tie a square of cloth over the mouth of the glass jar that held the queen's medicine.

Nessa laughed, a full-bodied sound that filled the stockroom with warmth. Blue raised a brow at her.

Kellan is my favorite. He'd be your favorite too if you gave him a chance.

Blue would rather suck on an entire bucket full of unripe shirellas than spend time with the insufferable, full-of-himself, rules-don't-apply-to-me Kellan, but she wasn't going to say any of that to Nessa. Instead, she said, "I'm glad you'll get to spend time with him this summer. We're going to have a short lesson today because Ana didn't show up to do the deliveries, so I'm going to have to do them myself."

I can help.

"I hardly think your mother would approve of you making shop deliveries, even with your guards in tow. Besides, I know you want to get back to the castle to see Kellan, may a wagon run over his"—she caught Nessa's eye—"um . . . enemies. Now gather up some bolla root, thorn fern, and essence of lyllis. I'm going to show you how to safely brew a batch of poison."

An hour flew by, with Nessa competently handling the ingredients and judging when the brew had coalesced enough to be transferred into glass jars for safekeeping. Once the princess and her guards left to return to the castle, Blue placed the deliveries in a large canvas tote and set off into the Gaillard quarter to bring the goods to the shop's customers.

A thick blanket of early summer heat shimmered against the cobblestone streets as Blue scanned the alley behind the shop for any children old enough to handle deliveries. The alley was empty. She sighed as she hoisted the tote over her shoulder and started walking.

She'd known it was a long shot. Most of the older homeless children who lived in the alleys and back streets of Falaise de la Mer were skilled at finding odd jobs each day or would take up begging on their favorite corners until the magistrate's guards chased them away. It was rare to find one of them still looking for work this late in the day.

She hated that they had to look for work at all.

The farther one got from the main roads with their pretty buildings and clean-swept cobblestones, the more the sordid truth about Falaise de la Mer and its head families became apparent. Some streets were full of ramshackle homes that were falling down around the people living in them. Some were full of children whose parents were gone—jailed by the magistrates, killed by the brokers who ran a host of dangerous, illegal enterprises throughout the city for being unable to pay their debts, or dead of starvation.

A familiar pulse of anger galvanized Blue as she hurried down the wide, gracious street that ran in front of the Mortar & Pestle, ignoring the gentle rustle of the iron bells that hung from every doorway to warn the city if Marielle the wraith, imprisoned in the wilds far to the west, returned.

The blood wraith that had terrorized the city sixteen years ago didn't currently worry Blue. The poverty and desperation of the children who were conveniently forgotten by the city's wealthy until they needed a job done, however, did.

A carriage rushed past her, the horse's hooves clip-clopping briskly along the road as Blue pulled a square box tied with twine out of her tote and turned down a street of two-story stone homes with red doors and polished iron filigree.

She had to find the key to turning lead into gold. Every day she failed was another day the children in her quarter were at risk.

THREE

KELLAN RENARD, CROWN prince of Balavata, was in serious danger of losing his lunch all over the beautiful interior of the royal carriage, an offense his mother would be slow to forgive.

It wasn't the fact that the road leading south through Balavata wound around the grass-covered hills like the curling sugar candy the cook made each Wintermass, though that certainly wasn't helping.

It wasn't that his mother had spent the past two hours lecturing him in great detail about the expectations on his shoulders now that he'd graduated from his boarding school in Loch Talam and would be permanently assuming his duties as heir to the throne, though that *really* wasn't helping.

It was the hint of sea salt in the breeze and the distant roar of the waves as they neared the seaside capital city of Falaise de la Mer, where both his home and his memories waited to swallow him whole.

And all right, *fine*, it was also the five pints of cheap ale and the scant two hours of sleep he'd had the night before after sneaking out of the inn while his mother slept. He'd only meant to have a single drink at the local pub, but a boy's best intentions could hardly stand up to the sparkling eyes and charming smiles of three pretty maidens who'd all wanted a dance partner. And if he'd needed more than one pint to face the idea of returning home to become king, who could blame him?

He'd made the long trip home from Milisatria Academy ten summers in a row. Each time, he'd been hit with a cold, sick feeling in the pit of his stomach once he got close enough to smell the sea, though a few ales, some pranks pulled on the castle staff, and a wild night or twelve in the more unsavory neighborhoods of Falaise de la Mer usually provided enough distraction to count as a cure. Or maybe it was simply because he'd known he only had to stay for nine weeks before he could head north again for another year at school with its rigid routine, his friend and roommate Javan, and so many glorious opportunities to break the rules and get away with it.

This time, Kellan was coming home to stay. This time, he'd have council meetings, power struggles, and worst of all—

"Are you listening to me, Kellan? Your birthday is a mere six weeks away. By law, you must be betrothed by then. We can do the betrothal proclamation at a ball, which we'll hold a bit earlier than your actual birthday. I thought we'd announce the ball at a royal reception for the head families. Say, in one week's time?"

Kellan sighed. Worst of all, he was bound by law to be betrothed by his nineteenth birthday to a girl from one of Balavata's nine head families. The law was designed to ensure that heirs to the throne were produced consistently, and that the head families had opportunities to increase their influence while one of their own sat on the throne beside the heir. It didn't matter if he liked any of the eligible daughters, or if they liked him. To be fair, Kellan rarely met a girl he didn't like, but enjoying some harmless flirting was a far cry from promising to love someone until he died.

That thought had him wishing he had another pint.

"Kellan." The queen's voice was a sharp warning that had him sitting up straighter and looking her in the eye.

She had his tall, athletic build, though she was rounder and softer than she used to be. Her dark eyes and brown skin were a match for his, as were her long, slim fingers and the deep dimples in her cheeks, but the rest of him was his father, from his close-cut black hair to his big feet to the restlessness coiled inside him, always longing for another adventure. Another risk.

"I've done all I can to let you have your childhood," his mother said quietly. His eyes flew open and found hers. There was a flicker of sympathy in her usually stoic expression. "I've let you be schooled far from home the way your father was before you. I've let you run wild in the summer months, ignoring all but the basic court functions that required your attendance."

"I mean . . . *wild* is maybe overstating things a bit."

Her eyes narrowed. "Do we need to have a discussion about who switched the kitchen's sugar supply for salt before the midsummer banquet? Or why my prize stallion was seen participating in an illegal race with someone who looked suspiciously like my son on his back? Or perhaps we should revisit the lovely morning when our esteemed butler woke up on the castle roof in nothing but his unmentionables?"

Kellan laughed, caught a glimpse of his mother's expression, and hastily pretended to be suffering from a coughing fit.

"Kellan."

He raised his hands in surrender. "No further discussion needed."

She leaned forward and wrapped cool hands around his. "You are the crown prince who will rule Balavata in the coming years. From the moment we step foot outside this carriage, you must act like it. One misstep, one appearance of weakness or vulnerability, and those who would love to take the throne for themselves, whether they have a girl of marriageable age or not, will not hesitate to pounce. They've only accepted me as their queen without your father for this long because they knew you, a true Renard by birth, would be of age soon enough."

His stomach lurched. He drew in a long, slow breath to calm his nerves and immediately regretted it. The air was thick with brine. The tang rested on the back of Kellan's tongue, bitter and dank.

"Kellan—"

"I won't fail you," he said. "I know the law, and I understand my duties."

It didn't matter if those duties felt like a noose around his neck. He was the prince. And it was his fault his father wasn't still alive to rule the kingdom.

The carriage topped the final hill leading to Falaise de la Mer, and Kellan stared out the carriage's window as his city came into view. He couldn't see the busy port from the carriage, but he could see the edges of the sea itself, stretching out along the horizon like a sparkling gold ribbon. Turning away, he watched as the castle came into view, perched on the hill directly to the north of the city, its white turrets, gleaming parapets, and silver filigree glowing in the midafternoon sun.

His mother tapped her finger on his knee to get his full attention. "You have ten minutes to change and greet Nessa, and then you have appointments at each head family's house. From the moment we leave this carriage, you are on display. Every word, every deed, every nuance must be carefully calculated. The head families will be watching you for any weaknesses they can exploit."

He definitely needed another pint. Queasiness be hanged. "I'm the Renard heir. Why would they be looking for weakness instead of opportunities to build alliances with me?"

"Your sister . . ." The queen's stoic expression slid back over her face. "They know you're the one who will rule this kingdom. If you don't prove to them that you have the strength to forge alliances and keep your enemies in check, both from within the kingdom and from without, some of them are ready to make a bid to put their own families on the throne. Permanently."

Kellan met his mother's eyes as a flame of anger ignited in his chest.

"Nessa isn't weak," he said quietly. "And she is perfectly capable of ruling should something happen to me."

"I know that, and you know that." The queen's voice was as unyielding as the stone beneath the carriage's wheels. "But to the head families, she's a girl who can't speak, and therefore can't rule. Unless they're trying to curry favor with me, they discount her entirely. Which means you have to be flawless, Kellan. If those who want the throne think they can take it from you, they will. And if that means they have to kill you and Nessa to have a clear claim on the crown, that's what they'll do."

His jaw set. Anyone who came for his sister was going to have to go through him first, but if he played the game well, it would never come to that.

Moments after reaching the castle, he'd changed into something suitable for greeting each head family and was impatiently waiting for his valet to finish tying his cravat when his sister came into the room, her face glowing with anticipation.

"Nessa!" His heart lightened, and the first genuine smile of the afternoon lit his face as she ran toward him. Sweeping her up in his arms, he laughed. "You've grown, little bird. One of these days you're going to pass me, and then how will I ever be able to show my face in public?"

She laughed, a full-throated, joyous sound he'd missed while he'd been away, and her arms tightened around his shoulders.

He closed his eyes as she murmured sounds that didn't quite sound like words, but that reached his heart all the same. He knew what she was saying. He always knew. From the moment she was born, through her toddler years as the nanny's calm proclamations that Nessa would talk in her own time became visits with the royal physician to see why she couldn't move her mouth the way other children could, to the summers when he'd choose her company over the company of anyone else in Balavata as she taught him the language she'd learned to sign with her hands, he'd always understood her.

Setting her down again, he stepped back and studied her. She looked happy. He was going to dedicate his life to making sure she stayed that way.

Nessa's hands moved rapidly. *Want to visit the garden with me? There's a new songbird nest in the rynoir tree. I want to climb up to see it.*

He grinned and signed back to her even as he spoke. "I'd love to, little bird, but mother has made appointments for me with each head family for the rest of the afternoon. Apparently, I'm supposed to act like a proper prince now."

She snorted.

"Exactly." He gave her another hug. "I have to leave now, but when I get back tonight, you and I can use the fire pit in the gardens and roast sugar puffs."

Her dimples flashed as she grinned.

He grabbed his silk afternoon jacket and then paused on his way out the door. "And don't climb the rynoir tree without me. Those branches break easily."

Her eyes narrowed. *You climb it every summer. Why do you get to climb it by yourself and I don't?*

"Because sometimes I'm an idiot."

I can't argue with that. Her laughter followed him as he hurried out of the royal wing and back down to the carriage waiting to take him to the first head family's home.

Four hours later, exhaustion pounded at Kellan's temples as the royal carriage left the Marcels' and headed toward the Gaillard quarter, the last on his list of required visitations. At least this visit would include time with a friend rather than the awkwardness of picking his way through conversations with girls whose parents eagerly watched to be sure their daughters did their best to catch themselves a prince. Even Kellan's considerable flirtation skills had been sorely tested.

Nothing said romance like being the fox at the wrong end of a hunt.

The Gaillard mansion was set on a gentle rise at the western edge of their quarter. Kellan disembarked from the carriage and was immediately greeted by their butler.

The man bowed low and said, "My Lady Genevieve is waiting for you in the gardens."

"Thank you." Kellan pivoted away from the front door and headed to the southern side of the house, where carefully manicured bushes, flowers, and trees were neatly arranged along paths of glistening white sand. He was nearly to the garden's entrance, his eyes on the ground, his thoughts full of navigating the betrothal season, assuming the crown, and protecting his family, when he ran full tilt into someone. His head snapped up, and his hand shot out to grab on to Genevieve Gaillard's arm as she stumbled.

She laughed. "You certainly know how to make an entrance, Your Majesty."

He grinned. "It's one of my many talents."

The late-afternoon sun glinted against her long red curls and shone against her golden skin as she gave him a proper curtsy. Her blue eyes danced with amusement as she cast a quick glance at the house and then whispered, "I'm positive my parents are huddled in front of my papa's bedroom window right now, taking notes. Why don't we stroll around the house instead of the garden? I don't feel like being on display."

They walked in companionable silence for a moment, and Kellan's headache receded. Technically, he wasn't supposed to be friends with any of the girls who qualified for the betrothal, as it would give them an unfair advantage, but he'd met Gen the previous summer when she snuck out to meet up with one of Kellan's friends and ended up spending plenty of time with their entire group safely away from the prying eyes of their parents. He might have felt bad about the brotherly affection he already held for Gen if she wasn't madly in love with one of his best friends. In his mind, that took her firmly off the list of contenders for the betrothal.

Leaning toward her as they rounded the corner of the house and headed toward the front drive, he said, "I assume you and Alexander are still . . . ?"

Pink bloomed on her cheeks. "We are." She cast him a swift look. "But of course, that doesn't mean you can't . . . I understand the law and what's at stake, and if you need to . . . if you decide to choose—"

"I'm not choosing you." He gave her arm a friendly squeeze. "I would never come between my friends. But we have to keep this quiet. If anyone suspects that I've already ruled you out, there will be trouble with your parents and their allies."

She nodded and then her face broke into another smile as she looked past him. "Oh, look! Blue is here. I guess she's making deliveries for the shop. Must have lost her errand girl again."

Kellan followed Gen's gaze and stopped walking. Blue de la Cour, the daughter of one of Kellan's father's dearest friends and the bane of his existence, was walking up the drive, her arms full of packages.

"Come on, Kellan." Gen pulled on his arm.

"I'd really rather not," Kellan said, but Blue had already heard Gen. Looking up, she made eye contact with Kellan. Her face twisted as if she'd sucked on a sour shirella.

"Hello!" Gen called, pulling Kellan forward with her as Blue reached the top of the drive.

"Ugh, this is happening," Kellan muttered as Blue came to a stop in front of them, her dark eyes full of faint contempt when she looked at him.

Gen let go of Kellan and reached for the packages in Blue's hands. "Let me help you, Blue."

"There's no need." Blue blinked as Gen whisked the packages out of her hands and turned toward the house. "Really. I can deliver them to the butler myself."

"There. You heard her. She can deliver them herself." Kellan turned toward Gen only to find that she was already halfway up the steps to the front door.

Silence fell between Blue and Kellan, and he couldn't think of a single courteous way to break it.

She arched a brow at him and said, "Nessa was excited to see you again." Her tone of voice made it clear she didn't share his sister's sentiments.

Fine by him. He could've gone another ten years without seeing the know-it-all, always-on-a-crusade-against-him Blue, but sometimes life gave you what you wanted, and sometimes it kicked horse manure in your face.

"I was happy to see Nessa too," he said, and dearly hoped they were done talking.

She tapped her fingers against her legs impatiently, opened her mouth, shut it, and then opened it again.

Kellan's words were rushed. "Before you say anything—"

"Try not to do anything foolish this summer," she said as if she hadn't heard him.

He glared. It was one thing to have to sit through her interminable lectures when he'd actually done something to deserve them. But to have her preemptively decide he was going to be a fool—never mind the fact that several very tantalizing and possibly foolhardy ideas had already occurred to him as the noose of his responsibilities tightened—was too much to bear.

"Try to give me a little credit, Blue," he snapped.

Her lip curled. "I give you exactly as much credit as you deserve."

He folded his arms over his chest. "You don't know me as well as you think you do."

She rolled her eyes. "I've known you backward and forward since we were kids. The only thing that still surprises me about you is how often others seem charmed by the things that come out of your mouth."

He took a step closer to her, and she fisted her hands on her waist and tilted her head back to meet his gaze.

"Maybe people find me charming because I am charming."

"Or maybe they act that way because you're the prince, and they don't want the consequences of getting on your bad side."

He barked a laugh. "What consequences, Blue? If there were any, you'd have been locked in the castle dungeons years ago."

"Hard to lock someone up for being right."

"In your case, I would find it remarkably easy."

Her eyes narrowed. "You know, you were named for Kellan the Great, the heroic warrior from the sea who arrived to rescue Balavata during desperate times centuries ago. Maybe that means nothing to you, but it means a lot to your people. Not the ones whose tables you sit at for tea or whose pretty little hands you hold while you dance at balls, but the ones who struggle each day just to find enough food to eat. They need a hero. Someone to rescue them. If you weren't so busy trying to get yourself killed with your pranks and your dares, maybe you'd see that."

The words he'd marshaled in his head to throw in her face dissolved, and he took a small step back from her as Gen came out of the mansion, her wide smile lighting up her face.

Maybe Blue was right. Maybe the ordinary citizens of Bala-vata needed a hero. But Kellan wasn't a hero, and he knew it. He was a pawn in a political game that was centuries older than he was. He was a piece of meat to be fought over by the head families who hungered for the power of the throne.

He was all that stood between his family and the wolves snapping at their door, and he couldn't lose focus on that for an instant. Not even to prove Blue wrong about the man she thought he'd become.

FOUR

BLUE WAS EXHAUSTED by the time she returned to the farm-house she shared with Papa. The deliveries had taken her the rest of the afternoon. She was annoyed that one of those deliveries had included a conversation with Kellan. He was still insuffer-able. Probably still planning some sort of stupid, risky adventure for the fun of it, regardless of the consequences.

And definitely none of her business. Not anymore. She washed her hands of him, his charming smile, and his reckless nonsense.

A shiver went up Blue's spine as far to the west of the city, the iron bells closest to the blood wraith's fae prison rang, a faint discordant melody that traveled through the perfect funnel cre-ated by the road that cut through the hills.

Sometimes she went months without hearing the bells. Some-times they rang every day. The sound didn't carry throughout the entire city, but those who lived on the western fringes, like Blue, heard it often enough. It was a stark reminder that even though the wraith Marielle was locked away, no one had figured out how to kill her, and so no one felt truly safe.

And it was a stark reminder of the woman on the market stage and what was at stake for Blue if she wasn't more careful.

Lanterns cast a welcoming glow in the front windows as Blue turned up the little lane that led to the farmhouse.

The farmhouse was painted a warm yellow with white trim. Flower boxes filled with cat's paws, pansies, dalliosas, and a sprinkling of wildflowers hung beneath the downstairs windows, and two large pots with herb gardens growing in them graced the wide front porch. Ivy climbed up one of the porch pillars and covered half of the veranda, and a wildly overgrown garden hugged the sides of the house. Blue had always thought it looked like the house had sprung out of the ground from a seed, just like the garden that surrounded it.

A dark streak launched itself off the porch and raced toward her. She laughed as her cat twined himself around her legs, managing to look furious with her for leaving him behind for the day even as he purred his joy at her return.

"Good evening, Pepperell, my handsome boy. Did you get into plenty of trouble today while I was gone?" Blue crouched to run her hand over Pepperell's fur.

His body bore the testament to his younger days as a street brawler before Blue had found him injured in the alley behind their shop and nursed him back to health. His gray fur always looked slightly unkempt, with a longer strip of brilliant white tracing the scar that started at his mouth, moved over his cheek, and ended where his left eye should've been. The tip of his right ear was missing, and one of his front teeth refused to stay hidden when he closed his mouth, but Blue thought he was beautiful, and Pepperell knew it.

Pepperell meowed as if to affirm that he had indeed been in plenty of trouble while his mistress was away, and then together they entered the farmhouse.

The inside of the house was neat and comfortable. Rich chocolate-brown floors scarred from years of use met walls painted a cheerful sage green, and darker green curtains hung on either side of the windows. The small entrance area met a hallway that bisected the downstairs and led to the kitchen, the office, the privy, and the sitting room. A set of simple stairs off to the right led to the second story, where the three bedrooms were located and then on to the small garret in the attic.

Blue sat on a bench in the entrance and switched her walking boots for her gardening boots, careful not to let the mud that had dried on them the night before get on Papa's clean floors. The smell of roasted fike and parslied turnips filled the air, and Papa poked his head out of the kitchen down the hall as Blue picked up her gathering basket.

"Dinner will be ready soon. Want honey with your oatcakes? Grand-mère brought a fresh jar with her."

"Grand-mère is here?" Blue's spirits lifted as a small, pear-shaped woman with sharp brown eyes, luminous dark skin, and a shock of tight gray-white curls peeked out of the kitchen. She was a full head shorter than Papa, nearly as small as Blue herself, and her full lips were lifted in a wide, welcoming smile.

"Course I'm here. Haven't seen you in at least a week." Grand-mère's stern voice belied the warm teasing light in her eyes as she walked toward Blue. "Had to come over and see if you had a boy who was taking all your time away from me, or if you were just neglecting an old woman."

Blue laughed. "No boy could ever be as interesting as you, Grand-mère. I'm sorry I've been so busy. I'm just going to gather a few things from the garden before they pass their peak. You're welcome to join me."

Grand-mère pursed her lips as Papa popped back into the kitchen to resume cooking. "Hip's bothering me tonight with that damp breeze. Why don't you plan to visit me when the shop is closed for the weekend? I'll make a pot of mashed sweetgrain and some fried apple cakes." Her hand reached up to tug Blue's headscarf aside, and her eyes narrowed. "Doesn't look like you're oiling your hair like you should be."

"It takes too long," Blue said as she leaned in to give Grand-mère a hug. "Besides, I'm barely awake in the mornings. I'm lucky to remember to change out of my nightdress before I leave the house."

Grand-mère made a noise in the back of her throat. "No excuse for letting yourself go. We'll fix that this weekend too."

"Yes, Grand-mère," Blue said, and then headed back outside in the purple twilight, with the last crimson rays of the sun to guide her steps. Pepperell shadowed her as she moved toward the garden.

Beyond the farmhouse and its wild garden stretched an orchard of apples, peaches, and shirella fruit. In the middle of the orchard, far from view of anyone who visited, was Grand-mère's little cottage. And at the end was a ragged cliff side with narrow steps carved into the side so that Blue could climb down to her beloved Chrysós Sea.

Humming the lullaby her mama had sung to her when she was a child, Blue let the crash of the distant waves and the delicate tang of the sea breeze wash over her as her fingers worked nimbly to lift vines and reach for fruit or gently brush at the dirt to dig for a bulb. Some of them leaped for her hand, eager to be harvested. But sometimes when she touched a bulb, a tiny pulse fluttered against her fingertip while the bulb remained still. Those she carefully re-covered with dirt and left for another day, just as Grand-mère and her mama had taught her.

The touch of fae magic in her blood came from them. It wasn't enough to send the iron bells ringing as she passed them. Not enough to count as a threat to those who feared magic, though she'd have no chance of convincing anyone of that if she got caught. Her magic was just enough to help her with the things she created for the shop, but not enough to help her when it had really mattered.

She drew in a deep breath and waited for the faint, bitter ache of grief to subside.

No, her magic hadn't been enough to help her save Mama's life as she lay dying in their root cellar so many years ago, but it was enough to lead Blue to the flowers and herbs that wanted to be harvested. It was enough to give her an instinct for which ingredients would work best together in the science of alchemy she loved so much. And as Grand-mère was fond of saying, it was useless wasting your time wishing for what you didn't have instead of using what you did.

When she was through gathering for the day, Blue returned to the farmhouse, left her gardening boots under the front bench, and carried her basket into the kitchen, where dinner was already set out on the small, polished kitchen table. Papa took the basket from her and set it beside the door that led down to the root cellar. Blue swallowed against the sudden hard knocking of her heart and looked away from the door as she washed her hands and sat down beside Grand-mère. Pepperell hurried to the corner of the room where a bowl of minced fish waited for him.

"How did the deliveries go?" Papa asked as he passed a basket of freshly fried oatcakes to Blue.

"They took forever, but I got them done." Blue took two cakes and slathered them with honey. "I hope Ana comes in tomorrow, because I don't have time to run packages across the city again."

"I'm sure she will," Papa said around a mouthful of fike. "She's been mostly reliable."

Blue savored her own bite of fike before saying, "I know. And I've also promised to teach her how to read and do her sums. I think she's excited about that. It would go so far in helping her to find an apprenticeship. She's nearly ten, and most merchants want apprentices to start at the age of twelve. That only gives us two years to fill in the gaps in her education and get her ready."

"Does she want an apprenticeship?" Grand-mère asked.

"Why wouldn't she?" Blue stared at Grand-mère while she swallowed a mouthful of turnips. "What other hope does she have? She'll be too big soon enough for begging. Too old for the wealthy to be willing to hire her for odd jobs here and there. If she doesn't have an apprenticeship, she'll end up working for the brokers, like so many homeless children who've gone before her, and you know that ends in violence more often than not."

"I know," Grand-mère said, her gaze finding her granddaughter's and holding. "But I also know that you can't save people unless they are willing to be saved. Maybe the thought of giving up the life she knows for the life of an apprentice scares her."

Blue slowly put her fork down on the table. She'd thought Ana was excited to learn the skills she needed to find an apprenticeship. Could Ana have skipped her job at the shop today because she was afraid of change? Was she so used to a life of desperation and faint hope that she couldn't see herself living any other way? If that was true for her, how many other children out there were struggling to envision anything better for themselves either?

Looking up from her plate, Blue found both Papa and Grand-mère watching her. Firmly, she said, "The only reason Ana or any of the other children would be scared of going after an apprenticeship is because they've lost hope that there's something better out there for them. If we give them shelter and decent food—if we treat them like people who are worthy of dignity and respect—then they'll be able to see that a better future is possible."

Papa's smile was wide and warm. "That's my girl." He reached across the table to squeeze her hand. "More turnips?"

"I'm full." Blue pushed her plate away and braced herself for the protest that was sure to come as she said, "And I need to figure out the next step in my experiments on turning lead into gold. Grand-mère, you can help with that." Blue drew in a breath and then said quickly, "I think it's time I had my own wand."

The older woman's gaze snapped to Blue's. "We've discussed this."

"I'd like to discuss it again." Blue held Grand-mère's eyes, though heat squirmed through her, and she had to concentrate on not shifting her weight.

Papa leaned forward. "Blue—"

"I can handle this, Pierre." Grand-mère's voice was soft, but there was stone beneath it as she ran her fingers along the wand she kept in a slim sheath beneath her left sleeve. "I've told you before, Blue. No wand for you. You don't need one. You already

43

focus your magic with the touch of your hands. That's good enough." Her voice was firm.

"It's not good enough!" Blue's voice rose, and a swift look of disapproval from Papa had her struggling to speak calmly again. "I can't figure out how to change lead into gold. My hands aren't telling me the secret. And if I can't figure that out, I can't buy shelter and food and tutors. I can't help Ana, or the other children on our streets, and somebody has to. *I* have to."

"And why do you have to?" Grand-mère pointed at Blue. "Who made that your job?"

"You did." Blue lifted her chin as Grand-mère blinked in surprise. "You're the one who always told me if I see something wrong, it becomes my responsibility to make it right."

Papa laughed, and then quickly choked it down as Grand-mère shot him a look. "She has you there, Destri."

Grand-mère snorted, but her eyes softened as she looked at Blue. "Your mind is so bright. So curious. Always hunting for something to understand, something to create, or something to fix. I know you look at a wand and you think you see all the possibilities, but I see the possibilities too. And not all of them are good."

"But—"

"If you use a wand in the shop and someone sees you, they could report you," Papa said quietly.

"I could use it only after hours, when the shop is locked up."

"It's too dangerous." He rose from the table, moved to her chair, and wrapped his arms around her. "I will not lose my daughter because of magic. You're a brilliant alchemist, Blue. You'll figure out how to help the children without risking exposing your magic to others. I believe in you, and I'll help you in any way I can. Something should've been done to help them long ago, and I'm ashamed it took my own daughter to open my eyes to it."

"Thank you." She leaned into him, and he held her for a moment before stepping back and reaching for her gathering basket.

"Shall we go down to the root cellar and store these together?" he asked as he did every time she brought in a harvest.

Her gaze flew to the root cellar door and skittered away as sharp teeth of panic scraped at her.

One day, she'd go back down into the root cellar, where she'd sat beside her mama's dying body when she was seven, unable to climb up the broken, twisted ladder to get help. Helpless to do anything but wait for her papa to return home far too late to even say good-bye to his beloved wife.

"I'm tired," she said, her voice a faint shadow of itself as the panic threatened to close her throat.

Papa smiled gently, though sorrow was in his eyes. "Perhaps tomorrow, then."

She nodded her thanks as he opened the door and descended into the root cellar with her basket.

"You're going to have to face that room someday, Blue." Grand-mère rose from the table and began clearing dishes. "Hiding from our ghosts only gives them the power to keep haunting us."

"I know." And she did. She knew it down in her bones, the way she knew when a storm was coming or when an animal nearby needed her. Something dark and frightening tethered her to the root cellar, tearing through her dreams with blood and teeth, and she didn't know how she'd ever be ready to face it.

But for now, she had something more pressing to face.

She had to figure out how to create gold before more children signed their lives over to the brokers or simply died in the warren of back alleys and dingy neighborhoods because they lacked the basics to survive.

FIVE

DINAH CHAUVEAU SWEPT into the royal council chamber ahead of the representatives of the other eight head families and dropped into a deep curtsy before the queen. Dinah's red gown contrasted beautifully with the emeralds she wore at her throat and wrist, and her brown hair was swept into an elegant updo with a sharp hairpin resting in its depths in case Dinah needed a weapon. She oozed power, wealth, and absolute confidence.

The queen smiled in welcome. "So lovely to see you, Dinah. Prince Kellan said he didn't get a chance to talk to Lord Chauveau yesterday. I hope your husband is well."

Dinah's teeth set, but she answered the queen's smile with one of her own. "Good morning, Queen Adelene. James is quite well, thank you, though he was a bit under the weather yesterday. He regrets not being able to meet with the prince."

Actually James, the true head of the Chauveau family, at least in name, had known nothing about the prince's visit, and neither had the extended members of the Chauveau family. Her plan had been to shine a spotlight on her daughters for the upcoming betrothal without reminding the prince that there were also several eligible nieces within the Chauveau family tree. Plus she intended to keep her feckless, irresponsible husband far away from the royal family. She didn't need the prince wondering if the strength of Dinah's empire rested on the shaky pillars of a gambler who would rather pursue his next pint of ale than the throne. Besides, Dinah had taken him well in hand—removing the bulk of their income from his solicitor to hers and making sure every bit of the considerable business empire she'd built in his name had *her* name on the property deeds.

Now she rose and moved to her assigned seat at the queen's right hand. It had taken her nearly a decade to earn it. To arrange the deaths of the three Chauveau heirs who came before her husband's claim to the family's title so that he could rule the clan and to expand their business interests until her income and holdings surpassed even those of the powerful Gaillards. Along with increasing the Chauveaus' wealth and position, Dinah had spent much of those ten years currying favor with the queen.

The queen had been cautious at first. She wasn't a woman with close friends outside the Barbier family she'd left when she'd married the king, and with good reason. She was surrounded by people who either wanted her favor, her coin, or her throne. Dinah had pretended to want nothing but the good of the kingdom itself so that her own empire would be protected.

And now all her work was paying off. She was at the queen's right hand for every council meeting. She and her daughters were frequent guests at the castle for private teas and brunches. No one dared bring up the fact that Dinah had been nearly penniless when she'd married into the Chauveau family. Not if they wanted their own empires to remain intact. Her wealth and position were rivaled by none, which made her family the strongest choice for an alliance with the Renards.

An alliance wasn't the thing Dinah truly wanted—sharing power was nearly as bad as having none at all—but it would open doors she couldn't open for herself, and one of those doors would lead her to the kind of power no one would ever be able to take away.

As the council members found their seats, the door opened one last time, and the crown prince entered. He was dressed in a royal-blue day coat with a purple cravat and the Renards' signatory ring on his right hand. The message was clear: he was their future ruler, and he expected each of them to remember it.

Dinah met his gaze and lowered her head respectfully.

The sniveling brat had never had to work for anything in his life.

He didn't deserve the power of the throne. He'd sacrificed nothing to gain it.

The meeting lasted nearly three hours. When it was over, Dinah swept out of the room, down the long hallway that led back to the entrance hall, and then out the front door. She was nearly to her carriage when someone yelled her name. Stopping short, she turned and found one of her household pages rushing toward her, a piece of parchment clutched in the girl's hand.

"My Lady, your solicitor stopped at the house and said this was urgent." She pushed the parchment into Dinah's hand and stepped back.

Lady Chauveau, please come see me immediately on a matter of some urgency.

Dinah read it twice and then stepped into the carriage. "Go

to my solicitor's office. Hurry."

Had one of her export ships been robbed? She'd heard there were issues with pirates on the stretch of sea between Llorenyae and Ichil. Had one of her buildings burned? Or was there an issue with payment from one of her many business interests?

The scenery flew by the window as the coachman drove the carriage quickly through the cobblestoned streets. Dinah settled against the cushions and forced herself to be calm. Whatever had happened, she would deal with it quickly and decisively before any hint of a problem reached the queen's ears and weakened the appeal of a betrothal to one of Dinah's daughters.

She wanted that throne. Needed it. It was the key to making sure no one could ever break her and leave her powerless again.

Her solicitor rented space above a bakery. The smell of warm, sugary bread followed Dinah as she marched up the outside stairs and entered his office.

He greeted her, gestured for her to take one of the wide wooden chairs that sat in front of his desk, and then gathered up five sheets of parchment. A bloody fingerprint marred the back of one sheet.

"A messenger delivered this to me earlier today," he said, fishing out a pair of spectacles so he could read. "I didn't send for you until I'd personally visited both your bank and the city clerk to ascertain the truth of the matter." His shoulders sagged. "I regret to inform you that your husband is dead."

Dead. The hit of shock faded quickly as a host of possibilities emerged. Without James in the way, Dinah would be the true head of the Chauveau family. She could make sweeping decisions without forging his signature or manipulating him to give the orders she wanted him to give. She could stop worrying that he'd make a mistake that could cost her everything she'd worked toward. She could—

Her solicitor cleared his throat, and Dinah's gaze snapped to him.

"Thank you for informing me. I suppose we'll have to wait for the reading of his will before—"

"James was murdered," he said. "By the creditors he was indebted to."

She drew back. "How could James possibly have accrued enough debt to be worth killing? I had him on a very strict allowance."

Her solicitor looked at the stack of parchment. "I'm afraid he fell in with someone far more clever than he. Whoever was floating him the money he used to gamble gave him the idea to forge your signature."

A quick slice of panic left her shaking. "What did he do?"

"He deeded all your property back into his name and then used it as insurance against his gambling. He also cleaned out your bank account. I'm afraid all you have left to your name is whatever coin you have at your home and whatever valuables you can pack up before the new owners move in."

"New owners." Her voice was a whisper of its former self. Stupid, self-serving, lazy fool of a man. If she'd known he'd cause this much trouble, she'd have killed him herself before he ever had a chance to ruin her.

"I'm afraid it gets worse." Her solicitor cleared his throat and handed her the parchment.

Worse? How could it possibly get worse? He'd bankrupted her right before her final bid for the royal betrothal. Everything she'd worked for, everything she'd sacrificed for, was disappearing in front of her eyes. She glanced down at the parchment and froze.

The solicitor's voice was sympathetic. "I'm afraid some of his debt remains, and as collateral, he put up—"

"My daughters." Her voice shook with fury.

"They will be claimed for their family name. Once the inquiry into James's death is finished, the creditor—a Mr. Dubois—will own your mansion, your business interests, and your bank account. When he claims a daughter in marriage, he'll own the Chauveau quarter as well."

"Not if he's dead." She stood abruptly, rage snaking through her blood like fire.

"He's quite well guarded, my lady. His message this morning said that he knows you are the force behind the Chauveau empire and that if he feels threatened in any way, one of your daughters will be the next to die."

Dinah crumpled the parchment in her hand, her pulse pounding against her ears until it drowned out every thought except for a single word: *powerless.*

Her vision narrowed, her mouth went dry, and every breath she took fought a battle against the fist of panic that was squeezing her chest.

Unless she could pay off James's debts before the inquiry finished, she would lose her wealth, her empire, and her quarter. Once word reached the queen about Dinah's ruined status, she'd lose any chance at the betrothal as well.

She had a few weeks before the estate would come up for review before the royal magistrate.

She needed coin, and she needed it fast. No creditor would loan her any. Not when she'd lost all her collateral. And she couldn't go to the rest of the Chauveau family because the bulk of their wealth had been tied to her empire, so they would be nearly destitute too. It was unthinkable to ask another head family for help. She might as well roll over and show a rabid wolf her soft underbelly and then wait for her blood to spill.

No, she'd have to find a different way to get enough gold to pay off her husband's debts, ransom her daughters out of Mr. Dubois's heinous contract, and restore her position before anyone was the wiser. Maybe there were businesses James hadn't known about that she could quickly sell. Maybe one of her contacts in Akram, Ravenspire, or Súndraille would be willing to float her a loan, though the thought of being so far in debt to any of them was sickening.

Or maybe there was a faster source of coin right here in Falaise de la Mer if she was willing to do whatever it took to get her hands on it. She'd killed before to get what she needed. She could do it again.

SIX

Restlessness churned inside Kellan as he dictated his response to yet another invitation for dinner or tea or . . . he'd forgotten precisely what he'd been invited to this time. It hardly mattered. It would be another test. Another game where the lies were pretty, the questions were pointed, and the calculation was shrewd. He'd smile, flirt, parry, and test the waters of loyalty and power with pointed questions of his own, just as he'd been doing every day since he'd returned home.

And then he'd return to the castle; navigate meetings with his advisers; hear concerns or offers from representatives of the head families, significant merchants, or magistrates from far-flung cities; and wear his careless charm like armor as he walked the castle halls. He never knew who'd be waiting and watching around every corner.

He caught himself sighing and tried to pay attention to his secretary, who was still discussing the invitation before him.

"The delightful Miss Cherise Sandovar, whom you played

cards with yesterday, should be in attendance, though I doubt that you'll get more than two words with her if Lady Chauveau has anything to say about it, even if Cherise is one of the Chauveau nieces. She is most keen on making sure you only spend time with her own daughters," the prince's secretary said as he wrote Kellan's response to the invitation in bold, slashing strokes, oblivious to the prince's wandering focus. "There are three other invitations to be dealt with, though each is from lesser families, so not as urgent. And the queen has requested your attention on the matter of the ball's menu. I've compiled a list of suggested dishes for your approval. If you have any friends from school you'd like to invite, give me a list so those invitations can go out on the morrow. I'd also like to . . ."

Kellan wandered to the window that overlooked the royal family's private garden, letting his secretary's words fade into the background. He'd been home for a week now, playing the part of the flawless prince, and it was wearing on him. There wasn't a minute of his day that hadn't already been scheduled before he awoke. Never an instant that he wasn't on display.

And there'd been no time to face the numbing void within him at the thought of taking his father's place when it was his fault his father wasn't still on the throne.

He needed to get out of the castle. Without his guards or his advisers or the seemingly endless parade of people who wanted his attention. He needed the space to breathe through the pain of being back where the loss of his father was a ghost that haunted every corridor.

He needed to feel alive, and there was only way to do that.

Turning back to his secretary, he found the man waiting for a reply to . . . whatever it was he'd just said. Kellan gave him an easy grin and said, "I'm afraid you lost me for a bit. So many girls to think about."

The prince winked, and Jacques chuckled. "Would that we all had your problems, sir."

Kellan's grin slipped.

Oh yes, he definitely needed to get out of the castle. By himself. And the only way to do that was to trick Jacques into leaving him alone while also tricking his guards into thinking the prince was still safely inside his office, working on the tasks his mother and advisers had set for him.

"Let's get started with the list of those to invite to the ball," Kellan said, walking to the desk and clapping Jacques on the shoulder. "Invite all my local friends, and also send an invitation to Prince Javan in Akram."

It would be good to see Javan again. The journey from Milisatria Academy in the northern kingdom of Loch Talam to his home in Balavata had only taken Kellan five weeks, but it felt like he hadn't seen his former roommate in months. Of everyone in Kellan's life, Javan—whose mother had died when he was young, leaving him with the heavy burden of living up to her final wishes and his father's high expectations— was perhaps the one person uniquely suited to understand the pressure Kellan was under now. It was almost a shame that Kellan had been too busy pursuing girls and mad escapades while at the academy to seriously discuss his future with his friend.

Almost.

He couldn't truly regret his many adventures at the academy. Especially the ones that had involved the kind of risk he craved now. At least at the academy, he'd only had to worry about evading the headmaster and the pairs of guards who'd patrolled the academy's grounds.

Here, everyone was focused on Kellan. Especially his mother.

Jacques finished his list and reached for a stack of requests from various advisers. The chain around Kellan's chest tightened, and he nudged Jacques's shoulder.

"You hungry?"

The secretary blinked up at him. "Hungry, sir?"

Kellan grinned. "You're only a bit older than me, Jacques. I walk around feeling like I have a hollow canyon for a stomach most days. We've been at this for hours. Are you hungry?"

Jacques smiled slowly. "I could eat."

"Say no more." Kellan leaned over the desk, shifting parchment until he found what he was looking for. "This list of dishes my mother wants me to approve for the ball seems very fancy."

"Quite fancy, sir."

"I've been eating academy food for so long, I'm not sure I remember exactly how each of these tastes." Kellan raised an eyebrow at Jacques.

"It would be a shame to approve a dish and then have it be a disaster on the day of the ball." Jacques spoke gravely, though there was a twinkle in his eyes.

"Exactly." Kellan handed the list to Jacques and stepped back. "Which is why I'd like you to go down to the kitchens and order a sample of each."

"Me, sir?" Jacques looked askance at the pile of work still waiting on his desk.

"Something like this requires a personal touch. Tell the staff you'll wait. No, tell them *I'm* up here waiting. That will get them moving."

And if there was any luck left in the world for him, cooking samples of each of the twenty-six dishes on the list would take at least two hours. Plenty of time for him to sneak out of the castle, figure out a way to feel truly alive, at least for a little bit, and then sneak back in with no one the wiser.

"But, sir—"

"I'll look over these while you're gone." Kellan took the pile of requests from Jacques's hand.

"But this could take hours."

Kellan was counting on it.

"My good man, do you have any idea just how many girls have been introduced to me in the past week? And just how fast my betrothal ball is coming? I have a lot of thinking to do." Kellan gave Jacques a meaningful look, and the man shook his head, a resigned smile playing at his lips.

"Very well, sir."

Kellan held his careless smile in place until the door closed behind Jacques, and then he whirled toward his bedchamber. It had been years since he'd last used his balcony to escape the castle, but the process couldn't be that different from the many times he'd done something similar to leave his third-floor dorm room at the academy after hours.

Several harrowing moments later, after nearly missing his leap from the balcony to the solid old oak tree whose branches painted shadows on his bedroom wall at night, and after almost being caught on the south lawn by a pair of representatives from the Faure family, Kellan slipped through the hedges that bordered the southern edge of the castle's estate.

He'd had no real plan other than escape, but he found his

feet hurrying toward the path he'd often taken as a child beside his father when they would go south, skirting the city, to visit his father's old tutor and friend Pierre de la Cour at his little farmhouse beside the sea.

Not that Kellan wanted to see Pierre today. Or, luck forbid, Pierre's interfering, know-it-all daughter, Blue, the tiny ruiner of many of Kellan's best adventures when he was younger. But there was a comfort in walking the familiar trail through wild seagrass and scattered groves, the city sprawling to his left. He could breathe in the delicate scent of salt and sun-warmed dirt and pretend he was eight again, his hand swallowed up by his father's, his world still beautiful and perfect.

He could pretend he'd made different choices. That he'd recognized the risks in swimming so far out that day. That Blue had seen him and tattled like she always had. Anything that would change the fact that he'd thrown himself into dangerous waters and that his father had thrown himself in after, desperate to save his son.

Kellan had been saved, but he'd felt lost ever since.

The thick, damp heat of the summer's day lay on Kellan's skin like a wet blanket as he neared the de la Cour farmhouse. Skirting the edges of the property, he took the well-worn path down to the cliff that overlooked the glittering expanse of the golden Chrysós Sea.

The waves hurled themselves at the strip of white sand that lay between the cliff and the sea. Beyond their foamy caps, a dark shadow threaded its way beneath the water, changing the color from light gold to a deep bronze.

That was the shadow that had taken his father from him.

The current that ran through the channel deep beneath the surface had snatched him. Flung him away from the prince and then sucked him under.

Kellan had been throwing himself into danger ever since. Daring the world to take the life it should've taken in the first place.

Ignoring the steps carved into the side of the cliff, Kellan stripped off his shirt and pants, and stood poised for a moment at the edge of the precipice.

It was a long, treacherous drop. He'd have to pull up out of the dive fast, or he'd slam into the sea floor and break every bone in his body. He'd have to fight the current that would want to drag him beneath the waves and into the channel. If he got hurt, there was no one to rescue him. If he was caught in the current, no one would ever know where he'd gone or what had become of him.

There were a hundred ways it could all go wrong, and for the first time since Kellan had set foot in Balavata again, he felt wonderfully, gloriously alive.

Spreading his arms wide, he drew in a deep breath of the salt-tinged air, and dove. The wind rushed past his ears, and then he plunged below the surface, the shock of barely warm water slapping at his skin and sharpening his senses.

He curved upward, angling his body so that his dive was as shallow as he could make it. Still, his stomach scraped the sand, a rough bite of pain that shrank the numbness inside until he could almost believe it didn't exist.

There was nothing but the dangerous waters of the Chrysós. Nothing but the sun on his back as he surfaced and the tug of the current against his legs.

For one brief moment, he stopped fighting. Let the current drag him toward the streak of bronze that marked the channel.

Maybe this time, he'd let it have him. Let it take what it should have taken nearly eleven years ago. A penance for the heavy price his actions had cost his family and his kingdom.

He closed his eyes and waited, his body buffeted by the waves even as the current dragged him closer and closer to the channel. Waited for peace. For a sense that he was finally doing the right thing after years of running from it.

Instead, he saw Nessa's face. Heard his mother tell him the head families didn't believe his sister could rule and would be only too happy to remove her from the line of succession permanently. And he felt a quiet, insistent desire to be alive, even though it hurt.

His eyes snapped open, and he was stunned to see the shadow was already gaping beneath him. Kicking, he began fighting the current with strong, measured strokes. For an instant, it held him, pinning him above the crevasse that had taken his father. But Kellan wasn't his father. He wasn't concerned with snatching a foolish child from the jaws of death, even at the expense of his own ability to survive.

He was young. He was strong. And he had more to live for than he'd thought when he'd come to the edge of the sea. He fought harder, coordinating his movements to harness the power of his height and physical strength, and in another moment, he was free.

As he swam toward the shore and the mountain of responsibilities that waited for him, the void within him throbbed, a single shaft of pain that tethered him to the shadow he was leaving behind.

SEVEN

BLUE STARTLED AWAKE as the weight of a grizzled, snaggle-toothed tub of a cat landed on her stomach.

"Oof." Groaning, she tugged her quilt over her shoulders and buried her face in its softness. "Go away," she mumbled. "It's barely light out, Pepperell."

Pepperell crept forward and pawed at her nose.

"Mmff." She tried to pull the quilt farther over her face, but the enormous cat made it impossible. When his paw swiped her nose again—this time with just a hint of claws to get her attention—she forced her eyes open and glared.

"Mornings are a plague."

Pepperell watched her out of his one good eye, whiskers twitching. She sighed as he lowered his face to hers and bit gently at the tip of her nose.

"Ugh. Stop breathing on me. You smell like you just cleaned the docks with your tongue." Blue pushed Pepperell to the side and rolled her eyes as he began to purr.

A quiet knock sounded on the doorframe, and then Papa entered the room carrying a large yellow mug. A smile tipped the corners of his mouth as he took in the sight of his disgruntled daughter and the huge cat purring beside her. Papa's skin was still damp from his morning shave, and flour dusted the front of the red apron he wore. Breakfast was no doubt already in the oven.

How Blue could be related to someone who willingly got up before dawn to bake and clean was beyond her.

"I see Pepperell already woke you." Papa sounded cheerful.

"No one should be up at this hour. It's uncivilized."

"You say that every morning." Papa's smile widened, and he raised the mug in his hands. Blue perked up as the warm, comforting scent of hot spiced chicory filled the room. "Maybe this will make waking so early worth it."

"I'm ashamed at how easily I can be bribed."

Papa laughed, set the mug on her dresser, and moved to her side to plant a kiss on the top of her head. "We have several large orders that need to be fulfilled, and if Ana doesn't show up again, we need to find a new delivery girl. Time to get moving."

Blue tossed off the quilt Grand-mère had stitched for her when she was a child and climbed out of bed as Papa left to go down to the kitchen. Her toes curled as they hit the cold wooden floor. Even though summer had arrived in Balavata, the sea breeze still carried a chill at night, and Blue loved to leave her windows open while she slept.

It had been a week since Ana had failed to show up. Blue had asked after her with a few of the homeless children she recognized in her quarter, but no one seemed to know where she'd gone or why she'd left. The entire thing had left Blue with hours of extra work and an uncomfortable worry in the pit of her stomach that Ana had left for another quarter because she was worried about Blue's plans to help her gain an apprenticeship. She'd thought that's what Ana wanted too, but now that she looked back on the conversation, she couldn't remember if the excitement she'd felt had been hers alone.

Pepperell seemed remarkably unconcerned with Blue's plight. Plopping down on the warm dip in the mattress where his mistress had recently been sleeping, the cat hoisted a leg and began to clean himself.

"You and I need to have a conversation about basic manners," Blue said as she slipped out of her muslin nightgown, splashed water from her basin over her skin, and dried herself briskly with the towel she kept folded on her dresser. "For example, jumping on someone to wake them up is generally frowned upon."

Pepperell's ear twitched.

Blue pulled a pink dress off a hook in her closet and slid it over her head. "Demanding breakfast at the crack of dawn is also rude. But neither of those is half as rude as cleaning your hindquarters on my *sheets*."

Pepperell sneezed on Blue's pillow.

"You are incorrigible." Mindful of Grand-mère's efforts to style her hair over the weekend, Blue uncorked her homemade almond oil, poured a coin-size amount in her palm, and rubbed her hands together. Carefully, she worked the oil into her scalp between the small rows of twists Grand-mère had put into the front portion of her hair. The rest of her hair was a riot of tangled black curls. She put more oil on her hands and ran her fingers through her curls, coaxing them into a halo of corkscrews that just brushed her shoulders.

Blue yawned as she made her way down the farmhouse's narrow hallway, her boots tapping against the scarred wooden floor. She'd have to hurry through breakfast. Hurry through the list of potions she needed to make at the shop. And then, if she still hadn't found a replacement for Ana, hurry through the deliveries so she could return to the shop and work on the formula for turning lead into gold.

She was getting closer. The night before, she'd produced a lump of metal that glowed golden yellow under the lamplight. Unfortunately, it had seams of dull gray running through it. Still, it gave her hope that soon she'd be able to put her project in motion.

And once that was accomplished, she'd turn the city over to find Ana, apologize if her enthusiasm had scared the girl away, and see if she could gently convince the child to move into Blue's new shelter.

The day flew by in a haze of potions, deliveries, and cleaning the storeroom to Papa's exacting standards. At one point, Dinah Chauveau entered the shop to purchase a few ointments. Blue overheard her asking Papa if they'd notified the magistrate yet about someone paying with fake gold, and had a moment of blind panic when Papa froze. She hadn't told him about trying to pay with the gold at the market, and that had been a mistake. He didn't have a story ready, and he'd had no idea the head of the Chauveau family had taken an interest. After several agonizing beats of silence, Papa smiled and assured Lady Chauveau that all was handled, but the look he gave Blue after Dinah left the shop promised a difficult discussion ahead of her once she got home that evening.

But before Blue could go home for the evening, she had to

handle a task she'd been avoiding. Ana hadn't shown again, and Blue knew it was past time to find a new person for the job.

The cathedral's heavy iron bells were tolling an hour far past Blue's usual dinnertime when she finally set aside her experiments. Five failures. Two that looked nearly like gold until you turned them over and saw veins of lead running across the surface.

And one that was a solid yellow throughout, though slightly harder than true gold.

She'd done it. Or very nearly. Hopefully, all she had to do was repeat the process the following night, fine-tune the pressure, the heat, and the inclusion of khravllin, a rare mineral from the faraway kingdom of Eldr, and she would have gold.

Blue locked the shop door, drew her summer cloak close against the chilly evening breeze, and bounced in place for a moment, excitement bubbling through her.

Countless hours of work. Of failure. Of having to pick her confidence up off the ground and convince herself to try again. And it was all about to be worth it. She couldn't wait to tell Papa.

But first, she was going to solve the problem of replacing Ana.

Turning north instead of west toward the road that led out of the city and to the farmhouse, Blue kept to the edges of the streets. Above her, fire crackled merrily in the torch lamps that were hung along the road, orange light pooling on the sidewalk beneath their iron poles. Carriages moved briskly, lanterns swinging from the coachman's perch, as their occupants went to dinner parties or dances or whatever it was wealthy people did when the sun went down.

Blue wasn't interested in the wealthy side of the Gaillard quarter. The children she was hoping to hire spread far and wide throughout the city during the day, begging, stealing, and working odd jobs, but at night, they returned to the crowded, dirty warren of streets that snaked their way through the city's heart.

Three blocks later, she turned left and began walking briskly. The buildings grew closer together, their fences leaning inward in places, their exteriors cracking here and there. The torch lamps grew few and far between, and a whisper of unease skated up Blue's spine.

Papa was not going to be happy with her, but it was too late to turn back now. She was already well within the neighborhoods of aging homes and old buildings that were now used for storage, for less than legal businesses run by brokers, or for shelter by people who had nowhere else to go.

Hopefully, she could quickly find one of the shelters and hire someone. She'd prefer to hire one of the children who already worked for the shops around hers. She knew them and trusted them, and surely at least one of them had time in the day to do deliveries for her shop as well.

Lost in her thoughts as she scanned a street corner by the distant light of the stars, she pulled up short when a shout echoed from the street to her right, followed instantly by cheers. Turning, she found a crowd gathered on both sides of the street. A square was roped off on the street itself, and a lantern hung from each of the square's corners. A broker in a striped top hat and matching dress coat stood at one corner calling loudly for bets as two young men entered the ring, stripped to the waist. One of them wore a black mask tied over the upper half of his face, leaving only his eyes visible.

An illegal street match. One of the dumbest gambling games that existed. Two fighters accepted a small fee to stand in a square and punch each other until one of them went down. The winner won some coin and the cheers of the crowd. The crowd won bets on the winner, on how many rounds it took to bring the loser down, and on stars knew what else. How anyone could find entertainment in watching two people pummel each other for coin was beyond Blue. Shaking her head in disgust, she kept walking, but stopped when an acquaintance caught her eye.

The boy was a few years older than Ana. Probably thirteen, though he was so skinny that it was hard to tell. He swept up for the bakery on the corner opposite of the Mortar & Pestle, and he'd visited the shop a few times with Ana over the months since Blue had hired her. Maybe he could take on an extra job. And maybe he knew what had become of Ana.

Moving to the outside edge of the crowd, she said quietly, "Lucian?"

Lucian turned, his brown curls bobbing, his pale skin white against the darkness. "Miss Blue? What are you doing here?"

"Trying to find someone to do the shop's deliveries." Blue craned her neck to look past Lucian's shoulder as the broker began shouting the virtues of each fighter.

Really, someone should alert the magistrate's guards before this got out of hand and a fighter was seriously hurt.

"I thought Ana was doing that," Lucian said.

"She was, but she stopped showing up." The taller fighter, the one in the mask, moved in a way that felt familiar. Blue tried to match him with one of the older boys she'd seen working around the quarter, but nothing quite fit.

"Do you know where she is?" Lucian asked.

Blue tore her gaze away from the fighters as the broker took in the final bets, his accountant scrambling to jot them down in her book as a bell rang and the fighters launched themselves at each other, fists flying.

"I was hoping *you* knew," Blue said.

Lucian shook his head, a frown digging into his brow. "Haven't seen her in days."

"Maybe she got a better offer in a different quarter," Blue said. "But that means I need a new delivery person. Do you want the job? Or maybe know someone who would?"

Lucian was still frowning. "I can do the job, Miss Blue, if you have the packages ready in the mornings. My afternoons are already taken. But I'm worried about Ana. She should've said something to one of us if she was leaving the quarter."

A shout echoed from the fight square, and the boy in the mask laughed and said, "If that's the best you've got, my friend, we should call this fight right now."

Blue stepped past Lucian and stared at the fight, dread heavy in her stomach. She knew that voice. That insufferable arrogance coated with a thin veneer of charm. No wonder he was wearing a mask. Punching the crown prince was a jail-worthy offense.

The other fighter charged, slamming into Kellan and nearly bringing them both to the ground. Blue winced as the boy's fists pounded into Kellan's stomach.

It was no better than Kellan deserved.

She hoped he hurt every time he drew breath for the next week.

But.

Closing her eyes, she said, "It's none of my business. It really isn't."

"Miss Blue?"

"Tell me it's none of my business, Lucian."

"Um . . . it's none of your business?"

"Of course it isn't." But what about the other boy? What if the guards came and everyone learned it was the prince in the fighter's square? And what if Kellan got seriously hurt right when he was supposed to be inspiring confidence in the head families that he was ready to take over leadership of the kingdom? Blue could think of a few families who wouldn't hesitate to remove Kellan and his entire family from the picture if they thought he was unfit.

Kellan answered the other fighter's attack with a graceful pivot followed by a devastating hail of blows but got caught by surprise when the boy delivered a powerful uppercut that grazed the prince's jaw.

"Mind my pretty face," Kellan said, laughing.

Laughing.

As if risking his life, the betrothal, the fate of the kingdom, and the freedom of the other fighter was all a game.

"That does it," she muttered, pushing past Lucian and storming toward the fight square.

"I thought it was none of your business!" Lucian called after her, but Blue wasn't listening.

Careless, charming, reckless idiot. How he could possibly be related to Nessa was beyond Blue's understanding, but the fact remained that he was the kingdom's heir. He was the brother of one of her best friends. His father and Papa had been close friends from the moment Papa was engaged to be the former king's tutor.

And Blue had spent her life trying to stop Kellan's foolishness before it exploded in his face. She'd thought he'd grow out of it.

She'd been wrong.

"Stop!" she yelled as she neared the rope. "Stop the fight!"

The crowd of people parted around her, their mouths agape as she swept past them to reach the square. The broker turned, the white stripes on his hat gleaming in the lantern light. His eyes narrowed, and his lips pursed beneath a razor-thin mustache.

"Don't tell me the magistrate sent a little slip of a girl to bring me back in line. Isn't she worried you'll be hurt?" he asked from his corner of the square, oily amusement covering the threat in his words.

Blue drew herself up to her full height and snapped, "This is illegal. And worse, you have no idea what you're doing." All pretense of amusement slid off the broker's face, and Blue hurried on. "Do you know who is underneath that mask?"

All eyes landed on Kellan, who shot her a glare and then laughed, throwing his arms out expansively as if to welcome scrutiny. "It seems I have an admirer. I told you not to ruin my pretty face." He winked at the other fighter, and Blue ground her teeth.

"You know very well I'm not worried one bit about your stupid face."

"Excuse me, gentlemen. I'll handle this and be back to the fight in a moment." Kellan gave the broker a quick, respectful bow, and Blue nearly choked. Then he whirled toward her, ducked under the rope, and gestured forcefully to the street corner where she'd just been. "After you."

For an instant, she considered standing her ground. Announcing his identity to everyone in the crowd and watching them either scatter like rats or fall all over themselves to fawn on him. But a quick glance showed her that he was there without any of his guards, and the broker looked furious enough to chew through iron. Unmasking Kellan would be more dangerous than just convincing him not to be an idiot.

Of course she'd been trying for years to convince him not to be an idiot, and nothing she did seemed to take. Still, it was better than putting him in more danger than he'd already put himself.

Quickly, she made her way to the deserted corner, ignoring the whispers from the crowd. The second they reached the corner, she snapped, "Have you lost your mind?"

"Have you lost yours?" His voice was low and forceful. "What are you doing walking by yourself in these neighborhoods after dark? Do you have any idea the kind of things that happen here?"

"We aren't discussing my choices. We're discussing yours. Hang it all, Kellan, what happens if you get seriously hurt?"

"I'm very quick on my feet." He grinned as if inviting her to admire his fighting skills.

"What happens if the magistrate's guards show up and catch you? What will the head families think of a crown prince who—"

"Keep your voice down." He glanced over his shoulder at the crowd, which was milling closer as if hoping to eavesdrop.

"And what happens to the other fighter if you're unmasked? He could go to jail. Is that worth you having a night of fun?" Blue planted her fists on her waist and glared up at him.

Kellan paused, looked once more at the square, and then swallowed hard. "I didn't think about that."

She threw her hands into the air. "You never do. Never. You just jump from one dangerous plan to the next with no thought to the consequences."

"Oh, I think about the consequences." The charm was gone from his voice, and in its place was something dark and lonely.

"I just didn't think about the consequences to *him*."

"And the head families? Nessa? Your mother?" Blue tugged at her curls as it occurred to her that she was now responsible to either inform the queen of Kellan's risky behavior or start keeping secrets from both her friend and her sovereign ruler. "Oh stars. What am I going to tell the queen?"

Kellan straightened abruptly. "Don't tell her anything."

"But—"

"Blue, please. For once in your life, don't run to someone in charge and tell them everything you know." His eyes beseeched her.

She set her jaw. "Give me one good reason why I should start keeping secrets for you."

He was silent for a long moment. The crowd behind them grew restless, and the broker shouted for Kellan to return to the fight.

Finally, Kellan said quietly, "Because we both love Nessa."

The righteous indignation that filled Blue slowly bled into resignation. They did both love Nessa. And Nessa would be worried sick if she knew what her brother was doing.

"Fine." Blue spat the word at him. "I'll keep this a secret on one condition."

"Name it."

"You never participate in another street fight again. Starting now."

"Now?" He shot another glance over his shoulder as the broker bellowed for him. "Blue, I can't back out of the fight. He'll send his enforcers after me in a heartbeat. I have to finish this."

"Then go lose. Quickly. Less risk for everyone involved that way." Blue folded her arms across her chest as Kellan glared at her.

"Fine." He flung the word at her in the same tone she'd used on him. "I'll go lose. And then I'll walk you back to the shop."

"I don't need an escort."

He stared pointedly at a group of men, all wearing the same black and white stripes as the broker, who were briskly moving in their direction. "The broker blames you for ruining the evening's entertainment. Come back to the square with me, watch me lose, and then we'll leave."

She sighed in annoyance, though in truth, the look on the broker's face made her heart pound uncomfortably.

Kellan poured the charm back into his voice as he turned them both toward the square. "My dear friends, a crisis has been averted. Who's ready to watch a fight?"

The crowd erupted into cheers as Kellan ducked under the rope, ignored Blue, and proceeded to gracefully lose.

EIGHT

Dinah couldn't draw a single breath without panic scraping at her thoughts. None of her plans had worked. The businesses she'd hoped her husband hadn't known about were mortgaged, the documents forged with his signature. Her contacts in Akram refused to extend the massive credit she needed because the economy in their own kingdom had declined sharply in recent months. Her contact in Súndraille had offered a much smaller loan than she needed but had pressed for assurances that she had collateral to back up the debt.

She didn't.

And while she'd yet to hear from her contact in Ravenspire, she had to assume they would demand collateral as well. She certainly would in their place. No one asked for the kind of loan she needed unless they were on the cusp of financial ruin.

She was running out of time. The estate, along with its debts, would go before the royal magistrate for review in less than two weeks unless she paid back every bit of it, according to the papers

Mr. Dubois, the creditor, had filed with her solicitor.

She didn't have any coin.

She didn't have any resources.

And so far, Mr. Dubois had been smart enough to thoroughly secure his home and walk the streets heavily guarded. He hadn't underestimated the lengths Dinah would go to reclaim what was hers. Under different circumstances, she would admire the ruthless cleverness it took to assess the value of the Chauveau empire, exploit its weakest link in her husband, and sweep the entire thing out from under her feet, all while staying safely out of reach of her dagger.

Dinah's back was to the wall, but she wasn't giving up. She'd sworn an oath to herself sixteen years earlier when she'd been alone on the streets of Falaise de la Mer, friendless, penniless, and powerless, that she would never allow anyone to put her in that situation again.

She intended to keep her word.

Pulling her black cloak close to her body, she tucked the hood over her head and looked at the ground as she walked briskly beneath the iron arches that led to the Gaillard quarter. Short of robbing every merchant in the city—a sure way to gain the notice of the queen and all the magistrates, especially when Mr. Dubois could then testify that she'd miraculously come up with a way to pay off her debt just after the robberies—Dinah had no way to get her hands on the coin she needed.

But someone in the city did. Someone was creating gold. She'd seen it herself a week ago when she was arguing with that old skinflint Maurice at the open-air market. The alchemist girl had tried paying for her purchases with it only to have Maurice realize the gold wasn't real.

Maybe it hadn't been real, but it had been close. And that meant whoever was creating it might have already perfected their methods.

Of course, it could have arrived in Balavata from another kingdom, either through the port or with a traveler who'd crossed their borders. But Dinah didn't think so. The girl—Blue, Maurice had called her—had seemed nervous when Maurice pronounced the gold a fake. Almost as if she already knew what he was going to say but had hoped to fool him anyway. And when Dinah had visited the girl's shop to inquire about the complaint the shop owner must surely have lodged with his local magistrate, he'd responded strangely. Freezing in apparent shock at the question and then quickly brushing her concerns away.

No merchant who'd been cheated out of coin would ever ignore the crime. There should've been a complaint filed with the magistrate in the Gaillard quarter, and there wasn't. Dinah's solicitor had checked.

Turning west, she walked quickly past a cathedral, the iron chimes that hung from its gate tinkling merrily in her wake. The moon hung fat and heavy in the sky, a pale orange ripe for the picking. Few people were still out on the streets at this hour, but Dinah took no chances. Ducking down side streets, crossing through alleys, doubling back over her tracks, she made sure no one was following her as she finally reached the Mortar & Pestle.

The door that led from the alley into the shop was solid, the lock secure, but Dinah had come prepared. Removing a metal crowbar from the deep inner pocket of her cloak, she pried, hammered, and smashed her way around the lock until the doorjamb was in splinters and the doorknob hung uselessly in its socket.

The streets might be deserted, and the shop might be

surrounded by businesses rather than homes, but Dinah couldn't take the chance that someone could've overheard her efforts and even now be on their way to alert the quarter's magistrate. She had to move quickly.

Pulling the door closed behind her, she quickly lit the candle she'd brought with her, found the closest lamp, and used the candle to bring the lamp to life. Soft golden light filled the store-room, and Dinah swiftly examined the room.

Well-stocked shelves. A worktable, chairs, a sink, and a small stove. What would someone need to create gold besides a hunk of metal? Fire? Acid? Some sort of magical concoction of herbs and minerals?

The thought that magic instead of regular alchemy was being used to create gold sent a shiver down Dinah's spine, and her gaze sharpened, searching the room for spell books or wands.

At a glance, the room looked free of any of the obvious trappings of a witch, but anyone using magic would be careful to hide the truth, even in their private storeroom.

Moving briskly, Dinah stalked past the shelves, muttering the names of the ingredients she recognized as she passed.

Bolla root. Tryllis weed. Beeswax. Minorate rock.

Bland. Ordinary. Nothing that would explain the gold Blue had tried to use with Maurice.

Dinah reached the stove and brushed her fingers over the strange little pot that sat on an unlit burner. The lid was held in place by five small latches, and a gauge rested on a slender pipe that disappeared through the center of the lid and into the pot itself. When Dinah picked up the pot, something rattled within. Quickly unsealing the lid, Dinah peered inside and smiled as grim triumph spread through her.

Three chunks of pale golden metal sat inside. They weren't quite the right shade of gold and there were faint lines of dull gray metal still threading through them in places, but they were close.

Dinah scooped up one of the rocks and pocketed it before returning the pot to the stove. Then she gazed around the storeroom, her mind racing.

She had to make it look like an ordinary break-in to disguise what she'd really been after. A stack of burlap sacks sat in the corner by the door. Dinah took one and faced the wall of shelves.

She could just take random things and discard them before she returned to her mansion.

Or she could take a few things she knew how to use in case her plan to have Blue create gold for her failed. It had been years since she'd had anything to do with witchcraft, but a competent woman never forgot her basic spells, and Dinah was far more than competent.

Snatching what she needed off the shelves, she filled the bag and then hurried out the door, her heart pounding. The streets were still deserted. Still silent.

The pale gold rock in her pocket bumped gently against her leg as she walked briskly toward her own quarter again, the burlap sack hidden in her arms beneath her cloak.

Should she try to force Blue to comply by threatening to reveal her experiment to the queen and the royal magistrate? The de la Cours were close to the queen, so that could go badly for Dinah.

Should she try appealing to Blue's father? Perhaps convince him that Dinah would offer protection for the de la Cours if he would get his daughter to produce gold for her?

There again she ran into the possibility of him reporting her to the queen. It was possible the queen would be upset with Blue's actions. But it was even more likely that she would be furious to discover the precarious position Dinah was in. Without control of her empire, she had no way to protect the people in her quarter or bolster Balavata's economy and outside business interests. Without control of her empire, she had nothing to offer in the way of an alliance for the betrothal season.

Without her empire, Dinah was perilously close to becoming friendless, penniless, and powerless once more, and this time, she'd be taking her daughters down with her.

No, whatever step she took next, it had to be bold. Decisive. It had to put her firmly in control of Blue and her experiments without anyone questioning a thing.

NINE

THREE DAYS AFTER the street fight that he would've *won* had Blue not stuck her nose once more where it didn't belong, Kellan stepped out of his carriage in front of the Mortar & Pestle and was instantly flanked by two guards. Lady Gaillard, who had both her daughter Genevieve and two of her nieces in tow, was waiting beside the shop's entrance. Someone in the palace must have been bribed into giving her the prince's schedule. How many other head families knew his every move and were waiting to ambush him? No wonder he couldn't get a single moment to himself without resorting to sneaking around like he was ten again.

The weight that had settled over his chest the moment he'd returned home to Balavata felt like it was crushing him as he straightened his shoulders and moved toward the shop.

"Prince Kellan!" Lady Gaillard swooped toward him, her delicate voice rising over the clip-clop of horse feet and the rumble of carriage wheels on the cobblestone street behind the prince.

"Lady Gaillard, you look positively delicious today," Kellan said with a wink, smiling as the color rose in the woman's golden cheeks. He'd quickly learned that flattering the mothers was an essential weapon in his arsenal.

"Oh, you rogue." Lady Gaillard swept into a curtsy that left her neckline gaping open before him. Kellan averted his eyes and found Blue standing at her shop's front door, one slim brow raised in scorn as she observed the situation. Her riotous curls framed her head, and her brown skin glowed in the sun. Her full lips twisted into a smirk as he stared. It should have made her look like the smug know-it-all he knew she was. Instead, he found himself wondering what she would look like if she smiled. A real smile, not the painfully polite version she usually trotted out when he was present.

It was an annoying thought, and a distraction he couldn't afford. Especially when a smile from Blue probably meant she'd found another way to drain the fun out of his life.

"Of course, you remember my daughter, Genevieve. My nieces also came along to the market today, but Gen especially has been anxious to see you again." Lady Gaillard shoved Gen toward the prince while managing to block her nieces' bodies with her own.

Kellan caught Gen's arms as she stumbled over her long skirt, and Lady Gaillard trilled with satisfaction. "How gallant of you, Your Majesty. I do think you favor our sweet Gen. Might we expect you to call upon us as her parents soon?"

There was no right answer to the question. If he said no, he would send the message that he wasn't interested in Gen, and the Gaillards might change tactics from flattery to threats in their efforts to secure the betrothal. If he said yes, it would take

Lady Gaillard less than a day to have the entire city discussing the prince's upcoming commitment to her daughter, which would infuriate the other families, who would feel they hadn't had enough of the prince's time to get a fair shot at the throne.

Fortunately, he'd spent the last ten years learning how to artfully dodge questions about his misdeeds at the academy. As Gen mouthed, "I'm sorry," with her face turned away from her mother, he gave her a charming smile and then extended the same to Lady Gaillard as he said, "I'm afraid my secretary keeps my engagement calendar. I really couldn't say if you are on it at the moment. But do send an invitation if there's an event you'd like me to attend."

A snort of laughter came from the shop's doorway, and Kellan sent Blue a withering glare. It wasn't like he was enjoying the situation. He was making the best of the responsibility he'd been given. She should be ecstatic.

She shook her head and disappeared inside the shop. Kellan moved to follow—picking up his mother's headache cream and finally seeing Pierre again were the reasons for his trip—but Lady Gaillard wasn't through with him yet. It was a full five minutes of flattery, compliments, and dodging questions before he was able to extricate himself and enter the shop.

The main room was a light, airy space with dark red shelves against the walls, polished tables to display larger goods, and a few bins of candy or little potted creams near Pierre's coin till. Pierre was busy explaining the differences between two types of powders to a woman who looked like a farmer. He looked up when the door's chimes sang, and his face split into a wide, welcoming grin as he saw Kellan.

The prince smiled back—a real, from-the-heart smile, the

kind he reserved only for family—and then nodded at the customer, giving Pierre permission to finish the transaction rather than bow and greet his prince. Fully expecting Lady Gaillard to enter the shop on his heels, Kellan made straight for the storeroom where Pierre had often welcomed him as a child.

As Kellan passed through the doorway, he motioned for his guards to remain behind and said, "Make sure no one but Pierre follows me."

And then he was in the long storeroom with its stocked shelves, its carefully stored tools, its worktable, and its stove with two pots of liquid bubbling on its burners. Behind him, he heard Lady Gaillard's voice rise above the shop's door chimes. Closing his eyes, he pressed his fingers against them in a futile effort to stave off a burgeoning headache.

"What are you doing in my storeroom?"

Kellan opened his eyes to find Blue standing beside some shelves full of amber jars with dried leaves inside. There was a scowl on her face, and her foot tapped impatiently. She made no move to curtsy. He had the sudden, inexplicable urge to laugh.

For nearly two weeks, he'd been courted, flattered, cajoled, and lied to by every person who saw him, with the exception of his family and Gen, in the twenty minutes he'd spent with her when he'd first arrived. It was exhausting to feel like he needed armor for every single interaction. But here was Blue, just as tiny and fierce as she had been the other night, and she had no intention of giving him pretty, meaningless words or soft lies. She would speak her mind plainly, whether he liked it or not. She always had.

"I came to see your father. I've missed him."

She sighed, clearly annoyed. "Well, don't touch anything."

"What's the fun in that?"

"Maybe you should think less about having fun and more about keeping your fool head attached to your neck long enough to be given the crown."

He deliberately leaned against the closest shelf just to see her eyes narrow. "Maybe you should learn to loosen up and find a little fun now and then."

"I have plenty of fun."

He rolled his eyes and picked up a jar full of a thick, dark red liquid. "Doing what? Mixing potions and making sure everyone around you is following every single rule? We need to work on your definition of fun."

"Well, I can promise you it doesn't include getting punched in the face. And unless you want to risk losing your fingers, I'd put the korash acid down."

Hastily, he returned the jar to the shelf, knocking over another jar in the process. As he set the shelf to rights, Blue said, "I *told* you not to touch anything."

Her tone was irritation personified, and it was like taking a breath of fresh air. The weight on his chest eased.

Maybe she interfered too much with his life, and maybe he deliberately provoked her just to make her mad, but here, he didn't have to parse through words for hidden meanings or worry that if he said the wrong thing, his sister would pay the price. Here he was just a boy irritating the girl who'd always ruined his best-laid plans. The rush of affection that warmed him was a surprise, but not nearly as surprising as the next words that came out of his mouth.

"You look beautiful today, Blue."

When she shot him a startled look, the words tumbled out,

faster and faster while a strange, unwelcome heat burned in his face. "I mean . . . you probably look beautiful every day, I have no idea. I've never really looked. I mean, I've *looked*, but not like that. Not that I'm looking at you like that, because of course I'm not. I just . . . It was an observation."

What was *wrong* with him? He'd taken pride in being able to charm any girl at the academy into a kiss, a dance, or both. And here he stood babbling like a fool in front of the one girl who couldn't stand him.

And he couldn't stand her either, he reminded himself. He really couldn't. He was just grateful that she wasn't playing games with his head the way everyone else seemed to be.

"What was all that?" she asked, waving a hand in the air as if to encompass everything he'd just said.

"It was a compliment," he said, and tried to play off the moment with an easy grin and a wink.

That was a mistake. Her scowl morphed into something dangerous, and she advanced on him, her eyes snapping.

He held his ground. Pride demanded it, but it took effort. She might be tiny, but that was easy to forget when her attitude took up the entire room.

She stood in front of him, hands fisted on her hips. "Were you *flirting* with me?"

"No!" Of course he hadn't been flirting. This was Blue. He'd rather pull out his toenails than try to flirt with her. Why would she twist a simple observation into something it wasn't?

He remembered the grin and the wink and silently groaned. She hadn't twisted anything. He had, and he was never going to live that down. Blue had a memory like a wolf trap.

"Are you going to tell me I look delicious too? It certainly seemed to work on Lady Gaillard." There was derision in her voice, and suddenly, he'd had enough.

"Trust me. I would never tell you that you look delicious. Angry? Yes. Scornful? Absolutely. But never, in a hundred summers, would I tell you that you look delicious."

"I don't believe you." She met his gaze.

"Oh you can believe it, Blue. I've never meant anything more in my life."

She cocked her head and studied him, and he had the uncomfortable impression that she was sifting through his character, looking for the pieces she was sure were missing.

"You toss careless words at people all the time, Kellan. Pretty compliments. Easy smiles. Winks that I suppose you think make people feel special." Her voice was calm and steady again. "I don't want your carelessness. I don't want easy. If you have something to say to me, then you'd better speak the truth and mean it. The rest of it is useless."

He took a moment to breathe. To rein in the flash of anger that left a hard knot in his chest. When he spoke, his voice was as calm and steady as hers.

"Do you have any idea what my life is like, Blue?"

She frowned.

"Those pretty compliments, easy smiles, and winks that you hate me for are the only way I can play a dangerous political game that ends with me being forced to choose a bride by weighing which head family is both the most advantageous ally and the best able to put down any violence from the families whose daughters aren't chosen." He closed his eyes and pressed his fingers against them again. The burgeoning pain he'd had before had turned into a raging headache.

"Everyone is lying to me. Flattering me. Testing me. If I slip up even once, it could cost me the rest of my family." His throat closed at the thought, and he told himself to be quiet. Stop telling the girl who despised him the things that weighed on him. He was just giving her more weapons to use against him, and he had no doubt she would if she thought he was in the wrong.

Her hand slid over his arm and squeezed gently. Startled, he dropped his hands and opened his eyes. She stood before him holding a little tin in her free hand. When she saw she had his attention, she opened the tin, and the sweet spice of wintermint spilled out. Her mouth tightened, and the pulse at the side of her neck beat rapidly as she dipped her finger in the cream and then raised it to his head.

"This will help that headache," she said quietly.

He let her rub the cream into his temples, and felt the tension start to leave his body as the pain lessened.

"I may have misjudged you in this instance," she said stiffly.

He blinked at her, and her eyes narrowed. "I can admit when I'm wrong, Kellan."

"Not in my experience," he said, but he smiled as he said it. A real, warm, reserved-for-family smile.

And miracle of miracles, she smiled back. Not the stiff, polite caricature of a smile he was used to seeing, but a wide, generous smile that welcomed him in and warmed him more than he wanted to admit.

"Thank you." He held her gaze as the shop's chimes rang to announce the farmer's exit, and the sound of Pierre's steps came toward the storeroom. "I'm grateful to finally have someone be completely honest with me."

"I'm here most days if you ever need to talk to someone who

is immune to your charms. Always happy to point out your many shortcomings." She sounded grumpy and sincere at the same time.

He laughed. "Be careful. I just might take you up on that."

Turning toward the rest of the storeroom, he frowned. The wooden frame around the back door was splintered, and the doorknob hung uselessly. "What happened?"

"Someone broke into the shop last night." For the first time in the many years he'd known her, Blue's voice trembled.

Anger rushed through Kellan as he stalked toward the door. "Did they take anything? Does the magistrate have any suspects? Was anyone here when . . . hang it all, Blue. You stay and work late on your own, don't you?" He rounded on her. "Were you here?"

She shook her head, but there was worry on her face. "It was the first night in nearly three weeks that I went home with Papa. And yes, they took some of my rarer ingredients, a few staples I can easily replace, and one of my new experiments." Her gaze slid toward the stove and then snapped back to him.

"We need to replace the door. Get a stronger lock. And you shouldn't stay here alone at night." He was pacing, anger a flush of heat beneath his skin.

No matter how annoying Blue could be, she and Pierre were practically family. No one threatened his family and got away with it.

"We've already ordered a new door. New lock. It'll be fine, Kellan. These things happen sometimes." She sounded unconvinced. He watched her for a moment as she bit her lip, but she said nothing more.

"I'll personally ask the Gaillard magistrate to post more

guards in the merchant district at night."

"Thank you." She offered him a small smile.

And then Pierre was in the storeroom, launching himself at the prince and laughing as he scooped the tall boy into a fierce embrace. Kellan leaned into it and let himself imagine, just for a moment, that the arms wrapped around him belonged to his father, and that the weight of his kingdom's future no longer rested on his shoulders alone.

TEN

BLUE STAYED IN the shop's storeroom long past sunset to get all the stock replenished and the morning's orders filled, humming Mama's lullaby as she worked. She refined silver and blended it with copper for strength and durability to fill an order from the Gaillards. Hung her recently harvested bolla root to dry and ground date pits into dust with her mortar and pestle before storing the dust in an amber jar. Crushed wintermint into tinctures of yaeringlei oil and sealed them shut with wax, her stomach churning as the spicy sweet scent filled the air.

And through it all she worried about the recent break-in.

She'd told Kellan the truth. These things did happen sometimes. But she worried that this wasn't a regular robbery. While a number of items had been taken, plenty of Blue's most valuable supplies had been left untouched. Supplies that were in easy reach on the shelves close to the damaged back door. Finished goods hadn't been taken from the shop floor, though they were in easy reach too. But the evidence of Blue's latest nearly successful attempt to turn lead into gold, evidence sealed inside a pot on the stove, had been taken.

Why would someone ransack the shop enough to find her almost-gold but leave so many truly valuable items behind?

Worry slithered through her, churning up her thoughts and sending her heart racing at odd moments. She hadn't told Papa that someone had taken the results of her experiments. Especially when he'd been so upset about Dinah Chauveau coming into their shop to question him about the magistrate's investigation into the fake gold Blue had tried to give Maurice at the market. If he knew someone had taken one of her failed attempts, he'd tell her to stop, and everything she'd worked so hard for would be lost.

Papa had been uneasy about letting her work late again, but she hadn't had much of a choice. Lucian wasn't able to start doing deliveries until the next morning, and she had more orders to fill than she'd had hours in her workday. Papa had only agreed to allow her to stay when she told him Kellan had requested extra guards in the area. He'd wanted to wait with her, but the shirella orchard needed harvesting while it was still light, and he'd already arranged to hire a crew of workers to help in the afternoon and early evening.

Blue had assured him that she'd stay alert and take no chances. Still, he'd made her promise to stay inside with the door locked and wait until he returned to escort her home.

Guilt sat heavy on her chest as she stirred the cream she was making and reached for its next ingredient. She'd never lied to Papa before. And she wasn't lying, exactly. She just wasn't telling him the whole truth. The guilt swirled into her stomach, slick and miserable, and she closed her eyes.

Not telling him the whole truth was the same as lying. Papa would see no difference between the two, and she couldn't bear to betray his trust in her. She'd tell him about the stolen experiment. Maybe she could keep working on it at the farmhouse instead of the shop. If the person who'd stolen the almost-gold broke in again looking for more and found none, maybe they would believe it had been a yellow rock Blue had purchased, rather than the result of alchemy.

Something scraped against the newly installed door that led to the alley, and Blue jumped, dropping the tincture she was holding. It smashed to the storeroom floor, releasing a thick wave of wintermint.

Cursing, Blue grabbed a rag and crouched below her worktable. She dabbed at the puddle of oil with its slivers of glass, blinking against the sharp sting of so much spice in the air.

The knob on the alley door rattled, and Blue froze. Lifting her eyes, she saw the knob turn back and forth as someone tested it to see if it was locked.

It was. Locked and triple bolted. The doorway itself was reinforced with a double layer of wood as well. Papa had taken no chances.

Had the same person who'd broken in before returned to see if there were more chunks of almost-gold to steal? Would they go away if they realized someone was still in the shop?

Panic blazed through her, making it impossible to think. Should she be silent? Be loud? Race out the front calling for the guards Kellan had said he'd ask the magistrate to post in the area?

Blue scrambled to her feet, the oil-soaked rag clutched in her hand. "Who's there?" she called loudly.

The knob stopped moving. Blue waited one breath, two, and then crept toward the door. Her heart thundered against her ears, and her entire body shook.

Pressing her ear to the wooden door, she strained to hear anything on the other side. It was quiet. Either the person was gone, or they were waiting and listening just like she was.

They were going to keep waiting. Blue had no intention of opening the door to check the alley.

Quietly backing away from the door, she tossed the rag she was holding into the trash and then returned to her worktable. Papa would be here soon, and Blue's concentration was destroyed. She'd pack up her ingredients and somehow pry herself out of bed earlier than usual so she could finish the orders Lucian was scheduled to deliver in the morning. She'd just begun sealing up her puffer bloom oil, when the knob on the shop's front door rattled.

Blue dropped the oil and reached for the halberd Papa kept on a hook beside the doorway that led back into the shop. The ax head was precisely balanced on a long, spiked shaft that was nearly as tall as Blue. Hefting it, she spread her hands wide along the shaft like Papa had taught her—one hand close to the ax head, and one just below the midpoint on the pole. If someone broke into the shop, Blue was going to make them immediately regret that decision.

The only light that came into the shop itself was from the braziers that were lit along the street poles outside the windows. The firelight glowed against the iron filigree that covered the windows from the outside. Blue crept across the dimly lit floor, holding the halberd steady, and then caught her breath when a shadow moved across one of the windows.

It was a figure in a hooded cloak. A woman, Blue was pretty sure. She moved with delicate confidence, seeming to be more shadow than human as she slipped past the shop and disappeared up the street.

Blue clutched the halberd close and rushed to the window. Peering past the iron filigree, she strained to see the figure on the torch-lit street, but the woman kept to the shadows and was soon lost from view.

What did it mean? Was it just a customer who'd seen the light pouring from the high windows in the storeroom and had hoped the shop itself was still open?

Blue shook her head as she swept the street with another look, searching for movement. No one who meant the shop any good would quietly try both doors in hopes of entering the store without being noticed. Whoever had stolen her almost-gold had come back hoping for more.

When would it stop? And how long before the rumor that she was creating gold at the Mortar & Pestle spread through the streets and reached the ears of a broker?

She should never have lied to Papa. Shouldn't have experimented at the shop in the first place. She could've figured out a way to do the same process at home. Bought a new stove with higher heat distribution. Taken tools and supplies from the shop to the house. Anything to keep the secret safe.

Now she'd put herself, Papa, and the shop in danger, and she didn't know how to fix it.

Blue stayed at the window gripping the halberd until her fingers began to cramp. Other than the occasional carriage, the street was deserted. Finally satisfied that she was truly alone again, she returned to the storeroom to finish cleaning up, but it was impossible to concentrate. She kept glancing at the door-knob, imagining it had moved. Jumping at tiny whispers of sound. Straining to hear footsteps outside the shop walls.

Finally, she gave up. Keeping the halberd at her side, she sat in one of the shop's chairs to wait for Papa.

The cathedral's iron bells tolled the hour, the sonorous notes rolling through the Gaillard quarter thick as cream. Blue counted the bells and frowned. It was well past the dinner hour. Papa should've returned by now. He liked to be in bed early, since he always got up before the sun.

She held herself still, watching the star-spun sky out the shop's window, leaning forward in anticipation every time she caught a noise that sounded like it might be Papa's footsteps.

Maybe he'd gotten caught up in a household project and lost track of time. Or maybe Grand-mère had needed his help at her cottage.

When even the occasional carriage stopped passing by the shop, Blue abandoned the chair and began pacing.

Maybe something had happened to Pepperell, and Papa was helping the cat before coming to get Blue. Or he'd fallen asleep while reading a book in his overstuffed arm chair as he did some nights, though Blue couldn't imagine Papa sitting down to relax while his daughter was still in town.

Maybe . . . Blue's heart dropped as the cathedral bells tolled again. Another hour had passed, and she'd run out of plausible excuses for Papa's tardiness.

Maybe he'd hurt himself along the way, and it was far too late for any passersby to take the road that led past their farmhouse and into the city, so he was just lying there waiting for help.

This last possibility latched onto Blue's thoughts and sent

a buzz of fear through her veins. Keeping the halberd in her hands in case the strange visitor from earlier was still lurking about the streets, Blue let herself out of the shop, locking the door behind her.

The day's warmth had long since cooled. A chilly wind scoured the street and tugged at Blue's hair with capricious fingers. She'd forgotten her summer cloak in the storeroom, but the fear that clawed at her now refused to let her return for it. Instead, she held the halberd close and hurried down the street, past the smithy and the tanner's shop, the cobbler's studio and the haberdashery. Turning left at the corner that housed a pub and a solicitor's office, she collided with the solid figure of a man.

For an instant, she thought it was Papa. Late, but still coming to retrieve his daughter and bring her home. The fear that had driven her out of the shop receded, and she took a hasty step back so she could see him clearly.

One heartbeat. Two. And the fear crashed into her again as she got a good look at the man in front of her.

Normand, a guard in the Gaillards' service whose wife was the magistrate of the quarter, stood before her, his fingers worrying with the edges of his uniform jacket. He was the same height as Papa, though wider in the middle, and his red-brown hair had long since gone mostly gray. She'd known him since she was a toddler sitting on the storeroom floor poking her fingers into her mother's potions. Usually, she'd greet him and let him tell her how big she was getting, how maybe he had a nephew who was looking for a girl with a steady head on her shoulders, how her mother had been the smartest person he'd ever known.

But she had no time for pleasantries tonight. Not until she found Papa.

"Excuse me, Normand," she said breathlessly. "I have to go. Papa didn't show up to take me home, and I'm worried."

"Wait a moment, Blue." His hands reached out to steady her, but his voice was all wrong.

It shook. Broke when he said her name. And there was an awful gentleness to it, as if he pitied her.

She backed up.

"Let's go to the shop," he said, his voice still gentle. His hands set carefully on her shoulders like she was made of glass.

She shook her head, her breath coming in quick, hard pants. "I have to go. Papa needs me."

His hands settled on her shoulders. Gripped. "I'm sorry, Blue."

"Sorry about what?" Her voice shook too, the fear that had pushed her out of the shop becoming a jagged knife that sliced into every thought.

"Your papa is . . . Carlson, the farrier two streets over, was out late shoeing horses. He found him. Found your papa, I mean."

"Where is he?" Her words came out loud and high.

"I'm sorry," Normand repeated. "I went to the farmhouse first, but you weren't there, so I thought I'd try the shop next."

"Normand, where is Papa?" She couldn't feel her lips. Couldn't understand how the words made it across her tongue when everything inside her felt paralyzed.

"He's dead, Blue. I saw it for myself. I'm sorry."

She wrenched herself out of his grip. "He's not."

"I checked and double-checked. I wish I had different news." Normand stood there, shoulders bent, hands hanging in the air like he didn't know what to do with them. Didn't know how to help her.

There was no help for her. Not if his words were true.

"Where is he?" She whispered the words as the terrifying idea that he was telling the truth took root and burrowed toward her bones.

"I've sent for someone to collect him—"

"*Where?*" She clutched the halberd so hard, her fingers ached.

Normand was silent for a long moment, and then he said quietly, "The side of the road, just beyond the merchant district. Looks like someone surprised him from behind and stabbed him in the neck."

She stood in front of him for a long moment, her heart thunder in her ears, and then the halberd clattered onto the cobblestones as she dropped it and ran.

Papa was right where Normand had said he'd be. His summer cloak had been arranged over his body. Normand's doing, she was sure.

She dropped to her knees and reached a shaking hand toward the cloak that hid his face.

Maybe it wasn't him.

It was so dark outside. Normand could be mistaken.

If she didn't move the cloak, if she didn't look, it could be someone else. She could get up and walk the rest of the way to the farmhouse, and Papa would be inside. Her dinner would be on a covered plate kept warm in the stove. Pepperell would complain that she'd been gone so long. And Papa . . . Papa would be asleep in his chair, his book fallen against his chest.

She held that image in her mind, let it glow with hope, as her hand slowly met the coarse linen of the cloak and pulled it back.

The image disintegrated, and a low sound of raw agony tore its way through Blue.

It was Papa.

His beloved eyes were closed. His neck torn open on one side. The heavy, metallic smell of blood filled the air.

It was Papa.

Her body shuddered and the dark corner of her heart where she kept her memories of Mama and the root cellar opened wide and swallowed her.

She curled herself over the top of him, clutching at his cloak, while the air left her body. She couldn't cry. Couldn't scream. Couldn't *breathe*.

It was Papa.

And she was utterly lost.

ELEVEN

IT HAD BEEN four days since someone had killed Papa. Blue had moved through the hours, a stranger in her own skin. She'd eaten when Grand-mère put something in front of her, though the food tasted like dust. She'd slept when Grand-mère gently pushed her toward her room. She'd said things when it was expected of her, nodded her acceptance of the funeral arrangements, and vaguely registered the presence of a steady stream of townsfolk coming by with food and iron chimes and kind words. Twice the warning bells along the road to the wraith's prison rang, their discordant melody scraping against Blue's nerves until she wanted to scream.

How could she worry about a distant, caged monster when a monster on the streets of her city had already taken what was most precious to her?

Through it all, her heart beat, though it sent a dull throb of pain through her every time she thought of Papa. Her lungs breathed, though it felt like there was a chain wrapped around her chest, pulling tighter with every passing day.

She'd spent most of those four days sitting at the edge of their property staring at the sea, pretending she hadn't stayed late at the shop. That Papa hadn't left to come bring her home. That someone hadn't torn his life away from him with one vicious choice.

That she hadn't lied to Papa about the real danger they were in.

Her eyes were dry. Her voice hollow. Somewhere inside her, a howling storm of grief threatened, but she shied away from it. If she didn't touch it, it couldn't hurt her. If she didn't look it in the eye, it wouldn't rip her apart at the seams.

The day of Papa's funeral dawned bright and golden. Blue stood on the little hill behind their garden and tried not to stare at the hole in the ground beside Mama's grave. The priest spoke his words, the bell girl rang her chimes in between homilies, and a crowd gathered behind Blue—a mix of the wealthy, the merchants, and the poor. Even the royal family was in attendance, though Blue couldn't remember when they'd arrived. It didn't matter. All that mattered was that she not look at his grave. Not listen to the words that praised his life of kindness and generosity.

Not let the storm within take control.

A sea hawk circled far overhead, and Blue followed his flight with her eyes. The summer heat was a damp, thick covering on her skin, and she imagined she was in the water. Swimming out to the field of golden sea vines that covered the floor of the Chrysós Sea and gave it its color. She'd swim with strong, sure strokes, farther than she ever had before. She'd dive, grasp the delicate rubbery vines with her fingers, and uproot them with a single tug.

They were good for potions that treated swelling. For hair loss or fatigue. They could even be used to season food if you sprinkled them with ginger and then dried them in the sun. Papa had shown her how.

Her throat closed, sending a sharp pain down her neck, and she hastily found the sea hawk again before tears could prick her eyes and the storm inside her could break free.

The priest finished. The bells fell silent. And then hands were reaching for her. Steering her away from the grave and into the crowd. Face after face.

"How are you?"

"I'm so sorry."

"He was a good man."

"Do you need anything?"

Blue couldn't find the words to respond to any of them. She was standing in front of yet another well-meaning townswoman, listening to yet another stream of platitudes, when a person beside her said, "Have they caught the person who killed him?"

The question wasn't aimed at Blue, but she turned toward it anyway and found the tall, sharp-nosed haberdasher talking to Normand.

Normand waved a hand to hush the woman, and said, "It was a lovely service, Blue. I'm sure your father would've liked it."

A frown moved slowly across Blue's brow, her muscles feeling ancient and unused.

"I think he would've much rather been alive," she said, the words sounding brittle and sharp. There was cotton in her throat, a chain around her chest, and as the last word left her lips, her breath caught on something that felt suspiciously like a sob.

"Of course," Normand said soothingly.

"But who killed him?" the haberdasher said. "Are we safe to walk the streets in our quarter?"

Blue felt something hot and sharp unfurl within her as she started shaking.

"I'm sure you don't mean to cause more distress to Miss de la Cour with thoughtless questions she can't possibly answer." The voice came from behind Blue, and both Normand and the haberdasher blanched as Kellan stepped to Blue's side.

Normand bowed, and the haberdasher flung herself into a curtsy while she babbled something that sounded like a cross between an apology and more questions.

Kellan simply wrapped his arm around Blue and led her away. He threaded them through the crowd, an easy feat when everyone was busy bowing and doing their best not to get in the crown prince's way, and then walked her to the far side of the graves until they were at the top of the hill overlooking the orchard and the distant glittering gold ribbon of the sea.

For a long moment, they stood in silence, and Blue was surprised to find herself leaning on the warmth of his presence, the solid strength he offered holding her up while her knees trembled and the hot, sharp thing inside her coiled and churned.

"Remember that time I tried to climb to the top of one of your trees and the branch was too small to hold me?" he said finally.

Blue looked at the orchard, remembering the pale blue flowers on the shirella trees and the shouts of Kellan and his friends daring each other to leap from tree to tree while Blue and Nessa dug in the dirt for worms and interesting roots. "You broke your arm. Papa was furious."

Kellan laughed quietly. "I'd never heard him raise his voice before. Told me he'd never forgive me if I broke my neck on his property and not to be cheeky when I asked if that meant I could break it somewhere else. I don't think he actually minded me being cheeky, though, because he laughed after he was done yelling."

Blue smiled a little, though her lips felt stiff. "He never could stay angry for long."

"Usually he never bothered getting angry at all. He had better ways to make a lesson stick. Remember the cider?"

This time she was the one who laughed—a faint, breath of mirth that died nearly as soon as it left her lips. "I remember that I'd never seen anyone be that violently ill before. How many times did you vomit in our front yard?"

Kellan sniffed. "I was nine. He made me drink the entire jug of fermented cider I'd stolen from his supply. Anyone would've been as sick as I was. Maybe worse."

"Ten times? Eleven?" Blue turned to look at him. "I remember thinking that we'd finally found the thing you'd be famous for."

His brows rose. "I remember thinking I was going to die by puking up my internal organs. Never did steal again, though."

"Did you ever drink fermented cider again?"

He shuddered. "Just the thought of it makes me feel sick. But he was right to make me drink it. I needed a father figure to step in and give me some limits. I can't count how many times he did that for me after my own father died."

She tried to smile, but the hot, sharp thing inside her was growing. Turning her face away, she gazed at the orchard again.

"I miss Pierre," he said quietly.

She pressed her lips closed and tried to swallow, but the thing in her chest had spread to her throat. Her voice sounded choked when she asked, "Why are you being nice to me?"

"Because I've been in your shoes, and I know how it feels."

She clenched her jaw as the hot, sharp thing surged, stinging her tongue with its bitterness.

"When my father died, everyone asked how I was. Told me things would be all right. Time would heal the wound, and it was lucky I had him for the time I did." Kellan's voice was steady. Every word felt like it was shredding a bit of her self-control.

"But I didn't feel lucky. I didn't want time to heal anything. I just wanted him back. I still do. I always wished someone would've told me it was all right to scream and cry and be broken over the heartache of it all." He turned to look at her, and her eyes were drawn to his. "So I'm going to tell you. It's all right to miss your father, Blue. It's all right to be angry that he's gone when he shouldn't be. You can fall apart for a little while if you need to. Nessa, your grand-mère, and I will be here to help pick up the pieces when you're ready."

She held his gaze for a long moment while her heart pounded and her knees shook. And then the hot, sharp thing that had been coiled inside her since the moment she'd pulled back the cloak to reveal Papa's face broke loose, and she collapsed against him and sobbed.

He held her. Let her cry and didn't tell her things would get better. Didn't say that he was sorry or that everything happened as it was supposed to. He just held on tight and let himself be her anchor as the grief tore its way out of her, raw and angry.

And when she was spent and weariness swamped her, he scooped her up in his arms and carried her back through the crowd and into the little farmhouse, Nessa at his heels. They tucked her into her bed, and Nessa crawled up beside her, her skinny arms wrapped firmly around Blue's waist.

Somewhere outside, the sea hawk cried, shrill and distant, and the crowd murmured while the iron bells brought to honor Papa chimed in the breeze, but inside Blue curled up beneath Grand-mère's quilt with Nessa on one side, Pepperell on the other, and Kellan's tall body folded up in her little desk chair as sleep took her.

TWELVE

THE DAY AFTER Papa's funeral, Blue woke to the noise of knocking on the farmhouse's front door. Stretching, she nudged Pepperell off her stomach as the sound of Grand-mère's footsteps left the spare room, where she'd been staying, and headed downstairs.

Blue wasn't sure when Nessa and Kellan had left. She'd awakened once well after sunset, and they were gone. It was strange that Kellan of all people had been the one person to see what she needed and give it to her. Or maybe not so strange since Kellan knew firsthand what it felt like to suddenly lose a father. Still, it was unsettling to realize she'd leaned on him so completely.

Before she could waste any more time thinking about Kellan, she sat up and tried to plan out her day. She needed to check on the shop, though the thought of retracing the route from the farmhouse to the Gaillard merchant district, passing by the place where Papa had been killed, made her feel shaky inside.

Still, she hadn't been there for nearly a week, and she was sure orders were piling up. She had no other means to support herself, so letting those customers take their business elsewhere while she grieved wasn't an option.

Grand-mère's voice rose sharply, and Blue scrambled out of bed.

It didn't take much to get Grand-mère riled up these days. She was furious over the death of her son-in-law and the hurt to her granddaughter, and anyone who caused her irritation was an easy target.

Yesterday, she'd snapped at the milkman and threatened to light his barns on fire. The day before, she'd insulted the magistrate's intelligence because the woman had no leads on who had killed Papa. Blue had no idea which hapless townsperson was currently irritating Grand-mère, but it was best to get herself downstairs quickly and intervene before Grand-mère forgot her own rule against pulling out her wand and reminding others that she could do magic.

Throwing a simple white muslin dress over her head, she shoved her feet into a pair of shoes, ran a damp cloth over her face, and rushed for the stairs as the sound of Grand-mère's wrath grew louder.

"This is preposterous, Nell, and you know it," Grand-mère snapped.

Nell. Blue grabbed the railing and began her descent. What was the magistrate doing here? Had they found the killer?

Nell's voice was a quiet murmur, quickly cut off by a vicious curse from Grand-mère.

"Over my dead body. The four of you can get right out of this house. Immediately."

Blue reached the bottom of the stairs and hurried toward the sitting room near the front of the house.

"I'm sorry, Destri." Nell's voice was soft but firm as she spoke to Grand-mère. "It's an official document. My hands are tied."

"Well, mine aren't." Grand-mère reached for her sleeve as Blue rushed into the room and grabbed her arm, stopping her before she could pull the hazel-wood wand free.

"It's all right, Grand-mère. Whatever this is, we'll figure it out together," Blue said as calmly as she could, a feat made difficult by the fact that it wasn't just Nell standing in her sitting room. Dinah Chauveau, head of the Chauveau family, sat on her little couch, flanked by two girls around Blue's age who looked remarkably like Dinah. Same pale-as-milk skin, sharp cheekbones, and long dark hair. The youngest had a smattering of freckles across her nose and gave Blue a sympathetic look. The oldest appeared bored.

Why would Lady Chauveau be in her sitting room? Was this another attempt to see if Blue and Papa had reported the fake gold? Or had she somehow found out about Blue's magic? The thought sent a shiver of fear through Blue, and she clenched her fists to keep her hands from trembling.

"What are you doing here?" Blue asked before remembering that manners dictated that she greet them and say something pleasant first.

Manners be hung. This was her sitting room, and they were upsetting Grand-mère. And besides, the worry churning through her made it hard to speak gently.

"They were just leaving," Grand-mère said firmly.

Nell sighed, and there was regret on her face as she lifted a piece of parchment she held in her hands. "Blue, this is a document signed and sealed by a solicitor in the Chauveau quarter and by both the magistrate in that quarter and in ours."

Blue frowned. "You're the magistrate in our quarter."

"I am now, but this document was signed sixteen years ago. It bears the signature of the previous magistrate."

"I bet my life that signature isn't real." Grand-mère moved as if to take the parchment from Nell, but the woman lifted it out of reach.

"I realize this is difficult, but I've already spent a great deal of time this morning comparing signatures and ascertaining the validity of this document. I'm sorry, but this is now binding."

Grand-mère stared her down for a moment and then extended her glare to the Chauveaus.

"What does it say?" Blue asked, her voice smaller than she intended. She'd never seen Grand-mère this upset. What could've been signed sixteen years ago that would cause problems now?

Nell cleared her throat and gave Blue a swift pitying look before saying, "It's an agreement between your mother and Dinah Chauveau giving Dinah full custody of you, your property, and your shop until you come of age, should both your parents die before your eighteenth birthday."

Blue opened her mouth. Shut it. Tried to corral her racing thoughts, but nothing made sense.

She didn't even know Dinah Chauveau. Papa had never mentioned her. Why would her mother sign custody of her daughter over to the head of the Chauveau family instead of to Grand-mère?

"That doesn't make sense," she finally said. "Grand-mère can take care of me."

"Exactly what I've been saying." Grand-mère stabbed a finger at the Chauveaus and then at the front door. "On your way, the lot of you. Blue is none of your concern."

"Oh, I couldn't bear to dishonor my good friend's wishes," Dinah said, her tone soft. "I'm sure she wanted Blue to have a mother and sisters if the unthinkable happened. We'll move in to the farmhouse so that she doesn't have to lose her home as well as her father in the same week."

Her daughters flinched at that, though the youngest kept her eyes trained on the scarred wooden floor that hadn't seen a broom since the night Papa died.

"I'm afraid there isn't room for all of you here," Grand-mère said. "And I'm sure a lady such as yourself wouldn't be satisfied with such a simple house. You just stay in your fancy mansion in your quarter, and if you're really that concerned, I'll send you reports each week on how Blue is doing. I'm sure you're very worried about a girl you've never bothered speaking to."

Something flashed in Dinah's eyes, so fast Blue almost missed it, and then the woman stood in a smooth, elegant motion. "I am Blue's new guardian. I am responsible for the farmhouse and the shop. I take my responsibility seriously. My girls recently lost their father to a violent crime as well. A change of scenery would do them good. We can all grieve together."

Grand-mère's lip curled. "Your girls need the change of scenery you just said shouldn't happen for Blue?"

Dinah's gaze sharpened, though her voice remained soft. "Valeraine also signed a document stating that she'd become guardian of my daughters should they lose both their parents before coming of age. Maybe I haven't stayed in touch with Blue over the years like I should have, but that doesn't mean her mother's wishes shouldn't be honored. I'd love for you to continue to be an important part of Blue's life, of course, but I must insist that the arguing stop immediately. We've all suffered a loss and arguing only makes it harder to cope."

Grand-mère's arm tightened against Blue's, and she stared at Dinah until Nell said softly, "I'm sorry, but there's nothing any of us can do. The document is legal and binding. Lady Chauveau can do as she deems best."

Blue held on to Grand-mère, her heart thundering in her chest, her throat aching. "I'll move in to Grand-mère's cottage, then. If your girls want to stay in the farmhouse, you can have it until I'm eighteen."

Dinah turned her gaze toward Blue. "Nonsense, my dear. I'm sure we're all going to become fast friends. I'm very curious to learn how to run your shop, and I'm sure we'll find common ground as you teach me. Now say good-bye to your grandmother for now. It's clear she needs some time to calm down. We can discuss arrangements for you to see her again sometime in the next week or so."

The next week or so? The air left Blue's lungs as if she'd been struck.

She'd lost Papa. And now she was losing her freedom, her privacy, and the person she needed most. Surely Dinah Chauveau couldn't think that was best for Blue.

"But—"

Stone crept into Dinah's voice. "Let's not start out our time together with conflict, Blue. I'm accustomed to my children obeying me. If you can't agree to stay peacefully with us in the farmhouse for the next little while, then I'll be forced to take you with us to our home in the city. Is that what you want?"

Before Blue could reply, Grand-mère gathered her close in a fierce hug and whispered against her ear, "Don't do anything that will make her take you away from here. It will be all right. We'll figure out how to contest that document. You know where to find me if you need help."

And then she was gone, and Blue was left standing in her sitting room facing the head of the Chauveau family, who inexplicably wanted to live in her house, run her shop, and control every aspect of Blue's life.

THIRTEEN

"I BEG YOUR pardon?" Kellan blinked at the page who'd met him at the bottom of the castle's steps just before he reached his carriage.

She bit her lip and dropped into yet another curtsy—her fourth in less than two minutes—and repeated, "My Lady Chauveau is temporarily staying at the de la Cour farmhouse just to the west of the city and asks that you meet her and her daughters there for your brunch date."

When Kellan didn't immediately respond, she dipped lower, wobbling precariously, and said in a shaky voice, "She said you'd know where it is, but I'm sure I can find someone to escort you if—"

"I know where it is." Kellan motioned for the girl to rise before she fell. "What I don't understand is why Lady Chauveau is *there*."

"I—she—My Lady Chauveau doesn't share her reasons with me."

Kellan offered the girl a smile, and she blushed prettily. "I suppose I'll have to ask her myself, then. Thank you for delivering the message."

She bobbed another curtsy, and Kellan turned toward his carriage. "The de la Cour farmhouse, please," he said as his coachmen held the door open for him.

"Yes, Your Majesty."

Kellan settled back against the plush cushions and sighed. Why was Lady Chauveau staying at Blue's house? And how was he supposed to conduct a betrothal meeting—complete with delicate political negotiations and a healthy side of charm and flirting—under Blue's scornful eye?

Not that she'd been scornful the last time he'd seen her. The numb corner of his heart that sheltered his own grief sent a shaft of pain through him at the memory of Blue's wild sobs as he'd held her after Pierre's funeral. Stars knew he didn't usually get along with Blue, but no one deserved the kind of pain he knew she was in.

Maybe she wouldn't even be present. Maybe she'd be hiding in her garden or seeking solace at Grand-mère's. He could visit the Chauveaus, do his duty, and leave without disturbing her.

And if the thought of not checking in on her left him with a faint twinge of disappointment, it was only because he'd loved Pierre too, and grief was easier to bear when it was shared with those left behind.

The scenery flew by, and before Kellan knew it, they'd pulled to a stop before the little gate that led to the farmhouse. As he stepped out of the carriage, the faint clamor of iron bells ringing far to the west drifted through the air. Kellan froze and looked down the long road that cut through farmland and hills before reaching the large expanse of the wilds at the base of the mountains. His coachmen lunged for the horses as if they might bolt, and his guards drew their swords as they flanked the prince, all of them staring at the distant shadow of the mountains.

The road was empty. The wraith was imprisoned in its fae forest, and nothing was going to change that. Kellan knew the bells were only ringing because the wraith was throwing its magic at the barrier that kept it inside its cage, but still a chill danced across his skin as he slowly moved toward Blue's gate, glancing twice more at the road, just in case.

He knocked on the door and nearly grimaced when Blue opened it. So much for being able to do his job without her watching his every move. She met his eyes, and a faint flicker of curiosity surfaced, but mostly she looked exhausted.

Kellan's irritation disappeared. Ignoring his guards as they moved into the house to check that it was safe, he stepped toward Blue. A tiny frown etched itself between her eyes, and he quickly cast about for something courteous and sympathetic to say. Something that would convey friendly concern for her well-being without intruding on her grief. Something charming and kind, but not overly intimate.

She cocked a brow at him as if to challenge his right to be standing on her porch, and he blurted out, "You look really worn out."

She crossed her arms over her chest, and he gave himself a mental head slap. What was it about her that made it impossible to be his usual charming, witty self?

"I didn't mean that. I was going to say something courteous and sympathetic. I don't know why I . . . Never mind. I'm sorry."

"Did you come here just to tell me I look like I haven't slept well in days?" There was a faint challenge in her voice, but the effect was lost when she scrubbed her hands over her face and pressed her fingers against her temples as if to stave off a headache.

"Have you slept at all?" He kept his voice quiet, angling his body to block anyone in the house from coming onto the porch and overhearing their conversation.

She blinked at the midmorning sunlight and yawned.

"I'll take that as a no." He extended a hand to rub her shoulders the way he did for Nessa when she was too tense to sleep, but then let it drop. She wasn't Nessa, and despite the fact that he'd known Blue since his earliest memories, he had no idea how to comfort her.

Something bumped against his ankles, and he looked down to find Blue's monstrosity of a cat winding through the prince's legs to get to his mistress. She scooped the cat into her arms, and he flopped against her chest, his one good eye glaring balefully at Kellan.

"I don't think your cat likes me."

Blue scratched the cat's head. "He's an excellent judge of character."

Kellan rolled his eyes. "Like you, I suppose?"

She shot him a look, and for a moment, he saw the old Blue—feisty, honest, and unafraid to tell the most powerful boy in the kingdom exactly what she thought—but then she yawned again, and her shoulders sagged.

"I don't want to argue with you," she said wearily.

Something warm awoke in his chest, and he smiled. "I don't want to argue with you either."

There was a beat of silence between them, punctuated by the

hum of bees in her garden and the sound of footsteps coming down the stairs inside the house, and then she smiled faintly.

"I have no idea what to say to you when I'm not mad at you or worried about you."

He tilted his chin down to meet her eyes. "You worry about me?"

She gave him the look that usually preceded an announcement about his general lack of common sense and said, "You climb high walls without safety harnesses, race barely broken stallions in illegal contests, get into street fights, and, to my knowledge, have yet to turn down a single, stupid dare from one of your equally foolish friends. I imagine everyone who cares about you worries plenty."

He frowned. "Wait. You care about me?"

She rolled her eyes. "Don't be an idiot. Everyone I love most loves you. Nessa, Grand-mère, the queen, Papa . . ." Tears glinted in her eyes, and she looked away. "I don't want anything to hurt them, which means I don't want anything to hurt you."

"Your Majesty, Lady Chauveau and her daughters are in the parlor, ready to receive you," his guard said from the doorway.

Kellan nodded, but didn't take his eyes off Blue. Quietly, he said, "I thought you hated me."

"Like you hate me?" She raised her eyes to his, and he swallowed hard at the stark vulnerability in them.

That was one of the things he both respected and dreaded with Blue. You always knew exactly where you stood. There were no pretty words, no artful deceptions, no games. She never bothered to hide the truth.

Choosing his words with care, he said, "I don't hate you, Blue. I never have."

"But you don't like me." She gave him a look that dared him to deny it.

"You don't like me either."

They held each other's gazes for a long moment, and then she laughed—a pure sound, unfettered by the grief that filled her. He grinned, and the warmth in him spread.

"Maybe you're not my favorite person in the kingdom, but I love Nessa, my mother, Grand-mère, and your papa too. And they all love you." Kellan let his hand rest on her shoulder and felt an odd sense of peace when she didn't flinch from his touch. "That means I don't want anything to hurt you, either."

Pepperell sniffed Kellan's hand and then rubbed his face against the prince's fingers. Kellan's smile widened. "You were right, as usual. He's an excellent judge of character."

Blue smiled. "Maybe a better judge than me sometimes." She scratched the cat under the chin and then said softly, "Thank you for what you did for me at Papa's funeral."

He squeezed her shoulder gently before letting go. "You're welcome. I'm happy to talk to you about Pierre whenever you need it."

She nodded. "You'd better get inside."

He gave the cat one last pet and then smiled at Blue. "It was nice not arguing with you."

She laughed a little, and he carried that sound with him as he walked into the farmhouse and found Dinah Chauveau seated on Blue's little brown couch, her daughters on either side of her. Dinah wore her signature red silk, but her daughters were dressed in pale blue gowns with intricately embroidered birds taking flight across the skirts. The younger daughter had gloves on, but Jacinthe, the daughter closest to his own age, raised a bare hand for him to kiss.

It was a subtle signal that Dinah preferred for him to court Jacinthe, though she'd offered Halette as well in case he preferred her.

What he preferred was hardly at issue. The true question was what was best for the kingdom, and according to his mother, the Chauveau empire spanned four kingdoms with significant wealth and allies in each of them. All that would be a considerable asset to a future queen, and everyone in the room knew it.

"So lovely of you to visit us out here as we take a small country holiday," Dinah said, her sharp eyes missing nothing as Kellan gave each girl a kiss on the back of her hand before taking his seat across from them. "I do hope Blue didn't bore or offend you when she answered the door. She lacks a bit of polish." Dinah cleared her throat delicately to convey her poor opinion of Blue's manners.

She wasn't wrong. Blue didn't feel the need to act like anyone was better than her because of their place in society. But she also never felt the need to act like anyone was worse. She was honest, passionate, and insistent on jumping headfirst into any wrong she thought she could fix—a trait Kellan had personally experienced countless times. Something about the powerful Dinah Chauveau taking advantage of Blue's hospitality so soon after Pierre's death and then insulting her hostess's lack of pretense ignited a flame of anger in Kellan.

Straightening his spine, he held Dinah's gaze and said crisply, "Do explain to me why you and your daughters are staying in the de la Cour farmhouse so soon after Pierre's passing."

Jacinthe shot her mother a quick look, and Halette stared at her hands clasped tightly in her lap. Dinah's smile was carved from stone. "It's a rather complicated situation and doesn't have any bearing on the betrothal season."

"Still"—Kellan flicked an imaginary piece of lint from his silk trousers and gave Dinah the lazy smile that drove the castle's butler to curse like a sailor—"I'd like to hear it."

Dinah inclined her head respectfully, though something flashed in her eyes. Interesting. She didn't care to obey him. She'd tried to deflect a request by telling him it was none of his business. If that was how she behaved when she was trying to win his approval of an alliance with her family, what would she do if one of her daughters became queen?

"Blue!" Dinah called, her voice gentle, though the smile on her face still looked carved from ice.

Blue returned from the porch, and Kellan was struck by the wariness in her expression when she faced Dinah. This was the girl who'd single-handedly stopped an illegal street fight, faced down one of Balavata's most dangerous brokers, and blackmailed the prince into doing what she wanted, and here she stood in her parlor looking unsure of her place in her own home.

"The prince and my daughters would like refreshments. Please bring what you prepared earlier. Thank you." Dinah's words weren't unkind, but the flame of anger within Kellan rose.

"Do you not have any of your staff here to wait on you?" he asked, his voice cold.

"There's hardly enough room in this house for the three of us, much less our staff," Jacinthe said sharply.

Dinah silenced her with a look and then turned to Kellan. "I appreciate how upsetting it must be to you to think that we're here taking over Blue's home and treating her like a servant. I assure you nothing could be further from the truth."

He cocked his head and waited in silence for more.

She leaned toward him and lowered her voice. "I was close to Blue's mother. She drew up a guardianship agreement since she and Pierre were a bit older than many childbearing couples. The agreement gave guardianship of Blue, the farmhouse, and the shop to me in the event that both Valeraine and Pierre died before Blue came of age. I didn't want to move Blue out of this home just yet, as she is very attached to it, so instead I moved us here temporarily until I figure out how best to uphold my responsibilities to Valeraine while still running the Chauveau quarter and my considerable business interests. I sent Blue for refreshments because I simply needed her out of earshot before explaining things to you. She's been through enough, poor girl. She doesn't need to hear it again."

"We've all been through enough," Jacinthe muttered. Halette elbowed her in the side, and Jacinthe subsided, though her brown eyes were fiery when they met his.

Kellan hadn't been aware that Valeraine and Dinah were close, but he'd been a child when Blue's mother died, and he had no clear recollection of her life outside of the times he saw her with Pierre and Blue.

Satisfied with her explanation, he leaned forward, his eyes on the sisters. "It was unforgivably rude of me not to offer my personal condolences on the death of your father the moment I walked into the room. I apologize. I was caught up in my own grief over Pierre de la Cour's death and in my concern over his family, but that's no excuse for my discourtesy."

Halette sniffed and looked away, but Jacinthe arched a brow

at him. "You'll just have to make it up to me with an extra dance at the Marcels' upcoming ball."

He was well and truly trapped. To refuse her now would be the height of discourtesy, but to accept would send a message to the rest of the head families that he preferred Jacinthe over their daughters. If he sent that message before his betrothal ball, he could have violence on his hands as other families sought to remove girls they thought might get the throne instead.

Dinah frowned at Jacinthe and said quietly, "The prince cannot afford to do that, darling. Not so early in the betrothal season. But I'm sure he could at least give you the first dance." She looked at Kellan as if to confirm that her request would be honored. "Especially since I'm sure he's well aware that I sit at the queen's right hand because our family's wealth and influence is second to none. A first dance with one of the Chauveau girls would be practically expected."

He smiled and winked at Jacinthe to mask his surprise that Dinah had offered him a way out. The other mothers would've leaped at the chance to secure an extra dance for their daughters. Perhaps Dinah was attempting to make up for her earlier resistance to his requests. Or perhaps she was gambling that showing an understanding of the prince's delicate position would make her family a more desirable choice in the end. Either way, he'd take the reprieve. Holding Jacinthe's gaze, he said, "Giving you my first dance would be an honor."

Blue entered the room with a derisive little sniff, a tray balanced in her arms. Pepperell hurried in behind her, twined around her legs as she carefully set the tray on the little table that stood between the sofa and Kellan's chair, and then hopped into Kellan's lap, purring loudly.

As Halette began to pour tea for the four of them, Kellan met Blue's eyes and grinned.

"Excellent judge of character," he mouthed softly, his hands buried in the cat's soft fur.

Blue rolled her eyes and left the room, but he caught the faint smile playing around the edge of her lips as she went.

FOURTEEN

It HAD BEEN a week since the Chauveaus had come to live at the farmhouse. Blue was miserable. It wasn't because she'd been kicked out of her room and relegated to an old mattress and quilt in the attic so that Halette, Dinah's youngest daughter, could have her bedroom, though Blue did resent that. It wasn't because Dinah stopped by the shop most days, though Blue was sick of her hovering about. It wasn't even that she hadn't seen Grandmère, though the older woman came to the door every day only to be turned away by Dinah, who said Blue needed time to bond with her new family members.

No, Blue was miserable because she knew Papa had died because of her.

It was the thought that sank into her bones every day, brittle and sharp. The accusation that chased its way into her nightmares until she woke choking on sobs.

If she had told him the burglar took the almost-gold experiment, Papa wouldn't have allowed her to stay late at the shop.

He would never have been on the road to come and fetch her. He'd still be waking her each morning with hot spiced chicory and cream. Still be chastising her to clean her work area between each potion. Still be *here*, instead of gone.

Blue couldn't bear the thought that he was gone.

She also couldn't bear the thought of trying to make gold again. Her pressurized pot sat gathering dust on the shelf by the stove, chunks of lead resting cold in its belly. She couldn't stand to look at it.

She nudged Pepperell off her stomach and slowly rose from her mattress in the attic to start yet another miserable day but paused as the glint of sunlight off the glassy surface of the sea caught her eye. Moving to the attic's garret window, she pushed the dusty curtains aside and stared at the distant water.

Mama had taught her how to swim. They'd spent hours playing in the foamy waves while Papa swam out, strong and sure, to harvest the sea vines Mama wanted to use in her potions. They'd swim, build elaborate castles in the sand, and then snuggle close as the sun sank beneath the horizon. Blue would fight to keep her eyes open for as long as possible, but Mama would wrap her in a quilt and sing the lullaby she'd written when her daughter was born.

Pain shot through Blue's chest, and she wrapped her arms around herself as she closed her eyes and imagined the sound of Mama's voice singing. The sound of Papa's gentle laughter. The feeling of belonging to people who loved her.

Tears burned her eyes, and she turned away from the window.

She still belonged to Mama and Papa, but she couldn't spend all day reminiscing. She couldn't spend all day blaming herself, either. Not if she wanted to survive Dinah's scrutiny and the strangers who were under her roof. Jacinthe never spoke to Blue unless she wanted something. Her dress washed and pressed. Food prepared. Someone to open the curtains for her because apparently wealthy girls couldn't lift a finger to do basic tasks.

Blue drew in a deep breath before anger could take root. Jacinthe might be difficult, but Halette wasn't so bad. She never treated Blue like a servant, and where Jacinthe behaved as if taking over Blue's guest room was an irritating inconvenience for her, Halette seemed genuinely sorry to be intruding on Blue's grief. In different circumstances, Blue imagined they might be friends.

But these weren't different circumstances, and Blue needed a distraction if she was going to survive the next few months until her birthday. She needed something else to focus on, and she knew just the thing.

Ana had never returned to the Gaillard quarter. Lucian hadn't seen or heard from her, and neither had any of the other children he'd spoken to. And yesterday, he'd reported that another child had suddenly gone missing. This time a five-year-old boy. Ana may have sought work in a different quarter, but it was very unlikely a child of five would leave the people and places he was familiar with.

Blue wasn't ready to try making gold again, but she didn't need wealth to search for a few missing children. All she needed was time, a familiarity with the streets of Falaise de la Mer, and the courage to go into the neighborhoods controlled by the brokers.

Hurrying to get ready before Jacinthe started yelling for her breakfast or Dinah thumped on the wall to summon her to sweep the floor, Blue formed a plan for the day. She'd fulfill the orders, send Lucian out with the shop's deliveries, and make enough potions to restock the shelves out front. And then she'd close up early and head out to start asking questions.

It was entirely possible that she'd find nothing. The children might have joined different shelters in other quarters. A kind person might have taken them in. They might have already signed up for jobs with a broker. But searching gave Blue purpose, and she needed that if she was going to get through her day.

The hours flew by as Blue worked hard to finish potions, restock shelves, and place orders to replenish her stock, all while running back and forth between the stockroom and the shop floor to deal with customers. Her nerves frayed until she thought she'd snap, and she desperately sang Mama's lullaby under her breath hoping to find a sliver of calm.

Lucian delivered the packages she had ready for him in the morning, but she deliberately kept a few back as an excuse to leave the shop early that afternoon.

She broached the subject when Dinah did her regular midday check-in to poke around the stock and ask Blue what new potions or experiments she'd like to try. "There are a few more deliveries that need to be made. I'll head out after Princess Nessa's tutoring session."

"Just get that boy back here to do that for you."

"I can't." Blue swept a rag over her worktable, sending a puff of fennel dust into the air. "He works at the bakery in the afternoons."

"So you expect to close the shop while we could still have customers?" Dinah's voice was impatient.

"Well, yes. Unless you want to take care of sales while I make the deliveries."

Dinah raised her chin. "Do I look like a shopkeeper to you?"

Blue shrugged, and the older woman's eyes narrowed. "It's past time for you to hire someone to run the shop floor. We can get one of the urchins who do odd jobs to take the packages while we post a Help Wanted sign."

"And how would we pay for that? Are you going to volunteer coin from your own coffers?"

Something flashed in Dinah's eyes. "Don't be daft, child. You know very well you can pay someone to work here."

Blue stared. "Pay with what? We make enough coin to cover the costs of maintaining the building, buying supplies, and keeping up the farmhouse. There really isn't much extra."

A muscle along Dinah's jaw ticked. "Haven't I been kind to you, Blue? Haven't I given up my home, divided my attention between you and my business empire, and looked after your needs?"

"I . . . You don't have to—"

"And you expect me to mind the shop. To believe there's no extra coin—"

"There isn't any."

"Don't lie to me!" Dinah's hand whipped across Blue's face. "I've done everything your mother would've wanted me to do."

Blue raised a trembling hand to her stinging cheek and blinked at Dinah in shock. Until today, the older woman had been demanding, and had certainly put her daughters' comfort ahead of Blue's, but she hadn't been cruel.

Dinah leaned forward, a wild light in her eyes. "I have an empire that desperately needs my attention. Daughters to position for the prince's betrothal. A family to run. All I want is for you to show me where the extra coin is kept so that we can hire someone to run the shop, and you sit there lying to me. I despise liars."

Blue scrambled out of her chair and backed away, keeping the table between them. "I'm not lying. We had enough to get by, but not much extra. And I never expected you to keep shop. I never expected you at all. You just showed up and took over my life!" Blue's voice rose. "You took my home, my bedroom, my time with my grandmother, and my shop. Well, I don't need you. Go back to your mansion. Go run your empire and find a way to marry one of your girls to Kellan. I don't care what you do as long as you leave me alone!"

Dinah lunged from her chair as Blue whirled toward the stockroom door. "Don't you dare leave without my permission."

Blue snatched up the three remaining delivery packages, flew into the alley, and slammed the door behind her. Before Dinah could follow, Blue raced to the main road, ducked around the bakery on the corner, and dove down a side street that broke into a dozen different streets within half a block.

Let Dinah try to find her. Blue knew this quarter far better than Dinah did.

Better yet, let Dinah realize the truth: there was no coin stashed away. Nothing to help Blue hire a replacement for Papa.

Before the thought of replacing Papa could burrow in, she turned down the second street she came to and headed east, forcing herself to think of nothing but the three addresses she needed to find. She'd deliver the packages. Ask questions of any street children she found. And see if she could figure out where Ana and the little boy had gone.

And maybe, after darkness fell, she'd return to the shop. She didn't know how she was going to return to the farmhouse. Not with Dinah still inside.

Her heart ached, a bright shaft of pain that stole her breath and brought tears to her eyes, and she blinked them away.

She wasn't going to be chased away from her home by fear of Dinah's unreasonable anger. Pepperell needed her. And besides, it was hers. Along with the shop and Grand-mère, it was all she had left.

She could endure the Chauveaus a bit longer. Surely, Dinah would soon grow bored of listening to Jacinthe complain about country living. Or at the very least, grow weary of worrying about a girl and her alchemy shop when she should be running the entire Chauveau quarter and chasing a betrothal to Kellan.

Blue winced as an image of Kellan standing beneath wedding chimes with Jacinthe on his arm filled her mind. Maybe Kellan wasn't her favorite, but she still couldn't wish a life with someone as unpleasant as Jacinthe on him. Especially when he'd been kind to Blue even though there was nothing in it for him. Once, she'd believed Kellan was incapable of turning on his charm for any reason other than to somehow benefit himself. Now she wondered just how much of his charm was the truth and how much of it was a shield he wore against the political expectations he faced.

The sky was a dusky purple pricked with stars by the time Blue finished her last delivery to a house on the far side of the Evrard quarter. She'd taken her sweet time, but even though darkness was swiftly falling, she didn't want to go home. Not yet.

Not when it meant dealing with the Chauveaus.

Instead, she wandered through the well-lit main streets of the

Evrard quarter, stepping aside as workers washed the day's grit from the cobblestones while others climbed iron poles to shine the glass lanterns that hung at regular intervals along the way. When she came to the corner that would lead her back to the Gaillard quarter, she hesitated.

Music poured from the building to her right, a bright, cheerful melody that danced along the air like laughter. She drew in the scent of roasted pork, spiced apples, and shirella wine and found her feet moving in that direction before she'd fully decided she was going inside.

A wall of noise hit her as she opened the pub's door—the din of voices, the sparkling notes of a violin, and the dull clink of glass mugs against the bar counter to her left. She took a few steps forward, letting the heavy wooden door close behind her with a thunk, and scanned the room for an empty seat.

Square tables with four chairs each surrounded a scarred dance floor on three sides. The fourth edge of the dance floor held a small stage with a pair of violinists in black dresses, their bows flashing as they coaxed a song from the strings. Most of the tables held at least two people, and there were five couples on the dance floor.

For a moment, Blue longed to join them. Dive into the dancing while music and laughter surrounded her. No Dinah. No grief. No accusation waiting to turn her dreams into nightmares. But there were no empty tables. No handy partners standing around hoping a young alchemist would walk into the pub alone and ready to dance.

She'd made a mistake coming here. Instead of offering comfort and distraction, the crowded pub was making her feel more alone than ever. Turning to leave, she bumped against the solid wall of someone's chest and stumbled back.

A hand shot out to steady her, and she looked up to find Kellan standing in front of her, surrounded by a group of his friends and several members of the royal guard, conspicuous in their blue-and-silver uniforms.

"What are you doing here?" he asked, looking over her shoulder as if he expected to find someone with her.

"Nothing. I was just leaving." Her voice broke, and she hastily cleared her throat and tried to step around him.

He waved his friends toward the bar, and then stepped in front of her again.

"Please don't be annoying tonight, Kellan. I'm really not in the mood." Tears burned, and she blinked rapidly, but still one chased a trail of heat down the cheek that Dinah had struck.

"Wait a minute."

"No." She didn't have a minute. She was going to break down in that stupid pub surrounded by music and laughter, and the hot, sharp thing that had lived inside her since she'd found Papa's body was going to shred her to pieces.

Spinning to the side, she skirted his body, wrenched the door open, and rushed into the night air, more tears stinging her cheeks. The door slammed shut behind her, and then he was at her side.

"Blue, please wait." His voice sounded warm and friendly, the way it had at Papa's funeral, and it made the hot, sharp thing inside her settle a little.

Quickly, she swiped at the tears on her face and then said, "What do you want?"

"To know what you want." He ducked his head so he could look into her downcast eyes. "I've never seen you at this pub before, and you've obviously come alone, so—"

"Yes, I'm alone, and you're with a crowd of your friends, all of whom are probably wondering why the prince followed the merchant girl outside." Her voice was brittle.

He rested his hands on her shoulders. "They're used to me chasing after a beautiful girl."

"Bet they aren't used to you catching one who is immune to your charms."

He gave her an exaggerated parody of the smile he'd trotted out for Jacinthe at the farmhouse. "Are you sure you're immune?"

She rolled her eyes and lightly smacked his shoulder. "Rarely have I ever been so sure of anything."

"You wound me." He winked.

"Wink at me one more time, and I'll wound you for real."

He laughed. "There's the Blue I know and almost like."

She surprised herself by laughing with him.

He dropped his hands from her shoulders, and she wasted a foolish second wishing he'd touch her again, if only to keep her from sinking back into her loneliness.

Quietly, he asked, "Will you tell me why you came here?"

She looked away as the violins took up another merry tune, the notes tumbling over each other in a mad dash up and down the scale.

She should leave now. Tell him she was fine and send him back to his friends while she walked the long trek back to the farmhouse, where no doubt Dinah waited to discuss Blue's disobedience.

But just like at Papa's funeral, there was something warm and comforting about Kellan's presence. When he wasn't trying to flirt or charm or get himself killed, he was actually a very intuitive person with a generous heart. How she could've spent so much time in his presence over the years without seeing that was a mystery. Maybe she'd been blind. Or maybe he'd always been in such a rush to implement another madcap scheme that he'd never bothered showing her another side.

It didn't matter. What mattered was that the hot, sharp grief within her had settled into a dull ache, and that instead of feeling irritated with him, she found herself telling him the truth.

"I wanted to dance. I thought the laughter and the music sounded so much better than walking home alone in the dark to a house full of strangers." She lifted her shoulders in a tiny shrug. "I guess it was kind of foolish since I didn't have a dance partner."

He met her gaze and gave her the charming smile that usually made her want to smack him. Bowing low, he offered his hand and said, "You have one now."

FIFTEEN

TIME WAS RUNNING out. Dinah had pressured every contact she had, but no one would loan her anywhere close to the amount of coin she needed. She had taken bold measures to kill Pierre de la Cour and forge a guardianship document that gave her control of his daughter and his property, but the girl had yet to even reach for the little pot, where Dinah knew for a fact the results of her experimental gold still lay. And she had less than a week before the estate's debts were turned over to the royal magistrate for review, effectively ending her bid for the throne.

In truth, she might not even have that long. Rumors had begun to spread. People wondered why she wasn't living in the Chauveau mansion, and even her lie about wanting a change of scenery for her daughters after their father's awful death wasn't enough to convince everyone. She could pack them up and move back home. It was still her house until the estate review was completed.

But if she did that, she put her daughters in close proximity to the odious Mr. Dubois, who'd taken to visiting all the business interests she owned, asking questions only a prospective owner would ask. True, he could ask the right staff members for her current location and find her easily enough, but at least her daughters wouldn't be subjected to the daily injury of whispered speculation about their father, their finances, or their future.

Plus, if she returned to the Chauveau quarter, she'd have to either give up on her plan to get Blue to create gold for her or take the girl and her ridiculous cat with her, and Dinah was certain Blue would fight tooth and nail to stay at her farmhouse. She needed the girl on her side. Needed her to start making gold again because she wanted to, not because Dinah was forcing her. It was the only way to ensure the girl didn't deliberately botch the experiment. There was a wide streak of independence in Blue, and Dinah needed the girl to feel like making gold for the Chauveaus was her own choice. Dinah just hadn't quite figured out how to do it.

Meanwhile, she needed a distraction from the rumors that were swiftly spreading. Something that would grab the attention of the queen and the entire royal council so completely that they never thought to look into any silly little whispers about the Chauveaus.

Blue leaving the shop early gave Dinah the perfect opportunity. First, she double-checked the locks on both shop doors. It would never do for the woman who'd championed for the death of those caught using magic to be seen doing magic herself.

When she was certain no one could interrupt her, she pulled one of Blue's pots onto the stove, lit the burner, and reached for some elfynrod, threffalk, mollywog, and charing root. A dusting of silver and a small thread of copper went into the pot next.

Then Dinah stood over the mixture, stirred counterclockwise thirteen times, and whispered the words to a spell she hadn't used in nearly two decades, praying the tiny spark of fae in her blood would be enough to infuse the mixture with magic.

Fat, glossy bubbles rose to the surface of the bloodred liquid, and Dinah smiled.

You could take a girl away from her cauldron, but you could never really take the witchcraft out of her heart.

Setting her spoon down, she leaned over the mixture and whispered her intent as the bubbles burst, their hearts blooming black until none of the red remained. Dinah cut a burlap sack into small squares and measured three drops of the spell onto each square. The thick, tarry liquid soaked into the squares and hardened. After quickly cleaning the pot, restocking the ingredients she hadn't used, and then wiping down her work surface, Dinah gathered the burlap pieces into her cloak pocket and left the shop as the sun sank into the distant horizon, disintegrating around the western mountains in ribbons of fire.

For a moment, Dinah stared at the far-off mountains, her heart beating in strange, heavy thuds.

That's where the true magic existed. That's where true power lived and breathed, trapped in a cage Dinah didn't know how to break.

If she had the wraith at her disposal, all of Mr. Dubois's carefully laid plans, all his guards and the many locks on his doors, would be nothing. Ash in the wind. A pile of twigs trying desperately to stop a fire from spreading.

But she didn't have the wraith, and it was no use dreaming about weapons that were out of reach. She had her own ingenuity, her own courage, and her own unflinching readiness to do what was necessary. It would be enough.

Turning, she began moving through the Gaillard quarter until she reached a small crowd standing outside a butcher's shop waiting to buy at a discount the poorer cuts of meat left over from the day's customers. She slipped a square from her pocket and whispered, *"Sruthán gan scor."* The square heated in her hand, the tarry black of the spell beginning to bubble. She dropped the burlap between the feet of those closest to the road and then hurried on.

She was just turning toward the next quarter when the screaming began.

SIXTEEN

DANCING WITH KELLAN was surprisingly fun. He escorted Blue back into the pub, waved at his friends, and then whirled her onto the dance floor without breaking stride. Before she knew it, she was laughing as they dipped and spun their way through the melody. He wore his charming smirk, the one that usually made her wish he'd trip and fall into a slop bucket, but somehow tonight, she didn't mind.

"You're a good dancer," she said as the musicians changed the tune, and the dancers glided into another rhythm.

"No need to sound surprised." He raised a brow at her. "I happen to have excelled at pub dancing while at school up north."

"There's a class for pub dancing?"

He laughed. "If there had been, I would've aced it."

"How did you do in your classes?" she asked because it suddenly occurred to her that all she really knew of his life away from Balavata were the few things Nessa had told her.

"I did well enough. Not as well as my roommate, Javan, but

that's what happens when you choose adventures over constant studying. You remind me of Javan, actually. You're both sticklers for rules and refuse to have fun unless all your other options are gone. Both champions of always doing the right thing. I guess the stars must think I need rule followers in my life to keep me in line." He winked.

"Every time you wink, I want to poke you in the eye."

"And every time you scowl at me, I want to dunk you in the rain barrel. Again." He spun her out and then in, his smirk back in place. "That was a memorable afternoon. What were you . . . eight? Nine?"

She rolled her eyes, but warmth was bubbling up inside her, comforting and safe. "Ten, and Grand-mère nearly flayed you alive for that."

He grinned, adjusting his grip on her waist. "How was I supposed to know your fancy curls would get ruined in the water?"

"She'd spent *hours* on those."

"Oh, I know. She told me in great detail." He turned them to the right as the violins chased another melody. "I don't know if I ever thanked you for intervening before she made good on her threat to throw me into the sea. I believe I might owe you my life."

"Please. You owe me your life a hundred times over." She gripped his hand and decided to ignore the fizzy feeling that was spreading through her veins. It was the dancing. The laughter. The way her complicated life suddenly felt as simple as following Kellan's lead across the floor.

"How do you figure?"

"The only reason you're still alive today is because I spent our childhood thinking two or three steps ahead of you so that I could save you from yourself."

He gave her a cocky grin. "Or maybe I just let you think those were my real plans so that you and my parents would be so busy putting a stop to one thing, you'd never think to look at what I was really doing."

"Or maybe those backup plans were safe enough that I decided not to tell on you because your chances of survival were acceptable." She returned his smirk with one of her own.

"Or maybe . . . wait. Is that true?" He pulled her near as another couple whirled past, the heat of his body a mere whisper from hers. The couple continued on, but Kellan kept her close, his big hands enfolding hers while he stared at her like she was a puzzle he was delighted to discover.

One tiny step forward, and the sliver of space between them would disappear. One tiny step, and she could lean against him, letting the thunder of his heartbeat drown out the violins.

Her breath caught, and her pulse quickened. She tilted her face up to see if he'd noticed, and found his dark eyes pinned to hers, a strange expression on his face. Her heart gave an odd little flutter, and she took a hasty step back to resume dancing.

What was wrong with her? This was Kellan. She didn't get heart flutters over *Kellan*. She especially didn't get heart flutters over Kellan when he was about to be betrothed to someone else. It was time to recover both her equilibrium and the thread of their conversation.

"You were a full-time job when I was younger," she said and cursed her voice for sounding breathless. Clearing her throat, she continued, "I take all the credit for the fact that you made it this far in life without breaking your neck."

He blinked. "What about the time I was planning on lighting

a bonfire in the ballroom so my friends and I could roast sugar puffs?"

"A cover for the sorry excuse for a lean-to you and your friends built in the woods outside the castle grounds. You just wanted to be handed a supply of sugar puffs and told to stay well clear of the castle for the rest of the day."

His brows rose. "We were going to light a fire in the lean-to instead but—"

"The wood was all wet. Such a shame." She grinned at the memory. It had taken her five trips to and from the little creek that ran through the castle's forested groves to soak that wood, but it had been worth it to hear the inventive stream of profanity that came from Kellan's mouth when he discovered there would be no lighting anything on fire that day.

And of course it was also worth it to make sure the foolish prince didn't burn down the grounds and kill himself in the process.

He gave her an appraising look. "How about the time I was planning to steal my mother's newest stallion when I was twelve?"

She snorted. "A ruse to get them to put extra guards around the best of the horse stock and leave you free to take one of the ponies and trade it for coin in the most questionable part of the Roche quarter. I don't know what you wanted to spend the coin on—something your mother didn't want you to have, obviously—but you never made it to the Roche quarter."

He shook his head, admiration on his face. "No, I didn't. Instead, there was a man waiting just outside the castle grounds with enough coin to buy the pony and make my friends and I feel rich until we spent it all on candy and fizzy cider. You did that?"

"Being the daughter of a shop owner has its perks. I knew our regular supply man could easily move the pony, and it was far safer for him to deal with the brokers than for the prince to be seen there."

"You are far sneakier than I realized, Blue de la Cour."

"Someone had to make sure the heir was alive to inherit the throne."

"Not all the plans you ruined were my backup plans. Sometimes you got me in far more trouble than any of those plans were worth." His brows drew together, but the warmth stayed in his eyes. "You were a thorn in my side."

"I take my joy where I can find it."

He grinned—that charming, easy Kellan grin she'd always thought was as shallow and useless as he was—and she found herself grinning back before she realized what was happening.

"I still don't like you," he said softly, his dark eyes on hers in a way that made her traitorous heart flutter again.

"I still don't like you either," she replied in a voice that sounded breathy and soft and very unlike herself.

"It seems I really do owe you my life," he said quietly as he pulled her close enough that she could feel the heat from his chest against her cheek. Releasing one of her hands, he placed his finger beneath her chin and gently raised her face to his. "How will I ever make it up to you?"

Her foolish, treacherous heart whispered several very tantalizing ideas, and she locked eyes with him as her breath quickened.

Before she could close the distance between them and do the kind of monumentally stupid thing she could never take back, the pub door burst open and a man stumbled inside. Black flames danced along his skin, and agony twisted his face. Screams rose as he turned toward the bar, hoarsely calling for water.

Blue jerked away from Kellan as they whirled to face the door.

"Magic!" a woman cried, and the crowd of people stumbled over each other, trying desperately to put space between themselves and the man. The music jerked to a halt.

The flames writhed like shadows made of wet ink, and the man dropped to his knees, his voice hoarsely calling for someone to help. Blue watched in horror as the flames licked up his arms and twined themselves around his throat like a necklace made of snakes.

Screams echoed throughout the building as people pushed and shoved, trying to get to the door without coming close to the man and his flames. Kellan wrapped one hand firmly around Blue's as people jostled against them and shouted, "Stop in the name of the queen!"

Obeying the prince was a reflex even the terror of magical black flames couldn't overcome. The crowd froze for the blink of an eye, but that was all the time Kellan needed. "Barkeep, throw some water on that man. You can keep the counter between you to protect you from the flames."

That was smart. Blue studied the inky fire, curiosity threading through her fear. Who knew how these flames would respond to water? Would they leap for another victim? Die out like regular fire? Or would the water make any impact at all?

"The rest of you quietly move toward the door," Kellan said. "We don't want anyone to be hurt while you exit the building."

The crowd did as he asked, giving the man on the floor a wide berth as they headed for the door. The barkeep tossed a pitcher of water over the man's head, but the flames barely flickered in response. The man crumpled to the ground, moaning in pain. The flames clung to him, devouring greedily. The harsh smell of burning flesh filled the air, and he wailed.

The crowd murmured fearfully as they moved toward the door. A woman opened it, took a step outside, and then shrieked in horror. "It's everywhere! The whole street!"

Blue and Kellan fought their way to a front window as the crowd surged back inside, buzzing with terror. All along the street, pools of glistening shadow flickered like flames beneath the golden light of the braziers. There were people scattered about the sidewalk, writhing in agony as the black fire ate into them. In the middle of the street, a carriage was tipped on its side, its owner sprawled motionless while the horse tangled in the carriage's traces shrieked as flames ate at its legs.

"What is this?" Kellan asked, horror in his eyes.

"It's a spell. Has to be. If I can get close enough to the flames, maybe I can figure out what's happening."

He shot her a startled look even as he shouted once again for calm. Leaning close, he said, "You can understand magic like this?"

She shrugged, pulling her hand from his so she could move toward the man on fire. "Depends. If this is a spell, then it has ingredients. I know how to work with that. If it's something else . . ."

If this was something else, then Blue had no idea what to do. The iron bells that hung throughout the Evrard quarter weren't ringing, so they weren't dealing with a fae monster. She couldn't speculate further without gathering more information.

"Be careful!" Kellan said as she neared the burning man, the prince on her heels. "Don't take any risks. We don't know if the flames can spread from one person to another."

"I never thought I'd see the day when *you'd* be telling *me* not to take risks." Blue circled the man, her stomach pitching at the way his eyes rolled back in his head while his body twitched in pain. There was a strong, sulfurlike smell and something sickly sweet—charing root, perhaps? It was highly flammable when combined with the right minerals. Several minerals would produce fire, but only threffalk could explain the inky darkness of the flames.

There was no counteringredient for burning charing root with threffalk. It simply had to extinguish itself over time.

"Blue?" Kellan kept his voice low and calm, though the horror was still in his eyes. He'd organized the crowd inside the pub and had them all in chairs, their gazes pinned to the man slowly dying at Blue's feet. She hadn't realized how easily leadership sat on his shoulders.

She took a step back, sorrow aching in her throat as the man began gasping for breath. "I can't help him. I think it's charing root and threffalk, probably with an accelerant or two involved. It's going to have to burn itself out."

It took several agonizing minutes for the man to die. And another twenty minutes after that for the flames to burn themselves out. The flames on the street finished burning around the same time, and Kellan immediately sent messengers to the quarter's magistrate and to the castle. Once he was sure the street was safe, he allowed the pub's customers to leave. As they scattered throughout the quarter, clinging to each other in shock, Kellan turned to Blue.

"Do you know who could have done this?"

"How could I possibly know that?" She glared at him as if he was responsible for the churning sickness that lingered within her as she took in the bodies strewn about the street.

"Because you're an alchemist." He gestured at the street. "This was alchemy."

"This was magic." She wrapped her arms around herself and shivered, though the air was still pleasantly warm. "Charing root and threffalk, combined with an accelerant, create the kind of fire that spreads to anything it touches. This fire stayed contained to living things. The pub is still standing. That carriage is untouched. The rest of the street is undamaged, and all of it should be destroyed."

"So maybe you're wrong about the ingredients that created the fire."

Blue shook her head. "I know what I smelled. But regardless of the ingredients used to create the fire, fire spreads. Magic is the only thing that makes sense."

Kellan pressed his fingers against his eyelids as if trying to stave off a burgeoning headache. "This is going to cause a widespread panic."

If Falaise de la Mer had someone practicing dangerous magic in its streets, then as far as Blue was concerned, the panic was warranted. She kept her thoughts to herself, however, and simply squeezed Kellan's arm in support.

She wouldn't take all the gold in the kingdom to be in his shoes right now. Everyone would be looking to him and to the queen for answers. For justice. For successfully capturing and hanging the perpetrator. And no one even knew where to start looking.

"I have to stay here," Kellan said. "My mother will be coming, I'm sure, along with the royal magistrate and plenty of guards. We'll have to canvass the street, question witnesses, if any of them are still alive." He swallowed. "And then we'll have to notify the families of those who . . . of the deceased."

"I'm sorry," Blue said softly. She could see the burden of his tasks weighing on his shoulders.

"Part of the job," he said, his voice heavy. Turning, he hailed the approach of the Evrard quarter's magistrate, complete with a dozen of his guards. "I'm going to have two of these guards escort you home."

"You don't have to do that."

"I really do."

"But you need all the manpower you can get." Blue lifted her chin and found implacable resolve on Kellan's face.

"I need to make sure you stay safe. This isn't a negotiation, Blue."

The warmth that had spread through her while they'd danced returned, and she nodded her thanks. How had she never seen that the prince who dared to risk himself cared deeply about not risking anyone else?

His fingers brushed hers gently as he led her toward the guards, and then he was off with the magistrate to examine the streets while Blue began the long walk home, flanked by solemn-faced guards wearing Evrard green.

SEVENTEEN

THE DAY AFTER the horrifying spell had destroyed so many of his people's lives, Kellan woke before dawn. A familiar restlessness churned through him, and he prowled his quarters, hunting for a way to quiet it. Usually, he'd sneak out of the castle and cliff-dive into the sea or get in a street fight, but he couldn't afford a single misstep today.

Today, he was running the royal council meeting. His mother would be watching him with sharp eyes that missed nothing. Hang it, the entire council of head family members would be watching him with sharp eyes that missed nothing.

When he'd agreed last week to head the meeting, he'd figured it would consist of the usual discussions of border issues with some of Akram's nobility, legal disputes within the quarters that needed a group consensus, questions about taxes, resources, imports, exports . . . the kind of things that could bore a man to tears, but that were essential to the running of a kingdom.

Now he'd been a firsthand witness to a magical attack on the streets of the Evrard quarter. And it turned out four other quarters had been hit with the same spell. Nearly fifty people dead. Eleven horses lost. And scores of traumatized people, many of whom remembered the horror of the blood wraith walking the streets sixteen years ago. Kellan might have been too young to remember the wraith personally, but he'd grown up with the stories. Last night's attack was different—nothing was feeding on the blood of innocents or leveling an entire contingent of royal guards with a clap of its hands—but it was terrifying all the same, and every single head family now had a full-blown panic on their hands.

Which meant Kellan had a full-blown panic on his hands.

And he was expected to have answers. Or at the very least, suggestions.

Instead, he had restlessness and pent-up energy and the memory of Blue's tiny hands in his, which shouldn't have been confusing, but somehow was.

He'd been surprised to see her in the pub, so far from her own quarter. More surprised to see tears on her face. But the biggest shock had been the instant urge to protect her. To wipe away the tears and make her smile instead.

This was Blue. The girl who'd acted like she was smarter than him and who'd made sure to get him in trouble every chance she'd had when they were kids. The girl who'd ruined his relationship with one of most interesting brokers in Falaise de la Mer by boldly interrupting a street fight and then forcing Kellan to throw the match.

But this was also the girl who'd taken Nessa under her wing with genuine love and respect. The girl who spoke up for those who couldn't speak for themselves and who defended justice like she was being paid to do it. And the girl who refused to fawn over him and who gave him absolute honesty, whether he liked it or not.

If someone had asked him at the start of the summer what he thought of Blue de la Cour, he'd have said she was a menace to good old-fashioned fun, but that she was a trustworthy friend for his little sister.

Now his thoughts were more . . . complicated.

And he couldn't afford complicated. He had political allies to soothe, a betrothal to manage, and a witch to catch. If he'd felt something bright come to life within him when he'd danced with Blue, it was simply the realization that they were becoming true friends.

As the first cracks of light broke through the dark sky, Kellan dressed and hurried out of the royal wing toward the kitchen. His valet would be mortified that the prince had let him sleep instead of waking him to assist with his morning, but Kellan wanted solitude a bit longer.

How were they going to find the witch responsible for casting the spells that had burned so many people? It had to be a witch. The iron bells hadn't rung like they would if it had been a fae monster, and he couldn't think of anything else capable of casting spells like that. To his knowledge, there hadn't been an active witch in Balavata since the two sister witches sixteen years ago. Marielle had become the blood wraith; the other had helped them trap the wraith in the Wilds and had then disappeared before the new law banning the use of magic could be used against her.

Had she come back? But if she had, why now? And why use harmful spells when she'd been instrumental in stopping her sister?

The truth was that Balavata was a healthy mix of people and cultures. Their port was busy, their borders active, their cities growing. Any number of witches could be living within the kingdom, and unless they chose to actively do magic in front of people, no one would ever know it.

Kellan reached the kitchens as the cook was lighting fires in the three enormous stoves while kitchen maids rushed about gathering ingredients for breakfast. When they saw him, they all froze, dropped into low curtsies, and waited for permission to continue.

The restlessness inside him scraped at his skin.

"Please don't mind me," he said as he reached for a shirella resting in a basket. The corkscrew-shaped fruit was larger than his palm, its pale blue skin smooth and inviting.

"That won't be enough breakfast for you." The cook, an employee at the castle since before Kellan's birth, nodded sagely. "I'll fry up some eggs and meat in a minute. Where should I send the plate?"

He smiled gratefully. "The council room, please."

He'd get an early start. Outline his thoughts. His questions. Begin organizing the tasks he needed to delegate to others. And he'd run it all past his mother before the meeting began. His handling of the matter had to be perfect. If he showed a single sign of weakness, he would sow doubt about his ability to be a strong ruler.

There were those who wouldn't hesitate to mount a coup against him if they thought they could get away with it.

By the time the council members began arriving, Kellan's breakfast was a distant memory, and he had a stack of parchment in front of him with notes, lists, and topics he wanted discussed. His mother had looked it over, added a few thoughts of her own, and then squeezed his shoulder in a show of support before moving to the door to greet everyone as they came in.

Kellan didn't waste any time. "Thank you all for being prompt," he began. "I'll get right to the point. We have a dangerous witch in the city, and people are panicking. It's important that we have a strong, measured response, and equally important that our response is highly visible."

"So we can give the witch plenty of warning that we're coming?" Martin Roche asked, his double chin wobbling as he spoke. The buttons of his jacket strained to cover the ample expanse of his belly, and his pale, stubby fingers tugged at his collar as if he found it constricting.

"Coming at whom? Do we even have any leads?" Dinah Chauveau asked, her mouth tight. Her quarter had been hit hard by the spell last night too, though she'd been safe at Blue's farmhouse, a situation that Kellan wanted to examine in more detail once he didn't have a crisis and a betrothal to manage.

"Do we really want to announce to someone capable of creating a fire that can't be extinguished that we're openly hunting for them?" Georgiana Faure spoke, her skin paler than usual against the black of her dress. Deep wrinkles dug in around her mouth, which was perpetually pursed as if she'd recently sucked an unripe shirella.

"I agree," Martin said, as if a decision had now been reached. "Best to move in secrecy, boy."

It was the first test. The first slice of a sword to see if the prince had any weaknesses to exploit.

Kellan cut his gaze toward Martin and said coldly, "Did you just refer to me as *boy*?"

Martin sat back. "I simply—"

"A yes or no will do." Kellan held the older man's gaze and waited.

Martin blinked first. "I'm sorry, Your Majesty."

To belabor the point would cost Kellan the ground he'd just won, so he turned away from Martin and said, "We need a public response because our people are panicking, and people do foolish things when they panic."

Senet Aubert tapped the polished table with her bold red nails, her graceful spine ruler-straight, and her close-cut dark hair covered with a crimson headscarf. "My guards had to stop a small mob this morning from dragging our quarter's alchemist out into the street on the accusation of being a witch. I think they might have tried to hang her if the guards hadn't intervened."

Kellan's skin went cold, and he found his mother's eyes in a moment of sheer, blind panic.

What if people in the Gaillard quarter were even now deciding that Blue might be responsible? In all his thoughts, his plans to approach the problem, it had never occurred to him that people might assume the city's alchemists were to blame.

The queen lifted her chin, a clear signal that he was to show no emotion beyond complete resolve. He drew in a slow, measured breath and looked to his notes for a moment. Took control of his voice. His expression. Looked up and said calmly, "First order of business, then, is to assign a guard to each of your alchemists immediately. Any other occupations at possible risk of being blamed?"

When no one had any suggestions, he continued, "As I said, we need a public response to restore confidence in the city's security. A show of going door-to-door, interviewing everyone, keeping an eye out for evidence of spell making within each home and business your guards approach."

"Do you honestly think the witch who devastated our quarters is just leaving spell ingredients lying about?" Dinah asked, her tone kind, as if he was too young to realize how things actually worked.

He met her eyes. "Of course not. But this is just our public response. Maybe we'll get lucky, but that's not the point. We have to show people we're working on this. That strong measures are being taken to assure their security."

"And our private response?" Warrane Barbier, his maternal grandfather, spoke from his seat beside the queen. His dark eyes found his grandson's, pride lurking in their depths, though his voice was gruff.

Kellan leaned forward, tapping his quill against the parchment in front of him. "You tell me. At least half of you occupied your family's council seat during the time of the blood wraith. How did we catch it?"

Several of the members exchanged glances, and then Georgiana spoke. "We had help. Her sister and the alchemist—"

"Valeraine de la Cour," the queen said quietly.

"Valeraine de la Cour?" Dinah sounded startled. When all eyes landed on her, she straightened her spine. "I've taken guardianship over her daughter, Blue, after the death of her poor father. I wasn't on the council at the time of the wraith, of course, so I didn't realize Valeraine's involvement."

The queen frowned. "But you were close enough to Valeraine

to have her sign guardianship over to you."

Dinah shrugged, though her jaw was clenched. "Valeraine was always very discreet. I'm sure she felt protecting her role in things was best for her family."

"Could an alchemist help us now?" Kellan asked, bringing the discussion back to its purpose.

"Perhaps with a potion to find lost things, but I believe that only works if you put something from the thing or person you want to find into the potion," Senet said, her crimson lips a slash of color against her light brown skin.

"I didn't realize you were a budding alchemist," Martin said.

Senet's nails tapped the table impatiently. "Read a book sometime, Martin. It's amazing the kind of things you can learn if you show the least bit of intellectual curiosity."

"So without knowing who we're looking for, we can't use a finding potion, and we're back to having nothing to go on." Warrane rubbed a hand over his face, scratching at the gray beard that covered his jaw.

"Not necessarily." Kellan pulled one of his parchment sheets free and glanced at the list he'd made. "We might not be able to track the person, but we can track the ingredients used in the spell."

The council leaned toward him as he read the short list of ingredients Blue had identified. When he'd finished, he looked up. "I've already done a bit of research. Charing root is fairly common, though we might have some luck if a merchant sold it to someone they hadn't seen before. But threffalk is rare. Rare enough that anyone placing a recent order for it should be memorable. Especially when there are maybe four suppliers in all of Balavata."

"Someone could've just brought it in with them at port," Preston Gaillard said from beside Kellan, his wide hands pressed flat against the table, his body leaning forward as if to emphasize his point. "The port traffic comes through my quarter, and I assure you that try as we might to stop illegal imports, we can't find everything."

"I know, but this is our best chance of finding a true lead." Kellan met his mother's gaze once more before moving rapidly through a list of tasks he needed each head family to do for both their public and private response to the threat. The meeting took another three hours as he worked through the other issues that faced the council.

Three hours he could've spent sending protection to Blue. Making sure Nessa didn't leave the castle early to see her friend until he was sure the shop wouldn't be attacked. Figuring out why there was so little difference between the fear of losing his sister and the fear of losing Blue.

By the time the meeting ended, the restlessness within him was at a breaking point. When Georgiana Faure demanded an audience to discuss the strength of her family's potential alliance with the throne, couched in terms that left little doubt that she was prepared to find another path to the throne should he prove unreceptive, Kellan turned on the charm, settled her in a side parlor with refreshments on the way, gave orders to send royal guards to watch over Blue, and then rushed to the royal suite for just five minutes of privacy so he could pace and think and *breathe*.

He needed to breathe.

How had his father done this? Managed every crisis with the steady calm needed to keep others tethered to their best selves, put the interests of the kingdom as a whole first, and played the political game without a single sign of weakness? Had he ever sat through a meeting because it was what the kingdom needed while inside panic bit deep over the few people in the kingdom he truly cared about?

Kellan pulled up short, his hand still reaching for the door that led to his bedchambers.

He cared about his mother. Nessa. Many of the castle staff and his friends.

But Blue?

They were becoming friends, yes. And it was true that she was the one person besides Nessa who made it easy to be himself. No bracing for lies, threats, or flattery. No worry that she would tell him what she thought he wanted to hear.

He laughed at the thought of Blue trying to flatter him, and then swallowed hard as the bright torch that had blazed to life within him while he'd danced with her came roaring back.

He couldn't afford to be anything but a prince dedicated to choosing a bride from the head families while proving he had what it took to step into his mother's shoes. Blue was becoming his friend, and he was grateful for it. And of course, he wanted to protect her. He'd do the same for anyone.

Except he hadn't. He'd assigned the job of sending protection to the various alchemy shops throughout the city to the representatives from each quarter, but he'd personally sent guards to watch over Blue. He could tell himself it was because her family had been a longtime friend of his, but the truth was that from the moment he'd heard Senet's report about her alchemist, the one person in all of Balavata he'd worried about was Blue de la Cour.

He turned and lightly smacked his head against the wall three times before someone delicately cleared his throat from behind him.

Slowly, Kellan turned to find his secretary standing in the hall, a bemused expression on his face.

"Problems, Your Majesty?"

"No." Kellan rubbed his forehead, caught Jacques's expression, and hastily dropped his hand. "Just a council meeting."

And a witch. And a betrothal. And shoes to fill.

And Blue.

Stars hang him, Blue.

EIGHTEEN

THE FARMHOUSE NO longer looked like a cozy, welcoming friend when Blue walked up the lane the day after she'd danced with Kellan in a pub and then watched a man die as magic shadow fire ate into his body. Dinah was on her heels, though she'd barely spoken to Blue since the night before when Blue had returned home, escorted by a pair of Evrard guards.

Dinah had spent half the day at the castle for an emergency council meeting and half the day in the Chauveau quarter dealing with the aftermath of the witch's attack, but on the walk to and from the city, she'd maintained a stony silence unless she was barking an order at Blue.

Pepperell still waited on the porch, though he wouldn't come to Blue when Dinah was near. The garden still framed the house with wild abandon, just waiting for Blue to walk its paths and let the magic in her blood tell her which things wanted to be harvested. Lanterns were lit in the windows—Halette's doing, Blue was sure. The younger Chauveau girl rarely spoke to Blue, but she'd started quietly handling a few of the household tasks when her mother wasn't around.

Dinah wanted a quick meal of the fresh bread, cheese, and plums she'd had Blue get from the market on their way home. Blue didn't mind making such an easy dinner, but first she had to harvest her garden. It had been too long.

And after she harvested, she had to either find the courage to bring the crop down to the root cellar or figure out somewhere else to safely store it.

Blue's hands trembled as she reached for the doorknob, Pepperell anxiously winding about her feet, his eye on Dinah as she carefully climbed their old porch steps.

Blue couldn't go down into the root cellar. It was impossible. Her stomach clenched, and her breath came in quick, hard gasps at the thought.

She couldn't be surrounded by those walls, standing on the floor where she'd kneeled in the middle of the spilled wintermint watching Mama die.

Pepperell meowed as Blue crossed the threshold, and she bit her lip as she scooped him into her arms. There was nowhere else to properly store her harvest. Not if she wanted the items to last while they dried. She was going to have to go down that ladder or give up harvesting from her garden.

Her heart beat too loud, and her breath came too fast as she made her decision. She'd find as much comfort as she could in the garden, and then she'd force herself to face the root cellar. Before her panic could blaze out of control, she whirled and nearly ran straight into Dinah, who was already closing the front door behind her.

"Where do you think you're going?" the woman demanded.

Blue snatched up the gathering basket that rested on the bench beside the coatrack. "I have some harvesting to do in the garden before sunset. If you want me to prepare dinner, I'll do it when I get back in."

"There's nothing to prepare. Seventh bell will ring soon. If you aren't inside for dinner, you don't eat." Dinah swept past her, and Blue hurried out of the house.

The door shut firmly behind her. Blue stumbled down the steps, raced along the little path that wound its way around the house and into the garden, and then simply sank to her knees in the dirt beside a clump of dancing ferns.

Pepperell climbed out of her arms and sniffed the ferns, his back twitching.

She smoothed his fur, and then rocked forward over her knees. For long moments, she remained still and silent, feeling the soft brush of the ferns against her skin. Smelling the richness of the dirt, the pungent green scent of the plants around her, and the sea salt that drifted in with the breeze.

Panic skittered through her.

"It's just a root cellar." She tried the words on for size, but they refused to fit. It wasn't just a root cellar. It was the dark, yawning chasm of her nightmares. It was wintermint and broken ladders and Mama dying.

And she was going to have to climb down into it because there was no one else to do it for her now.

Grief closed her throat, and she drew an unsteady breath.

Her home now felt like an unwelcoming stranger to her. She hadn't seen Grand-mère in almost a week. Papa was gone. Dinah watched Blue's every word, every movement, both at the shop and at home, and none of it made sense.

None of it.

Dinah should have been too busy running her businesses, managing her quarter, and chasing the betrothal to be bothered with spending her days at the alchemy shop. She should have been unwilling to move herself and her daughters into the little farmhouse when they had a beautiful mansion of their own. And if she was so close to Mama, surely Papa would have mentioned her.

Leaning forward, Blue pressed her bare hands into the dirt at the base of the fern clumps, wiggling her fingers until they disappeared beneath the loamy soil. She closed her eyes and let the magic in her blood settle into her fingertips. Let the grief and confusion settle too.

The soil became alive beneath her skin. Roots, seeds, fruits, herbs—every living thing in a wide circle around Blue strained toward her. She could feel tendrils of dancing fern root curling toward her hands. Sensed the buzz of walla berries ready to harvest from the bush to her left. The hum of wintermint and sage tucked beneath the hanging vines of the garden's rynoir tree, its frothy pink blossoms brushing the ground as it swayed in the sea breeze.

Blue pressed her hands deeper in the ground, willing herself to be calm. Be steady.

All she had to do was go into the root cellar and store a few things.

Her throat closed on a bubble of fear, and she swallowed hard. Drew in a shaky breath. Thought of the ways Papa had used to calm Blue when her nightmares hit.

Hands in the soil, grounding herself to the plants.

Slow, deep breaths, paying attention to the rise and fall of her chest instead of the frantic beat of her heart.

Mama's lullaby, sung soft and gentle, connecting Blue to the best memories she had of her mother. Memories of warmth and safety. Blue's clearest memory of Mama was of walking the garden path with her, listening to Mama sing the lullaby she'd written for her daughter.

Blue drew in another slow breath, kept her hands deep in the soil, and began to softly sing.

> *Hush now, baby, don't you cry.*
> *Your little tears I'll always dry.*
> *A branch of myrrh and bolla root*
> *To strengthen you in all you do*
> *With silver and gold, and a strand of rose*
> *And plenty of magic to keep them close.*

Tears stung Blue's eyes as the memory of Papa sitting by her bedside singing to her overlapped her memories of Mama in the garden. She let the tears fall, let the grief in her chest unfurl as she sang the second half.

> *Hush now, baby, I'm right here*
> *To chase away your every fear*
> *With a drop of mint and a sprig of yew*
> *And three little precious drops of blue.*
> *You'll grow straight and swift and true*
> *And I will always be with you.*

Dancing fern roots brushed against her fingertips, and she drew in another shaky breath.

166

"That's a strange lullaby," a voice said from behind her.

Blue jumped and felt a quick bite of pain on her index finger as she pulled her hands free of the soil and turned around.

Halette stood there, a small plate of food in her hands. Her dark hair was swept into a long tail down her back, and her silk day dress was covered with Papa's red apron.

"My mother wrote it for me. She was an alchemist too." Blue eyed Papa's apron and struggled to keep her voice even. "Why are you wearing that?"

"I've never heard an alchemist's lullaby before." Halette walked closer. "Why were you singing it?"

Blue brushed dirt from her hands and grimaced as blood smeared across her palm. She'd cut her finger on something in the soil. "Because I wanted to."

Halette shrugged like she hadn't really wanted a true answer in the first place. "I saved some dinner for you. Mother expects you to come inside soon." She glanced at Blue's empty gathering basket. "She also expects you to come in with things you harvested."

"That's my papa's apron." Anger sparked within Blue, and she grabbed a few fronds of the dancing fern plant, tore them loose, and threw them into her basket.

Halette looked down at the apron she wore, the freckles on her cheeks catching the fading rays of the sun. "Oh. I didn't realize—"

"You've already taken my house." Blue snatched walla berries from the bush beside her and tossed them into the basket. "My shop. My bedroom. My ability to see my grandmother." More berries landed on the ferns inside the basket. "You've taken everything from me. You're not going to take my papa's things too. That's *his* apron. Take it off."

Halette stared at her for a long moment, her expression carved from glass. And then she slowly set the plate down and reached for the apron's ties. A small serving of buttered bread, several slices of cheese, and a glossy purple plum sat on the plate. Pepperell immediately rushed forward and began licking the cheese.

"You know, you aren't the only one who's lost everything." Halette's voice cracked, and she pulled viciously at the apron's ties. "I lost my father too. And my home. My life in my quarter with my friends. My household staff—don't look at me like that. I know you're used to doing everything for yourself, but I'm not."

Blue started to say that the two situations weren't the same, but then stopped at the look of furious grief in Halette's eyes. She knew that grief. It lived inside her, sending an ache through her veins with every heartbeat.

Carefully, she plucked a few more walla berries, giving herself time to calm down and think about her words. Finally, she said, "I'm not used to doing everything for myself. Papa did all the cooking and most of the cleaning. One of the worst parts of missing him is waking up in the morning without the smell of hot spiced chicory in the air. It's a daily reminder that he's gone." She met Halette's eyes. "I'm very sorry you lost your father and the life you knew."

Halette folded the apron with care and gently pushed Pepperell away from the cheese. "I'm sorry you did too."

Blue hooked the basket over her arm and got to her feet. "Do you know why your mother moved you out here?"

Halette picked up the plate, tossed the cheese to Pepperell, and then balanced the plate on top of the folded apron. "My mother only does things that benefit her, so either she thinks this will somehow help get Jacinthe the betrothal, or you have something that will add to her business empire."

"I can't imagine living in my farmhouse will help your sister win the betrothal, so it must be the latter." Blue looked into her basket and frowned. One of the berries had burst, and its bright purple juice had run in rivulets down a fern leaf before sinking into the veins and turning them the dusky purple of a twilight sky. "How did that happen?" she murmured, reaching in to pull out the leaf.

"How did what happen?" Halette stepped closer, holding the apron and the food plate in front of her like a peace offering.

"This leaf." Blue held it up. The sun painted it with a nimbus of gold, lingering on the fern's pointed edges like bits of fire. "The walla berry juice alchemized with the fern sap. The two are compatible, and I often use them together for skin creams and topical ointments, but the process of alchemizing them takes hours of boiling them together in a pot of yaeringlei oil and some essence of tryllis. I've never seen them bond like this without help."

"Maybe you still had some of that oil or whatever in your basket."

Blue examined each side of the leaf. "No, I make the oil from seeds I get from Llorenyae. And I don't keep essence of tryllis at the farmhouse."

"Well, then I guess this is convenient and saves you some work," Halette said.

"This isn't convenient. It's impossible." Blue turned toward her. "This is completely impossible, but here it is."

Halette opened her mouth to respond, but then both girls jumped at the sound of a man's harsh, angry voice echoing from the front of the house. Exchanging a quick glance, the girls quietly crept along the side of the house until they could just see a pair of polished black boots standing on the porch. Dinah's slender gray shoes faced his.

"How dare you come to this house of grief with your mundane complaints." Dinah spoke quietly, her words coated with ice.

The man's laugh sent a chill over Blue's skin. "I'd hardly call the list of debts in your name a mundane complaint, Lady Chauveau."

"Not my debts." The ice in her voice hardened. "My late husband's. And there are a number of legal questions regarding signatures—"

"There are no legal questions. I've had everything verified by your husband's solicitor. In three days, the royal magistrate will review the estate and verify that every single piece of property you own was signed over to me as collateral against his debt."

Dinah's voice trembled. "I happen to be coming into a large sum shortly. I just need a few more weeks."

"And I need a palatial estate in the gorgeous kingdom of Súndraille, but it looks like we're both out of luck." Papers rustled, and the man's boots edged closer to Dinah's. "Once the magistrate reviews the estate and authorizes me to seize all of your property, there will still be the matter of the additional debt your late husband accrued. If you do not have the coin to pay it at that time, as per my contract with your late husband, I will then exercise my right to claim one of your daughters in marriage."

Blue shot a look at Halette, who was trembling beside her. The girl's eyes were full of tears, and she'd chewed her lower lip until it began to bleed. Blue quietly shifted her basket and wrapped an arm around Halette's shoulders.

No wonder Dinah had moved here with her daughters. No wonder she'd been so angry to learn that the shop only made enough coin to support itself and the farmhouse. Her mansion and extensive businesses had been signed over to this odious man. Blue didn't know what that meant for the running of the Chauveau quarter, but it didn't matter. What mattered was that a man who sounded nearly old enough to be Halette's father might have the legal right to force her into marriage unless Dinah found a way to pay off the debt.

Blue knew a way to pay off the debt. She just hadn't quite accomplished it yet. For the first time since Papa's death, Blue began thinking about ways to perfect her attempts to turn lead into gold. As Halette leaned against her and Dinah sent the man on his way, Blue resolved to try the experiment once more. Maybe it would lead to nothing.

Or maybe it would save Halette and Jacinthe, restore Dinah's property, and finally rid Blue of living with the Chauveaus.

NINETEEN

"I'm GOING TO try to help you."

Blue stood across from Dinah in the farmhouse kitchen, the faint clamor of the wraith's bells drifting in through the window and sending a chill across her skin. The bells had been ringing for hours, now. Far longer than they usually did. Maybe the recent spells used in the city had somehow set it off, though Blue had no idea how it could sense magic from that far away. Or maybe the wraith was just restless for reasons that made no sense to anyone but it.

Either way, Blue wanted it to stop. She was already exhausted and on edge. She was behind in refilling the shop's stock because she had to divide her time between the floor and the storeroom. She was behind on filling orders for deliveries too, and Ana still hadn't returned. And Blue had spent the better part of the previous night jumping between memories of Halette's tears, the hardness of the man's voice as he'd said Dinah had three days left, the strangeness of the dancing fern leaf that had bonded with the walla berry juice without the usual alchemy, and the warm, fizzy feeling that danced through her stomach when she thought of Kellan.

Which was ridiculous. He was *Kellan*. Not only would he probably break his neck doing something reckless before she ever saw him again, but he was about to choose a bride from one of the head families.

Not that she wanted to be Kellan's bride.

In fact, stars save the girl who did.

When Blue realized she couldn't actually dredge up any charitable feelings toward whichever girl Kellan eventually chose for his betrothal, she ordered herself to stop thinking about him entirely and focus on Dinah, who stood across from her with pinched lips and fingers that worried with the lace edges of her dress sleeves.

"Help me how?" Dinah asked, scorn filling her voice.

Blue drew in a deep breath as her heart thudded against her chest.

The shop had been robbed for this. Papa had died because Blue hadn't told him about the almost-gold experiment being taken. The thought of going back to work on it made her chest ache, but the thought of Halette or Jacinthe being taken by the man in the black boots was worse.

"I . . . overheard the man who came to the house last night."

Dinah's gaze sharpened. "I should have known you'd eavesdrop."

A tiny thread of anger slid through Blue, and she straightened her shoulders. "You should've kept your voices down if you didn't want me to overhear. Are you going to listen to my plan?"

"Plan for what? Finally going to show me where your father

kept his extra coin?" Dinah snorted in derision, but her eyes locked on Blue with an unsettling fervor.

"There is no extra coin." Honestly, could the woman be any more difficult to talk to? "But I don't want Halette or Jacinthe to be forced into marriage with that awful man, and there may be a way I can help. I can't promise it will work, but I can try."

"Try what?"

Blue hesitated. Once she told Dinah, there would be no going back. She had no doubt a woman as desperate as Dinah would hound her day and night until the experiment worked. But Dinah wouldn't spread the word to the rest of the city. She'd want the gold all to herself to pay off her debts, restore her property, save her daughters, and remain in position to win the betrothal.

"How can you help me?" Dinah's voice was hushed, but there was a spark of anticipation within it.

Blue met her gaze and remembered what Grand-mère had always taught her. If you saw a wrong and had the ability to make it right, it became your responsibility to do so.

"I can try to turn lead into gold."

The words sounded ridiculous. A far-fetched dream that an alchemist could chase for her entire life and never see come true. For a moment, Blue thought Dinah would laugh in scorn or berate her for talking nonsense when the Chauveaus were in desperate need of a real solution.

But Dinah smiled. A slow, cold curving of the lips that made the hair on the back of Blue's neck stand up.

"I can't promise." Blue's words were rushed as Dinah clasped her hands in front of her chest as if praying and then turned to survey the kitchen. "I've come close, but haven't actually succeeded yet, so there's a good chance I won't be able to figure out the key to it in time. But I'll try."

"Of course you will." Dinah turned back, that unsettling smile still locked in place. "It's what you do, isn't it, Blue? You rescue the strays. The desperate. It's the purpose that gets you out of bed and keeps you moving forward even after unspeakable loss."

Blue opened her mouth to reply but couldn't think of a single thing to say. This was a far cry from the reaction she expected. Should she smile back? Agree that Dinah was desperate? Remind her that it might not work?

Dinah gestured toward the front door. "Well, let's head to the shop and get started. I'm sure your abilities rival those of your mother, and as I've recently learned, she was quite the talented alchemist. One would almost believe she combined alchemy with magic. Almost like the person who unleashed that terrible spell on my quarter the other night."

Blue froze as Dinah's gaze landed on her with startling ferocity. Her heartbeat was thunder in her ears as she faced the older woman. What she said next could be the difference between life and death, both for herself and for Grand-mère. If Dinah learned that Blue did indeed possess magic handed down through her mother's side, she could decide that reporting Blue to the authorities and taking credit for capturing the person responsible for the carnage would put her in a better position than waiting for Blue to hopefully create gold.

It wouldn't matter that Blue wasn't guilty. Not if they could prove she possessed magic. She'd heard the stories about the alchemists in other quarters who'd already been beaten, threatened, or had their shop burned after the spell. It wouldn't take much to convince the city that she should be put to death.

Taking a calming breath, Blue said quietly, "My mother was simply a talented alchemist. As am I. Now, do you want my help or not?"

Dinah's eyes narrowed, but she simply said, "Of course."

Today, Dinah's carriage waited to take them into the city. Blue guessed that since the creditor had found them at the farmhouse, there was no use in Dinah continuing to hide her presence. They spent the ride in silence, Dinah staring out one window, while Blue stared out the other. When they came abreast of the shop, the carriage rolled to a stop, and Dinah sucked in a sharp breath.

"Blue," she said, her voice low and urgent.

Blue scooted to Dinah's side of the carriage and peered out the window at the Mortar & Pestle. Someone had painted *Death to Witches* in red sand paint across the front windows. Ice crept over Blue's skin, and she hugged her arms close to her body as she shivered.

"I'm not a witch," she whispered.

"These peasants don't understand the difference between an alchemist's potion and a witch's spell." Dinah sounded furious. "And they've damaged the shop with their ignorance."

"It will come off," Blue said, rubbing heat back into her arms. "I'll hire Lucian to get a crew of kids to scrub it."

The words would come off, but the message would still linger in the back of her mind. And if it lingered in hers, how many others would walk by her shop and remember it? How many believed it? And would she ever feel truly safe until the witch responsible for the carnage was caught?

Not for the first time, she was deeply grateful to Kellan for assigning extra guards around her shop during the day.

Hours later, Blue had rushed Nessa through her regular

tutoring session, thankful that Kellan hadn't come with her that day as he had the four previous days. She didn't need any distractions. Not with Dinah suspicious that Blue might have magic.

Not that Blue's magic was anything spectacular. Certainly nothing dangerous. Just a little affinity with harvesting and combining plants. Still, she couldn't afford to take any chances.

Once Nessa and her guards left to return to the castle, Blue turned her attention to the painstaking process of alchemizing ordinary metal into something precious. She heated the stove, prepared her pressurized pot, and pulled down the Eldrian mineral that had nearly worked last time. Soon, she lost herself in the rhythm of her work, forgetting about the passage of time or the fact that Dinah sat at the worktable, her sharp eyes following Blue's every move.

The first attempt produced a rough chunk of milky white metal with streaks of gray. The second produced a faint golden sheen, but the threads of gray were still there. She was working on the third experiment when Dinah got up from the table and moved to the stove.

"Why do you keep singing that ridiculous song?"

Blue startled, nearly dropping the tongs into the pressure pot. She hadn't realized she'd been singing Mama's lullaby. And she certainly hadn't realized she was singing it in front of an audience. She'd been caught up with her experiment, and everything else had faded away.

"Habit," Blue said.

"I've never heard it anywhere else," Dinah said as she approached the pressure pot and peered inside. "The rhymes could use some work."

Blue shrugged, irritation flaring. "My mother wrote it for me when I was a child. It's not meant to be critiqued."

Dinah stared at the lump of metal Blue held. "Fine. Who else knows that you're working on this?"

Blue was about to say no one but paused. Did she really trust Dinah enough to let her think she was the sole person involved in this secret? Blue wasn't sure how it could be used against her, but Dinah was both desperate and used to manipulating others to maintain order and control. Cautiously, she said, "Some members of the royal family."

The lie tasted like ash in her mouth, and she promised herself that she'd make it the truth as soon as she could.

Dinah's brows arched. "Really? And the queen has no issue with it?" She turned away before Blue could answer, pacing the storeroom as she tapped her fingers restlessly against her legs. "Of course she doesn't. Why would she? It's the perfect answer to any problem. If she has an unlimited source of gold, she'd never need another alliance with a head family if she didn't want one. Is that the plan?" She rounded on Blue, who was standing beside her pot staring at Dinah with wide eyes. "Get a supply of gold so that the rules of betrothal become about personal preferences instead of about which family can offer the strongest alliance?"

Blue shook her head.

Dinah closed the distance between them, her expression cold, though her eyes were still lit with fervor. "You listen to me, girl. The gold belongs to me first. You remember who you owe a debt to. I took you in when you had no one."

"I have Grand-mère." Blue lifted her chin, anger sparking along her nerves.

Dinah slapped her hard enough to send her stumbling back into the stove. Her arm grazed the side of the pot, and she hissed in pain. Pulling her arm toward her stomach, she tried to move around Dinah, but the woman blocked her path. Blue's pulse thundered in her ears, and she braced herself in case Dinah lashed out again.

"You have nothing," Dinah said calmly. "Just like me. Your property belongs to someone else. Your standing in the city is at the mercy of someone else. We're the same, except that I've taken care of you. I've made sure you were able to keep working in your shop and living in your house. The gold comes to me first. Once I've paid off my husband's debts and restored my standing, you can report your success to the queen."

Blue didn't plan to report anything to the queen at all, and she trusted Nessa and Kellan not to either unless they thought somehow it would protect Blue to have the queen know. But Dinah wasn't going to listen to reason, not when she thought someone else might take what she now desperately wanted for herself.

So Blue simply nodded her agreement, cradling her burned arm against her body while she waited for Dinah to move so she could get the burn cream and treat her wound. As Dinah hovered over the stove, anxiously awaiting the results of the next experiment, Blue bandaged her arm and reminded herself that she hadn't offered to help for Dinah's sake. She'd done it for Halette and Jacinthe. She'd done it because no one deserved to be gambled away like that.

And she'd done it because it would free her of Dinah's violent mood swings and constant interference. She wasn't sure how much more of the woman she could take.

TWENTY

DINAH THREW AN empty jar at the back wall of the Mortar &
Pestle's storeroom, where it shattered into thin shards of amber
glass.

She had one day left to pay off her late husband's debts, and
she still didn't have the means to do it. The stupid girl had tried
no fewer than seventeen times in the past two days to turn metal
into gold, and each time she'd failed.

Dinah's gamble had failed.

She'd killed Pierre de la Cour and moved herself and her
daughters into that old, drafty farmhouse far from her quarter,
lived like a peasant, and checked on the alchemy shop like a
common merchant day after day, just waiting for a chance to
catch Blue working on the one experiment that really mattered.
But Blue hadn't returned to work on the gold, and Dinah had
grown desperate. It was clear that the girl wasn't motivated by
coin. She wanted to stay in her simple little house with her quiet
life.

What she cared about was rescuing others. So when Mr. Dubois, the collector who held the notes to all her husband's debts, came calling unexpectedly at the farmhouse to deliver the news that her time to pay off the remaining balance was nearly up, she'd insisted that they talk on the porch. And she'd raised her voice, which encouraged him to raise his, hoping Blue, out harvesting in her little garden, would be drawn in.

Grabbing another empty jar, Dinah slung it against the wall, her teeth clenched as the glass shattered.

Her plan to gain Blue's sympathy had worked. But even though the girl was working frantically to help Dinah, she couldn't seem to get it right. Maybe the true talent had died out with her mother. Blue was still trying, but Dinah was out of time. Tomorrow, Dubois would deliver a record of her husband's debts and the signed documents that listed all of the Chauveau properties and coin as collateral against them to the royal magistrate.

Dinah could break every jar in the shop, and it wouldn't do a thing to help her. If she didn't stop Dubois tonight, everything she'd worked for would be ruined. She would be ruined. Without the authority of the throne at her beck and call, the true power she craved more than the breath in her lungs would be lost to her.

Abandoning the shelf of spare jars, Dinah grabbed a broom and stalked toward the pile of broken glass. A thread of white-hot anger sparked along her nerves as she quickly swept up the mess.

Maybe Blue had failed to create gold. And maybe Dinah had failed to find a creditor willing to loan her anything. But Dubois had made a critical error in coming to see her personally. He'd been heavily guarded, of course, but when he saw that it was just her on the porch, he'd come close enough to discuss things with her face-to-face.

Close enough for her to reach out as he turned to walk away and pluck a single loose hair from the back of his cloak.

He'd known he was dealing with a cunning, ruthless woman. He had no idea he was dealing with a witch. How could he? She'd stopped practicing when the law against magic went into effect. With everyone so sure another Marielle might rise to wreak havoc, Dinah had found it prudent to become one of the most vocal proponents of the law. What better way to hide one's true nature than to campaign viciously against it?

Baring her teeth, she threw the glass into the trash.

She'd had a taste of her true nature a few nights ago, when she'd created the fire spells to cause chaos across the city, and already she hungered for more. If magic could solve one problem, it could solve another.

And Mr. Dubois's strand of hair gave Dinah the perfect opportunity to craft the spell that would destroy him.

The cathedral bells tolled midnight as she slipped into the storeroom of the Mortar & Pestle, locking the door behind her and lighting a lamp. She had to give Blue credit: the girl kept her shelves well stocked. Quickly gathering her ingredients, she combined them in a pot on the stove, added the strand of hair, and whispered the incantation that would be the death of Mr. Dubois.

The mixture bubbled and hissed, sending a puff of dark green smoke into the air where it writhed like a snake. Dinah held a small glass vial up to the smoke, focused on her purpose, and said, "*Scrios*."

The smoke drifted into the vial, where it coiled and churned. She capped the vial, cleaned the pot, and made sure the storeroom looked undisturbed. And then she left the shop and moved briskly toward the Aubert quarter, where Mr. Dubois lived.

When she reached the corner closest to his home, she stopped. Any closer, and his guards might see her. Uncorking the vial, she focused once more on her desperate wish for Dubois to die in agony, and then set the smoke free.

It burst from the vial, whirled in place, a tiny dust devil spinning in the midnight air, and then it arrowed toward the distant redbrick home that sat a comfortable distance from the cobblestoned street.

Dinah didn't wait. Nothing could stop the spell she'd put in motion, and she couldn't be seen anywhere close to the home when his body was discovered.

He was as good as dead, and once the spell had finished killing him, it would utterly destroy everything within his home. Including the Chauveau estate debts her fool of a husband had signed.

She was free.

TWENTY-ONE

"WE HAVE TO do something!" Senet Aubert paced the castle's east receiving parlor, where an emergency meeting of the royal council had gathered. The ends of her red headscarf trailed in the air behind her as she moved. "Another magical attack happened in my quarter last night. The Dubois house and everyone inside it were destroyed. Disintegrated into dust! People are terrified they'll be killed in their own homes while they sleep, and I certainly don't know how to convince them they're safe."

"They aren't safe," Georgiana Faure said flatly, her mouth pursed as she turned to face the prince. "None of us are. You told us you were investigating the source of the first spell's ingredients, but you have nothing to show for it, and now we have another attack."

"We've had less than a week to investigate," Kellan said. "We have an expert helping us identify the ingredients used—"

"An alchemist?" Martin Roche's lip curled. "Seems to me that's the same as asking another witch to turn on their own kind."

"It's not the same, Lord Roche," Kellan said firmly. "One is science. The other is magic. We need all the help we can get, including any alchemists willing to identify the spell's components so that we can trace them to their source."

He turned to Senet. "I appreciate the awful position you're in, Lady Aubert. I'm certainly open to other ideas, but short of finding another witch willing and able to ferret out the one causing us problems—"

"The last thing we need to do is invite more use of magic," Dinah Chauveau snapped.

"What we need is a workable plan, and a leader capable of putting that plan in motion." Georgiana gave Kellan a look that was pure challenge.

He straightened his shoulders and held her gaze. "We have a workable plan, Lady Faure. No one said it would be easy, or that it would yield results immediately."

"I'm not sure a boy of nearly nineteen is the best person to catch a witch," she said.

Silence blanketed the room, and Kellan stared the woman down. Here was the challenge he'd been worried would happen. A family without a daughter of marriageable age who still wanted a shot at the throne. A direct hit at his leadership abilities, at the confidence the council had in him to be their next king. A hit that had to be answered without a single show of weakness.

Praying he was making the right choice, he said in a voice as cold as the marble floor beneath his feet, "Lady Faure, you are dismissed."

Her eyes widened in furious disbelief. "You can't dismiss me."

He kept his gaze steadily on hers. "I am your sovereign prince, soon to be your king. This is my kingdom, my castle, and my royal council. You are invited to participate as a representative of your family only so long as I allow it. You have made it clear that you do not wish to cooperate with the plan the council agreed upon, and further, you have insinuated a lack of confidence in my leadership. I will not tolerate advisers who are not fully committed to the good of the kingdom. If you do not cooperate, the Faure family will lose its seat on the council. If you make amends for your disrespect, I will allow you to choose another representative for your family at the next council meeting. You are *dismissed*."

He turned from her, as if fully confident she would leave without a fuss and focused all of his attention on discussing the previous night's attack with Senet. His shoulders knotted with tension as he waited for Georgiana's response.

Either he'd passed the test, humbling Georgiana and leaving her without allies on the council and with no choice but to obey him or lose her family's seat entirely, or he'd made an enemy of both her and anyone who secretly felt as she did and given them a flag to rally around.

After a moment that felt as long as a year, she said quietly, "I beg your pardon, Your Majesty. My son will take my place at the next council meeting." Her voice seethed with bitterness, but she left quietly, and Kellan decided to count it as a victory. He turned to meet the eyes of the rest of the council and found respect, wariness, and speculation in equal measure.

"Let's get to work," he said, and no one argued.

Two hours later, the council meeting adjourned, and Kellan slipped out the door, even though his mother, Dinah, and Martin were heading toward him from three separate corners of the room. He didn't know what each of them wanted to discuss with him, but he needed a minute to breathe. To think.

He ducked into the east library, cut through the sitting room attached to it, and ended up in the smaller hallway used by the castle staff.

"Your Majesty?" His secretary spoke from behind him.

Kellan shook his head, waving his hand in the air as he kept walking. "Not now, Jacques. And also it's spooky how you always seem to know where I am."

"I find it a useful skill since you tend to be . . . somewhat difficult to pin down at times." Jacques hurried after the prince.

Kellan turned a corner and walked faster.

"Your Majesty, I apologize, but there are several important documents you need to review, and your mother has requested that we immediately set up a meeting between you and the new Faure council member."

"The new Faure . . . I left the meeting less than three minutes ago. How did she already get word to you?" Kellan shot Jacques an irritated look.

The man shrugged. "She had me sit just outside the room so she could brief me on anything you might need assistance with once the meeting adjourned."

"Well, schedule the meeting, then. You know my calendar. And leave the documents on my desk. I'll see to them later." He took another step and sighed. "And stop following me, Jacques. That's an order."

He cut through the conservatory and reached the main hall- way just in time for Dinah to call his name as she moved out of the east wing.

Was it too much to ask that he have one single minute to himself?

Pretending he hadn't heard her, he increased the distance between them, nearly jogging by the time he reached the corridor that led to the kitchen. She called his name again, and this time he heard Martin too.

Rounding the corner out of their view, he sprinted down the corridor, burst into the anteroom that led to the kitchen, and nearly collided with Blue.

"Kellan!" Her mouth dropped open in shock. "What are you doing? Why are you—hey!"

"Shh," he said as he flung open the door that led to the kitchen maid's closet and pulled both of them inside. Shutting the door quietly behind them, he said softly, "I just need a minute."

"A minute to do what?" she spoke as quietly as he had. "Hide in a closet?"

"If that's what it takes." He strained to hear footsteps, but if Dinah and Martin were intent on following him to the kitchen to have a conversation, they hadn't reached the anteroom yet. "I just finished with an emergency council meeting, and I needed a minute to myself just to breathe, but my secretary kept following me, and then Dinah Chauveau and Martin Roche came after me, and I'm sure they want to discuss what happened with Georgiana Faure, but I need to think before I have another fraught political discussion."

His words tumbled out too fast, and his heart was racing like it did when he dove off the cliff to swim in the sea. He could lead. He could navigate difficult political relationships. And he could hold his own in a crisis. But stars curse him, couldn't he have the space to catch his breath in between them?

In the dim light that seeped in under the closet's door, he could just make out Blue crossing her arms over her chest.

"Fine, you needed a minute to yourself. Why drag me in here with you?"

"I—it seemed like a good idea at the time."

"Are you insane? If we get caught in here together, they'll call you a rogue and wink about your ability to charm girls, but they'll call me something much worse, and my reputation will be permanently damaged."

He leaned toward her, keeping his voice low. "Dinah is on a rampage about the attack that happened last night. She's calling for a purge of anyone with magic, whether they use it or not. And Martin doesn't believe there's a difference between witches and alchemists. He wants them both put to death. So yes, I pulled you in here with me because I didn't want either of them to see you in their current moods. There's a lot more at stake here than your reputation."

Footsteps echoed from the corridor, and Dinah's voice drifted toward them. Blue stiffened. Her hand shot out, grabbed a fistful of his shirt, and pulled him with her to the back of the long closet, behind the row of aprons and dress uniforms that hung on a rod. Her back hit the wall, and she tugged until he closed the distance between them and let the flimsy fabric barrier close behind him.

He braced his forearms against the wall above her head and tried not to notice the way his body pressed against hers. The way her chest rose and fell with every breath, or the delicate scent of vanilla, wintermint, and dried herbs that filled his senses as he leaned his head down to whisper beside her ear, "This seems far more compromising to both of our reputations if we're found."

"Then we'd better not be found. I'm not going to be known as the girl who seduced the prince in a maid's closet." Her voice trembled, and her breath caught—a tiny little hitch that sent heat swirling through him. He laid his forehead against the coolness of the stone wall and ordered his heart to stop pounding like thunder in his ears.

Her hands were still fisted in the front of his shirt, though there was no need to pull him any closer. The door to the closet opened, and Martin said crossly, "The prince wouldn't have gone into a closet, Dinah. He must've grabbed a snack from the kitchen and then left through the staff entrance."

"He would've had to move incredibly fast to do all that before we arrived." She sounded impatient.

Blue shivered, and Kellan pressed his body closer, as if to promise that he'd stand between her and the council members at his back.

Heat from her skin spilled over onto his, and the warmth swirling through him exploded into flames. She tightened her grip on his shirt, and he turned his head until his lips were a whisper away from the side of her neck.

Her hands moved slowly, sliding over his chest until she was gripping his shoulders, and all he could think, all he could feel was *Blue*. Her scent, the warmth of her skin, the way she held on to him like he was the anchor keeping her safe, and the tiny catch of her breathing that fanned the flames within him until he thought he'd explode with the ache of wanting her.

Dinah moved a few steps into the closet, her heels tapping a sharp, staccato rhythm on the stone floor. Blue dug her fingers into Kellan's shoulders as they waited in silence to be discovered.

"This is a waste of time, Dinah. If the prince isn't available, we'll have to make appointments with his secretary," Martin said.

Another agonizing minute passed, and then Dinah's footsteps receded, and the closet door shut.

Kellan stayed right where he was. He told himself it was because Dinah or Martin could decide to check the closet once more before leaving the anteroom, but he knew the truth.

He wanted Blue.

More than wanted. His heart was a lit torch, and Blue was the match.

He was in way over his head.

Her hands released his shoulders and slid down to his chest again, but she didn't push him away.

"Blue," he whispered against her neck.

She turned her face toward his, leaving nothing but a thin sliver of air between her mouth and his. He closed his eyes and fought a war with himself.

"We can't." Her voice was soft. Breathless. And the fire within him felt like it would turn his bones to ash.

"I know," he breathed.

She fell silent, and he ordered himself not to close the distance between them. He'd kissed more girls than he could remember over the years. Harmless little flirtations on a dance floor. Nothing serious. Nothing permanent. He'd always known he didn't have that right until he chose a girl from one of the head families to be his queen.

But this was different. This was Blue, the girl who demanded honesty. Who wanted only what was real. He was standing on a precipice, and though everything in him wanted to dive off the cliff and take Blue with him, there were a hundred reasons why he shouldn't. Why he *couldn't*.

"I still don't like you," she whispered. The affection in her voice made him want to gather her in his arms and leave the castle behind, rogue witch, royal council, and betrothal season be cursed.

"I still don't like you, either," he said and waited another moment, memorizing the feel of her hands on his chest, of her mouth a breath away from his. And then he stepped back, opened the curtain of uniforms, and struggled to get his heartbeat under control.

She followed him out of the closet into the empty anteroom. In the kitchen, the cooks were busy calling out instructions to the maids as preparations for lunch got under way. Kellan turned and met Blue's eyes. She wore a strange expression—half regret, half wonder—and he understood exactly how she felt.

"Blue—"

"I have to go," she blurted, already backing away. "I came here to petition the queen for help searching for homeless children who've gone missing. Nessa told me I should. And maybe the queen needs my help identifying the ingredients of the spell that was used last night."

"I'm heading up that investigation," he said. "You can go to the Aubert quarter with me—"

"I'll just . . . I'm going to go find Nessa and see the queen. If you still need my help, maybe Nessa and I can go together."

She was right. It was better that he didn't spend any more time alone with her today. Not while his heart was still blazing and his thoughts kept wandering to the feeling of her body against his. He opened his mouth to agree with her, but she was already gone, hurrying down the staff corridor toward the main hall without a single backward glance.

TWENTY-TWO

"LADY CHAUVEAU." A man wearing the blue jacket and golden shield pin of the royal magistrate's office stood beside Dinah's carriage as she exited the castle. He sketched a quick bow as she approached, and then handed her an envelope sealed with blue wax and pressed with the magistrate's emblem.

Dinah's throat tightened as she entered her carriage and tore the envelope open with shaking fingers. She read the words, blinked back furious tears, and then read them again, her heart thudding painfully.

That snake of a creditor had turned the Chauveau estate debts over to the royal magistrate a day earlier than planned.

It didn't matter that Dubois was dead. His next of kin would inherit Dinah's holdings instead. The empire she'd built would soon be taken from her, her chance at the throne would be lost, and, with it, the guarantee of absolute power that would keep her from ever being at the mercy of others again.

She hadn't fought this hard only to lose. Maybe the Chauveau name would soon be worth nothing, and her chance at winning the betrothal for one of her daughters would be out of reach. But there was still a way she could get what she'd desperately wanted for so many years. Still a way to become too powerful to hurt.

It was going to take all of her courage and cunning to make it happen.

Dinah had left Blue on her own in the shop after giving the girl a taste of the punishment she deserved for not figuring out the secret to creating gold fast enough to save Dinah from all this trouble. Now she left the farmhouse gate and turned west. The road wrapped around the gentle swell of vineyards and orchards, hugged the rugged coastline briefly, and then turned toward the mountains and the dark prison that lay before them. A summer rainstorm flattened tufts of grass beside the road as Dinah took the curve around the first vineyard.

Icy fear filled her stomach, pricking along her skin until she shuddered as she glanced around. The sky was a flat slate of dark gray, the landscape blurred into vague, indistinct shapes, and whether because of the storm or because it was nearing the noon dining hour, no wagons were on the road.

She was alone.

The vow she'd made sixteen years earlier to never walk this path again, never retrace these cursed steps, blazed across her thoughts, and she forced it away.

Everything she'd worked for was in jeopardy, and Dinah refused to fail. Not after all she'd sacrificed.

Turning on her heel, she faced the closest orchard. Her breath clogged in her throat as she reached past the fear and clung to the thorns of anger that sliced into her like splinters of fire.

Maybe these steps were cursed, but they were familiar, and

the witch at the end of them was the only person who could help Dinah now. She had every right to be here, and she wasn't leaving until she got what she came for.

Wearing that thought like armor, she left the road and hurried through the orchard, the leafy apple branches rattling above her as her boots sank into the muddy ground. The neat rows of trees ended in a tangle of wild rosebushes, overgrown fennel, and windswept hazel trees. To the unpracticed eye, it appeared to be impassable, but Dinah knew better.

Angling her tall, thin frame, she edged between two leafy hazel trees, their wide skirt of leaves swallowing Dinah whole for a moment before spitting her out the other side. Brushing at a stray twig caught on her cloak, Dinah raised her face to stare at the tiny weathered cottage that was tucked in the center of a garden that was part vegetables, part flowers, and part herbs.

The cottage listed to the right now, and there were shingles missing from the roof. Two steps leading up to the porch were caving in, and cheerful clusters of bluebells grew out of cracks in the home's foundation.

Dinah's hands shook as she slowly made her way to the porch and knocked hard on the faded blue front door. The last time she'd been here, she'd made a bargain thinking she understood the strength of the witch she was dealing with.

She'd been wrong, and it had cost her dearly.

She wasn't going to make the same mistake twice.

The door swung open. The woman who stood on the other side barely reached Dinah's shoulder. Her belly was wide, sagging toward the floor beneath the cover of her stained apron, and wrinkles furrowed their way across her brow now, but her dark eyes were as sharp as they had been sixteen years ago.

"You!" The witch moved back a step, and Dinah took that as permission to crowd her way into the cottage.

Dinah's face was a cold mask, her gaze as unrelenting as the rain that fell outside the cottage's windows. She could show no fear. No weakness.

"What are you doing here?" The witch asked, though she'd stopped backing up and was reaching for a slip of hazel wood that rested on a table beside the door.

"I came to buy spells, Riva," Dinah said, her voice as cold and steady as her expression, though she was surreptitiously glancing around the cottage, searching for something she already knew Riva would have the good sense to keep hidden.

Riva grabbed the hazel wood and raised it, one end pointed at Dinah's chest. Her voice was a low hiss. "Liar."

The barbs of anger became a flush of rage pressing against Dinah's skin, and she raised her chin. "I've never lied to you."

Riva's mouth tightened. "You think I don't know what you're really after? I've had sixteen years of silence, and now you show up stinking of desperation and greed, and it isn't for a few small spells from me. You want to let the blood wraith out of its cage in the Wilds. You want to sacrifice innocents for the promise of the wraith's dark power again. Let me tell you this: I wouldn't help you open its cage even if I could."

"Even to save my daughters?"

Riva's eyes narrowed.

"I've been to the gate that holds the wraith in the Wilds. I know the spell that was used."

Riva froze, the pulse in her neck pounding. "That's impossible."

Dinah waited for Riva to glance toward wherever she'd hidden the spell, but the witch held Dinah's gaze, a frown digging in between her brows. Dinah glanced around the cottage, taking in the tumble of books on the shelves, the loose piles of parchment where Riva had written spells for every conceivable situation.

Every situation but one that required her to take a life. That had always been her weakness. So much power, so little will to use it.

"You're bluffing," Riva said, her voice low and furious. "Trying to trick me into giving something away—"

"One strand of silver, one of gold, and one of rose lead," Dinah said. She drifted toward the closest pile of parchment, but pulled up short when a brilliant green spark shot from Riva's wand and nearly collided with Dinah's face.

"Anyone can look at the lock and see which metals were used. You're fishing, and it isn't going to work."

Dinah turned the full force of her gaze on Riva. Pretending she was in the council room with the queen instead of facing a witch who could destroy her, she lifted her chin and armed herself with absolute confidence. "Burnt bolla and myrrh. Ground yew with notes of wintermint."

She leaned toward Riva, ignoring the wand that was pointed at her chest. This was it. Her big gamble. If Riva didn't fall for it, if she didn't give Dinah a clue she could use, there were no other cards she could play. "And one very special ingredient. Very rare. It took me forever to isolate it."

Riva paled, and Dinah smiled, slow and cruel, though her knees were shaking. "However did you come by it, Riva? It's not like you to be quite that creative."

As soon as she said the words, Dinah saw the truth on Riva's face.

Riva truly wasn't that creative. And whatever had been used to bind the spices to the metal had been something so far out of the ordinary that even Dinah, with all her years of experience with such things, couldn't identify it.

"You didn't make the lock, did you?"

"Of course I did."

Riva was a terrible liar. She blinked repeatedly, her chest rising and falling rapidly.

Now it was Dinah who hissed, "Liar."

Riva took a step forward and jabbed the wand into the skin above Dinah's heart. A jolt of power leaped from the hazel wood into Dinah, and pain crashed through her. She clenched her teeth to keep from crying out.

"I told you I wouldn't help you, even if I could." Riva's voice was steady, though something dark haunted her eyes. Grief? Remorse?

"I'm going to lose everything," Dinah said quietly, hoping to appeal to the part of Riva that had once welcomed Dinah with open arms. "My home. My businesses. Maybe even my daughters too."

Riva closed her eyes as if pained by Dinah's words, but when she opened them again, they were hard. "The blood wraith isn't the way to solve those problems."

"I just need the wraith for one day. One single day."

"No."

"Riva—"

"Leave it be. I can't help you."

"Then the person who made the lock—"

"She's dead." Riva spat the words at Dinah. "Been dead for years. There's nothing you can do to change that. The blood wraith is out of your reach."

Dinah held Riva's gaze and waited, but the witch's breathing remained steady, her stare unwavering.

She was telling the truth.

Which meant Dinah's plan was once again falling to pieces all around her. Her head swam, and a faint ringing sounded in her ears.

Sixteen years of planning. Of living for the revenge she was so justly owed. Of flattering and pretending and living next to those who'd taken the wraith from her and, with it, the power that Dinah had sacrificed so much to get.

"If that's all, then you'll be on your way." Riva stepped closer, and Dinah's eyes were drawn to the beads of sweat that dotted the witch's brow. The way her pulse fluttered rapidly in her neck. The tremble in the hand that held the wand.

Riva was afraid.

Dinah cast about for a reason, searching through their conversation until she found a thread that didn't belong.

Riva had known all along that the person who'd created the lock was dead and couldn't undo it or share its secrets with Dinah. So why had she insisted that Dinah leave it alone? Why had she lied about being the one who made the lock in the first place?

The answer hit Dinah, a wave of sickening relief that nearly brought her to her knees.

Maybe the original creator of the lock was dead, but someone else still knew the secrets. Someone else still had the power to open the wraith's prison. And Riva knew it.

The queen had said Valeraine de la Cour helped Riva lock the wraith into the Wilds. If Riva hadn't created the lock, then it must have been Valeraine, which meant she had the potion written down somewhere in her shop or in her home.

Dinah smiled as she turned to leave the cottage.

Maybe Valeraine and her talent were out of Dinah's reach, but she had something nearly as good.

She had Blue.

TWENTY-THREE

KELLAN WAS CORNERED. Flanked on both sides by girls from rival families, his back against the south parlor's wall, his tea coat itching in the miserable summer heat that rolled in through the open doors that led to the veranda. The girls' parents weren't far from their daughters, their eyes trained on every move the prince made, even as they exchanged pleasantries with the queen and each other.

His smile felt permanently carved into his face as he offered each girl his arm and led them toward the tea table in the corner where dainty apple puffs, fig twists, and tiny bolla jelly sandwiches were arranged on plates the same color as the warm summer sun.

"I've been stitching my own ball gown for your birthday party," Marisol Evrard said as she let go of his arm in favor of picking up a small plate and filling it with food.

On Kellan's other side, Jacinthe Chauveau's pretty lips twisted into a sneer. "Why would you do your seamstress's job?" She kept her arm tightly laced through Kellan's.

Marisol frowned. "Stitching a gown is slow, careful work. It develops patience and attention to detail, both of which are important qualities for a queen."

Kellan gave Marisol a real smile. "I can attest to the depths of both my mother's patience and her remarkable ability to keep track of every single thing that happens in her kingdom."

Marisol grinned and popped an apple puff in her mouth.

Jacinthe leaned against him. "I think I've shown remarkable patience with you already, Prince Kellan."

His brows rose. "Is that so?"

She gave him a pretty little pout. "I've entertained you twice in my home in the past few weeks, and I've attended four functions at the castle, and you've barely danced with me."

He gave her a slight bow. "A grave oversight on my part."

"And one you can remedy now." She gently pulled him in the direction of the veranda, where a trio of musicians played stringed instruments. The soft melody wrapped around the thick summer air, a ribbon made of song.

He paused and turned back to Marisol, who looked suddenly bereft. Winking, he offered her his other arm. "A dance with one pretty girl is lovely, but a dance with two makes me the luckiest boy in the kingdom."

Jacinthe's grip tightened painfully as Marisol set her plate down and reached for Kellan. He led them past the small clusters of people talking, catching Gen Gaillard's eye as he reached the doorway that led to the veranda. She assessed his situation with a quick glance and hid a laugh behind a raised hand.

Oh, she thought it was funny that every head family representative in the room was watching the prince with microscopic intensity and that he didn't dare give more attention to one girl than another, did she? He stopped walking halfway out the door and turned back, earning murmurs of confusion from both Jacinthe and Marisol.

He'd danced with more than two girls at a time at the academy. No reason he couldn't do that here as well. "Miss Genevieve," he called, silencing the conversations directly around them. "Would you do the three of us the honor of joining us in this dance?"

Jacinthe's grip felt like claws digging into his arm as Gen's eyes widened. She couldn't possibly refuse, though. Not without infuriating her parents, who watched eagerly from behind her. With a gracious smile, she made her way to Kellan, Marisol, and Jacinthe.

"Of course, Your Majesty. Though I'm not sure how you're going to accomplish this when you have but two arms." Gen was still laughing at him, and he gave all three girls a cheeky grin.

"Ladies, there's enough of me to go around. Shall we?"

Marisol's blue eyes darted between Gen and Kellan, as if trying to figure out how this was going to work. Jacinthe had yet to let go of his arm. He was going to lose all feeling in the limb soon. He swept onto the veranda, gently shook himself free of Jacinthe, and bowed to each girl as the musicians picked up the beat.

Taking Marisol's hands first, he swept her into the dance for eight beats before turning midspin to Jacinthe. The girl's dark eyes were angry as she grasped his hands and leaped into the flowing movements of the dance.

"Must you always divide yourself between us?" she asked, her tone as delicate as a bird in flight, though there was fire in her expression.

He spun her into a turn. "Unless I'd like to have the other

parents in the room decide to start removing the competition to give their daughters a better chance at the throne, I'm afraid I must pay equal attention to each." Which meant he needed to be sure to give Nathalia Roche a dance next before moving on to the various nieces who were in attendance. Martin Roche had already twice insinuated that Kellan was neglecting the courtship of his daughter.

The fact that Kellan could barely stand more than a few sentences of conversation with Nathalia had no bearing on his duties. At least both Leona Aubert and Emmaline Perrin were in attendance as well. Dancing with them would give him something to look forward to once his time with Nathalia was finished.

He let Jacinthe go and pulled Gen into his arms. Her smile sparkled. "You make it look easy."

That was the point. He'd spent years flirting and charming his way through the academy because his mother had been very clear that the ability to appear attentive and attracted to multiple girls at once was the only way to avoid bloodshed in the weeks leading up to his betrothal ball.

Sending Gen a careless wink, he said, "Dancing with the three of you could never qualify as a hardship."

When it was Marisol's turn again, she clung to him as they dipped and swayed. "Do you really think other families would kill some of the eligible girls to give their own daughter a better chance?"

"It's happened before," he said quietly. Three girls the year his mother had won the betrothal. Four boys leading up to the betrothal ball that had happened for his grandparents. He was determined to do whatever he could to keep bloodshed from happening now.

"Why doesn't anyone do anything to stop it?" Marisol asked.

He met her gaze. "Murder is already illegal. If the family behind the killing is caught, they're punished to the full extent of the law. Short of stripping the head families of their right to pursue the betrothal in the first place, there's not much else we can do."

When he returned to Jacinthe, her smile was in place, and the fire in her eyes at having to share the dance had been banked. "A family must prove itself worthy to rule by showing itself to be the strongest ally. If there is anything my mother and I, and by extension the entire Chauveau clan, can do to help protect the eligible girls, please count on us. Our mothers are great friends. Whether you choose me or not, we should work together to make sure no one dies over this."

He nodded, holding eye contact with her as a tiny vein of doubt wormed its way through him. She sounded sincere, but he'd spent enough time coating his own words with a veneer of sincerity to recognize it in someone else. Did she think pretending to care about the cost of competing for his hand would win him over? Or was she simply upholding her responsibility to prove that her family was his strongest ally?

His mother certainly favored the Chauveaus for the betrothal, though she'd also told him the Gaillards and the Perrins would make very strong allies as well. As the music entered its final stanza, he released Jacinthe and turned to Gen.

Her smile had disappeared. She stepped into his arms, and said in a voice too quiet for the others to hear, "I don't want to die for this."

He kept his expression neutral, though his grip on her hands gentled. "I don't want you to die for this, either. I don't want anyone to die."

Especially his sister. All the more reason to keep the charm flowing, watch his words with care, and hide his intentions until the night of the ball, when bloodshed would be pointless because the announcement would already be made.

"The worry must weigh on you," Gen said softly, and he gave her a startled look. She hurried on. "I'm sure you must be starting to care for some of them, at least as friends."

"Of course I am."

She smiled. "Does the choice feel impossible?"

Yes.

He couldn't bring himself to answer, so he smiled and spun her into the final measure of the song.

When she returned to his arms, red hair flying, cheeks pink, she said softly, "If the choice feels impossible, ask yourself which person, besides your mother and sister, you'd be most heartbroken to lose."

Blue's face flashed across his mind, and he frowned as he bowed to the girls, thanked them for the dance, and turned away.

He couldn't think about his complicated feelings for Blue. Not now, when he needed to guard his every word, expression, and move.

The tea lasted for another hour. By the time Kellan made his way to his suite, he was exhausted, and a headache was brewing behind his eyes. He allowed his valet to remove his tea coat and cravat, then sat on the bed and unlaced his shoes.

Movement caught his eye, and he looked up to find Nessa in his doorway, her fingers already moving.

Send out your valet. We have to talk.

"Thank you, Bayard, that will be all," Kellan said. His valet nodded, laid the folded coat over the back of a chair, and backed out of the room. Nessa shut the door behind him and hurried to her brother, her expression distraught.

"What's wrong?" Kellan was on his feet again. "Did something happen? Did someone do something to you?"

He was going to kill whoever had put this expression on his sister's face. Avoiding bloodshed be hanged. If one of the head families had threatened Nessa, they were going to discover their future king had a sword for a spine.

I'm all right. But Blue isn't.

Slowly he sank back onto the edge of his bed, his heart still thunder in his ears. "I know she isn't. It's going to take a long time, Nessa. You were really young when our father died, but it's the kind of pain that lasts."

It still hurts you.

He studied his hands. Of course it still hurt him. It was his fault. He deserved to have it hurt him for the rest of his life.

She sat down next to him and leaned against his side, her curls pressed against his shoulder. He wrapped one arm around her. "Yes, sometimes it still hurts me. I expect it always will."

She lifted her hands and signed. *You could talk to me about it.*

His heart squeezed, and he pulled her closer. "You would be the very best person to talk to, little bird. You know I love you, right?"

She snorted. *Of course you love me. I'm amazing. Now how do you feel about Blue?*

"Blue?" he pulled back so he could look at her face. There was a gleam in her eyes that made him uneasy, though he couldn't put his finger on why. Carefully, he said, "I feel sorry that she lost her father and glad that we're all friends."

You protected her at the funeral. Helped her cry.

He shifted his weight. "Someone had to."

Maybe, but you're the one who saw what she needed.

"Is there a point to this, Nes?"

She turned to face him. *Blue's in trouble, and I need the right person to protect her.*

He straightened, his heart pounding again. "What kind of trouble?"

She made a sign he couldn't interpret. When he frowned, she changed the movements.

Head family. Woman. Widow. You danced with her daughter.

"Dinah?" He mimicked the first sign she'd made. "That's your name sign for Dinah Chauveau?"

Yes. Dinah is making Blue afraid.

"Afraid of what?"

Afraid of Dinah. Blue had a bandage on her arm when she came to the castle yesterday. And when I showed up at the shop today, there was a bruise on her face, and she said tutoring was canceled.

Kellan's blood felt too thick, his pulse too fast, as he climbed to his feet. "How did she get those injuries?"

She told me not to ask questions and to stay away from the shop until Dinah was out of her life.

He reached for his coat, his jaw set.

You're the right person to protect her now, aren't you? Nessa's eyes were fierce as she watched her brother button his coat.

"*We're* the right people. Get your shoes on. We're going to find Blue."

TWENTY-FOUR

It was past the dinner hour, and Blue was working on yet another attempt to turn lead into gold. She'd lost count of how many times she'd tried in the past few days. The shop floor's inventory was depleted, and she was behind a full day in fulfilling orders for delivery, but Dinah didn't care. She was obsessed with Blue's success, and while Blue couldn't blame her, she flinched every time Dinah came into the room. She had bruises in multiple places now, a burn on her arm, and a shallow cut where Dinah's nails had pinched the skin of her arm when yet another experiment ended in failure.

Earlier in the afternoon, Blue had sent Nessa home without a tutoring session for the first time in three years. Even though Dinah had been gone from the shop as she was every day, Blue hadn't been sure when the woman would return. There had been something wild, something dangerous, in Dinah's mood that morning, and she didn't want her around the princess. And the truth was, Blue didn't want anyone to see her new reality.

She'd never imagined herself in a position where someone with power over her could slap her, pinch her, and shove her against the hot stove, but she'd always thought she was the kind of girl who wouldn't take that kind of abuse without a fight. But somehow things were more complicated than that. Dinah was bigger, stronger, and had the ironclad legal power of Blue's guardianship on her side. The woman could simply claim she was disciplining her charge, or that it had been an accident, and the law would support her.

And while deep down Blue knew Dinah would never hurt Nessa because it went against her self-preservation instincts, she didn't want Nessa to see Blue helpless to protect herself.

She reached for another small hunk of ordinary metal, heat billowing from the stove beside her. Maybe she wasn't yet able to protect herself against Dinah's fury, but she might still be able to help Halette and Jacinthe and get the Chauveaus out of her life. She just had to get this experiment right.

Especially because there were others out there who also needed protection. Ana hadn't been seen by any of her friends now for weeks. The little five-year-old boy from the streets in the Gaillard quarter had disappeared completely as well. And Lucian had informed Blue the day before that he'd started asking questions of children in other quarters and had discovered that in the Chauveau, Roche, and Barbier quarters, street children regularly going missing had been happening for years.

Blue wanted to get to the bottom of it. Guilt over Ana's fate and Blue's lack of focus on the girl's disappearance sat in her stomach like a stone. She'd petitioned the queen yesterday for help, and the queen had agreed to bring it up at the next council meeting, but at the moment, their hands were full trying to hunt down the witch who was killing people throughout the city.

Blue needed to thoroughly search for Ana and the others. She needed to help Halette and Jacinthe escape the man in the black boots. She needed to take breaks from the shop, swim in the sea, spend the day with Grand-mère, and have her house back. And all that required that she get her experiment right.

Dinah had returned an hour ago, still in her strange, dangerous mood, and was spending her time on the shop floor, sifting through boxes of receipts and sorting the contents of every shelf, cupboard, and chest. Blue had left her to it. As long as the older woman was busy, she was leaving Blue in peace.

Adding another log to the stove, Blue carefully placed the metal in her pressurized pot and screwed the lid into place. She was setting her tongs to the side when Dinah swept into the storeroom.

"I know it's past dinner bell, but I wanted to try adding a different mineral to the procedure," Blue said before Dinah could complain about the time or demand to know why Blue hadn't yet produced gold or slap her because she'd decided Blue must be dragging her feet on purpose.

"Where are your recipes?" Dinah scanned the room.

Blue blinked in surprise. "Um . . . in those books." She jerked her chin toward a set of five bound books of parchment on a shelf by the spare jars. "Why?"

"I don't have to tell you why." Dinah moved to the shelf of books and began looking through them.

"If you tell me what you're looking for, I can help you find it much faster," Blue said carefully.

"I'm interested in recipes that contain rare or very hard-to-find ingredients. Preferably an older recipe. Maybe one of your mother's."

Blue frowned. What would Dinah want with an older potion recipe? The woman caught Blue's expression and snapped, "Vintage alchemy recipes containing rare ingredients are a collector's item, girl. I can fetch a good price, which I'll obviously need since you still haven't improved on the first yellow rock you made."

Blue didn't think vintage alchemy recipes were worth enough to satisfy Dinah's debts, but she kept her thoughts to herself. Joining Dinah, she took one of the books and began searching its pages, careful to stay out of striking range. They worked in silence for long moments, punctuated by the occasional discovery of a recipe that required something rare. Every time, Dinah perused the spell, said it wasn't quite what she was looking for, and then asked Blue to help her find more.

By the time they finished going through all five books, the cathedral had already rung another bell, and they hadn't found a spell that satisfied Dinah. Blue checked the progress of her experiment, and then asked, "Would you like to go home for dinner while I finish up here?"

"I'd like to find the rest of the potions your mother owned," Dinah snapped.

"What potions?" Blue unscrewed the pot's lid, careful not to burn herself with the escaping steam, and added more water, plus another pinch of rhasvedot, a brittle green mineral mined in the northern mountains of Loch Talam.

"Your mother was brilliant." Dinah sounded nostalgic, but there was an urgency to her voice. "She told me about several spectacular potions she designed, but I don't see them in the shop. There must be another place she kept things."

Blue glanced around the storeroom and shrugged. "We don't have any storage beyond the shelves you can see in here and the cupboards you already searched out front."

"Not here." Dinah gestured toward the door. "At the farmhouse." She looked at Blue as if waiting for her to reveal where the rest of Mama's spells were kept.

"She died when I was seven," Blue said quietly. "I don't have any memories of her keeping potions around the house, and Papa never mentioned it."

Dinah's jaw clenched as she approached Blue. "All right, forget about potions. Think about where your mother kept things. Important things. Things she didn't want to lose or forget or have damaged in any way."

Blue's heart lurched, a sudden, sickening ache in her chest, and she took a step away from Dinah. There were little reminders of Mama all through the farmhouse. A quilt she'd helped Grand-mère make one winter when Blue was a baby. The painting of a ship at sea she'd picked out for the room she shared with Papa. A pair of goggles hung on a nail in the kitchen where she'd sometimes done experiments.

But the rest of Mama's things were packed up in chests and kept in the root cellar.

"You know where she kept things." Dinah's voice was flat.

"I'm not helping you look there." Blue's hands shook as she curled them into fists.

"Look where?"

Blue pressed her lips closed. Dinah rushed forward, grabbed Blue's shoulders, and shook violently.

"Where are her things?"

Blue shoved Dinah's hands off her shoulders. "No. You've

taken my home, my grandmother, and my shop. You've hit me, pinched me, and burned me all while I'm trying to *help* you save your daughters. And now you want to drag me down into the root cellar to hunt through Mama's things so you can sell one of her spells for a little bit of coin. I'm not going to do it."

"The root cellar." Dinah smiled coldly. "Was that so hard, Blue? We'll search tonight."

"You can search without me."

Dinah slapped Blue, sending her reeling. "You'll watch your mouth."

"Lady Chauveau!"

Kellan's voice, thick with anger, filled the storeroom. Dinah froze.

"Oh! Prince Kellan, how did you get in here? Not that you aren't welcome, of course, but it is a surprise." Dinah sounded flustered.

"I spent half my youth in this shop. The de la Cours are close family friends, and we have a key to both the farmhouse and the Mortar & Pestle. The true surprise is finding you in this storeroom striking my good friend Blue."

Blue turned toward the sound of Kellan's voice. He stood in the doorway, anger blazing in his eyes. Heat flooded Blue, a spinning, tingling kind of warmth that made her want to smile and cry at the same time.

"Blue is my charge now. Her dear mother left the girl's guardianship to me." Dinah all but simpered as she stepped toward the prince. "I'm afraid her father spoiled her, and I've had to take measures to teach her the manners and courtesy that a girl of her station should display. I'm sorry you had to see that."

She sounded as smooth and polished as river-washed stone

now, but the fire in Kellan's eyes remained bright and burning.

"On the contrary." Kellan sounded as smooth as Dinah. "I'm glad to know exactly what kind of family the Chauveaus are. I have to take every aspect under consideration for my upcoming betrothal decision, as I'm sure you know."

Blue blinked. Had he really just threatened to ignore Dinah's daughters for her sake? The heat in her veins felt like sunshine, soft and pure.

What was she supposed to do with the reckless, charming prince who'd grieved with her over Papa, danced with her in a pub, nearly kissed her in the maid's closet, and then stood up for her when she needed it most?

Dinah straightened her spine and spoke in a voice like honey. "If striking a disobedient girl upsets you, Your Majesty, then I will of course choose other ways to manage her."

Kellan moved into the room, and Nessa hurried in behind him. She took one look at Blue and rushed to her side.

Are you hurt? The princess's hands moved rapidly.

The pressurized pot behind Blue began rocking as the metal inside bounced against its sides. Blue took the pot off the burner and banked the fire before turning to sign to the princess.

It hurts, but I'll survive. Why are you here? I told you to stay away from the shop until Dinah was out of my life.

Nessa's face was grim. *I don't need your protection, Blue. She wouldn't dare strike me. We're here to take care of you. I told Kellan about you getting hurt, and he got mad and said we were going to find you.*

Blue lifted her face and met Kellan's eyes. Once again, he'd surprised her. She'd never dreamed she could count on the prince to be firmly at her side through the worst days of her life.

"I would appreciate it if you spoke clearly in front of me," Dinah said, a gracious smile on her face, though her eyes were burning embers of fury. "I find it rude to have conversations going on that exclude some of the people in the room."

And I find it rude that you've spent so much time in the castle as one of my mother's closest friends and never bothered to learn a single sign. Nessa's chin lifted as she aimed the signs at Dinah.

Blue opened her mouth to interpret, but Kellan got there first. "If your daughter is interested in being queen, perhaps she can learn Nessa's signs. I couldn't ever marry someone who didn't make an effort to speak my sister's language."

That's not what I said. Nessa glared at her brother.

He signed rapidly. *I'll deal with Dinah, but I don't want her to be angry with you.*

Who cares if she's angry with me?

Something dark flashed in Kellan's eyes, and Blue scooted closer to Nessa. *Let Kellan handle Dinah. She has a mean temper, and there's more at stake here than just how she treats me. She's part of his royal council. He has to be able to work with her.*

Fine. But I don't want her in our family. Nessa aimed a glare at Dinah.

Dinah's eyes darted between Nessa and Kellan, and then she said, "I do apologize again, Your Majesty, for upsetting you. And I'm afraid Blue and I have a rather pressing task waiting for us at her house. Perhaps we could invite you to tea with Jacinthe and Halette tomorrow afternoon?"

Kellan smiled, though it didn't reach his eyes. "I would be delighted, but I'm afraid all invitations must go through my secretary, as I have no idea what spaces are available on my calendar."

Dinah matched his smile. "I'll send word to the castle, then. Now if you'll excuse us—"

"I beg your pardon, Lady Chauveau." Kellan's charm was back in his voice as he sketched a quick bow for Dinah. "But I'm afraid I'm in need of Blue's time for a short while tonight."

Blue's eyes widened.

"May I ask why?" Dinah said, her fingers pulling at the edges of her dress sleeves.

"Royal business." Kellan nodded solemnly, and Blue quickly wiped the surprise off her face as Dinah shot her a glare.

"What kind of royal business could Blue possibly have with you?"

What kind of business could you possibly have asking all these questions? Nessa stared Dinah down, but the older woman never looked her way.

"Important royal business." Kellan was using his I'm-the-prince-don't-you-dare-argue tone of voice. Once upon a time, Blue had found that tone insufferable. Now she cheerfully wished Dinah luck in getting around Kellan when he'd made up his mind.

Dinah gave Blue another look, one that promised retribution, and then curtsied to the prince and stalked out of the shop. Kellan immediately turned to Nessa and said, "I'll have the guards bring you back to the castle."

What about you?

His eyes met Blue's, and that traitorous heat danced through her veins as he said, "Like I said, I have business with Blue."

TWENTY-FIVE

KELLAN PROWLED THE storeroom, looking at the shelves, the stove, the potion books . . . anything but Blue. His restless energy filled the space, humming through the air like a chord Blue was just beginning to understand. Nessa had left several minutes earlier with her guards. A pair still waited outside to escort their prince home. Dinah was long since gone.

The silence expanded between them, a bubble that pressed against Blue until she itched to just pop it and be done with the strange tension that filled her body like lightning skimming over her skin.

"Are you just going to examine my storeroom all night?" she asked.

"Maybe." He stared resolutely at a row of empty jars.

Why wouldn't he look at her? And why did the thought of what might be in his eyes make her cheeks feel like she'd been hovering above a hot stove?

"Why are you here?" she asked before she could think better of it.

He moved away from the shelf and tapped his long fingers against the potion books that still lay on the worktable. "I came because Nessa said you might need help with Dinah."

She folded her arms across her chest and said, "I know why you came. I want to know why you're still here."

"I don't know." He flung the words at her and then cradled his head in his hands and whispered, "I don't know."

His shoulders bowed as if carrying a burden he could no longer bear, and she hurried to his side. Laying her hand on his arm, she asked quietly, "Are you all right?"

"Do you know how I spent my last few days?"

Her cheeks warmed at the memory of hiding in the maid's closet with him, feeling the weight of his body pressing against hers while he whispered in her ear, sending shivers of delicious heat through her. Ordering her voice not to betray her thoughts, she said, "Tell me."

He scrubbed his hand over his face and then let it come to rest on top of hers. "I met with the Marcels to discuss what benefits their family could bring to the throne. I had lunch with the Gaillards and their extended family, all of whom made sure to make their family's wealth and influence perfectly clear, and then I met with the royal magistrate to discuss the rule of law regarding the transfer of power from my mother to myself and to organize the search for the witch who cast those terrible spells across the city."

His fingers slowly twined with hers, and he turned her hand over so that her palm was pressed against his. She sucked in a little breath at the sudden jolt of fire that sizzled through her veins. He raised his head and looked her in the eyes for the first time since Nessa's departure.

"I held royal council meetings, revoked a council member's representative privileges, and attended an afternoon tea where I charmed the Roches, the Gaillards, the Evrards, the Perrins, and even Dinah Chauveau. I tiptoed through questions designed to trap me into an early commitment, steered conversations away from anything that might inflame more tensions between the head families, and danced with every girl in the room, all while fielding baited questions about my handling of interkingdom trade agreements, the hunt for the witch, and of course which families would get future royal contracts."

His thumb traced a circle over the back of her hand, and her stomach danced in slow, lazy circles. "I even nearly kissed my friend in a maid's closet."

She tried to smile, though there was a question in his eyes she wasn't sure how to answer. "I'm sure that wasn't a first for you."

"Oh, it was. First time I wanted a kiss for reasons that were real." He gave her a ghost of his charming smile, then let it die. "Blue, I don't know what to do."

She swallowed hard. Trying for a steady, calm voice, she said, "What do you want to do?"

His gaze met hers and held. His brown eyes were full of longing, and her foolish heart leaped because apparently she didn't care that he was a prince and she was a commoner. That he was set to be betrothed to someone else and she was set to live a quiet life with her alchemy, her farmhouse, and her one-eyed cat. That it was impossible.

Quietly, he said, "I don't get to do what I want. I have to do what the kingdom needs."

What did that mean? That he wanted her too? Or was he still talking through his problems with his friend?

She frowned. "So then you're here because . . . ?"

He was silent for so long, she didn't think he'd answer, and then he finally said, "Because while I was meeting with the Marcels, I was wondering if you liked picnics. And while I was lunching with the Gaillards, I kept overhearing things I wanted to share with you. And while I was dancing with every girl in the room, I kept wishing the only girl in the room was you."

"Kellan—"

"I know!" He broke away from her to prowl the room again. "I'm an idiot. How many times have you called me that? This time, you'd be right."

"I was right plenty of times in the past as well." She turned slowly to follow his progress, her heart racing, her body aching with longing to touch him again. "But this is different."

"This is . . ." He turned to face her, his eyes wild as he gestured like he couldn't find the right word.

"Impossible," she said, because it was true. It would always be true. But somehow that didn't change the way she wanted to trace his shoulders with her hands or spin with him on the dance floor or whisper her secrets in his ear, trusting that he'd be the rock she needed him to be.

"I don't even know how this happened." His words sounded like an accusation, and she gave him a stern look.

"Don't look at me. You're the one who was kind at Papa's funeral."

"You're the one who gave me the freedom to be myself."

"Well, you're the one who cared enough to dance with me."

"Well, you're the one who makes me want to come to the shop each day with Nessa just to see if I can make you laugh." He pointed at her as if the argument had been handily won, and she stalked toward him.

"Nobody asked you to always see when I need a friend." She raised a finger of her own and began ticking off her list. "Nobody told you to show me that you're a natural leader or that you're generous and protective. And certainly, nobody said you should drop your shallow, flirtatious ways around me and make me fall for you."

The words left her mouth before she'd realized what she was going to say, and her eyes widened as Kellan slowly dropped his arm and stared at her.

"Not that I'm falling for you," she said quickly, but her voice, unsteady and entirely unconvincing, betrayed her.

"Blue." He breathed her name like it was hope and pain and joy all at once.

In three steps he was in front of her, his arms lifted in a clear invitation. She could walk into them and give her heart a taste of what it wanted, knowing it would break her later. Or she could walk away, her heart disappointed for now, but still whole for when he announced his betrothal to another girl.

Her heart ached as she slowly stepped back.

His arms fell to his sides. "You've always been the one to keep me in line."

"I don't want to keep you in line." She took another step back before her resolve crumbled. "But you can't belong to me like this. And I don't want to sacrifice what we already have. I love our friendship, Kellan. I don't want to lose it."

He smiled, though his eyes were sad. "I don't either."

Silence once more fell between them, and this time it was Blue who turned to restlessly prowl the room. She put the potion books away. Checked her inventory for morning deliveries. And then opened the pressurized pot that had cooled beside the stove. The nugget of metal had turned a rosy pink.

She sighed as she dumped it onto the counter. The new mineral she'd tried had taken her results even further from actual gold. She needed to figure out how to get back to the first almost-gold result and then improve on that.

A thought scratched at the back of her mind while she tidied up, and she stared at her tools while she struggled to pinpoint what was bothering her.

The first time she'd offered to experiment with making gold for Dinah, she'd produced a rock that was milky white. But tonight, Dinah had complained that Blue hadn't improved on the first golden rock she'd made.

Her breath quickened. She hadn't made a truly golden rock since the almost-gold experiment that had been stolen. Perhaps Dinah was simply referring to what she'd seen at Maurice's stall so many weeks ago.

Or perhaps Dinah's avid interest in the shop and her lack of surprise when Blue offered to try turning lead into gold meant something much, much worse.

"Blue?" Kellan was beside her, his hands on her shoulders. "Are you all right?"

"I need to get back to the farmhouse." She turned toward the door.

"I'll walk with you, but . . . Wait a minute." He rushed to

her side as she whipped open the back door. "What's the matter? Is it me? Did I . . . I'm sorry. I shouldn't have said anything. I shouldn't have—"

"It isn't you." She turned and nearly bumped into his chest. He caught her arms to steady her, and she laid her palms against his chest.

"Then what is it?" he asked softly.

For a moment, she drew on the silent comfort of his presence while she sorted through her thoughts. Did she really believe the head of the Chauveau family had broken into her shop and stolen the first nearly successful experiment? How would that have benefited her?

Unless.

Unless she'd had Papa killed so that she could use her guardianship papers to take over Blue and the shop.

It was a sickening thought, but it was also a string of unlikely coincidences. It was strange that the head of the Chauveau family had bothered to travel to an alchemy shop in a different quarter to ask if they'd filed a complaint with their magistrate about someone paying them with false gold. Stranger still to have someone break into the shop shortly thereafter and steal the failed experiment while leaving so many other valuables behind. If Dinah had been the thief, then it was awfully convenient for Papa to be killed and for her to happen to have guardianship over the one girl who might have the solution to her financial crisis.

Awfully convenient.

"Blue, please talk to me."

She met his eyes. "I need your help with something."

"Anything."

"Maybe you should hear what it is before promising."

He met her gaze and said firmly, "Anything."

"I need you to have the royal magistrate look into Dinah's guardianship document. Make sure the signatures are real. Try to date the parchment. That sort of thing."

And then she explained what she'd been doing at night in the shop. Listened to him swear as he realized the risks she'd been taking, especially after having been robbed once. Watched something cold and deadly move into his eyes when she told him she thought Dinah might have killed Papa because of the almost-gold.

"I'm taking you to the castle with me," he said as she finished talking.

"You can't."

"Watch me."

"Kellan, right now she has the law on her side. And if you make a single wrong move, you could incite the head families into declaring you unfit or going to war with each other based on which of them want to remain your allies and which are furious that it looks like you're stripping the legal rights of someone who is one of them." She took a step back and dropped her hands to her sides. "You told me you don't get to choose what you want. You have to choose what the kingdom needs. It needs you to follow the law."

He sighed. "I really hate how often you're right."

"You'll get used to it. Could you also look into reports of homeless children going missing across the quarters? My own delivery girl hasn't been seen in weeks, and she's just one of several from this area. Some of the other quarters have had street children go missing quite regularly. I broached the subject with your mother, and she said she'd bring it up at the next council meeting, but I don't want to wait that long. Maybe the magistrate could put some guards on the case."

"I'll check into it. Anything else?"

There were a hundred other things she wanted to ask. Could he hold her hand again? Promise to visit the farmhouse like he used to, even after he was betrothed?

Could they somehow remain close friends even while she had to watch him walk away?

Keeping her silence, she shook her head, put an acceptable distance between them, and together they turned to meet his guards at the mouth of the alley and begin the journey to the farmhouse.

TWENTY-SIX

TWO HOURS LATER, Kellan found his mother on a settee in the receiving room off her bedroom suite. Even reclining, she looked regal. Her spine remained straight, her evening gown draped elegantly across the settee and onto the floor, and her hair, thick as Nessa's, was still secured in an impeccable twist at the top of her head.

"Good evening, Mother," he said as he walked into the room and dropped a quick kiss on her cheek before settling into a chair close by.

She gave him the smile she reserved for times when she was alone with her children and sat up straight. "I see you received my summons."

"Nessa refused to listen to any of my excuses."

The queen's smile widened. "That girl is just as stubborn as I am."

"How am I to survive in this castle with two such formidable women watching my every move?" Kellan stretched his legs out in front of him and considered how best to approach his mother about Blue's situation.

The queen had spent the day hearing requests from citizens of the realm, advising magistrates on difficult cases with the help of the castle's solicitors, and meeting with her steward and the royal event planner to discuss final preparations for the ball that was to happen in one week.

One week to sift through all the pros and cons each head family brought to the table and choose a girl to be his queen. One week to get used to the idea that his heart wanted someone he could never have. The thought made it difficult to breathe.

One week, and the course of his life would be set in stone. He'd have to cajole goodwill out of the families whose girls weren't chosen. Offer prestigious diplomatic posts to the girls and whichever man they eventually chose to marry. Give the families more contracts for royal goods and services. Choose their favored children, nieces, and cousins for upper level military or magisterial positions.

"How are you?" his mother asked. "And give me an honest answer."

He took a moment to think before he spoke. "Tired. Worried. Ready for this to be over, but unsure that I have enough time left to make the best choice."

"That's what I thought we'd work on tonight." She gestured toward some parchment sitting on a small table beside his chair. "I thought we could list pros and cons for each girl to help you make your decision."

He shifted in his chair. "That makes it sound like a business transaction with the girls as goods we're evaluating. I don't like it."

"You don't have to like it. This is how things are done in your kingdom."

"But we can't just discuss the girls like they're horses we're thinking of buying. It's disrespectful. They're people, and they deserve to be treated with dignity."

His mother smiled again. "My sweet boy, your heart is going to make you a great king. Beloved by all and remembered through the ages. But part of being a king is knowing when you have to do things you don't want to do because it will keep the peace."

He met her gaze for a moment, and then sighed. "Fine. But we are going to discuss each girl with respect. I'm not going to treat them like goods I'm buying at the market."

"I would expect no less from you. Now, which is your favorite?"

Blue's face flashed across Kellan's mind, and he tugged at his collar. He couldn't choose her as his favorite, but he could do something about her situation now that he had his mother's undivided attention.

"Let's talk about Blue first," he said.

His mother drew back, her eyes narrowing. "Why are you thinking about Blue when I ask you which girl is your favorite?"

Hang it all. His heart was causing him enough confusion on its own. He certainly wasn't going to try explaining the problem to his *mother*.

"I've been meaning to discuss her with you all day, but we were both so busy, I never found the chance." He kept his voice steady, his gaze even. Blue was a family friend. Of course he was concerned about her. Anyone would be.

His mother watched him carefully. "What would you like to discuss about Blue?"

"I think we should look over the guardianship document that gives Dinah Chauveau control over Blue," he said.

"You think it's a fraud?" Her voice lowered, though there was no staff in the room to overhear.

"I'd like us to be absolutely sure." Kellan leaned forward, splaying his arms across his thighs. "I can't understand why a woman with Dinah's wealth and power would move herself and her daughters into the de la Cours' farmhouse, or why she'd have any interest in the alchemy shop. And I don't like the way she treats Blue."

The queen met his gaze. "How does she treat Blue?"

"She hits her, though I think I've put a stop to it."

"Hits her?" The queen's lips pressed into a thin, hard line.

"Nessa and I went to the shop to check on Blue, and walked into the storeroom in time to see Dinah slapping Blue." A hot flash of anger stirred in his gut at the memory.

"And how did you put a stop to it?"

He kept his eyes on hers, though he was pretty sure she wasn't going to like what he had to say. "I subtly threatened to not choose Jacinthe for the betrothal if I ever heard of her laying a hand on Blue again."

The queen's expression remained unreadable for a long moment, and Kellan waited to hear that he'd been foolish. That the all-important betrothal and the nuanced, political games-manship that went into it, couldn't be sacrificed for the fate of one commoner.

Instead, the queen said softly, "Good for you."

"I had to try . . . Wait, what? You aren't upset with me?"

"Blue is Nessa's dearest friend, and has been a staunch help to me with my headaches and fatigue of late. Her father was my sweet Talbot's most trusted friend, and the two of you grew up together. Blue is practically family, and we protect our family."

Kellan shook the tension out of his shoulders. "So what do we do about this?"

"I'll speak with Dinah. She'll listen to reason. Staying at the farmhouse instead of in her quarter doesn't meet her duties as head of the Chauveau family."

"And the guardianship document?" Kellan asked.

"Her solicitor will have had to file it with the magistrate in Blue's quarter. I'll ask our royal solicitor to request it so it can be examined."

"Doesn't the entire situation seem strange to you?"

"It does, but there could be any number of legitimate reasons for it." The queen leaned forward and tapped the parchment sheets beside Kellan. "Now, let's discuss your betrothal options."

Starlight filtered in through the windows and candle lamps glowed soft against the walls by the time Kellan and his mother were finished discussing each family's strengths. Six of the nine head families had daughters or nieces who were close enough to Kellan's age to be in the running for the betrothal, though the Barbier family was out of the running since the current queen had come from them. The other three had vested interests in the betrothal based on their own alliances.

The Chauveaus owned the largest business empire, with significant holdings and contacts in the kingdoms of Akram, Súndraille, and Ravenspire, which could only help to strengthen the throne's relationships with those realms. Plus they had enough wealth to help award contracts to some of the families who'd lost out on the betrothal, which would alleviate the pressure on the royal coffers.

The Perrins had decent holdings and a reputation for excelling at military strategy. Most of Balavata's head generals had come from the Perrin family, and having a strong alliance with those who ran the military was a smart move for a king worried about a revolt. The queen had heard rumors that the Faure family, which had no one close to betrothal age, was whispering about ousting the Renards and putting the Faures on the throne instead. Those rumors had strengthened in the wake of Kellan's dismissal of Georgiana from his council. Kellan couldn't afford to overlook strong ties to Balavata's army.

The Roches and the Gaillards were both solid leaders in commerce and law and would be able to deepen the crown's interests in both arenas. And the Evrards' oldest son had recently married into the royal family in Loch Talam far to the north, where Balavata had few diplomatic or commercial ties.

"Now that we have the pros in place, let's look at the cons," the queen said while the faint tolling of cathedral bells from every quarter drifted through the wind, their sonorous chimes proclaiming the tenth hour.

Kellan looked longingly out the window. It was a clear summer night. Perfect for slipping out of his bedroom window, scaling the wall, and heading to the sea for some dangerous nighttime cliff diving.

His pulse kicked up at the thought, and the numb corner of his heart warmed. He could chase death one more time. Look it in the face and dare it to take him like it should've done years ago. And then he could beat it and return to the shore remembering what it was like to feel fully alive. If he was lucky, the risk would chase his longing for Blue into the background of his mind as well.

"Don't even think about sneaking out tonight," his mother said calmly.

He wrenched his gaze from the window and stared at her. "I wasn't . . . That's not . . . How did you—"

"How long have I been your mother, Kellan?"

He squinted. "Is that a trick question?"

"Don't be cheeky. I've known you for nearly nineteen years. Do you really think I'm not aware of how often my son ditches his guards and disappears to do stars knows what for hours at a time?" She sat up straighter, an edge to her voice. "Don't tell me you're sneaking out to see a girl."

"What? No! I just—"

"Is it Blue?"

"Mother."

"If you're sneaking out to spend time with Blue and the head families find out—"

"I'm not sneaking out to see a girl. Blue or otherwise." He enunciated each word with exquisite precision. "I just go swimming."

She sat back. "Swimming?"

He nodded.

Something flickered in her eyes, and Kellan looked away as she said softly, "Are you swimming because you love it? Or because it's where you feel closest to your father?"

He shrugged.

She reached across the distance between them and wrapped one cool hand around his. "Be careful, Kellan. That's all I ask. I know you need moments of freedom from the pressures of being the crown prince, but I don't want to get a message that my son has disappeared beneath the water and isn't coming back."

He nodded but couldn't trust himself to speak around the sudden tightness in his throat.

"Why don't we resume this discussion another night?" she asked, and her voice sounded suspiciously shaky at the edges.

He risked a quick glance at her and grimaced at the tears shining in her eyes. "I'm sorry. I didn't mean to make you cry."

Her smile wobbled but remained intact. "Crying over their children's hearts is what mothers do."

He stood, pulled her from the settee, and wrapped her in his arms. She hugged him fiercely and laughed. "You grew taller than me this past year. We're going to have to have the tailor look at your dancing clothes to make sure your suit fits for the ball."

He stepped back and smiled, but whatever he was going to say in response was cut off by a knock at the door.

"Enter," the queen said.

A page hurried in, handed the queen a folded parchment with the yellow wax seal of the magistrate in the Evrard quarter, bowed, and then exited. The queen moved to her desk, slit the wax seal open with a small knife, and then read the message.

A thick sense of foreboding settled over Kellan as his mother's shoulders slumped briefly before straightening into her regal, queen-in-charge stance.

"What is it?" he asked.

"It's Marisol Evrard," she said.

The girl who was sewing her own ball gown, who'd unabashedly enjoyed both eating snacks at the tea table and dancing with Kellan, Jacinthe, and Genevieve. He liked her. "What's happened?"

"She's dead."

TWENTY-SEVEN

DINAH HAD BEEN waiting for Blue when she got home. The moment Kellan and his guards walked out of the farmhouse gate and back toward the city, Dinah grabbed Blue's upper arm and dragged her to the kitchen.

"We're going to find that spell of your mother's," she said.

"I can't," Blue said, pulling with all her strength, until Dinah faced her, tears shining in her eyes.

Her grip on Blue's arm gentled. "Please, I'm going to lose everything if I can't find a way out of this. Getting an old, rare potion of your mother's could be the key."

Blue didn't think an old potion would be worth as much as Dinah seemed to think, but maybe she was wrong. Maybe this would get the Chauveaus out of her life. And she'd promised Papa that one day she'd face the root cellar.

Reluctantly, Blue allowed herself to be pulled toward the root cellar's door.

The cellar smelled of drying herbs, pickled roots, and dust.

Blue clung to the ladder, her breath coming in shallow pants as she slowly eased her way down. A lantern hung from the crook of one elbow, and her gathering basket hung from the other.

"Please hurry," Dinah said from above her. "You spent far too much time in town. I want enough time to search the whole cellar tonight."

The whole cellar? Blue's heart slammed against her chest as she took another shaky step toward the floor. The cellar ran along the entire length of the farmhouse. There were walls full of shelves, crates stacked higher than Blue in two corners, and several chests lining the center like a row of soldiers.

The chests hadn't been there the day Mama died. Maybe Papa had moved them so that he wouldn't have to walk over the place where she'd last been. Or maybe he'd just run out of space elsewhere.

"Move faster, girl. I know you know how to get down a ladder."

Blue carefully slid down another step, her knuckles white with strain as she gripped the rungs.

There was no wintermint. No spilled herbs.

No Mama.

She was going to be fine. Papa had always wanted her to face her fears, and now she was. Of course she'd never imagined facing them in front of Dinah Chauveau, but she couldn't afford to think about that. Not if she wanted to keep her nerves under control.

Her foot found the dirt floor, and she slowly pried herself off the ladder. Her knees shook, and she nearly stumbled, but caught herself in time. Panic skittered through her at the thought of landing on that cold dirt floor where Mama had lain dying.

Dinah stepped off the ladder and faced Blue. "What are you waiting for? Light the room."

The faster she obeyed, the faster she could get through this ordeal.

Blue turned and made her way to the wall torches in their glass hurricane shades. Pulling a candle from her pocket, she touched the wick to her lantern's flame and then carefully lit each torch along the walls. Before long, the cellar was bathed in a warm golden glow that did nothing to calm the frantic beat of Blue's heart.

"Where would your mother's things be kept?" Dinah asked, sweeping an arm out to encompass the towering stacks of crates and the wooden chests.

Blue shrugged as she gently blew out the flame on the candle she held.

Moving rapidly, Dinah wrapped her hand around Blue's hair and yanked the curls back until Blue staggered, her face tilted toward the ceiling.

"Maybe I can't leave a bruise on you for the prince to see, but there are plenty of other ways to make sure you're compliant." Dinah's voice was cold. "Don't underestimate how far I'm willing to go to right the wrongs done to me."

Blue winced as Dinah pulled on her hair, and tears stung her eyes, but she refused to let them fall. Not here. Not for this woman. The tears Blue shed in the root cellar belonged to Mama alone.

"Let's try again. Where are your mother's things kept?"

"I don't know." Blue's voice trembled, and she swallowed hard.

Dinah's nails dug into Blue's scalp. "Do you know what

happened to the last servant of mine who refused to obey me?"

"I'm not your servant." Blue blinked her tears away and met Dinah's gaze.

"Close enough." Dinah's voice was stern. "I own you, Blue. I own this house, the shop, and everything inside them. If I want, I can burn all of it to the ground and send you far away."

The panic threading through Blue's veins burst into a thin flame of anger. "Might be hard to explain to the royal family why you destroyed their friend's home and then got rid of her."

Dinah's smiled winked out. "I don't explain myself to anyone. Show me your mother's things."

"I don't know where they are." Blue winced as Dinah's grip tightened.

"Of course you do. We're surrounded by drying herbs, bottles of roots, and satchels of ground flower petals. There are several old cauldrons on that upper shelf. This is an alchemist's cellar, and you are the alchemist of the house."

"I never come down here." Blue's throat felt like it was stuffed with cotton, and the panic took over again, sending shivers across her skin. She looked away from Dinah and tried to simply breathe.

Dinah released Blue's hair and cocked her head. "Are you afraid of this place? Is that why you tried to refuse me?"

Blue clenched her jaw and remained silent. Hang this monstrous woman and her demands. What Blue felt, what she feared, belonged to her alone.

"What happened, Blue?" Dinah's voice was soft and compelling. "Did you get locked in here as a child?"

Blue drew in a deep breath. "If you find what you're looking for, will you leave me alone?"

Dinah's smile prickled the hairs on the back of Blue's neck. "Oh yes. When I find what I'm looking for, I'll leave."

Something about Dinah's tone left a slick, oily coat of unease in Blue's stomach, but she ignored it. If all Dinah needed from her were a few of Mama's old spells that used rare ingredients, Blue would somehow find the courage to turn the root cellar inside out searching for them. As far as Blue knew, Mama had never designed a dangerous potion, so while Dinah might be able to make some coin off it, there would really be no harm in letting her take it.

Not that Blue could stop her anyway.

"I guess we should start with the crates. I think they've been here the longest," Blue said.

Hours passed as the two dragged down crate after crate. They found old clothes that might have belonged to Blue as a child. Books full of childish drawings and early attempts at recipes, all with a big *B* scrawled in the lower right-hand corner. Parchment with old bills of sale from the shop, Wintermass decorations, and a dusty supply of knitted socks with holes in the heels, a darning needle threaded through one of the socks as if someone had stopped repairing it midstitch.

"This is useless." Dinah glared at Blue as if holding her personally responsible for their failure to find any of Mama's things. Dread sank into Blue as she watched Dinah turn from the crates to size up the chests in the center of the room.

She couldn't do it. Couldn't sit on the packed dirt floor again, pulling items from the chests as if the thing that lived in her nightmares wasn't pressing into her skin.

"It's past bedtime," Blue said, her voice shaking. She pushed the last crate back against the wall, her hands like ice, her breath clogging her throat as the room started collapsing in on her.

"There will be no sleep until we finish searching this place."

Blue tried to stand. Tried to find her balance as the walls rushed toward her and darkness loomed at the edge of her vision.

Her heart was thunder trapped in her chest.

A noose of panic was tightening around her throat, cutting off her air.

She closed her eyes, and wintermint saturated the air. The ladder twisted away from the wall. And Mama . . .

Blue's eyes flew open.

"I can't stay here." She choked the words out as she stumbled past Dinah, her vision going gray at the edges.

"Blue!" Dinah reached for her, digging her fingers into Blue's arm, but panic was a monster with teeth and claws, and Blue wrenched herself out of Dinah's grip.

"You come back here this instant. We have to go through those chests." Dinah's voice was full of fury.

Blue rushed for the ladder, smacking her knee into one of the chests and nearly toppling to the floor.

"No, no, no." She breathed the words under her breath. Latched on to them as if the litany could save her from the nightmare that was closing in on her.

Mama lying at her feet, broken and bleeding. Blue screaming for help that never came. Magic in her blood that couldn't do a single useful thing on the day she needed it most.

Mama trying to smile at her. Singing for her one last time.

And then Mama's chest falling silent, and her face going slack until she barely resembled Mama anymore at all.

"I will punish you in ways you can't even imagine if you leave this cellar!"

Blue's hands found the ladder's rungs. Hung on with desperate strength, though her palms were slick with sweat.

She moved up a rung, her body trembling like a leaf caught in a rainstorm.

The darkness pressed closer, and there was a strange ringing in her ears.

She couldn't think. Couldn't breathe.

Couldn't stay in the root cellar another instant.

Dinah screamed at her as Blue scrambled up the ladder and burst through the door into the kitchen. Her knees gave out, and she collapsed onto the floor, but the panic that owned her wouldn't let her stay there. Climbing to her feet again, she ran out of the kitchen and down the hall toward the front door, Pepperell at her heels.

The house was dark and quiet. Halette and Jacinthe had long since retired for the night. Kellan had made it clear to Dinah that Blue should have her bedroom back again, and Dinah had grudgingly told Blue she could sleep on the floor while Halette took the bed, but Blue couldn't stand the thought of being inside. Of having walls around her or other people close by.

Snatching her summer cloak from the hook beside the door, she let herself onto the porch, closing the door after Pepperell, who hopped down the front steps and began sniffing the puffer bloom bushes, whose flowers were slowly opening to the moonlit sky.

Blue intended to escape into her garden, but her legs refused to hold her. She sank onto the front steps, pulled her cloak tight, and focused on breathing.

In.

Out.

No walls collapsing in on her. No memories waiting to swallow her.

In.

Out.

The delicate scent of puffer blooms, Mama's favorite flower and the source of Blue's nickname, wrapped around her, and the soft, salt-washed air pressed close.

She didn't think about Dinah. About the price she'd pay for running away. Didn't think about the cellar and all its awful memories.

Instead, she thought of Papa. Of his warm hands and big smile, and the love in his eyes when he looked at her. Grief bubbled up, drenched in the residue of the panic that had driven her out of the cellar, and she let it take her. Let the hot, sharp thing inside her burst into sobs that shook her entire body.

As the stars spun slowly across the night sky and the sea crashed against the not-so-distant shore, Blue curled up against the porch rails and cried herself to sleep.

TWENTY-EIGHT

THE QUEEN SENT guards to notify the other head families of Marisol's death so that extra precautions could be taken for the daughters and nieces who were vying for the betrothal, but Kellan couldn't rest until he'd seen for himself that all of them were safe.

He'd sworn to keep this betrothal period free of bloodshed, and he'd failed.

Not that he took responsibility for someone choosing to kill Marisol. That was on the shoulders of the killer. He knew that. But knowing that didn't stop the horror of Marisol's death from leaving a wash of sickness in Kellan's stomach. And it didn't stop the weight of guilt that sat on his shoulders like a stone. He'd been going back over his every action, his every word for the past few weeks, hunting for a misstep that could have led to this.

Had he paid her more attention than anyone else? Looked at her too often at the expense of the other girls?

He didn't think so, but maybe his actions hadn't mattered.

Maybe it was simply a matter of narrowing the field of potential queens, and nothing Kellan said or did would've changed the intentions of the killer.

One of the head families was behind it. They had to be. No one else could possibly have benefited from Marisol's death. And since the weapon of choice was a knife instead of a spell, he doubted the rogue witch was to blame. His mother had assured him that she'd asked the royal magistrate to investigate, and the man had connections throughout the kingdom. Someone would know who was hired to kill the Evrard girl. Those ties would eventually lead back to the family responsible. It was just a matter of time before they figured out the truth.

Kellan was afraid the other girls didn't have that much time left. If someone was willing to kill one of the betrothal contenders, they were willing to kill more. Taking a contingent of royal guards with him, he'd ridden through the streets of Falaise de la Mer, stopping at each head family's home, including those without anyone vying for the betrothal, to discuss the murder, additional protection, and his expectations moving forward.

For the families with girls of eligible age, he'd checked on their security protocols and encouraged them to change their habits, their patterns, to throw off any additional attempts at murder. He'd comforted distraught mothers and anxious fathers without once losing sight of the fact that one of those who leaned on him for reassurance might be the person who'd ordered Marisol's death.

And for every family, both those who were in the running for the throne and those who weren't, he'd stated in unequivocal terms that when he learned who was behind Marisol's murder, he would charge them with treason against the crown and ask the magistrate to sentence them to death.

The cathedral in the Gaillard quarter was tolling midnight when he rode up to the Gaillard mansion. He had Gen's security to see to, and the security of Lord Gaillard's nieces, and then he'd leave the city proper and head to the farmhouse to check on Jacinthe and Halette.

He frowned. He hadn't seen any of the Chauveau staff, including guards, when he'd visited the farmhouse just after they'd moved in. Perhaps the guards had remained hidden at their stations across the property, and Kellan simply hadn't seen them. He certainly hadn't been looking for them at the time. It would be immensely foolish of Dinah to allow her daughters to be unprotected, and Dinah was anything but foolish.

Still, he decided to make his visit with the Gaillards as quick as he could manage. Looping his horse's reins over the hitching post at the top of the drive that led past the Gaillards' front door, he motioned for his guards to remain behind and jogged up the steps. The door opened before he could raise his hand to knock.

The Gaillards' butler swept into a bow as he backed into the entrance hall to give the prince room to enter. His voice shook as he said, "I will ask my lord and lady to join you in the receiving parlor in the east wing. If you'll follow me, please."

There was a palpable hush pervading the house as Kellan followed the butler through the halls. He caught sight of a maid rushing past, her arms full of white sheets, tears on her cheeks, and his throat tightened.

"Genevieve Gaillard," he said as the butler opened the door to the parlor. "I want to see her too."

The butler's lips trembled. "I'm afraid . . . That is, I will ask that her body be prepared for visitors." He broke off, and looked at the ceiling, his jaw clenched.

"Her body . . ." Kellan sagged against the doorframe.

Lord Gaillard entered the parlor from the opposite end, his face flushed, his eyes full of tearstained fury. "My daughter. My beautiful Gen." He choked on a sob and then gestured wildly, his voice rising. "What is being done about this? I demand justice. I'll run the coward through with my own sword." He looked around as if vaguely surprised to find himself clad in his nightclothes with no weapon in sight.

"Lord Gaillard." Kellan moved into the room, trying hard to look as if he knew how to handle the entire situation.

Of all the girls in the betrothal race, she'd been the one who felt most like a true friend. The thought that someone could snuff out her life for a chance at the throne was sickening.

"Who did this?" Lord Gaillard's voice shook. "Who killed my daughter? My beloved Gen." He lingered over Gen's name, and then collapsed on the sofa, his entire body shaking.

"I'll find Lady Gaillard for you," the butler said softly from the doorway behind Kellan.

"No." Kellan cast the man a quick glance, and then returned his focus to Gen's father. "Let her be. I don't wish to intrude on her grief."

Kneeling beside Lord Gaillard, Kellan said, "I'm so sorry for your loss." The words weighed an entire kingdom, but they were still far too small. Gen—sweet, smiling, exuberant Gen—was gone. It was impossible to imagine the world without her, and Kellan couldn't bring himself to try. How was he ever going to be able to look Alexander in the eyes again knowing the betrothal season had cost his friend the girl he loved? Grief settled into his heart, sharp and raw, and he blinked as tears stung his eyes.

"I don't want sorry." Lord Gaillard's gaze was fiery. "I want justice. Which family did this? I'm betting on the Roches or the Marcels. Whichever one it is, they owe us a blood debt, and I will be paid in full."

Kellan drew in a shuddering breath and nodded. "I want to personally assure you that our royal magistrate is on the case, and it won't be long before we know who was responsible for this heinous crime. They'll be charged with treason and punished accordingly. An attack against any girl seeking the betrothal will be treated as an attack against the crown. Someone will hang for this."

Misery banked the fire in the older man's eyes, and he reached for Kellan's shoulder. "She was a good girl. Kind and smart and strong."

"Yes, she was," Kellan whispered, his own grief aching in his chest. "There are no words for the depths of my anger and horror over this. You have my promise that the crown will pursue her killer until he or she is caught."

He sent guards to check on the Gaillards' nieces, and waited with Lord Gaillard until he had confirmation that the girls were safe and protected. Then he took his leave, mounted his horse, and turned toward the west, where the Chauveaus and Blue waited.

Blue. Would she be protected by the Chauveaus' guards too? Living under the same roof as Jacinthe and Halette might put her in danger. He couldn't trust that whoever was trying to take out eligible girls hadn't issued orders to wipe out every girl of marriageable age within each household.

Worry buzzed through him, and he nudged his horse into

a canter. The hoofbeats of his guards' horses clattered against the cobblestones behind him as he sped through the Gaillard quarter, out the western gate, and down the winding dirt road that lead to the de la Cours' house. As if to reinforce his fears, the bells along the road began clamoring, and Kellan could swear he heard a faint wail rising above them, like a trapped beast keening for its freedom.

Setting his jaw, he ignored the bells and nudged his horse to move faster. He didn't have time to worry about a caged monster. He had a human monster on the loose killing his friends.

When he reached the farmhouse gate, he pulled his horse to a stop and dismounted in one fluid motion. Tossing the reins to one of his guards, he wrenched opened the gate and ran toward the front door.

He couldn't see any obvious guards in the vicinity, and the worry in his gut blossomed into full-blown fear. There was no way a guard could've identified Kellan as the prince with nothing but faint starlight to illuminate the darkness. Anyone protecting the Chauveaus should've stopped him by now, weapon out, demanding an explanation for his presence.

Was he already too late? Had a killer been here sometime between the royal messenger and his own arrival?

He vaulted up the steps and then froze, his heart slamming against his throat.

A body was lying on the far end of the porch, its back to the wall, a huge lump of a cat sitting on it and glaring at Kellan out of its one good eye.

"Oh no," Kellan breathed as he forced himself to move forward on legs that felt suddenly unsteady.

He was too late. He should've come here first, even though it was the farthest distance from the castle. He'd made a grave mistake, and the inhabitants of the farmhouse had paid the price.

The cat meowed as he approached, and Kellan sank to his knees, the grief that had taken root in his heart for Gen spilling over until his entire body ached with the pain of losing Blue.

It had to be Blue. Her cat wouldn't guard anyone else.

Reaching out, he brushed her cloak back and pressed his hand to her cheek.

Her eyes flew open, and she sat up, sending the cat thudding to the porch beside Kellan. He swore and nearly fell over in surprise.

"What are you doing?" she demanded.

"What are *you* doing?" His heart refused to settle, and his hands shook as he fisted them against his knees.

"Sleeping!"

"You could've been dead!" His voice broke over the last word, and he cleared his throat.

She blinked. "That makes no sense, Kellan."

"It makes more sense than deciding to spend the night asleep on your porch." His eyes narrowed. "Did she kick you out of the house?"

"No." There was something aching and lost and very un-Blue in her voice.

He made a conscious effort to gentle his tone. "What happened?"

"I didn't want to be inside anymore." She drew her cloak around her and reached for the cat, who curled up in her arms but kept his eye on Kellan.

"You can't stay out here alone. It isn't safe."

He couldn't see her well enough to know if she rolled her

eyes, but her tone sounded like it was a good guess. "It's safer out here than inside. I promise."

"Someone killed Marisol Evrard and Genevieve Gaillard."

"Oh no." She reached for him, wrapping one hand around his. "I'm so sorry. They were your friends, weren't they? I really liked Gen."

"Yes." He turned his palm up and laced her fingers through his, taking comfort in the steady warmth of her skin. "They were some of the girls vying for the betrothal. It means one of the families is making a bid to remove their competition. They could target the girls in this house next. You have to be careful."

"They'd target Jacinthe or Halette, not me, but I appreciate the warning." She squeezed his hand once and then let go.

"They might target every girl of betrothal age, just to be sure. Where are Dinah's guards? I want to speak to them about increasing security."

"I haven't seen any guards since she came to live here."

"That can't be right. Why would she take that chance?" He glanced around as if somehow the Chauveau guards would materialize.

"Maybe she can't afford to pay them."

"That's right. She's in financial trouble." Kellan drew in a deep breath but kept his hand in hers. Strange how her hand was small enough to be nearly engulfed in his, but still somehow made him feel twice as strong as he'd been moments before. He'd forgotten to mention Dinah's financial difficulties to his mother. Mostly because his mother had started asking pointed questions about his time spent with Blue, and it had thrown his thoughts into a complicated spiral.

"All right, then I'll speak to Dinah about moving some of the royal guards out here. And I really would feel more comfortable knowing you were inside the house with the doors locked."

"I'm not going back inside." Her tone was defiant, but the ache still lingered.

"Blue—"

"I'm not."

"Then let me take you to Grand-mère's. No one targeting the head families' girls would think to look there. You can stay there tonight, and tomorrow I'll have security arranged with Dinah so you can return home."

"Dinah will be furious."

"She can take that up with me. Come on. I'll walk you there."

He let go of her long enough to stand up while she scooped up the cat, who laid his head on her shoulder, and then together they left the porch and began the long walk through the orchard to Grand-mère's house.

TWENTY-NINE

BLUE WOKE TO the smell of hot chicory with cream, and for one glorious moment imagined she was home. Papa was in the kitchen making breakfast and planning ways to gently wake his sleepyhead of a daughter, and all was right with her world.

"I see you're awake," Grand-mère said from the doorway of her spare room. She held a steaming mug in her hands. "Come to the kitchen, and I'll fix us some breakfast. You still like fried apple cakes with a dusting of sugar, don't you?"

Blue pulled the quilt closer to her chest and snuggled down into the bed. "Can I stay here now? Kellan was able to make Dinah let me go last night. Maybe he can make it so I can live with you now."

Grand-mère approached the bed. "There's nothing I'd love more, though you'd better stick with your usual routine until we know for sure. Don't want that Chauveau snake sending you away. Prince Kellan seemed quite concerned for you last night. I didn't realize the two of you were that close."

Blue's face warmed. Yes, they were close. Somehow they'd moved from animosity to grudging respect to true friendship over the past month. Not that she'd ever almost kissed any of her other true friends.

Her skin tingled as she remembered the look in his eyes when he'd held his arms out to her. Reckless Kellan taking a chance to have what he wanted instead of what the law dictated, at least for a week. Her refusal still stung, the bone-deep ache of regret burrowing into her.

She'd obeyed the rules. It was better that way, and they both knew it. If it left her feeling just a little hollow over the loss of what might have been, all she needed was to remember that what might have been would have had to disappear the night of the betrothal ball.

Belatedly, she realized that Grand-mère was waiting for a response. Quickly, she sat up and reached for the mug. "We've become friends. Or maybe we were always friends, but now we've come to understand and appreciate one another."

"Well, it's about time. I'm going to get started on those fried apple cakes. You can wear one of your mother's old dresses until you get to the farmhouse. The dress you wore last night needs washing. Sleeping on the porch." She tsked. "What were you doing out there?"

It was on the tip of Blue's tongue to tell her grandmother about being forced to go down into the root cellar. How the panic had become an all-consuming beast beneath her skin, and how she hadn't been able to bear the thought of having walls around her again.

But if Grand-mère had been angry enough to nearly pull her wand in front of the magistrate at the thought of Dinah having guardianship over Blue, how would she respond to knowing that Dinah had forced Blue into the root cellar? Or the knowledge that Dinah wanted to steal some of Mama's old, rare spells and sell them or use them for herself? Or worse, the fact that Dinah sometimes slapped or pushed Blue in a fit of temper?

Swallowing the words she'd been about to say, Blue took a sip of the chicory root and then said, "I just wanted some fresh air, and then I guess I fell asleep."

It was the truth, just not all of it. She hadn't seen Grand-mère for more than a few minutes at a time for weeks. She wasn't going to ruin this perfect morning with talk about Dinah.

Grand-mère nodded briskly, sending her halo of tight graying-black curls dancing. "The faster we get that snake out of your house, the better. Come down for breakfast soon. Apple cakes are best when they're fresh."

Blue set the mug on the bedside table, nudged Pepperell off her knees, and slipped out of bed. Grand-mère's words rang in her head as she opened the closet her mother had used when she was a girl.

The faster we get that snake out of your house, the better.

Dinah wanted old potions with rare ingredients. Blue's mind raced as she reached for a dress in faded yellow cotton with tiny sprigs of purple pansies dotting its surface.

Dinah didn't have a specific potion in mind since she hadn't given Blue a list of ingredients she expected to see on the recipe parchment. She'd simply turned down any potion that didn't have a rare, hard-to-procure ingredient on its list.

Blue donned the yellow dress, tied its sash behind her, and considered her alternatives. She could keep cowering under Dinah, required to account for her every moment to a woman who treated her harshly. She could be forced to return to the root cellar to go through the chests that lay where Mama had died. She could endure the Chauveaus' interference with her life for the foreseeable future.

Or.

She could create a fake potion, write it on some of the old parchment sheets Grand-mère had kept in the closet for Blue to scribble on when she was little, and pretend she'd found it in some of Mama's old things. Dinah wouldn't know the difference, and hopefully it would get her out of Blue's life for good.

Energized by her plan, Blue hurried to splash cold water on her face, rub some of the oil Grand-mère kept on the dressing table into her curls, and brush her teeth. When she was finished, she sat on the floor in front of the closet and began pulling out the wooden boxes that lined its floor.

Quilting squares, yarn, and pieces of muslin with designs half stitched onto them filled the first box. Neatly organized headscarves filled the second. Blue pulled out a purple scarf with silver beaded fringe and tied it around her head before reaching for the next box. That one contained a collection of books, their spines cracked with age.

"Apple cakes are ready!" Grand-mère called.

"I'll be right there." Blue pulled out another box and took off the lid. A heavy velvet cloth in shimmering blue covered the contents of the box. Blue lifted the cloth and gasped. Nestled in the folds of more velvet lay the most beautiful pair of shoes she'd ever seen. The heels were thin spikes encrusted with gold filigree embedded with blue sapphires. The body of the shoe was a delicate swoop of fabric dusted with real gold and laced at the ankle with a golden chain encrusted with tiny diamonds. A large purple-blue feronghe jewel rested above the tiny opening that would allow the wearer's toes to peek out.

They were extravagant. Feronghe jewels were a rare find on Llorenyae, prized by witches and alchemists alike for their ability to accept protective enchantments, and the other jewels on the dancing slippers would bring more coin than the alchemy shop saw in profit for six months.

"Blue, these cakes aren't going to eat themselves!"

"Coming!"

Blue put the shoes back into the box and slid them into the closet. She'd ask Grand-mère about them later. Pulling out the final box, she found the old, yellowed sheets of parchment she needed. Taking several, she hurried to the kitchen where fresh apple cakes were flipping themselves in the skillet, the sea breeze was tangling with the row of chimes hanging by the open window, and just outside the window, Dinah Chauveau was striding up to the cottage.

Grand-mère whipped around to face the front door, her wand already raised. "Thinks she can come to my house and tell me what's what, does she? I'll turn her into a real snake."

"You can't turn her into a snake." Blue snatched a handful of apple cakes from a platter on the table, hastily shoved the folded pieces of parchment into her dress pocket, and ran to get between Grand-mère and the door.

"Watch me. The spell might wear off in a few hours, but I'll certainly feel better about things."

"But then she'll turn back into a woman, and she'll know that you use magic. She'll bring the royal council down on your head, and even the queen's friendship can't save us if you break the law. Especially now that a witch is doing harmful spells in the city." Blue gently pushed Grand-mère's wand arm down. "Dinah just wants to go to the shop for the day, I'm sure. I'll leave with her. Kellan is already looking into the guardianship document. Maybe he'll find a way to get me out of it."

Grand-mère grudgingly sheathed her wand as Dinah rapped smartly at the door. "Maybe I'll pay a visit to the castle myself. Your mother saved Balavata once. It's time they remembered the kind of favors they owe us."

Blue wrapped her arms around Grand-mère, holding tight for as long as she dared while the knocking behind her grew more impatient. Finally, she said, "I love you. Don't use your wand outside the cottage."

Grand-mère snorted, but her voice was warm as she said, "I love you too. Now get that woman off my property before I decide to have snake stew for lunch."

Dinah was silent on their carriage journey from the farmhouse to the shop. Her lips were pinched tight, her fingers restlessly tugging at the lace that hemmed the sleeves of her expensive yellow day dress. At first, Blue figured Dinah was still angry with her for running away from the root cellar and sleeping at Grand-mère's at Kellan's behest, but then she remembered the reason Kellan had arrived so late to the house in the first place.

Clearing her throat, Blue tried to sound compassionate. "I was sorry to hear about Marisol Evrard and Genevieve Gaillard. I'm sure you must be worried about your girls."

Dinah sniffed. "Marisol was a silly girl, and Genevieve wasn't anything remarkable. Their deaths narrow the field of competition." Her fingers worried the lace, and her voice softened. "But yes, my girls are in danger. Jacinthe especially, since she's spent

258

more time with the prince. And I no longer have the resources to protect them."

"Can't you just bring your guards from your quarter and assign them to your daughters?" It seemed like the most obvious solution.

"If I could, don't you think I'd have done it already?" Dinah snarled. "Guards must be paid."

"But—"

"Prince Kellan left two guards on the property to watch them while I'm gone today, which means the queen will now know about my financial situation even before the royal magistrate's report is finished." There was rage in her voice.

"I'm sorry," Blue said sincerely, though she had no idea what report Dinah was talking about.

"I'm not discussing any more of this with you." Dinah's tone was final, but she kept picking at the lace, shredding the edges into loose threads.

Blue took a deep breath, reaching for calm. Dinah was an awful woman. And if the guardianship document somehow proved false—a faint hope since Nell had already verified it— Dinah might have had a hand in Papa's death. If that was true, Blue could give herself permission to hate Dinah. To work hard to make sure she was brought to justice as publicly as possible.

But until then, she was still a mother worried about her daughters. Blue was worried too. Not just for Jacinthe and Halette, but for all the other girls vying for Kellan's hand. She might not be close to the members of the nine head families, but the idea of someone murdering girls her age because they wanted the throne made sickness crawl up the back of her throat.

She couldn't hire guards to protect the girls, but she could still help. Yesterday, Maurice had finally delivered the pink sapphire she'd ordered. Blue had planned to use it in a complicated new potion meant to tremendously strengthen the lifespan of any potions created in the pot where the now-enchanted sapphire sat, but pink sapphire could also be used as a conduit to harness the qualities of certain herbs and minerals and transform them into a powerful protection charm that worked directly with the energy of the person it was meant to protect.

As they rode past the place where Papa had died, Blue sent a silent prayer that he could see her and was proud of her, and then said, "I'll help your girls."

She'd expected Dinah to laugh, to say something cruel and scornful. Instead, the older woman stopped tugging at the loose threads on her lace sleeves. "How?" There was caution in her voice, but there wasn't disbelief.

"I'll make a protection charm for each of them. I just got some pink sapphire. It will concentrate the potion, but I'll need a strand of hair from each of them so I can personalize the potion."

They turned into the business district in the Gaillard quarter, the road already full of wagons, carriages, and riders hurrying toward their destinations. The harsh clang of the smithy's hammer striking molten metal filled the air, and the scent of freshly baked ginger pudding wafted out of the bakery. The slight wind that drifted in from the sea sent iron chimes hanging from balconies ringing merrily as Dinah and Blue rode past.

Finally, Dinah said, "Why are you offering to help me?"

"Because it's the right thing to do. Papa taught me that I can't help how people choose to treat me, but I can always control how I choose to respond." Blue cut her gaze toward Dinah, but the woman's expression looked carved from stone.

As they turned up the street that led to the shop, Dinah said quietly, "I'll return to the house in a bit and get a strand of hair from each of them."

When it became obvious that she would say no more, Blue sighed. Dismounting from the carriage, she unlocked the shop, flipped the sign from Closed to Open, and hurried back to her storeroom, leaving Dinah out front.

She wasn't just going to make charms for Halette and Jacinthe. She was going to make them for every girl vying for the betrothal. And, she decided in a sudden burst of inspiration, she would make one each for Nessa and Kellan. That would take some of the weight off his shoulders and some of the worry out of Blue's heart.

First, she'd need a sample of hair from each of them. Quickly, she jotted a note to Kellan, explaining what she was doing and asking him to help collect the strands and send them to her at the shop. Then she went into the alley and found Lucian waiting outside.

With Lucian running to the castle with the note for Kellan, a copper coin in his pocket for his troubles, Blue turned her attention to the basic ingredients she'd need for the charms. She pulled herbs from one shelf, dried leaves from another, and several strands of pure rose lead wire from the coil she kept by Mama's old cauldron. Then she took the largest of the pink sapphires Maurice had brought her, fitted it into her rock splitter, applied pressure, and broke it into small shards.

"I'm leaving to get what you need from the farmhouse," Dinah said from the doorway. Blue nodded, her attention on the potion she was devising.

Feeling sentimental, she pulled down Mama's old cauldron. Setting aside her own copper pots, she lit the burner and placed the cauldron on top.

Yaeringlei oil went in first, then thresh moss, carpa leaf, yew, bolla root, and a dash of myrrh. Bringing the mixture to a boil, she added silver flakes to bond the ingredients, and then let it simmer.

While it cooked, Blue sat at the worktable, pulled the old pieces of parchment from her pocket, and grabbed a quill. She needed a potion that could look like something Mama would have used. Something with at least one rare ingredient.

Quickly she dashed off a recipe that was close to the one she'd just used, though she added more myrrh, required both gold and silver, and took out the carpa leaf. It would make for a decent protection potion, though without the pink sapphire to concentrate it, it wouldn't last very long.

Now she needed a rare ingredient. Something hard to find. Something that would interest Dinah enough to hopefully convince her she had what she wanted and could leave Blue alone.

Should she use a stone? A rare mineral? Or something even more exotic?

A hazy memory surfaced. She was with Mama in the castle garden while Papa and the king played thistles and thieves at a table set up on the lawn, and Kellan tried to catch snakes on the creek bed that wound along the edge of the grounds. The queen was resting in the shade with baby Nessa in her arms, and the royal guards were posted nearby.

Mama had lowered her voice, as if telling Blue a secret, and had asked if she wanted to see the most special plant in the entire garden. Of course Blue had said yes, and the two of them wandered deep into the heart of the castle's garden, where flowering bushes and budding trees lined paths of crushed seashells. When they came to a single rynoir tree, its flowing branches resembling a long, wispy gown dressed in extravagant pink blooms, Mama ducked under the branches, and Blue followed.

Beneath the skirt of branches, close to the trunk, a small, thorny bush with heart-shaped blue leaves and dark red berries grew. Mama explained that it was a volshkyn bush from the far north, gifted to the previous queen from the then-queen of Morcant. It was said to be good for healing ointments, protection potions, and potions to help the lost find their way home, but was only used in rare instances because the plant took years to replace the leaves that were harvested from it.

Blue added it to the ingredient list, and then jumped as she heard the shop bells chime. Quickly putting the quill away, she left the recipe out to dry and hurried into the front of the shop. Dinah shut the door behind her and turned to Blue.

"I have it." She held out two small squares of muslin, one with a strand of hair from Halette and one with a strand from Jacinthe.

"And I have something for you," Blue said, her heart hammering as she led Dinah back into the storeroom.

This had to work. Blue needed her life back. Needed time to herself to grieve, to heal, and to figure out how to move forward.

"What is this?" Dinah's eyes focused immediately on the sheet of old parchment sitting on the worktable, creased and yellowed. The ink had dried, Blue noted with relief.

"It's a potion recipe."

Dinah shoved the muslin squares into Blue's hands and hurried to the table. Picking up the spell, she examined it for a long moment, and a smile sharp enough to cut glass spread across her face.

"Where did you find this?" she asked, raising her eyes to pin Blue where she stood.

Quickly Blue cast around for inspiration and then turned to stir the potion that was brewing on the stove. "I pulled Mama's old cauldron down to use for the protection charms. Nostalgia, I guess."

"And it was inside," Dinah breathed. "I didn't think of looking there."

"Are vintage alchemy potions really worth enough money to help you?" Blue asked carefully, afraid to hope that she'd finally found the key to getting the Chauveaus out of her life.

"You let me worry about that." Dinah looked carefully at the list of ingredients, pausing when she came to the last one. "Do you have any volshkyn leaves?"

"No, but the queen has a volshkyn plant in her garden. If you need a leaf or two, I'm sure she could help you."

Dinah brushed past Blue without another word, and in moments, the shop chimes rang again as she walked out, leaving Blue blissfully alone.

THIRTY

BLUE'S MORNING FLEW by, and soon Lucian was there to gather the deliveries.

"Did the prince have a message for me?" Blue asked Lucian as the boy hurried to stack packages into a large bag he could strap onto his back.

Lucian shrugged. "Didn't see him in person. The man who answered the door said he'd deliver the message for me."

Blue nodded. Of course Kellan hadn't seen Lucian himself. He was probably in meetings or wooing one of the head families.

Before that thought could linger, she said, "I've been meaning to discuss Ana and the other children with you."

Lucian's big brown eyes found hers, and she winced at the hope she saw in them. "You found them?"

Setting her tongs aside, she moved toward him. "I'm sorry, Lucian, but no. I've asked around in a few quarters as I've had time, but—"

"No need to explain yourself, Miss Blue. I know you're busy, and they're just street kids. No one really notices when one is gone." His voice was parchment-thin as he resumed loading his bag, his eyes firmly on his task instead of on her.

She closed the distance between them and softly put her hands on his shoulders. They were thin, the bones jutting up to push against her palms. Quietly, she said, "I notice, Lucian. And I care. About Ana, about you, and about all the children who've been left to fend for themselves. It isn't right, and I'm trying hard to do something about it."

He shrugged and began tying the mouth of the bag closed over the last package.

"What I wanted to tell you was that I talked with the prince about the problem, and he's going to have the royal magistrate look into it."

Lucian's hands stilled, and he slowly raised his eyes. "The prince himself said that?"

"Yes."

Suddenly, he abandoned his bag and threw his skinny arms around her waist. She blinked, and then gently hugged him back, resting her cheek against his mop of curls.

"Thank you," he whispered.

Her heart squeezed. No child should carry the burdens Lucian bore. Maybe she should stop trying to force lead to change into gold. Maybe she should go straight to the queen with her idea for a large home that could accommodate the city's orphans safely and ask for the royal coffers to finance it.

Lucian pulled away and roughly cleared his throat. "I better get these deliveries out the door, Miss Blue. Don't want to miss the docks today."

"The docks?" Blue squinted at him.

He gave her a questioning look. "It's the day the bounty hunters from Llorenyae come through with their shipment of monsters for Akram. I thought the whole city knew about that."

"It is?" She glanced at the wall calendar that was nailed beside the sink, but she hadn't changed the date on it since the night Papa had died.

"See you there!" he said as he rushed out the door.

Abandoning all thoughts of running the shop for the afternoon, Blue made sure the protection potion was ready to soak for the next two days, turned the shop's sign to Closed, and hurried toward the docks.

Seeing the bounty hunters from Llorenyae on their twice-yearly journey through the port of Falaise de la Mer to the northern kingdom of Akram with the monsters they supplied to one of Akram's prisons was excitement few of the city's inhabitants missed. But in addition to seeing the monsters who weren't completely hidden in their crates, Blue was interested in the other wares that might arrive on the ship. Usually there were yaeringlei seeds, maelsa wood, and an assortment of unusual gems and minerals mined deep in the mountains on the fae isle. Sometimes, Blue and Papa had even found fae-made jewelry or clothing, though Grand-mère had forbidden them from wearing anything made by a fae. Something about possible curses woven into the threads.

Sunlight stung Blue's eyes and heated her skin as she made her way through the merchant district and south toward the docks. Already the streets were choked with people. Carts set up along the main road that led to the port sold iced shirella drinks with crushed walla berries floated at the top of the cup, fresh ginger cakes, and bags of spicy popped corn. If Papa had been with her, they would've purchased a bag of the popped corn and cooled their tongues with iced shirella as they took in the sight of the busy docks, the ships coming into port, and the fascinating pair of bounty hunters who handled terrifying monsters with ease.

But Papa wasn't here, and Blue wasn't ready to do their traditions by herself. Bypassing the food carts, she made her way through the crowds to the edge of the docks. Several ships were coming in, but she was only interested in the black vessel with five sails and a flag that was ice blue on one side and sunshine yellow on the other. The symbols of the Winter and Summer courts were embroidered into their respective colors, and the sculpture of a water nymph clung to the bow as if she'd just risen from the sea itself.

Another boat was docking while the black ship from Llorenyae approached. A fancy dark blue craft with brass trimming and the crest of Súndraille's ruling family on its bow. Blue was surprised to see Kellan, Nessa, and the queen, all dressed in formal afternoon attire, standing at attention in the center of the dock where the blue ship was being tied to several posts. A dozen royal guards surrounded them, keeping onlookers at bay.

Nessa was looking at everything, a huge grin on her face. When her eyes found Blue, she lit up and waved Blue over. Blue hesitated, shaking her head, but the queen noticed and lifted her hand in a regal summoning. Quickly, Blue crossed the dock until she was beside the royal family. She risked one glance at Kellan, found his warm brown eyes on hers, and quickly looked at the queen instead before the telltale racing of her heart could somehow show on her face.

"Blue, I'm glad to see you here, though we can't talk long.

The royals from Súndraille will be disembarking soon as part of their tour of the western kingdoms, and we'll need to greet them and escort them to the castle."

"It's good to see you too, Your Majesty." Blue curtsied.

The queen smiled. "I wanted to thank you for the headache cream you created for me. It's worked wonders."

Blue returned her smile. "I'm so glad. I thought moss glider venom might be the key. I can get more next week and make another batch if you'd like."

"Moss glider venom?" Kellan's voice sounded strangled. "You put lethal snake venom in a cream and gave it to my mother?"

Blue frowned at him. "It has numbing properties."

"It has *killing* properties."

She tapped her foot impatiently. "It's a perfectly safe dosage. I tried it on myself three times to be sure."

His eyes widened. "You tried it on yourself? You're nearly half her height!"

"Which is why I knew if it didn't kill me, it wouldn't kill her."

"And you call me reckless." He glared at her, but she could see the worry and care in his eyes.

Praying his mother couldn't read his face as easily as she could, she said quietly, "I'm fine. And your mother's headaches are better. Everyone's happy."

He didn't look happy. He looked miserable. She understood the feeling perfectly. It was awful to stand next to him and be aware of every bit of space between them. Awful to long for him and make herself turn away.

The slap of a gangplank hitting the dock brought Blue to her senses. Tearing her gaze away from Kellan's, she turned to see a young man who looked around Kellan's age and a girl with

269

long, sun-streaked brown hair and a wide, easy smile walking toward them. Quickly, Blue moved out of the way so the royal families could greet each other. Nessa caught her eye, her hands discreetly signing.

Why is Kellan mad at you?

Because he thought she'd risked both herself and her mother. Because he had to greet royals and go choose a bride instead of spending time with Blue.

Because her emotions had been too easy to read, and he knew she longed for him too.

She gave Nessa a little smile and signed, *He was just worried. He worries about you a lot.*

Blue didn't know what to say to that. The pair from Súndraille reached the royal family, and Nessa turned her attention to them.

A page raised his voice and said, "Your Majesties Queen Adelene, Prince Kellan, and Princess Vanessa of Balavata, may I present Their Royal Highnesses Thaddeus and Arianna Glavan of Súndraille."

While the families greeted each other, Blue turned to find the black Llorenyae ship docked and its passengers disembarking. There were a few merchants, a handful of children dancing around a harried-looking woman, and some small loads of crates coming down the gangplank on carts, but Blue's eyes were drawn to the twin bounty hunters who stood on the deck, legs braced as if they were still at sea, their dark auburn hair glowing in the sun like halos of fire. Behind them, a train of wagon beds were being loaded with cages and crates full of creatures who howled, hissed, growled, and screamed in unearthly tones that sent a wave of stunned silence over the crowded dock.

Near Blue, the princess of Súndraille sighed dramatically and said, "Hansel and Gretel always bring the most terrifying creatures with them when they travel. I could never strand myself on board a ship with those monsters. I need a slice of pie just *thinking* about it."

Her brother laughed. "I'm not sure pie would do you any good if one of their creatures got loose."

The princess snorted. "I think you're seriously underestimating the value of dying while doing something you enjoy."

Kellan laughed. "I have to agree with Princess Arianna. Seizing the moment is never a bad decision."

"It's Ari, please," the girl said, "and you sound like a wise prince."

Blue laughed, choked when all five members of both royal families turned her way, and then laughed again at the smirk on Kellan's face.

"You don't think I'm wise, Blue?" he called, daring her to join the conversation. To tease him. To act like they were alone in her storeroom instead of standing on a dock in front of the city and worse, his mother.

"I . . . really couldn't say."

"Ooh, that means you must have some very interesting stories to tell," said a bold, bright voice behind her. She whirled and found herself face-to-face with the bounty hunter Hansel, his blue eyes dancing with glee. There were dark runes inked into his arms and iron charms tied in his shoulder-length hair. A single white streak of hair grew from his left temple.

His sister stood behind him, a matching streak of white at her temple, along with matching runes in her skin and charms in her hair. The way she held her lithe, graceful body reminded Blue of

Pepperell's sudden stillness as he stalked prey across the garden.

"Hansel! Gretel!" Ari rushed to them and threw her arms around them. "It's been ages since you've visited."

Hansel grinned, lifted her in the air, and spun her once. Gretel simply gave her a serious smile and squeezed her shoulders once. Hansel slung an arm around Ari's shoulders and looked around. "Where is your silent, predatory partner in crime?"

Ari grimaced. "Still on the boat, lying down. Turns out Sebastian doesn't handle sea travel well."

"Vomited, did he?" Hansel asked.

"If I were you, I wouldn't tease him about it," Gretel said quietly. "Cornering Sebastian is a good way to get hurt."

Hansel included everyone in his smile. "Speaking of getting hurt, Your Majesties, if I might suggest clearing the dock before we bring our beasties off the boat? While our cages are solid and our crates are strong, Akram has ordered some of its most vicious monsters yet. If one of them gets loose, you'll need all prey . . . I mean people, of course . . . out of the way so we can catch it."

"What happens if you can't catch it?" Kellan asked, frowning.

"Then we hunt it down and kill it," Gretel said in a voice that left no doubt she was capable of doing exactly that.

Blue thought of the witch hurting people in the city and blurted, "Can you catch a witch?"

Kellan met her eyes and nodded his agreement with the direction her mind was heading.

Hansel's eyes lit up, and he cracked his knuckles. "Witch hunting happens to be a specialty of ours. What's the problem? You have one going a bit rogue?"

"We have someone who released a spell in multiple parts of

272

the city. It caused black flames to burn on whatever living being it touched until it extinguished itself, long after the person or animal was dead," the queen said. "Then, a few nights later, a house and everyone inside it simply disintegrated into dust."

"I hate witches who hurt people," Hansel said, for once sounding nearly as serious as his sister. "Any clues to the witch's whereabouts?"

Kellan shook his head. "We sourced the ingredients and followed up, but no one sold those items to anyone besides their regular customers within the last year."

"How did you know which ingredients were used?" Gretel asked, the stillness of her body somehow going from aware to menacing without Blue being able to identify what specifically had changed.

"I identified them," Blue said, flinching a little when all eyes landed on her.

"Are you a witch?" Ari asked, sounding more curious than afraid.

"I'm an alchemist."

Hansel grinned again. "Smart *and* beautiful. Please tell me you aren't spoken for."

Blue didn't dare look at Kellan. Instead, she said, "If we could focus on catching the witch—"

"Well, that's a lot less fun than what I was going to suggest, but I suppose we can't have everything we want." Hansel winked at her, and Blue folded her arms across her chest.

Gretel laughed, a solemn, quiet sound. "This girl is immune to your charms."

"Or maybe you aren't as charming as you think," Kellan said, and then hurried on when his mother shot him a questioning look. "I'm concerned about catching a witch when we can't follow the ingredients. How do we find this person?"

Gretel met Kellan's gaze. "Since magic is illegal in your kingdom, I'd start turning over every rock to find where a witch interested in hurting people might hide to practice magic in secret."

Hansel nodded as the queen gave orders to her guards to clear the dock in preparation for the bounty hunters' crates. "It's unfortunate that you have a witch using spells to hurt people, but as long as you don't have one feeding on the blood of children, you'll be able to put the witch down easily once you find him or her."

Blue froze, her eyes finding Kellan's, the horror on his face a mirror for what she felt inside.

Hansel's grin disappeared, and his body took on the eerie, predatory stillness of his sister's. "You have a witch feeding on children, don't you?"

"We have children disappearing," Blue said softly. "Orphans. Homeless. The kind who won't be missed by those with enough power to find them."

Hansel and Gretel exchanged a long look, and then, finally, Gretel said, "We have to deliver this shipment to Akram on time. They run a tournament in a prison there, and the beasts can't arrive late. But once we finish, we'll return as quickly as possible and help hunt down your witch before it turns into a blood wraith."

"The good news is that it takes months, sometimes even years, of feeding on the blood of innocents before a witch goes full blood wraith," Hansel said. "We have time before this gets out of . . ." He looked from Blue to Kellan to the queen, took in their uneasy expressions, and sighed. "You already have a blood wraith, don't you?"

The queen nodded, her lips pinched. "We caught and imprisoned it sixteen years ago."

"Imprisoned?" Gretel sounded skeptical. "They're practically invincible. You'd need powerful magic to do that."

The queen cut her eyes once to Blue and then looked away. "We had . . . help."

"And you're sure this blood wraith is still in its prison?" Hansel asked.

When Blue, Kellan, and the queen remained silent, he shook his head. "That's the first place I'd check. If children are going missing, and your wraith is still locked away, then we're back to having another witch aiming to turn wraith. And if that's the case, Gretel and I can help when we return."

"Either way, we can help you kill the wraith you have," Gretel said, a dark violence lurking in her voice.

"How do you kill a blood wraith?" Blue asked.

Hansel winked, though it looked more like habit than glee this time. "I don't know. It's hard to kill something that gets stronger every time it feeds on an innocent's blood, but we'd figure it out, wouldn't we, Gret?"

"We do love a challenge," Gretel said quietly.

The queen nodded briskly. "We'll do as you say. I'll find someone to check on the wraith, and we'll continue to look for places a witch might practice in secret. Thank you for your expert advice."

As the crewmen began carefully bringing wagonloads of beast cages down the gangplank, Hansel and Gretel turned to oversee them, and Blue waved a little good-bye to Kellan and

Nessa, who were already being drawn into conversation again with the royals from Súndraille.

Children going missing. A witch practicing in secret. A wraith no one had seen in years.

A chill went down her spine as she made her way back into the city and toward her home, all thoughts of watching the monsters in Hansel and Gretel's cages forgotten.

How had her mother locked the wraith away in the first place? Blue had a feeling it was knowledge she might soon desperately need.

THIRTY-ONE

THE CASTLE WALLS were closing in on Kellan. He'd spent the morning checking with the royal magistrate about the state of the investigation into the murders as well as the investigation into the witch, triple-checking Nessa and his mother's security protocols, and dealing with a steady stream of visitors from the various head families before heading to the docks to greet the new ruler of Súndraille, who couldn't be much older than Kellan himself.

Most of his early afternoon had been spent lunching with the Glavans, fielding requests for investigation updates from various members of the head families, and answering correspondence from trade and political ambassadors across the ten kingdoms.

Everywhere he turned, there was another question to answer, another problem to solve, and another demand on his already limited time. And through it all, the knowledge that he had less than a week before he needed to choose a girl to marry, keep the other families from turning against each other or the crown, and help Blue with both her guardianship situation and her worries over children going missing throughout the city spun through him, a tightly wound coil that made it difficult to breathe.

When his tailor arrived to measure Kellan for a new dancing coat and trousers, followed immediately by his secretary with a long list of documents to approve, choices to make, and invitations to reply to, the coil exploded into a desperate need to get out of the castle so he could have a moment to think.

And to wrestle with the grief that kept sneaking up on him when he wasn't looking.

His father should've been here. Attending the ball. Holding the throne as the true Renard until he was old enough to feel that passing the crown to his son was the right move to make. Helping Kellan decide which girl to marry and maybe understanding the hollow space within him at the knowledge that the girl Kellan thought he might like to marry was off-limits.

Kellan held himself still for the tailor and rattled off a quick list of instructions for his secretary—yes, he approved next week's meeting schedule, no, he was unavailable for brunches this week and wouldn't be until after the funerals, yes, leave the documents on his desk for him to sign later. When the tailor left and his secretary looked ready to bring forth another list of demands, Kellan pleaded a headache and asked for two hours to lie down.

Two hours before he had to shoulder the mantle of crown prince again, pretend he had all the answers, and somehow figure out how to walk the thin line between suspecting every head family of murder and convincing them he held them all in the highest esteem.

The instant his secretary left his suite and informed the

guards posted in the hall that the prince was unwell and would be lying down for two hours, Kellan locked the door and hurried out the window. In the time it took him to climb down to the castle grounds and slink away, the restlessness had become a churning storm of panic, edged with despair.

What if he couldn't protect the rest of the girls? What if he couldn't protect his family or Blue? He was surrounded by help—his mother, his guards, the royal magistrate, and his allies within the head families—but he'd never felt so alone.

He wished his father was here.

The thought sent a shaft of pain straight into the numb corner of Kellan's heart where his grief for his father lived.

He just needed to feel alive for a little while. Truly alive. Needed to stare death in the face, dare it to take him once more, and survive. It was the only way he'd learned how to find an ounce of peace.

He headed south, skirting the city proper, until he'd reached the de la Cour farmhouse. Careful to stay on the edges of the property, where Jacinthe and Halette wouldn't be able to see him, he made his way to the cliff that overlooked the sea.

The water seemed as restless as he was—rocking in its berth, its waves choppy, its current strong. A storm was coming. The sky was a thin gray-blue, the horizon darkening with clouds, though the storm itself wouldn't break over land for another hour or more.

It was a terrible time to swim out to the shadowy line that lurked beneath the water. The current could change at any moment. The tide could snatch an unwary swimmer and drag him beneath the waves, holding him prisoner until he stopped struggling.

Kellan couldn't wait to face it.

Stripping off his shoes, belt, and tunic, he rolled his pants up above his knees, aimed at the deepest section of the water, and dove.

The water was a slap of coolness against his skin as he broke the surface. Quickly pulling out of the dive, he scraped his stomach along the bottom of the sea and then shot toward the open waters where the shelf fell away and the shadow loomed.

He'd been right. This was a terrible time to be in the water. The current snatched him, propelling him toward his destination with terrifying speed. He rode it for a moment, feeling the numbness inside disintegrate before the rush of danger. When the land beneath him fell away, and the shadow stretched as far as he could see, he began kicking. Fighting. Struggling toward the surface while the water did its best to swallow him whole.

He broke free, his mouth clearing the water so he could drag in a much-needed breath before the current slammed into him, dragging him under again.

For an instant, he drifted with it. Spinning into the shadow, feeling the slap of the rubbery sea vines that grew beneath the waves, his chest constricting as his air began to run out.

How long had his father held his breath?

Two minutes? Three?

Or had he fought so hard to get back to the surface that he'd used up his air before he even realized he was drowning?

Something brushed against his back, and he kicked hard, turning sharply in time to see a small hand latch onto the waistband of his pants and pull.

He lifted his face and the rush of danger flowing through his veins froze into stone-cold panic.

Blue was caught in the shadow too. Her body was buffeted by the current as she kicked and struggled. Her cheeks bulged with her last breath.

He grabbed her hand and fought for the surface with every bit of strength he had. Gone was the glorious blaze of life that burned away the numbness. In its place was absolute terror.

He couldn't watch another person he cared about drown.

The current was colder than the rest of the water. It dragged against him, its grip relentless, but Kellan was relentless too. He kicked, shoved at the water with his free arm, and begged Blue with his eyes to hold on. Keep her breath locked inside where it would hold the water at bay. She kicked right alongside him, her expression fierce. Her glare could shatter glass, and he prayed that determination kept her fighting as the current pulled them farther from the safety of land.

His lungs burned, his chest ached, and panic was lightning in his veins.

He wasn't going to lose Blue to the insatiable appetite of the sea. If that meant he pushed her to safety while the current snatched him away, he was prepared to do it.

With a final kick, he broke the surface, pulling Blue up with him. The second her face cleared the water, she sucked in a deep breath, wrapped her free arm around his chest so that she was snug against his back, and started swimming toward the shore.

He was far too big for her to pull, but he kicked as hard as he could, propelling both of them out of the shadow and over the shelf of land where the waves were still choppy, but the water no longer felt as if it was tearing their bodies apart.

When they reached the shore, he stood, tried to help Blue out of the water, and then simply fell to his knees in the sand, as his legs refused to hold him.

Blue struggled to her feet, her shirt and trousers clinging to her body, her eyes blazing. She stumbled to his side and poked a finger in his chest. Hard.

"What do you think you're doing?" she snapped.

"Me?" He pushed her finger aside and wondered if he had the strength to stand yet. "What do you think *you're* doing? You could've been killed!"

Hang it all, he was shaking. Her hand was so small. What if he'd lost his grip?

He closed his eyes against the image of Blue spinning away into the depths of the shadow, swallowed up by the arms of the uncaring sea. They flew open again when she tapped him smartly on the shoulder.

"Are you even listening to me at all? This is serious, Kellan."

He glared. "This is absolutely serious. What were you thinking going out that far in the water with a storm coming in? Do you want to drown?"

The thought hit him like a punch to the gut, and he sank back onto the sand. "You want to drown, don't you? Pierre's death, Dinah in your home, all of it felt overwhelming, and you thought you'd just swim out and never come back. Stars, Blue, you could've just come to me. To Nessa. You're family. We don't want to lose you."

"I'm not the one who was trying to drown." She sat down on the sand beside him, her expression serious, and he frowned.

"Then what were you doing swimming so far out on a day like this?"

"Rescuing you."

He stared at her. "Blue."

"You're lucky I closed the shop early today because of the bounty hunters. And lucky that Dinah's been gone all day, so I had the freedom to come home after visiting the docks. And especially lucky that I had already changed into my gathering clothes, or there would've been no one here to see you jump into the sea like a fool with a death wish."

"And you jumped in after me?" His eyes found the cliff top, and his stomach dropped as he measured the distance between it and the water. What had felt like freedom, like daring death to take him so he could feel the rush of life when he survived, suddenly felt terrifying when he imagined Blue doing the same.

"Don't be an idiot. I ran down the steps. It's amazing that you didn't break your neck with that dive. I wouldn't have been any help if I'd broken mine."

"But you swam out beyond the shelf. The current today . . ." The current was a death trap. He'd known it going in. He'd never planned for someone else to come in after him.

"I know what the current is like today." Her voice was sharp. "I swim here often. Storm's coming in, so it's a dangerous time to swim. But I guess that's why you went in, isn't it?"

He couldn't answer her. Couldn't even look at her.

It was one thing to risk his own death. It was something else entirely to see the lengths someone who cared about him would go to save him from himself.

"You could've died," he said quietly, clenching his fists to hide how badly they shook. "If I hadn't been able to kick us free—"

"You would never have been able to free us both, Kellan. I fought for it too." Her voice gentled. "We beat it together, because that's what people do when they face trouble as a team. I've always known you were reckless, but I never realized you were dangerous to yourself. Why did you do it?" she asked, the softness of her voice whispering against a wound he'd never figured out how to close.

He closed his eyes, and for one long moment there was nothing but the crash of the waves hurling themselves against the shore and the faint call of a flock of seabirds overhead. He wanted to keep his eyes closed, keep the sound of the present firmly in his focus, but her words had already sent him spinning into the darkness of the memory that refused to let him go.

"You don't have to tell me," she said quietly.

His heart clenched. He opened his eyes, but he couldn't look at her. Instead, he stared at the sea as it tossed restlessly in its berth. At the seductive surge and retreat of the waves he'd been swimming in since he could walk.

"This was his favorite spot." His throat closed, and he dug his fingers into the sand to ground him. To hold on to the faint trace of his father that he was convinced lingered here still. "We came here almost every morning unless it was storming. Usually we arrived after you and your family left for the shop, but sometimes you were here with Grand-mère, and you'd join us."

"I remember." She stretched her legs out beside his.

"Father would swim with me for an hour and then sit and watch me play for a bit on my own. There were others with us, of course. Our assigned guards and sometimes the castle steward or father's secretary so he could work while I played, but I never saw them when I looked at the shore. I only saw him."

"He was your hero." Blue's voice held everything he needed at that moment. Understanding. Grief. Permission to keep his memory a secret if that's what he needed.

He wanted it kept a secret. He'd been guarding it for so long that letting the words out into the open felt like stripping bare in the dead of winter. But the secret was already bubbling up. Already scraping past his grief-closed throat and clawing for its freedom.

"There were dark clouds on the horizon. Heavy winds. He wanted me to get out of the sea when he did, but I begged him to let me swim just a bit longer. The waves were choppy, and I wanted to see how fast I could reach the edge of the shelf. I wanted to test myself."

The pain in his heart shot through his veins as he remembered the slap of the waves against his skin, the thrill of pushing himself to beat the sea as it turned against him, and then the sharp surge of panic as a current—different from the normal rhythms of the sea and twice as strong—snatched him and flung him away from the shelf and deep into the bowels of the Chrysós.

Blue's small hand wrapped around his, and he squeezed as if he were holding on to a lifeline.

"There was a crosscurrent, like there is today. It was moving away from the shore, and it caught me. It was so strong." He blinked as tears burned his eyes, blurring the sea before him into a shimmering ribbon of gold. The numbness in his heart was gone, and in its place was a firestorm of grief and regret. "I couldn't find the way up to the water's surface. I couldn't break free. I tried. I was a strong swimmer, but I was only eight, and there was no way out."

"You were drowning." She rubbed her thumb along the back of his hand, and he drew in a shaky breath, but the rest of the words were caught behind the terrible grief—fresh and jagged as the day he'd recklessly thought to challenge the sea and win— and he couldn't find a way to give them life.

He met Blue's brown eyes for a moment, and a tear slipped down her cheek. She whispered, "You were drowning, and he couldn't let that happen. No father could."

Turning back to the sea, he forced himself to say, "He was the strongest swimmer in the kingdom. He reached me just as I thought my lungs would burst."

Hands reaching for him, grasping his shoulders with iron strength and pulling him to the surface as he kicked and struggled. As he panicked and tried desperately to beat back the sea that was determined to drag him to his death.

"He saved you."

The secret trembled at the edge of his tongue, coating his mouth with bitterness, before spilling from his lips. "I killed him."

"Oh, Kellan."

He pulled his hand from hers and slammed his fists into the ground, his heart thundering in his chest.

"I was so scared, so panicked for air, that I kicked and fought the entire way up to the surface." His voice was raw. "I kicked him, just as our heads broke through. There were people in the water coming for us. The guards. One of his stewards. But all I could see was him."

Shoving Kellan out of the current's grasp even as he spun away from his son, the water dragging him under.

"He surfaced once, and I tried to go after him, but a guard had reached me and was holding me back. I never saw him again."

He'd screamed himself hoarse, beating against the chest of the man who was doggedly dragging the prince to the shore even as others ran to sound the alarm and call the king's fleet of ships to scour the sea for their ruler.

"How many times have you come back here to swim in that same current?"

Swallowing hard, he said, "More times than I can count. When I was younger, I thought that somehow if I could just be strong enough and fast enough, I could undo what happened. If I could be the kind of boy who doesn't need rescuing, I wouldn't lose anyone else. But for the past few years, I've felt so numb inside whenever I returned to Balavata, that risking death and surviving it was the only way to truly feel alive. Stupid, I know."

"I don't think it's stupid." Blue's eyes brimmed with tears, but her voice was steady. "I'm so sorry for all you've lost."

"I'm sorry for all you've lost too." He reached for her hand again and pulled her closer. She leaned against him, her head tipped against his shoulder, and for a moment he wasn't a prince, and she wasn't a commoner. They were just two grieving souls finding safe harbor in each other as they silently watched the storm rush toward them across the sea.

THIRTY-TWO

DINAH STOOD IN the front receiving parlor of the castle, Valeraine's spell safely tucked in her chemise.

She'd done it.

She'd removed every obstacle. Every roadblock that had tried to sabotage her plans. She'd taken over the de la Cours' shop and their talented and useful daughter. She'd caused confusion in several quarters with her fire spell to keep attention on something other than why she'd moved herself and her girls to a farmhouse. And she'd found the spell that Valeraine had used sixteen years ago to seal the wraith into the Wilds out of Dinah's reach. She didn't even need the betrothal anymore. Power—the kind that sent others to their knees regardless of their rank—was so close she could almost touch it.

Now she simply had to take a walk in the garden with the queen, something she'd done hundreds of times over the years, and harvest a bit of the volshkyn bush, and she could do what she'd longed to do every moment since the wraith had first been imprisoned: open the gate.

Footsteps sounded on the stone corridor outside the receiving parlor as Dinah went over the spell's ingredients. She'd been off on her guesses about what formed the wraith's lock, but not by much, and that could easily be attributed to the burned smell and the strange, bittersweet scent she hadn't been able to identify as volshkyn. The other ingredients were stocked in the de la Cours' shop, so once she had the volshkyn, she could head to the Wilds. She'd have to go at night. Until she had the wraith by her side again, it wouldn't do to be seen going so far west by herself. Should anything go wrong with her plan, there would be no explaining why she'd gone to the Wilds, and she'd lose any chance at the betrothal.

Not that she'd need to put one of her daughters on the throne once she had the wraith. She could put herself on the throne and punish everyone who'd had a role in destroying what she'd secretly worked so hard to gain so many years ago.

She'd start with the queen.

"Dinah," the queen said as she swept into the room, leaving her guards posted on either side of the doorway. Adelene's expression was smooth and regal, but there was something in her eyes that raised the hair on the back of Dinah's neck.

"Your Majesty." Dinah swept into an elaborate curtsy while her mind raced.

The queen knew she was staying at the de la Cour house. Kellan would have informed her of that. Perhaps the strange look in her eyes was because she wanted to discuss Blue's situation without overstepping the legal bounds that gave Dinah guardianship.

Or perhaps she wanted to talk about why Kellan had stationed royal guards at the farmhouse to protect Jacinthe and Halette in the absence of Chauveau staff. The parchment in her chemise rustled against her bosom as she rose from her curtsy, and her thoughts steadied. It didn't matter if the queen knew about the debts. Soon, all that would matter would be those whom the wraith killed and those she chose to spare.

"We have much to discuss," the queen said as Dinah moved toward her.

"Shall we walk in the garden?" she asked Adelene. "It would be nice to get some air before the storm hits, and it would give us some privacy for our conversation."

The queen nodded, and together they left the castle and moved to the crushed-seashell path that wound through the royal garden. The sky was a dark blue streaked with gray, and a damp wind slapped at their faces. They'd only gone a few paces past the flowering hedges that bordered the garden when the queen said softly, "I thought we were friends."

Dinah drew back in surprise, and said quickly, "Of course we are, Your Majesty."

"Then why did I have to find out from my son that creditors are going to take your mansion and much of your business interests once the estate review is finished?" The queen's tone was gentle.

When Dinah was quiet, the queen asked, "It was James's gambling, wasn't it?"

Dinah sighed as if weary beyond words. "I tried to stop him. I took over the accounts. Had everything transferred to my name so he couldn't do anything more than lose the coin I allowed to be kept in our coffers at home."

"And he agreed to that?" She sounded surprised.

"I didn't give him a choice." Anger threaded through Dinah's words. "He was going to destroy us. Destroy the entire Chauveau family if given half the chance. My solicitor copied his signature on the documents. I had to. It was the only way to save my daughters and my quarter."

"But it didn't work?"

Dinah took another three steps into the garden, scanning the plants for the dark blue diamond-shaped leaves that marked the volshkyn bush. "He must have copied my signature on documents as well, and he pledged everything we owned to his creditor. When James couldn't pay, his creditor had him killed and served me notice that they would be taking everything owed to them. Including marriage to one of my daughters."

The volshkyn bush wasn't here. She pulled on Adelene's arm to guide her farther into the garden.

The queen brushed past a stone bench with tendrils of ivy snaking up its back. "Of course you couldn't let the other families know, or they'd have tried to buy it out from underneath you. But you could've come to me."

"I know," Dinah said. "But the betrothal period had just begun, and—"

"And you thought you'd trick me into thinking your family would make the strongest alliance to the crown?" Adelene's voice sharpened.

Dinah gritted her teeth and worked to sound like she regretted her choices. "I thought I could turn it around if I just had a little bit of time. And frankly, I was more concerned with how to protect my family and my quarter than with whether we still qualified for the betrothal. I should have thought about how that would appear to you. I'm sorry."

The queen was silent for a moment as they walked. Finally, she said, "I'm concerned about protecting your family and your quarter as well. I'll have the royal magistrate request the debt sheets from James's creditors so we can verify the authenticity of your signature."

They turned toward the center of the garden, where tall oaks with fat trunks spread their limbs over clusters of cheerful yellow, purple, and red flowers. The sky was more gray than blue now, and the wind had a bite to it.

Dinah scanned the area for the volshkyn bush but didn't find it. "Thank you for your help, Adelene."

The queen patted her arm and said quietly, "I'm getting into the habit of asking the royal magistrate to verify signatures lately."

Dinah's skin went cold. "Are you?"

She had to find that volshkyn bush. Quickly, before the queen became more suspicious of her and refused to let her harvest any. Her heart pounded in time with the far-off rumblings of thunder that shook the air over the distant sea.

Drawing in a deep breath, Dinah steadied herself. If the queen knew the truth about Dinah's actions, she'd have already thrown Dinah in the dungeon.

"Tell me," Adelene said, "how did you know Valeraine de la Cour?"

Dinah sent the queen a look of surprise and prepared to lie through her teeth. "We were girlhood friends. You know I was part of the merchant class before I met James. We drifted apart a bit after our marriages—hard to stay close when one of you is running an alchemy shop and the other is learning how to be a member of one of the head families—but we never lost touch. Why?"

Adelene frowned. "I was friendly with Valeraine. Our husbands were close. I never heard her mention you, and yet here you are with guardianship over Blue and the de la Cour property."

Dinah matched the queen's frown with one of her own. "And so you had the guardianship document checked for authenticity? You could have just asked me for the story behind it."

"I did just ask you for a story behind the loss of your mansion and your business titles, and I learned that you had your solicitor fake James's signature on official property deeds." The queen's voice was still soft, still sympathetic, but there was stone beneath it now.

Dinah infused her voice with hurt. "And you think that the fact that I had to stoop so low to avoid utter humiliation and homelessness means I would stoop that low again? For what? To have to take care of some mouthy girl and her decrepit farmhouse? How does that benefit me?"

The queen stopped walking and turned to face Dinah. "I don't know. How does it benefit you?"

Dinah clenched her fists. Let the queen see anger. An innocent woman would be furious at the accusation. "It doesn't benefit me, Adelene. I lost my husband, my home, my business empire, and my income in one fell swoop. A week later, I had to take guardianship over an old farmhouse, an alchemy shop, and a defiant girl who won't even help me clean out her own root cellar, much less be of any assistance with anything else. My girls are miserable. I'd much rather be living at one of James's cousins' homes in the Chauveau quarter, but my responsibility to Valeraine keeps me at the de la Cours'."

The queen held up her hand to stop the flow of Dinah's

words. "You made Blue go down into her root cellar?"

Dinah blinked. "Of everything I just said, that's what you want to discuss? I realize the girl is a friend to your children, but, Adelene, she must be taken in hand. I asked her to do something as simple as go through the boxes of old belongings in the root cellar so we could organize them, and she barely spent twenty minutes working with me before she ran out of the house entirely."

"Valeraine died in the root cellar. Blue was with her for hours after she died until Pierre got home and could fix the broken ladder and get to her." Adelene's tone was a slap, and Dinah quickly blinked a few tears into her eyes.

"Oh no. I didn't realize Blue was with her when she died. Poor thing, I wish she would have just told me."

"Blue doesn't like to talk about it." Adelene shivered as the wind picked up.

She was going to suggest turning back, and Dinah couldn't leave. Not without a leaf from the volshkyn bush.

Quickly, Dinah said, "Speaking of Blue, she asked me to get something for her from your garden. A leaf of some plant from Morcant. Volsh . . . something."

"Volshkyn?" Adelene looked puzzled. "She's never asked me for that. Why does she need it?"

Why would she need it? Dinah scrambled for an acceptable reason and came up with the task Blue had set herself earlier in the day. "She's making protection charms for the betrothal girls. I guess she needs that plant for the potion."

The queen smiled. "That's Blue. Always ready to try to fix what's wrong."

Dinah made herself smile in response. "Perhaps I've been too hard on her in my own grief. The upheaval of my world has been difficult to withstand."

"Your guardianship document held up to examination," Adelene said.

"Of course it did." Dinah promised herself she'd give her solicitor a lovely bonus once the wraith laid waste to her enemies. A man with his talents should be rewarded.

"I won't tell the council about your financial situation, though unfortunately, this takes Jacinthe out of the running for the betrothal." The queen's voice held regret. "I'd so hoped to unite our families, but we must do what's best for the crown."

Dinah nodded, careful to keep her expression blank. What was best for the crown had cost Dinah everything once. It wasn't going to cost her again.

"We should go inside," the queen said, rubbing her arms briskly as a chill descended and the first drops of rain began to fall.

"Agreed. But first, I'll need to get the volshkyn for Blue," Dinah said.

"Over there beneath the rynoir tree. Only take a little bit. It's very potent and takes years to grow back."

"Thank you," Dinah said as she walked toward the rynoir tree, envisioning Adelene's blood and the blood of her children staining the seashell path red.

She had a dinner party to attend tonight at Lady Faure's, and a brunch with Lady Perrin in the morning, but her schedule the following night was clear. Once the midnight bells rang, she would head to the Wilds, and then the people of Balavata would get the reckoning they deserved.

THIRTY-THREE

THE DAY AFTER Blue and Kellan had nearly drowned at sea, he showed up at her doorstep just before breakfast. She opened the door to his knock, Papa's apron wrapped around her, a wooden spoon in her hand.

"Are you cooking?" he asked, his expression hopeful.

"Are you telling me you didn't already eat half the castle's food supply this morning?"

"I only ate one-third of the food supply, so clearly I'm nearly starving at this point." He gave her his charming smile. The one that weeks ago would've made her want to slam the door in his face. This time, something warm and fizzy ignited in her chest and spiraled into her stomach.

She stepped back to let him in and said, "I'm trying to make Grand-mère's fried apple cake recipe."

He sniffed the air. "Smells good. I'd say you're succeeding."

"Papa always did the cooking. I'm still trying to figure out if I'm any good at it, but I think it's a lot like alchemy. It's just the science of making sure the right ingredients go together the right way." She turned toward the stairs. "Should I tell Jacinthe and Halette that you're here? Dinah didn't tell me you were coming for brunch today."

His hand shot out and wrapped around her arm. "I'm not here to see them."

She paused. "Dinah?"

"Nope."

Turning, she gave him a slow once-over as Pepperell wound himself around the prince's legs.

"Obviously, I am here to see your adorable monstrosity of a cat and eat some fried apple cakes." He winked, and she felt a strange heat in her cheeks.

He leaned closer and said softly, "In case it isn't already apparent, I'm here for you, Blue."

The fizzy feeling gushed through her veins, and she winced inwardly. How was she supposed to keep walking away from him when he'd bared his soul to her the day before at the sea and then showed up on her doorstep just to eat breakfast with her? Turning quickly toward the kitchen before he could see her expression, she cast around for something to say. Something normal and non-fizzy-feeling.

"Do you think this is a good idea?"

Ugh. Look who she was asking. The boy who got in street fights and jumped off a cliff into a stormy sea just to feel alive. The gap between his definition of a good idea and hers was an entire canyon.

She stopped at the counter, where her batter bowl rested, and then he was there beside her, leaning on one elbow, his dark eyes boring into hers.

"I'm here because you jumped into the sea to rescue me yesterday, and because I was able to tell you things I've never told anyone else." He stuck a finger in the bowl, dabbed a bit of the batter onto his fingertip, and licked it clean. "And I'm here because I've decided you and I should go west to check on the wraith like the bounty hunter suggested yesterday. Things are hectic right now between the ball in three days and hunting for whoever murdered Marisol and Gen, but knowing if the wraith is still imprisoned, or if we have a much bigger problem on our hands than a rogue witch, is a priority, and we should go there together."

"We should?" she asked in a soft, breathy voice that sounded nothing like her.

Hang it all, she wasn't the type of girl to swoon over a boy. Especially a prince who in three short days would be betrothed to someone else.

But if she was swooning over him, it was his own fault. Defending her from Dinah. Helping her grieve. Caring deeply about her, about his family, and then trusting her with his darkest secret. She'd been so sure she knew him nearly as well as she knew herself, but she'd been wrong, and now she didn't know what to do with him. She couldn't have him. Not the way she wanted. And she also couldn't seem to figure out how to walk away.

"We should," he said. "It will take hours. Hours where there will be no one with us but the pair of trusted guards I brought with me. We'll have a picnic on the way."

Her brows rose. "You want to spend hours with me and go on a picnic three days before your grand ball? Your mother would kill you."

"My mother will get what she wants. I'll do what I have to for the good of the kingdom." He leaned closer to her. "But what I said yesterday at the docks about seizing the moment? I meant it. And I haven't been doing it. Neither have you. I want one day with you, Blue. Just one. Besides, we have to know if the wraith is still locked away before we know how to continue to search for the missing children."

West. To look for Ana and the other children, and to pray they found the wraith locked away where it should be. And to spend hours alone with Kellan. To have a picnic and seize the moment.

Her pulse raced at the thought, and she turned to pour four even circles of batter on her hot skillet. The homey scent of frying apples and vanilla cake surrounded her, reminding her of waking on weekend mornings to Papa making an extravagant breakfast for just the two of them, and sudden tears stung her eyes.

"Are you all right?" Kellan asked quietly.

She sniffed. "I'm fine."

He took the spatula off the counter, edged it under the cakes as bubbles formed and popped along the top, and flipped them as if he spent every morning cooking himself breakfast in the castle.

Maybe he did. She wouldn't wish his appetite on any cook in the kingdom.

"Are you crying because I want to take you on a picnic or because you're cooking apple cakes?"

She dashed an errant tear off her cheek. "Papa made these on weekends."

He rested his hand on the small of her back and rubbed it in gentle circles for a moment before stepping back. "Remember that time he left extra cakes under a towel on the counter?"

"And you and your friend Michel crept in through the open kitchen window and stole the lot." She smiled.

"We crept back out the window, thinking we'd scored the best meal of our lives, preparing to take it to the makeshift tree fort we were building at the back of your orchard, and there was Pierre, standing right behind us, a bucket of water in his hands."

Her smile stretched wider. "I'd never heard you scream like that."

He assumed a regal expression. "I'm a prince. I never scream. Even when a bucket of cold water is thrown over my head, ruining my stash of stolen apple cakes."

She laughed and bumped him out of the way so she could slide the cakes onto a plate. "And then Papa took you both inside, made you clean the kitchen, and then promptly cooked you lunch."

He accepted the plate from her and began hunting for butter and honey.

"It's already on the table." She waved him toward the table and then sat beside him to the plate of cakes she'd been about to eat when he'd knocked.

"Yours are cold," he said and tried to switch plates with her.

"I like them cold." She shoved his plate back in front of him and took a bite. They were good. Nearly as good as Grand-mère's, which was no small feat seeing as how Grand-mère used her wand to transfigure the ingredients into cake, and Blue was stuck with a bowl and a spoon for the same task.

They ate in companionable silence for a few moments, and the fizzy feeling in Blue's veins settled into a warm glow.

Footsteps sounded on the stairs as they finished, and Blue hastily checked that the skillet was still hot. Dinah and Jacinthe were both ill-tempered in the mornings when they were hungry.

"Time to go," Kellan said as he rinsed off the dishes they'd used.

"Go where?" Dinah asked from the doorway. "Are you leaving us already, Prince Kellan? We haven't even had a chance to say hello. Or perhaps your mother has told you there's no need to be courteous to us anymore given our current financial situation."

Dinah's words sounded defeated, but her expression was lit with the same kind of vicious fervor that had sent Blue down into the root cellar hunting for her mother's old recipes.

Kellan met Dinah's eyes, his voice quiet. "A person's wealth doesn't dictate how much courtesy they're owed. A person's treatment of others, however, does."

Dinah moved to sit at the table. "Where is my breakfast, Blue?"

"In the batter bowl," Kellan said before Blue could turn toward the stove. "The skillet is hot. I just flipped my own cakes and can testify that it is remarkably easy to do. I'm sure you'll get the hang of it. Come on, Blue."

"Where are you taking her?" Dinah demanded. "There's work to be done. A ball to prepare for. Maybe we aren't in the running for the betrothal anymore, but we still have appearances to keep up, and Blue is needed to help get my daughters' gowns ready."

"Blue and I are going out." Kellan held Dinah's gaze. "We'll be gone most of the day, so you'll need to see to the gowns yourself. I'm sure, just like flipping cakes in a skillet, it's a skill you'll easily acquire."

Kellan offered his arm to Blue. "Shall we get started? It's going to be a long day."

Blue untied Papa's apron and hung it on its hook. Then she scooped up Pepperell, took Kellan's arm, and walked out of the house. When they reached the porch, she said, "I'm going to leave Pepperell with Grand-mère today. I don't trust Dinah with him."

Kellan followed her down the steps and through the garden. Flowers unfurled for her, vines curling toward her skin as she passed, and Kellan laughed. "It never gets old."

"What doesn't get old?"

"Seeing how plants respond to you. It's like they know you're a friend who understands them. They want you to choose them for your next potion."

As this was precisely what happened with Blue's magic, she gave Kellan a long side-eye. "That's some pretty imaginative thinking on your part, Prince."

He grinned. "We've known each other since we were toddlers, Blue." His voice lowered. "Since before you knew you had to hide your magic."

Her eyes widened, and she shot a quick glance at the house, though they were too far from it now for anyone to overhear them.

"Don't worry. Magic was outlawed because of the wraith. Because it was easier to say all of it was bad than to try to figure out where the line stood between harmless magic and someone who could turn their magic into something deadly. I know your magic is harmless. More than that, I know that you are the kind of person who'd rather die than cause someone else harm."

"You just keep surprising me," she said as Pepperell batted at a butterfly that had circled Blue's hair.

"You keep surprising me too," he said quietly as he lifted a curtain of vines out of the way and then followed her into the apple orchard.

"How?"

He took his time answering. The crash of the sea came closer, and the buzzing of bees flitting from one thing to the next filled the morning air. Blue drew in a deep breath, savoring the sweetness of the apple trees, the tang of sea salt, and the rich soil beneath her. They were nearly to Grand-mère's house, when Kellan said, "I thought you only cared about rules. About getting people in trouble if they didn't see the world in absolutes. I thought you believed you knew all the answers and that you were better than other people."

"Ouch."

He ran a comforting hand down her arm, tangled his fingers briefly with hers, and then pulled away. "But now I know that you're passionate about justice, you're willing to work hard to help anyone who needs it, and you care deeply about what really matters. Maybe we've come at life from different perspectives, but at the core, we're very similar. We love deeply, we fight for those we love, and we put ourselves at risk if that's what it takes to protect others."

She absorbed his words, letting them linger and take root as they walked up the path to Grand-mère's cottage, where the older woman was already out on her porch, a mug of hot chicory in her hands.

"I'm glad we're friends," Blue finally said, though her heart wanted so much more.

"I am too." He smiled.

And then Grand-mère was making a fuss over both of them, getting Pepperell a breakfast of thinly sliced pheasant, and feeding Kellan again, though Blue rolled her eyes and said he'd already eaten enough that morning to feed a small army.

"I would stay and eat at your table all morning long, Miss Destri, but I've promised to take Blue on a picnic out west, so we must be going," Kellan said as he pushed away from the table and carried his plate to the sink.

Grand-mère's eyes sharpened. "What's this about going west?"

"We're looking for Ana," Blue said. "And I need to leave Pepperell with you because I don't trust Dinah with him."

"If that girl hasn't already shown up, Blue, I doubt you'll be able to find her. It's been too long," Grand-mère said. "And if you go too far west, you'll reach the Wilds, which is too dangerous. You know that."

"I'll be with her," Kellan said. "And so will my guards. Including at the Wilds. My mother needs assurances that the wraith is still in its prison."

Grand-mère grabbed Kellan's hand. "Promise me you two won't touch the wraith's gate."

Blue frowned. Of course they weren't going to touch the wraith's gate. She didn't plan to get close enough to be an arm's length away from the thing in case the wraith could somehow reach through the bars. She didn't have a death wish.

Kellan squeezed Grand-mère's hand and met her eyes. "On my life, I swear we won't touch the wraith's gate."

And then they were out the door, down the steps, and heading back to the lane, where Kellan's guards waited to escort them west.

THIRTY-FOUR

SCATTERED ALONG THE road that led west away from Falaise de la Mer, there were a handful of cottages, a number of farms, and a small road that snaked north to skirt the mountain range that loomed ever closer. A long, dark shadow spread across the base of the mountains, growing larger as they left the city far behind.

"Are you nervous about seeing the Wilds?" Kellan took her hand and gave it a comforting squeeze.

Blue nodded and tried not to pay attention to the fact that he still hadn't let go of her hand. "More nervous about the wraith than the forest my mother grew to imprison it."

"She used magic for that, didn't she?"

Blue squinted against the glare of the sun. Surely that was the cause of the heat dancing along her skin like tiny bits of fire. But just in case, she slowly pulled her hand free of Kellan's. "Yes, she did. I know she created the potion that locked the wraith away, but Grand-mère said she had help from the witch's sister, so I have no idea where one magic started and the other ended."

And she wished she did. Her magic worked differently from her mother's. Mama's magic had encouraged things to grow and ripen quickly, which would explain how she grew a dangerous fae forest from a handful of seeds in minutes—but didn't explain how she'd managed to create a lock the wraith's powerful magic couldn't break.

"I don't understand how the lock held. Nothing is ever permanent," she said as they crested a hill and stared at the landscape spread before them. Orchards, vineyards, and a few farmhouses dotted the plains, with the road cutting through the center. In the far distance, the Giant's Fist mountain range was a smudge of green against the sky. And at the base of the mountains, spread along the fringes of the plains, the dark shadow of the Wilds waited for them.

"What do you mean?" he asked as they began moving down the hill, his guards behind them on horseback. Kellan's horse had a large bag of food strapped to its back behind its empty saddle. He'd offered to let Blue ride in the saddle with him, but she'd opted to walk. If she sat that close to him on his horse, she was going to start imagining things that would never be true for her.

"I mean even the most closely bound ingredients can be unbound if you can find something strong enough to break them apart."

He gave her a troubled look. "That's not very reassuring."

"Mama didn't write down the potion she created for the lock. Without knowing the list of ingredients, it would be really hard to find a way to reverse the spell."

"And someone couldn't figure out the ingredients used?

Maybe by taking a sample or by experimenting or something?" he asked. "You figured out the ingredients for the fire spell just by smelling it."

Now she sent him a troubled look of her own. "Actually . . . that's not impossible. It would be difficult if the ingredients were uncommon, but certainly not impossible. Mama must have planned for that, but I can't figure out how."

"Let's hope her plan worked," he said as they passed the next farmhouse. He reached for her hand again, and she gave up pretending she didn't want to keep her hand in his. They spent the next hour walking in silence, his skin warm against hers.

"Let's stop here," Kellan said abruptly and gestured toward a lovely patch of wild meadow grass dotted with purple and yellow flowers. "We need to eat before we go into the Wilds."

Blue didn't argue. Her knees felt strangely shaky, and her heart seemed to tremble in her chest when she looked at the yawning expanse of darkness that spread out before them just past the edge of the meadow they were in.

Was the wraith still there? Would it approach? Blue didn't want to find out. She wanted to turn around and go back. Ride on Kellan's horse with his warm, solid body behind her to anchor her to something better than the sick fear that was crawling up the back of her throat. Close her eyes to the possibility that the wraith was still locked away but that another witch was trying to turn into one.

She wanted to turn away, but she couldn't. Wouldn't. Someone had to check the Wilds, someone had to look at the gate and make sure all was secure, and Blue wouldn't be able to look herself in the eye again if she didn't find the courage to face what was in front of her. For Ana's sake. And for the sake of all the innocents in Balavata who deserved to be safe from the terror of a blood wraith.

"You look like the weight of the kingdom just landed on your shoulders," Kellan said as one of his guards handed him a blanket and the bag of food. He spread the blanket out on the grass, took generous helpings of fruit, cheese, and bread from the bag and gave it to his guards, and then sat and patted the space beside him.

Blue eased down next to him, her eyes still on the Wilds. "I'm afraid of what this means for Balavata." She swallowed hard and made herself say the rest. "And I'm just afraid."

"I know." He leaned forward and tucked one of her curls behind her ear. "But whatever is waiting for us in the Wilds will keep for another few minutes while we eat and steady our nerves. And whatever is there, we'll face it together."

She leaned against his hand before she thought better of it, and his eyes softened. For a long moment, they stared at each other. He leaned closer. She caught her breath, a tiny sound that shattered the silence between them, and he jerked his hand back and looked away.

"Do you want fruit? Bread? I think there are pastries in here too, but I'm not sure. Maybe not. I forgot to check, though I know you love pastries. There might be . . . here. Take what you want. Just . . . look. Pastries." He dumped the bag's contents onto the blanket and then stared at the food, while her brows rose.

"Are you nervous?" she asked, her nerves still tingling, her skin alive in a way it hadn't been a moment ago.

He'd almost kissed her again. Worse, she'd almost kissed him back. And that would mean nothing but heartbreak. Kellan wasn't hers. Would never be hers. The fizzy feeling in her veins, the heat sparking along her skin . . . all that was trouble, and she didn't need this kind of trouble.

Kellan grabbed a peach that was rolling toward the edge of the blanket, and then slowly looked at her again. "I don't want to admit that you make me nervous."

"Too nervous to seize the moment?" she asked, her stomach flipping the way it had when she'd seen him dive off her cliff.

His eyes darkened. "I'm caught between wanting to do and say all the things I think about when I think of you and knowing that I should just enjoy this time with you because in three days, I won't get to be with you like this again. If I do or say too much, it will hurt us both in the end, and I don't want to hurt you."

Blue's lips parted, and he rubbed his forehead before saying, "I'm not supposed to be thinking about you like this. About wanting to talk to you and listen to you and kiss you instead of wanting to spend time with . . . to do the other things on my schedule."

She was going to tell him to stop thinking about her. To pay attention to the girls vying for the betrothal and to the decision he faced in three days. It was the only way to be fair to both of them and to the kingdom.

Instead, she opened her mouth and said, "I'm not supposed to be thinking things about you either."

"You think about me?"

She blew out a breath and grabbed an apple. "Maybe."

A smile tugged at the corner of his lips. "What do you think about when you maybe think about me?"

She took a bite of apple before she was tempted to tell him that she thought about the way he filled a room just by entering.

The kindness in his eyes when he talked about Papa. The way he'd protected her as if she was precious. The fizzy warmth that spiraled through her at the thought of kissing him.

"You're avoiding the question." His smile grew.

She swallowed and said, "Maybe you should tell me what you think about me instead?"

He looked at the peach in his hands, rolling it back and forth across his palm. "I think that you're one of the bravest people I've ever known. And that I like the way I feel when I'm around you. And then sometimes I think maybe . . ." He looked up, and Blue was struck by the sadness in his eyes. "I think I want to dance with you again. I want to hold you. I want to kiss you even though I know I can't."

"No, you can't," she whispered, though she leaned closer to him as she said it.

He stared into her eyes for a long moment, and Blue could see his torment.

She wasn't the only one with that fizzy feeling when they were close.

But he was the prince. She was a commoner. There would never be anything more than friendship between them, and if she really cared about him, she'd help him enter his betrothal with a clear conscience.

Pulling back, she said as casually as she could muster, "We should probably eat lunch instead of kiss."

"That doesn't sound half as fun."

She smiled. "No, it doesn't. But I think spending the day together is as much of a moment as we should seize."

He laughed a little. "You're probably right."

The tension between them eased as they shared a lunch

beneath the hazy summer sun, surrounded by meadow grass and butterflies. And then lunch was over, and it was time to face what waited for them in the Wilds.

Kellan held out his hand. "We go in together, and we stay together. No matter what."

"No matter what," she said, and let his hand swallow hers, his fingers tangling between hers like they belonged.

The meadow ended at the edge of a spongy marshland with scattered stones and tall grass growing in clumps. To the left, the marsh met a cliff that overlooked the glittering expanse of the Chrysós. To the right, the mountains loomed. Kellan and Blue began trekking up the incline that led through the marsh and into the Wilds.

The Wilds spilled across the marsh's edge in a tangle of thick trees, rubbery vines, and dark patches of moss that covered the ground and the bottom of the tree trunks with black. The tree limbs locked together at the top, forming a dense canopy that allowed the faintest slivers of sunlight to drift past. As Blue and Kellan stepped into the Wilds, brushing vines and thorny bushes out of the way, the guards behind them drew their swords.

The gate was at the top of the incline that led deep into the Wilds. Blue and Kellan walked forward, the sounds of the sea, the buzzing of bees in the meadow, and the breeze that had tugged at their clothing all disappearing, absorbed into the thick shroud of silence that held the Wilds in its grasp.

"Oh." The word escaped Blue as if she'd been struck as they climbed past a rotted log, the sunlight barely illuminating their passage, and looked up at the gate.

The path was strewn with bones. Some were still vaguely shaped like small humans. Some were just scattered pieces lying about. Closer to the gate, there were three shapes that still had clothing on. All the shapes were smaller than Blue.

Kellan cursed, and one of the guards behind them turned and vomited into the bushes.

"Children," Blue said, her voice catching on a terrible grief that was rising to choke her. "Someone is bringing the children here and killing them."

Kellan pulled her closer to his side, though it was hard to tell if it was for her comfort or for his. His eyes were dark pools of horror, and his mouth was grim. "We'll find whoever is doing this. We'll put a stop to it."

Blue pulled free of Kellan and walked closer to the gate. Closer to the bodies that still wore clothes.

"Blue, stop."

"I have to see." Her voice was ragged. Tears gathered in her eyes as she passed a bundle of bones from a child who couldn't possibly have been more than three years of age.

What kind of monster did something like this?

She reached the first clothed body. A boy who looked to be about five years old. Probably the one Lucian had told her about. Dread sank into her as she moved on, shivering as the gate came fully into view.

It was a narrow thing made of iron. No wider than her own front door, and wedged between two massive oaks, their bark entirely covered by black moss. The lock was a metallic rope woven in and out of the bars—she could see a strand of silver, a strand of gold, and a strand of rose lead, which was smart. A good way to bind the potion. The triple strength of the metals combined with the other ingredients would make it harder to break.

But someone must think it could be broken. Someone must believe they could free the wraith, and that the monster would be grateful enough for the many sacrifices brought to this gate that it would do its releaser's bidding.

Kellan joined her, and they stepped closer, their harsh breathing the only sound.

Blue stared at the bodies that lay just in front of the gate. One was a young boy with a thatch of curly black hair not much different than Kellan's. One was a slender girl with long brown hair and pale skin.

Ana.

Blue's heart broke, and the last shred of hope she'd been desperately clinging to dissolved. She fell to her knees beside Ana's body and carefully smoothed the girl's hair away from her face.

"Her arms," Kellan breathed, and Blue looked down.

Ana's arms had been torn open, two perfect circles with jagged edges. Blood stained her arms, though the rest of her skin was incredibly pale.

"She was drained," Kellan said. Neither one of them needed help remembering the stories. The wraith had once been a witch who longed for more power than she had, and so she'd begun drinking the blood of innocents, taking their lives, their energy for her own. It had increased her power, but it had also turned her from fully human into a wraith who needed blood to survive.

The stories said the mark of the wraith was a circle with jagged edges—teeth marks. The blood would be drained from the body, leaving the skin gray and translucent. Any doubt that the blood wraith was killing again, and indeed from the look of some of these bones had been killing for the past sixteen years of its imprisonment, was gone.

"They should have just killed the wraith," Blue said, anger warming her voice. "Destroyed it like the monster it is, and then this would never have happened."

"I think they tried," Kellan said. "But it was too powerful. The best they could do was contain it."

Blue straightened Ana, holding her nose when a wave of sickly sweet decay hit her.

"Leave her be, Blue. We know the truth now. We should go."

"It's disrespectful." Blue swallowed past the tears, the anger. "Leaving her like this. She should at least look like she's at peace, instead of being discarded like she was nothing."

She tried to fix Ana's dress, to have it lie over her body gracefully like it would had she been given a proper burial. Something pricked Blue's finger, and she drew back, shaking her hand as blood welled.

"All right. It's all right." Kellan sank to the ground beside her. "I'll help."

He gently combed Ana's hair to lie neatly around her and then worked on smoothing her dress. Blue watched Ana's face, a strange buzzing gathering in her blood and heading toward her hands.

She turned her head and stared at the gaping maw of the Wilds. At the gate and the threads of metal that held it closed.

A shadow detached itself from the darkness behind a clump of vines, and the buzzing within Blue became a scream of pain and power as a shimmering, smokelike human shape undulated closer. The dark pits where its eyes would have been were fixed on Blue.

The bells on the road behind them rustled gently, a soft melody that sounded like wind chimes. The wraith moved closer, and the bells rang faster, their clappers striking their iron sides with relentless fury. A wild, discordant song swirled into the air, filling Blue's senses with rage and longing as she locked eyes with the wraith.

She needed to touch the monster. To press her skin to the gate and reach through it. The need was a craving—a powerful ache rising from some dark, unfathomable place within her—and it would not be denied. The monster would know pain then. It would know punishment for its heinous crimes. All she had to do was touch it. Her magic, usually an ember in her palm, was liquid fire in her veins. If she could just wrap her magic around the wraith, she could destroy the monster. She was sure of it.

"Blue, no!"

Kellan slammed into her, knocking her to the ground and wrapping himself around her. She blinked and stared around her in confusion.

When had she stood to her feet? Why had her hand been a breath away from the lock at the gate? She didn't realize she'd actually been reaching for it.

The wraith opened its mouth and wailed, a scream of fury and anguish that scraped the air like a sword, blending with the bells, a storm of anguished rage trapped in its prison.

Kellan pulled back, his eyes wild. "What were you doing?"

"I don't know!" She looked over his shoulder as the wraith rushed for the gate, its wail shaking the ground beneath her. "I don't even remember standing up and moving toward the gate."

"We're leaving." Kellan rolled them away from the gate and then climbed to his feet, keeping her hand securely in his.

She didn't argue. She was shaking, and the magic in her blood was still hurling itself toward the wraith.

What did that mean? Was it just a response to another creature with magic? Or had Grand-mère suspected something like this might happen all along when she warned them not to touch the gate?

"You scared me more than any stupid risk I've ever taken," Kellan said as they left the Wilds and entered the marsh again.

"I scared myself." Her hands were still trembling.

Abruptly Kellan stopped walking and dragged her into his arms. Burying his face against her hair he said, "Promise me you'll stay away from here. Forever."

"I promise," she said as she wrapped her arms around him and held on until the shaking stopped, the bells went still, and the wraith eventually fell silent.

THIRTY-FIVE

KELLAN WAS STILL shaken when he returned to the castle after dropping Blue off at the farmhouse. Even the knowledge that she was safe, that the wraith couldn't break out of its prison and come for her, didn't make him feel any better.

Children had been regularly sacrificed to feed the appetite of a monster. To keep it strong.

And Blue had nearly touched the gate. Nearly reached through it to where the wraith was waiting on the other side, its miserable pits for eyes focused solely on her.

A chill raced down his spine as the truth hit home. The wraith hadn't looked at him once. Hadn't acknowledged the guards with their swords. It only had eyes for Blue, and Blue had somehow only had eyes for it.

There was a mystery there that needed to be unraveled, but he wasn't sure where to start.

And one look at his mother's face when he entered the family's wing of the castle told him he wasn't going to have time to think about it.

"Where have you been?" she demanded, giving him a look that usually prompted him to start making amends even before he'd figured out just how much of his crimes she knew.

"I had something important to take care of."

"Oh, did you?" Her brows rose, and he stilled his hands before he could reach up to adjust the collar of his shirt, which suddenly felt too tight.

"Yes. And you'll be glad I did." It was always best to sell his misdeeds as something that would benefit her. It didn't always stop the sword from falling, but it often softened the blow.

"I'll tell you what I'd be glad of." She rose from the settee where she'd been waiting for him. The window at her back let in the rays of the dying sun, painting her tall profile in orange and crimson, like a warrior of fire.

"Mother—"

"I'd be glad if my son kept to his schedule so that I didn't have to reassure head families, reschedule the hairdresser, and make excuses to any number of people who showed up at the castle today for their appointments only to be told the prince wasn't in residence."

"I left a note for—"

"For your secretary. Yes, he showed me. Unfortunately, it was far too late to notify your morning appointments. And so three days before your betrothal ball—*three days*—you had members of various head families here to see you, to bring you their concerns or their suits, but you weren't here. What do you think they assumed from that?"

He risked a look at her face and wisely decided not to reply.

She was far from finished.

"Now you have the Roches thinking you've already chosen against them since you didn't bother to meet with them. You have the Evrards thinking you aren't committed to finding justice for Marisol. And—"

"Now, wait a minute—"

"And you have Dinah Chauveau here spreading the word that instead of being in the castle where you belong, you were on a picnic with Blue. A *picnic*." She threw the last word at him like it was a weapon.

"Not just a picnic," he said and waited to see if she was ready to listen.

She frowned but stayed silent.

"After our conversation yesterday on the docks, I decided I should check the Wilds. Make sure the wraith was still there. And yes, I took Blue with me. She was able to identify the spell used to burn people. If there was something wrong at the wraith's prison, I thought she could be helpful."

And he'd needed a day with her. Maybe he hadn't kissed her like he'd dreamed of doing, but he'd had her by his side. No Dinah. No mother. No interruptions. It was the closest thing to getting what his heart wanted as he was ever going to have, and he refused to regret it.

"Kellan," his mother said on a sigh, "didn't you think that three days before your ball, with the head families pressing their suits and a murder investigation underway, wasn't the best time to go?"

"Yes," he said, and her brows lifted in surprise. "But when will there be a good time, Mother? After the ball when I'll be busy placating the families who weren't chosen while simultaneously taking over control of the throne? After I'm crowned king and all the responsibility lands on me? You heard Hansel and Gretel yesterday. We have to get control of this situation with the missing children and the rogue witch, and we have to do it fast."

A tiny frown etched into her forehead. "You could've sent anyone to check on the wraith."

"I don't want to be the kind of king who uses others to do the most dangerous tasks."

"And it didn't hurt that you got to spend the day with Blue."

His pulse jumped, and this time he couldn't stop himself from tugging at his collar.

"Son, I'm not blind. I see the way you light up when you talk about her. I noticed how you two looked at each other yesterday. I adore Blue. But she's a commoner. You can't fall in love with—"

"We found the children," he blurted, as much to get the news out as to stop her from saying what he didn't want to hear.

He knew he wasn't allowed to be in love with Blue. Unfortunately, he wasn't sure his heart was paying attention to the laws of his kingdom.

"You found them?" The queen took a step toward him. "Where?"

He met her gaze and tried to keep his voice steady, though the horror of what he'd seen was a slick, oily rock lodged in his stomach. "At the wraith's gate."

She stumbled back, hit the edge of the settee, and sank onto its cushions. "No."

"It was horrible. There were . . . someone has been feeding the wraith all this time." His voice shook.

"All this time," she repeated, staring at him with horror in her eyes. "The gate?"

"Still closed. Locked securely, as far as I could tell, though I'm not an expert."

"No, but Blue is. Her mother created the spell that locked it. Did Blue seem to think it was weakening?"

He was in no mood to discuss Blue's strange reaction to the wraith or the gate or whatever had happened to make her stretch her hand out toward the lock. "She didn't say anything either way."

The queen drew a shuddering breath. "The wraith—*Marielle*, that cursed witch—cannot be loosed again, Kellan. It took Valeraine, Marielle's sister, and nearly one-third of your father's army working together to lock it away the first time. The streets ran red with blood spilled by that creature."

He nodded. "Then we have to figure out who is feeding it. Stop the food supply"—he choked over the memory of all those small bones and cleared his throat roughly—"and you weaken the wraith. Maybe even starve it to death."

"I'll order the magistrates to continue efforts to round up any homeless children in their quarters. I've already found acceptable housing for them. For now, I'll send some of our staff to run the children's shelter, and after the ball, we'll figure out how to make it all work so they can be safe and cared for."

"I'll talk to Blue and—"

"I think you and Blue have done enough talking for now."

He fell silent. She was right. He knew she was. But his traitorous heart wanted to argue. Wanted to sneak out of the castle window and go see Blue again that night.

His mother stood and nodded toward his bedroom suite. "You're dismissed. And if you disappear off these castle grounds again anytime between now and the ball without my express permission, I will make your life absolutely miserable. Are we clear?"

"Yes, ma'am," he said, and made a hasty escape to his bedroom. He shut the door behind him, allowed his valet to undress him, and then dismissed the man so he could fall onto his bed and close his eyes.

So many bones.

Blue reaching for the gate, a fevered light in her eyes.

The way she'd leaned toward him in the meadow, her lips parted.

He should have kissed her. He was never going to get another chance, and he'd spend the rest of his life regretting it.

A hand tapped his shoulder, and his eyes opened. Nessa stood there in her pink nightgown, fluffy white slippers on her feet. Her hands flew.

You still know how to make Mother angry.

He sighed. "I know."

Was it worth it?

"Maybe." He wasn't going to tell his little sister about the graveyard of children's bones. About the wraith kept strong on the blood of innocents. Or about wishing he'd kissed Blue just once.

She hopped up onto the bed beside him, and he scooted until he was sitting with his back to the headboard to make room for her.

Who are you going to choose at the ball?

He closed his eyes again. "I don't know."

She smacked him lightly on his knee. He opened his eyes.

Pay attention. I'm going to help you.

He smiled, though it felt so much harder to do than it had a few weeks ago. "My little sister is giving me marriage advice?"

I'm old enough to understand how love works.

He ruffled her hair, and she batted his hand away. "So what is your advice, O wise one?"

Which girl would make you want to move back to Loch Talam if you had to sit across from her every morning at breakfast?

He laughed, and Nessa's eyes sparkled. "I'm not going to answer that in case I end up having to choose one of the girls who makes that list."

Nessa's expression grew serious. *All right, new question. Which girl would you regret not joining for breakfast every morning?*

Blue's face flashed across his mind, and he shook his head. "I don't know."

She gave him a perfect imitation of their mother's glare. *Yes, you do.*

"Nes, I like several of the girls enough to enjoy eating breakfast with them."

That's not what I asked, but fine. I'll change the question. Ready?

"Always."

Who do you want to kiss?

He stayed quiet.

She smiled, wide and triumphant. *I knew it. There is someone you want to kiss. Wait. Have you already kissed her?*

"I am not discussing kissing with my little sister."

But I want to know!

"We don't always get what we want."

She rolled her eyes. *Who do you want to tell your darkest secrets to?*

"Who says I have any dark secrets to tell?" he said, though Blue's eyes, filled with understanding as he unburdened himself to her, filled his thoughts.

I'm your sister. I know you have secrets. All right, last question, and this is most important.

"Hit me with it."

Which girl would you die to protect?

He quit trying to get Blue's face out of his head. She'd taken up residence when he hadn't been paying attention, and now it seemed impossible not to think of her with every question Nessa asked.

Well?

"I'd die to protect you," he said, and meant it with every fiber of his being. Pulling her into a quick hug, he said, "Thank you for your help, little bird, but I'm afraid you've missed one very important thing."

What did I miss?

"I don't get to make this decision based on who I love. I have to decide what's best for our kingdom. If I'm lucky, my emotions will follow my decision like it did for our parents. If I'm not lucky, well, then at least I'll have brought peace and prosperity to Balavata."

But what about you?

"What about me?" He pulled back to look at her. At her nimbus of curls and her big brown eyes. At the dimple in the corner of her left cheek and the joyful energy that radiated from her.

You deserve to be loved. You deserve someone who would die to protect you.

"Then let's hope the girl I choose eventually feels that way. Now, off to bed with you." He gave her a quick kiss on the cheek and watched her leave his room. And then he blew out the light beside his bed and lay in the dark for hours thinking of bones, magic, and kissing Blue.

THIRTY-SIX

BLUE ROSE WITH the sun, though it took immense effort to force herself out of bed without Dinah's furious prodding. She wanted to leave the house before Dinah or the girls woke and began giving her a long list of chores to complete. Or worse, before Dinah decided she needed yet another spell of Mama's and made Blue go back down into the root cellar again.

Dressing in one of her plain gardening shirts and pants, she wrapped a blue headscarf over her twists and crept out of the bedroom. Halette turned over as Blue crossed the threshold into the hall, but the girl remained asleep.

Pepperell meowed, twining around her legs, and she hushed him. Scooping him up, she hurried down the hall, careful to miss the boards that creaked. When she got to Papa's office, the room Dinah had claimed as her own, she froze.

The door was already open. The blankets Dinah used as she slept on Papa's sofa were tossed carelessly onto the floor. Dinah was already up.

Blue's shoulders slumped, and she pressed her face against Pepperell's fluff as her plans to escape early and spend the morning with Grand-mère discussing the wraith, her magic, and Kellan dissolved into a weary resignation.

Pepperell purred, digging his claws into her shoulder as he kneaded happily.

"Watch yourself, you great lug," she said as she moved down the stairs. There was no point in avoiding the creaking boards now. Dinah would be waiting in the kitchen for her breakfast or pacing the little parlor with a list of tasks in her hand. Not tasks for her or her daughters, of course. Just for Blue.

For what felt like the thousandth time, Blue wondered what Mama had been thinking. How had she ever been close to a woman like Dinah? Had Dinah changed that much in the sixteen years since the guardianship agreement was signed, or had she simply fooled Mama into thinking she would be the motherly sort?

They were useless questions. Mama wasn't here to ask, and Blue had to either find her own way out of this or endure it until her next birthday. She'd thought Dinah would be satisfied with the spell she'd given her. Dinah had said she'd leave Blue alone once she had what she wanted, but it had been several days, and Dinah showed no signs of leaving yet.

Resolved to ask Dinah about her plans to move herself and her daughters out of the farmhouse, Blue rounded the bottom of the stairs and peeked into the parlor. Empty.

She sighed. That meant Dinah not only had a list of tasks, but she also wanted breakfast. Blue trudged into the kitchen, Pepperell hanging over her shoulder like a sack of bolla roots, and then stopped. It was empty too.

Slowly turning in a circle, Blue held her breath and strained to hear anything. The house was quiet. Was Dinah in the garden? On the porch? The root cellar? Blue eyed the door that led to the cellar and then backed out of the kitchen.

If Dinah wasn't present to force Blue into doing her grunt work for her, Blue certainly wasn't going to seek her out. Grabbing her gathering basket, she hurried outside.

No Dinah on the porch, in the yard, or in the garden. Blue didn't wait for her luck to change. Hurrying through the garden, ignoring the buzzing of magic in her veins as the plants reached for her, she moved into the orchard.

Yesterday's trip west was at the center of Blue's thoughts, a sharp-edged knife worrying at her seams. She'd found Ana, though now she wished she hadn't. She'd seen the horrifying proof that someone was feeding the wraith. She'd nearly kissed the crown prince and still wished she had, though she knew it would break her heart.

And somehow her magic—her small, plant-loving magic—had turned into a firestorm that had her reaching for the wraith, who would devour her without hesitation.

If Kellan hadn't been there . . . She shuddered and steered her thoughts away from the horrible images that played out in her head.

If Kellan hadn't been there, she'd be dead. One more body collapsed at the gate, a sacrifice to a monster who preyed on the innocent. And somehow, Blue was sure, Grand-mère had suspected that might happen.

The sky was the pale blue of shirella fruit, and the rhythmic shush of the waves rolling in soothed Blue as she reached the little grove that hid Grand-mère's cottage. This time the older woman wasn't waiting on the porch, but by the time Blue and Pepperell reached the steps, she'd opened the front door.

"Are you alone?" She squinted past Blue.

"Pepperell counts." Blue climbed the steps, plopped Pepperell onto the porch, and set her gathering basket down. She'd forgotten to empty it out the last time she'd harvested because the second she'd gone indoors, Dinah had forced her down into the root cellar.

"Of course Pepperell counts, the handsome boy. I was wondering if the other handsome boy was with you again."

"Kellan?" Blue ordered herself not to blush. "Why would he be with me?"

"Because my granddaughter is up at the crack of dawn, and that takes either a very handsome prince—"

"Grand-mère!"

"Or an emergency." Grand-mère's mouth tightened. "Is this an emergency? Has that snake of a woman done something? I'll get my wand."

"No emergency!" Blue pulled her grandmother into a tight hug. "I thought I'd get up early enough to get out of the house to see you before Dinah woke up and told me I couldn't go."

"That was smart of you." Grand-mère reached a hand up to stroke Blue's hair. "We'll need to redo these curls soon. You've been swimming, haven't you?"

Swimming. Rolling in the dirt outside the wraith's gate. Riding home on horseback, pressed close to Kellan's warmth. Blue had been up to any number of things, only one of which she wanted to share with Grand-mère.

"We can do that soon, but I don't have time this morning. I'm making protective charms for the girls who are trying for the betrothal, and for Kellan and Nessa, and the potion will be ready this afternoon."

"So you thought you'd come out here and enjoy the fresh, early-morning air with an old woman?"

"There's nothing enjoyable about early morning. Unless you have peach tea and a fritter or two?" She gave Grand-mère her best hopeful look, and the older woman laughed.

"Come inside. I'll fix you a meal. And then we can talk about whatever brought you here."

"How do you know I want to talk about something?" Blue asked as they went inside, Pepperell at their heels.

"Because I have my granddaughter memorized." She waved her wand and set the teapot on to boil while the ingredients for maple fritters began assembling in a batter bowl. "Which is why I also know that you're starting to look at Kellan like he's something special."

"He is something special, but not for me," Blue said firmly, and willed herself to believe it. To let it be the truth that ruled her instead of the pointless longing to wrap herself around him and listen to him share the things that were hidden in his heart.

"You'd best keep that in mind." Fritter batter hit the skillet that had warmed itself on the stove while a teacup left its hook and floated over to the teapot. "He's a good boy. That reckless impulsiveness and thirst for proving himself that got him in trouble when he was younger has grown into steady courage and a strong will bent toward protecting his kingdom. But that same strong will is what will keep him from acting on the feelings he seems to be developing for you."

Blue risked a quick look at Grand-mère. "Kellan can't have feelings for me."

Grand-mère snorted. "That boy was in and out of this cottage as much as you were over the years. I have him memorized too."

The fritter flipped itself, and the tea poured into the cup, releasing the juicy sweet scent of peaches. Grand-mère whisked open the kitchen window, letting the breeze dance through her wind chimes.

Blue held the idea of Kellan truly having feelings for her close for a moment, letting its bittersweet ache pierce her, before gently setting it aside. She couldn't change what was written in stone, and neither could he. And there were far more important things at stake than the way she felt for the prince.

"I didn't come here to talk about Kellan," she said as the fritter flipped itself onto a plate and headed toward the table. "I came to talk about the wraith."

Grand-mère's lip curled.

"And about my magic."

The older woman slowly pivoted away from the window, pinning Blue with a look. "What do the two have to do with each other?"

"Don't you have a guess?"

Grand-mère held Blue's gaze for a long moment while the plate clinked against the tabletop and Pepperell heaved himself onto the windowsill, his tail sending the closest wind chime swinging. Finally, the older woman moved to the table and sat heavily in the chair across from Blue. "Tell me what happened."

Careful to include every detail from the moment they'd entered the Wilds, Blue told the story of finding the children's bodies, trying to arrange Ana so that she looked peaceful, and then suddenly finding herself reaching for the wraith until

Kellan tackled her and held her back.

Grand-mère reached her arms across the table. "Let me see your hands."

Blue laid her hands in her grandmother's and sat quietly while Grand-mère examined them. When she got to the small cut on Blue's index finger, she stopped.

"When did this happen?"

Blue frowned. "While I was trying to fix Ana's dress. I guess I caught it on a thorn or something beneath her. I'm not sure—"

"Your magic turned from a buzzing to a firestorm after you cut yourself?"

Blue nodded slowly.

"And that's when you felt like you should touch the gate?"

"Not just the gate. The wraith itself. I thought if I just touched it, I could destroy it. And it seemed to be waiting for me to do that because it looked right at me. Came straight for me. I don't think it ever looked at Kellan once."

Grand-mère pulled her wand and waved it over Blue's hand, muttering under her breath.

"What is it? What do you see?"

Grand-mère lowered her wand. "Nothing. I thought if there was some kind of curse on you, some spell that would cause you to be the wraith's next meal, then we'd have a clue as to who was behind it all. Only one person with a motive has been close enough to you lately to have cursed you."

Blue considered her words. "You think Dinah could be behind this?"

"You don't?"

"I know she's a disagreeable person, but it's a big leap from disagreeable to murderer. Kellan told me her guardianship document held up under our verification process, so while she's difficult to be around, I can't accuse her of anything else."

Grand-mère made a noise of disgust. "I don't believe for one second that she was friends with my daughter. Certainly not close enough for Valeraine to give guardianship to her instead of to me. Maybe she did a good job of it, but Dinah faked that guardianship agreement, and it must be because she wants something. But what could you possibly have that she wants?"

A chill scraped over Blue. "A recipe. She wants one of Mama's old potion recipes. Something with a rare ingredient."

Grand-mère's eyes sharpened. "Does she, now?"

"She made me go down into the root cellar to look through Mama's things."

"Oh, Blue." Grand-mère grasped Blue's hands tightly. "I'm sorry."

Blue blinked away the sheen of tears that gathered, and said, "I took some old parchment from the closet in Mama's old bedroom here and created a potion that I passed off as one of Mama's. Added volshkyn bush as the rare ingredient. Dinah was thrilled, and we haven't had to search through anything else, so I think she was satisfied."

"So maybe she was looking for something to sell, like she let you assume." Grand-mère turned Blue's hands over again and looked at the healing cut. "Or maybe she was looking for a very specific old potion, and once she realizes she didn't get it, she'll be furious."

Blue's breath caught in her lungs as terrible possibilities unfurled before her. "You think she wants the spell Mama used to lock away the wraith? Why would anybody want that?"

Grand-mère looked grim. "I think we have far too many

coincidences here not to acknowledge it as a possibility. Of course, she won't find the spell. Valeraine never wrote it down. Wouldn't even tell it to me in case someone thought to force it out of me."

"But that also means that if the person who is feeding the wraith figures out the spell's ingredients, we won't know how to reverse their spell. We won't know where to start."

"Oh, I think my granddaughter would know where to start." Grand-mère turned Blue's hands over again and looked at the cut. "I've always wondered something."

"What?"

"Your magic helps you find ingredients that want to be used. Helps you instinctively know how to bond them into something new." Grand-mère lifted her eyes to Blue's. "Magic is in our blood."

Blue's heartbeat thundered in her ears. "And you think when my blood was exposed to the wraith that it wanted to bond with me?"

"Have you ever had anything strange happen when you've bled on your ingredients?"

Blue flashed back to the dancing fern leaf in her basket. The one that had mysteriously bonded with the walla berry juice without the usual alchemy she used to combine them. She'd cut herself right before harvesting them. "In my basket on the porch."

Blue explained what had happened as they hurried to the porch. Grand-mère lifted the leaf and examined the deep purple veins where the walla berry juice had fused with it. "You bled on this?"

"I must have. I'd cut myself, and there was blood smeared across my palm."

Grand-mère held the leaf up to the light and then said softly, "You know what this means?"

Blue shivered. "That my blood not only calls to plants but somehow performs alchemy on them too?"

"Yes. And the wraith is a living being, just like everything else you harvest. Your magic must be interpreting the monster's longing for freedom as a need to be harvested." Grand-mère's voice shook. "If you had touched it, if it had sunk its teeth into you and drank your blood, it could've bonded with anything else you were touching."

Blue's knees trembled, and she abruptly sank onto the porch beside her basket. "I was touching Kellan."

Grand-mère lowered herself to the step beside Blue. "And you were touching freedom. You were touching the world outside the gate."

"Did you suspect this? Is that why you didn't want me to go?"

Grand-mère gave a short, hard laugh. "If I'd suspected this, you would never have come within an hour's walk of the Wilds, Kellan or no. No, I didn't want you to go because I saw what the wraith did to children while it walked our streets. And I heard your mother cry for months afterward whenever she tried to talk about locking it away. She made me promise I would keep you from the wraith. I thought it was simply because she didn't want to risk losing you. Now I wonder if she already knew what your blood could do."

"She wasn't trying to protect me from the wraith," Blue said softly. "She was trying to protect all of Balavata from what the wraith could do through me."

THIRTY-SEVEN

THE PROTECTION SPELL Blue had begun two days ago was ready. She donned gloves, grabbed a pair of tongs, and set out fourteen small glass vials. She'd already placed a hair from each person who needed protection into a vial and marked the bottom with their initials. Now she lifted each vial with the tongs and carefully poured an ounce of the spell inside. The liquid swirled in streaks of pink and silver and smelled like honey and musk.

When each vial held an ounce, Blue scraped the bottom of the cauldron she'd used to brew the potion and came up with slivers of the pink sapphire she'd used to concentrate the power of the spell. Slipping one tiny shard of the jewel into each vial, she corked them, sealed them with a dab of black wax, and pushed one end of a silver chain into the wax so the chain would be permanently attached once the wax dried.

Lucian waited by the storeroom door. Dinah still hadn't made an appearance, and Blue decided that meant the woman had what she wanted and would now leave her alone.

"Lucian, could you come here, please?" she called. When he joined her at her counter, she gathered all the vials except for Kellan's and Nessa's and showed him the labels. "I need these delivered to each of the head families. They should be expecting them since they willingly gave up a strand of each girl's hair three days ago."

Lucian packed them into his bag, but before he could leave, Blue pulled him close. "Remember what happened to Ana. Don't go anywhere with anyone. Not even for a job. Promise me."

"I promise," he said, and Blue's heart ached.

She'd told him about finding Ana when they'd first entered the shop. Asked him to warn the other street kids. Held him while he cried and shed some tears of her own.

"Hurry, now. And stay safe," she said as she sent him on his way.

As soon as he left for the long trek to each head family's home in Falaise de la Mer's nine quarters, Blue packed up the other two vials and locked the shop. Then she hurried through the city streets toward the castle. She'd give the necklaces to Nessa and ask her to pass Kellan's along to him. It was better that way. If she didn't see him, she wouldn't be tempted by what she couldn't have.

The sun hung heavy in the sky, a ripe orange waiting to be plucked. Soon dusk would fall, and Blue didn't want to be alone on the city streets after dark. Not after seeing the wraith come for her. Not after hearing it scream while she was surrounded by the bones of the children it had devoured.

She picked up the pace and was nearly out of breath when she approached the guards at the castle's entrance. They nodded respectfully to her and let her pass. The advantages of being a frequent visitor.

She didn't want to be a frequent visitor once Kellan married someone else. Didn't want to see him walking arm in arm with his chosen bride and imagine all the things she wished she'd said to him. The things she wished she'd done with him when she had the chance.

The butler informed her that Nessa was in the royal garden, and Blue opted to skirt the south side of the castle rather than walk its halls, where she might run into Kellan. She reached the garden's main path soon enough and ducked beneath the hanging roses that twined around the raised arch that spanned the entrance.

The path wound through regal oaks, large iron pots with cheerful collections of flowers in riotous colors, and small groves of cypress and shirella trees. She hadn't found Nessa yet, and nerves sparked as the shadows stretched longer, and the sun dipped closer to the horizon.

She'd just entered a grove of gently swaying shirella trees, their branches laden with the pale blue fruit, their glossy green leaves blocking out all but fragments of the sunlight, when she heard footsteps on the path. Turning to face the way she'd just taken, she said softly, "Nessa?"

Something rustled behind her, prickling the hair on the back of her neck. Whirling, she ran straight into Kellan. His arms shot out to steady her, and he tipped his face down to look at her.

"Blue? What are you doing out here? Are you all right?"

"You aren't supposed to be here."

He cocked his head. "I live here."

"Not in the garden." How was she supposed to avoid the

longing she felt for him when he was standing right in front of her? "You should leave. Or I should leave. I'll leave."

She stayed exactly where she was. His hands ran down her arms, and the fizzy feeling exploded through her. She narrowed her eyes.

He really was making this impossible.

"I'm leaving."

"So you said." He leaned closer, until all that stood between them was the faint, hazy glow of the sun sifting in through the shirella trees. "But here you are."

"Kellan."

"Blue." His voice was soft with longing, and his hands found hers, pressed close, and held. "Just stay here with me for a moment. One moment where we pretend nothing else exists. Will you do that?"

"Yes." She breathed the word against all her better judgments.

Two more days, and he would belong to someone else. He wouldn't hold her hand or show up for breakfast at the farmhouse. She wouldn't ride horseback with him or sit with him on the shoreline while he trusted her with his heart.

His skin was warm against hers, and she tilted her head up to look at him. He smiled, though his eyes were sad.

"I'm not coming to the ball," she said quietly, the decision made as the words left her mouth.

"But—"

"I can't." She met his gaze, begged him to understand what she didn't want to say. What she had no right to say. "It will be hard enough without being there to witness it myself."

"I'm sorry," he said, his fingers still tangled with hers. "I've made a mess of this whole thing. I shouldn't have spent so much time with you. I shouldn't have told you my secrets. And I shouldn't have asked you to stay here with me. I had no right. I thought it was only my heart on the line, and that whatever time I spent with you would be worth the heartache afterward. I didn't consider the possibility that your heart was on the line too. Please believe me. I didn't mean to fall in love with you."

Love. The word pierced Blue's heart with all of its pain and possibilities. Two more days of possibilities with Kellan was all she had.

It was going to have to be enough.

She closed the distance between them and pressed her lips to his. For an instant, the kiss was soft and sweet, and then he let go of her hands so he could wrap his arms around her and drag her against him. Nothing existed but the rough pressure of his mouth and the heat of his skin. She tilted her head to get a better angle, and someone cleared their throat behind her.

Blue jerked away from Kellan, and he took one look behind her and hastily dropped his arms. Turning, Blue found herself face-to-face with the queen.

"Your Majesty." Blue fumbled into a curtsy, her cheeks flaming.

The only thing worse than being caught kissing the prince she had no claim to was being caught by his *mother*.

"Mother, I can explain," Kellan said.

"Oh, I don't think an explanation is needed." The queen's voice was calm, but there was fire in her eyes. "I'm not so old that I don't remember stealing kisses in a garden."

"It was one kiss," Kellan said quietly. "It doesn't change what has to happen in two days."

The ache that had opened in Blue's heart when Kellan said he loved her grew into something sharp.

"It's not just one kiss," the queen said firmly. "It's you giving your heart to someone you can't marry at the expense of the girl who will be your bride. And it's you taking the heart of someone who can never have you."

"He didn't take what I didn't offer," Blue said. To her horror, tears threatened, and she blinked rapidly to keep them at bay.

"He shouldn't have taken anything at all." The queen smiled sadly at Blue. "We all love you, Blue. If I could pick the perfect girl for my son, I couldn't find anyone better. But we would have a mutiny on our hands if the throne went to someone outside the head families. I have to think about the political consequences and the good of our kingdom. *Kellan* has to think about the good of our kingdom." She aimed the last sentence like a dagger at her son.

"I have been," he shot back, his voice rising. "I've played every game. Listened to every veiled threat, every pretty lie, every attempt to sway my opinion for the benefit of one head family over another. I've smiled and flirted and tried to protect all of us from dying over this."

He turned and began pacing, frustration vibrating through him. "I've accepted that my own feelings can never be a priority. That what my heart wants isn't important if that's not what the kingdom needs. But for one moment—just one—before I commit to the betrothal, before I have to start playing another political game to bribe, cajole, or strong-arm the other families back in line, I wanted to kiss the girl I love."

"Oh, Kellan," his mother said.

"I'm sorry." He turned to Blue. "I never meant to hurt you."

She studied the torment on his face, felt the sharp ache of love in her chest, and decided their one moment wasn't going to end with him apologizing.

"You didn't hurt me." She walked up to him and wrapped her arms around him. "I kissed you, remember? I know I can't have you, but I didn't want to regret not having that one moment with you." She pulled back, and before she lost her courage said, "I'll always be your friend, Kellan. And you'll know you always have someone who loves you, even if you don't see much of me from now on."

She fished the vials out of her pocket and pressed them into his hands. "These are protection spells for you and Nessa. They can't save you if the wraith itself gets loose, but they will help keep you safe from any person who means you harm. Please wear them at all times until the threat is gone."

"You made one for yourself too, didn't you?" he asked as he glanced at her neck where no cord hung. When she took too long to answer, he frowned and began handing his back to her.

She made herself smile as she backed away. "I'm protected, Kellan. You don't really think I'd go to the trouble of creating such a powerful spell and not leave enough for me, do you?"

Before he could reply, before the queen could lecture them again, and before the warmth that still lingered on her skin from his kiss could fade, she turned and left the garden.

THIRTY-EIGHT

KELLAN SWALLOWED HARD and met his mother's eyes as Blue left the garden. "I can explain—"

The queen raised her hand in a command for silence. "We can discuss your poor choices with Blue later. I came to find you because the magistrate's guards caught the person who killed Marisol and Genevieve."

All thoughts of finding a defense for his actions fled, and Kellan moved toward the castle, his mother walking briskly by his side. "We need to call a special council meeting."

"I've already sent messengers out. All representatives who are available will be present."

"We need six for a quorum," he said, though of course, she knew that. Still, it helped to think through what was coming. He couldn't make a single mistake as he presided over the council meeting. He owed it to Gen and Marisol to deliver on his promise to get justice for them.

"Six shouldn't be a problem," his mother said as they left

the grounds and entered the castle. "But we'll want to discuss the proceedings with the magistrate before the representatives arrive."

"Especially if one of the representatives is guilty of murder." His voice was hard. Which one of them had given the order to slit the throats of innocent girls in their quest for power? Who had sat across from him at teas and meetings and balls, smiling while they plotted the murder of someone else's daughter?

And would the person responsible show for a meeting if they thought they would be sentenced to death by the end of it?

Turning, he placed a hand on his mother's arm and said softly, "What reason did you give for calling the meeting?"

"An urgent update on the situation with the rogue witch," the queen said grimly. "I'm not willing to tip our hand and let someone flee the kingdom rather than face justice."

He nodded. "Then let's hear what the magistrate has to say and prepare for the meeting."

An hour late, Kellan and his mother stood side by side in front of the council table. Seven members were in attendance. Dinah Chauveau hadn't been at the farmhouse to receive the royal messenger, and Senet Aubert was two cities away dealing with a business issue.

That didn't matter. The person who needed to be in attendance was seated two chairs down from Kellan, patting Lord Gaillard's arm as he offered condolences on the terrible loss of his daughter.

Anger, bright and burning, filled Kellan as he said, "I'll come straight to the point. We have no update on the rogue witch."

The room fell silent, and seven pairs of eyes turned toward him.

Martin Roche frowned. "Then why—?"

"You'll speak when you are given permission to speak," Kellan snapped.

Martin's cheeks flooded with color, but Kellan didn't give him a chance to respond. "You've been called here because the royal magistrate has caught the woman who was hired to kill Marisol Evrard and Genevieve Gaillard."

Conversation erupted across the room, and Pieder Evrard lunged to his feet. "Where is she? I'll kill her in this very room."

"You'll do no such thing." Kellan's voice was stern. "She was the weapon, not the mind behind the crime. She will be sentenced to death by hanging, according to the law, but she is not the one who owes you a blood debt. That person is seated here among us."

Kellan motioned sharply, and a trio of guards marched into the room and stood behind him. Looking out at the council members' faces, he said quietly, "I'll give you one chance to confess your crime and ask those you've wronged for mercy. You will still hang for your crimes, but you may yet spare your family the pain of paying off your blood debt."

The room was absolutely silent. Slowly, Kellan's gaze moved from face to face until he came to Martin, who was subtly trying to edge away from Louis Gaillard.

"So be it," Kellan said, nodded toward the guards. They moved rapidly to flank Martin's chair as Kellan said, "Martin Roche, you are hereby accused of paying an assassin to have Marisol Evrard and Genevieve Gaillard murdered. The magistrate has collected sworn testimony and evidence of payment. Proof will be offered to this council for review, but I will tell you now that I have already reviewed the proof, and there is no doubt in my mind that you are guilty."

Martin leaped to his feet, his fist lashing out at one of the guards. The other two slammed him into the table and pressed him forward until he was bent at the waist, his arms held firmly behind his back, his cheek lying against the wood as he locked eyes with the prince.

Pieder made a strangled noise in the back of his throat and began crawling across the table toward Martin, while Louis drew his sword.

"Stop!" Kellan held up his hand and waited until he was sure he had both Pieder's and Louis's attention. "You will have justice, but you will have it within the confines of the law. He owes each of you a blood debt. The crown offers to strip his immediate family of their noble titles and their place on this council and allow the two of you to choose which distant relation of his may have his place here. Further, his wealth and business holdings will be divided between the two of you, though we will hold in escrow an amount sufficient for the upkeep and security of the Roche quarter and kingdom holdings until we are satisfied that the person you've chosen as his replacement is capable of sustaining their obligation to their quarter and to the crown."

"How could you?" Louis spat, his voice trembling with rage as the guards pulled Martin to his feet again. "You have a daughter of your own."

Martin clenched his jaw and looked at the floor.

Kellan waited as Pieder and Louis hurled questions and accusations at Martin, their grief a wild, feral thing that filled the room until it seemed the air was growing thick with its fury. When the two men were spent, Kellan said quietly, "Martin Roche, pending the presentation of evidence to this council, you are hereby sentenced to death by hanging. I will give you one day in our dungeons so that your family may visit you to say their good-byes. It's one day more than you gave to Marisol and Genevieve, and I want you to know that I do that as a courtesy to your family, and not to you."

Martin spat at the floor, and the guards dragged him from the room. Kellan waited until he was sure the guards had had enough time to secure Martin in the dungeons before presenting the evidence, taking a vote on the verdict, and then dismissing the meeting. Once the last representative left, he sagged into the closest chair and covered his face with his hands.

The queen's dress rustled as she sank into the chair beside him. Softly, she said, "You did well. I'm proud of you."

He dropped his hands and met her eyes. "He didn't even have it in him to apologize to them. To own the fact that he was willing to sacrifice their children for his own lust for power."

"It's an awful thing to see someone so corrupted by their own desires that they stop caring about how their actions affect others."

Kellan stiffened. "If you're comparing what happened with Blue in the garden to Martin—"

"I'm not." She wrapped one hand around his and squeezed firmly. "There's a vast difference between killing someone for power and kissing someone you can't have because you've fallen in love."

He was quiet for a moment, and then he said, "I didn't mean to fall in love with her."

The queen laughed sadly. "I know you didn't. And if I'd ever dreamed there was a possibility of the two of you dropping your constant bickering in favor of kissing, I'd have put a stop to you visiting both the farmhouse and the shop long ago."

"I don't know how I'm going to offer to marry someone else."

She gathered him to her and held him. For a long moment, he let himself be comforted, but then he pulled away. She didn't have to tell him that he was going to have to master his heart and do his duty. He already knew it. His destiny was a long corridor carved from stone, and there was no changing it.

As if she could see the direction of his thoughts, she said quietly, "The ball is coming, and we'll need to make the betrothal announcement."

"I know."

She waited as he scrubbed his hands over his face again before finally saying, "I'm going to choose Emmaline Perrin. I like her, she's kind to Nessa, and I think we're going to need a strong alliance with the military between our current problems with the Roches and the Faures."

"That's a good choice," she said quietly, stone threading her words with the strength that had kept her on the throne long after her husband's death, fighting to keep her kingdom together while she prepared her son to take his father's place. "Now, let's get some rest so we can be at our best during the ball."

He rose, offered her his hand to help her to her feet, and then left the council room with purpose in his thoughts and a lonely ache in his heart at the thought of dancing at the ball with anyone but Blue.

THIRTY-NINE

BLUE DIDN'T RETURN home after kissing Kellan in the garden. She couldn't face the thought of talking to Dinah, or worse, being asked to go down in the root cellar again. Instead, she went to Grand-mère's, where Pepperell waited on the porch and dinner was quickly magicked onto the table.

If Grand-mère wondered why Blue was so subdued, she didn't ask. Instead, she filled the evening with hugs and pastries and lovely stories about Blue's mother as a child. When bedtime came, she tucked Blue in the way she'd done when Blue was small, sang her the lullaby her mother had written, and left a very sleepy Pepperell curled up on one side of Blue's pillow to guard his mistress's dreams.

The day before the ball dawned bright and clear. Or at least, Blue assumed it did. She'd stayed in bed until long past breakfast. Part of her kept waiting to hear Dinah knock on the door, demanding that Blue return to the farmhouse to work or head to the shop even though it was usually closed on weekends. But as the morning went on and Dinah never showed, Blue dared to hope that maybe since Dinah had what she thought was one of Mama's old spells, the Chauveaus had returned to their quarter. Surely they needed to be in their own mansion, surrounded by a team of seamstresses, hairdressers, and maids as they prepared for the betrothal ball.

Before the thought of the ball could cut into the wound left by her love for Kellan, Blue rolled Pepperell's thick body off her chest and sat up.

It was good that she didn't need to prepare for the ball. Her garden was overdue for harvesting. She had dried herbs to grind. And she hadn't had a good swim in the Chrysós since she'd gone in after Kellan.

Shying away from the memory of the fear that had gripped her when she'd seen him dive into the stormy waves and the affection that had swelled within her when he'd shared his truth with her, she dressed in another of her mother's old gardening dresses. Sparing a quick moment to open the wooden box that held the gorgeous golden dancing slippers, she ran her finger over their jewels, careful not to catch her skin on the sharp prongs that held the stones in place.

The last thing she needed to do was cut her finger and have her blood bond the shoes to the box.

Her brows furrowed as she put the shoes away. That was another thing she could do instead of prepare for the ball. She could experiment with bonding different compatible substances using her blood as the alchemy.

Really, she had a very full day ahead of her. Even if she'd wanted to get ready for the ball, she'd have been far too busy.

After eating a quick breakfast with Grand-mère, Blue and

Pepperell headed back to the farmhouse as the sun was rising to its peak in a clear blue sky.

Blue ran through her list of tasks, prioritizing them by necessity and interest. The garden needed the most attention, but she was most interested in experimenting with using her blood as the alchemy between compatible ingredients. Maybe she could do both at the same time. And then she'd swim as far out as she dared, letting the soft shush of the waves and the vast expanse of the horizon be a balm on a wound she didn't know how to heal.

Kellan would dance with all the girls at the ball. Or at least all the girls who would dare catch his eye. He would smile and flirt and charm. And then he would announce his chosen bride and escort her onto the floor for the betrothal dance.

Everyone would believe that he meant every word. Every gesture.

No one would see the boy who dared the sea to take him because he felt responsible for his father's death. No one would think of the boy who'd shone a light on the dark chasm of her grief for Papa and made it all right to laugh, to cry, and to remember. No one would see the prince who'd faced the blood wraith so he could protect everyone in his kingdom, including the street kids, or the prince who'd kissed the commoner because he loved her even though he knew he could never let his heart make his choices for him.

No one would see the real Kellan, and that made her ache for him.

He should be known as the brave, protective, conflicted boy that he truly was, not as the slick charmer who navigated political warfare with practiced ease.

As she entered her garden, feeling the buzz in her veins as

flowers bent toward her and branches lowered themselves to brush against her hair, she let the ache she felt for Kellan sink into her bones, where it would stay.

Maybe it was enough that she saw him. That she understood him.

Maybe it was enough that she'd kissed him, and she'd meant it.

She hopped up the porch steps, opened the front door to grab her gathering basket, and flinched as Dinah stepped away from the wall beside the open door. The woman reached one pale hand to slam the door closed, and then skewered Blue with a look that was pure venom.

"Where is it?" she asked, biting off each word and flinging them in Blue's face.

Blue froze, her heart racing. "Where is what?"

Dinah's arm whipped out, her palm connecting with Blue's face in a stinging blow that crushed Blue's lips against her teeth. Blood welled, and Blue stumbled back.

Dinah advanced slowly, her tone vicious. "I am done with your games, Blue. I know you faked the spell you gave me."

"I . . . What?" Blue looked wildly around for help as Dinah came closer, but they were alone.

Dinah's lip curled as she mimicked Blue's voice. "Oh, I just happened to look inside my mother's old cauldron and see what I found! Look at the rare ingredient you can easily find at the castle! Will you leave now that you have what you want?"

Blue's back hit the wall beside the receiving parlor, and Dinah slammed one palm onto the wall beside Blue's face. The other hand grabbed a handful of Blue's dress and anchored her in place.

"You wanted an old spell, and I gave you one!"

"You faked an old spell to trick me." Dinah's tone sent a shiver down Blue's spine. "That means you've known all along what I was looking for, and you thought you could keep it from me."

"I don't . . . You said an old spell. That's all I know."

Dinah laughed, cold and cruel. "Liar. You've been getting in my way from the moment I walked through this door. Mouthy little brat. Saying you don't know where your mama kept things. Refusing to look through the chests in the root cellar. And then giving me a fake spell."

"It wasn't fake—"

"It was fake." Dinah wrenched Blue's dress, bringing the girl's face next to her own. "You think I don't have ways of figuring that out? I tried it, and it didn't work. Not for what it was supposed to do. And then I had another alchemist analyze the ink. Fresh ink, Blue. Which means you wrote that spell on old parchment because you wanted to trick me. You wanted to keep me from what's mine."

Blue shook her head, her heartbeat pounding in her ears. "I don't know what you want."

"Of course you do." Dinah's eyes blazed, and her voice rose with every word. "And you tried to keep it from me. You, your papa, your mama, the queen and her little brats—all of you trying to keep me from what's *mine*."

"I . . . I don't understand. What do my parents and the royal family have to do with this?"

"Everything! Your family and the Renards ruined my life, and you're trying to do it again." She shoved Blue against the wall, her expression wild.

"How? How did we ruin anything?" Blue's voice rose. "Your

husband was the one who gambled everything away. None of us had anything to do with that."

"Not now, you fool. Sixteen years ago. Your precious mother, the king and queen, and the witch took the blood wraith from me. All that work, all that *power*, and it was just gone."

Sixteen years. Blue's stomach dropped as the pieces fell into place. Papa's sudden death and Dinah's unexpected guardianship. Her desperate search for one of Mama's old spells.

Not just any old spell. The one spell that mattered. The one that opened the blood wraith's gate.

Blue lifted her head as the truth rushed through her, full of fire and rage. "You killed Ana. Killed all those children by bringing them to the wraith."

Dinah laughed in scorn. "Bratty whelps who didn't deserve the glorious destiny I gave to them."

"You killed Papa!" Blue shoved Dinah, and the older woman stumbled back a few steps. The hot, sharp thing that had risen inside Blue when Papa died exploded into a blistering fury. "You took him from me because you thought he had something you wanted. You can't just take things because you want them."

The cut on her lips stung, and Blue reached for it. Maybe she could use her blood to bind Dinah to something awful. Something that would destroy her. She glanced around for inspiration and nearly fell to her knees as Dinah collided with her.

The older woman wrapped her hands around Blue's throat and squeezed. "If your papa didn't want to lose his life, then he shouldn't have helped your mother and the queen ruin mine. Where is the spell to open the wraith's gate, Blue? Tell me, and I'll spare you."

Blue's throat burned. Her chest constricted, lungs begging for air. She clawed at Dinah's wrists, digging in and drawing blood.

Dinah threw her to the floor. "Where is it?"

Blue coughed, drawing in ragged gasps of air. "I don't have it. No one does. Mama didn't write it down because she knew someone like you might come looking for it one day."

"Liar." Dinah leaned down and snatched Blue's hair in her fist. Yanking on it, she forced Blue to look into her eyes. "The answer is here. Valeraine was too smart an alchemist not to leave her spell with someone. Knowledge of the ingredients would be the only way to shore up the gate's defenses if they failed. Where is it?"

Blue spit blood in Dinah's face. "Even if I knew, I'd never tell you."

"Then you'll die."

"Better me than the thousands the wraith would devour if it got free." Blue raised her chin and reached for a sense of peace as murderous rage settled over Dinah's face. She would die without begging. Without flinching away from the sacrifice that was necessary to keep those she loved safe. And at the end of it, she'd be with Mama and Papa again. Holding on to that bright spot of hope, Blue kept her gaze steady as Dinah drew a dagger from a sheath at her waist.

"Oh, I'm not going to kill you yet," Dinah said as she stepped away from Blue and toward the kitchen. "I'm going to kill the little friend of yours who's waiting for you in the root cellar."

Blue shot a glance down the hallway toward the kitchen. "Who—"

"And when I've fed your precious little Lucian to the wraith, I'll head to the castle and kill your beloved prince and princess next."

Blue's heart seemed to stop beating, and the air refused to leave her lungs.

Lucian.

Dinah turned on her heel and stalked toward the kitchen. Blue scrambled to her feet, her knees shaking as the bright, blinding light of terror rushed through her. Not Lucian. Blue couldn't bear the thought of losing her friend to Dinah's treachery. Taking off at a dead run, Blue caught Dinah in the kitchen. Sprinting past her, she threw herself in front of the door to the root cellar.

"You aren't going to hurt him."

Dinah simply smiled. "What's going to stop me?"

Dread sank into Blue, and she pressed her back against the door as if her body would be enough to stop Dinah from reaching Lucian. She should've made more potion. Given him some. Simply warning him to stay safe had been a terrible miscalculation.

Dinah tapped her dagger against the counter. The ingredients Blue had included in the fake spell were strewn across its surface, including a small leaf of volshkyn. "Do you know, I almost admire your ingenuity?"

Blue glanced around, hunting for a weapon. Papa's apron hung on a hook to her left. To the right was the dish rack with a few bowls and mugs still set out to dry from the Chauveaus' breakfast.

Dinah picked up the ingredients one by one—thresh moss, bolla root, yew, myrrh, and bergamot, along with the small volshkyn leaf. "This created a good protection spell, though carpa leaf would've been better than bergamot, don't you think? And adding the volshkyn . . . that was inspired. Guaranteed to give me hope."

She threw the ingredients at Blue and rushed toward her.

Blue twisted to the right, grabbed a mug, and dashed it against the counter. It burst into pieces, leaving the jagged shard of a handle in Blue's grasp. Dinah slammed into her, trying to reach the doorknob. Blue slashed at her with the pottery, slicing through the woman's sleeve and into her arm. Blood welled, and then Dinah was grappling with her, trying to stab the hand that held the pottery with her dagger.

Blue threw herself at Dinah, ramming the bony part of her shoulder into the woman's stomach. Dinah's breath wheezed, and she slashed at Blue with the dagger. Its blade bit into Blue's chest, tearing open a small wound.

Blue pressed a hand to her chest, but the blood was already spilling faster than she could stop it. Dinah shoved her away from the door, and Blue grabbed the woman's wounded arm for balance. They went down in a tangle of limbs, and the weapon Blue had been using flew out of her hand.

"Just tell me where it is, and I'll spare you and Lucian," Dinah snarled as Blue slapped her hands against the floor, hunting for another shard to use.

Her hand, covered in her own blood and blood from Dinah's wound, hit something sticky, and she pulled back, leaving a bloody handprint on the volshkyn leaf.

The leaf sizzled, its edges curling up as the blood bubbled into tiny crimson beads, danced across the surface, and then sank into the thin veins that ran through the leaf.

Beside her, Dinah gasped and then lunged for Blue, knocking her onto her back.

"How did you do that?"

Blue swallowed hard and put every ounce of fury she possessed into her face. "Go crawl off and die."

Dinah's smile sent ice down Blue's spine. "You had your blood and mine on your hand when you touched that leaf. And now that blood is bonded with the plant." Her eyes widened as her smile grew. "You have magic, don't you? So did your mother. It's the only way she could have locked up the wraith. The only way she could have permanently bonded all those ingredients, because believe me, I've tried everything to break that lock. All the antidotes to the things she used to build it have failed." She dipped her face closer to Blue's, the dagger's tip digging into the soft skin of Blue's throat. "And now I know why. The rare ingredient wasn't a stone or a leaf or some rare mineral from another kingdom. It was *you*."

Blue couldn't breathe. Couldn't speak as the truth blazed through her mind like lightning.

That's why Mama never told anyone the spell. Not even Grand-mère.

She wasn't protecting the kingdom from the wraith's return. She was protecting Blue from those who might want to free the wraith, foolishly thinking to harness the creature's power for themselves.

Dinah started humming, and Blue's throat closed at the look of vicious triumph on the woman's face. Mama's lullaby. The one she wrote just for Blue. The one with the scattered mention of plants and metals that Blue had always assumed meant nothing more than a way to connect a budding alchemist child with her mother.

"She did leave the spell behind, didn't she?" Dinah asked

softly. "It's in that atrocious lullaby you sing to yourself every time you harvest in the garden. How does it go again? I'll just skip to the important parts. A branch of myrrh and bolla root, silver, gold, and rose, a drop of mint and a sprig of yew."

She leaned closer, pressing the dagger until blood flowed down its blade. "And three little drops of Blue."

Standing, she wrenched open the root cellar door. Blue rolled to her knees and reached for Dinah, desperately trying to stop her from going after Lucian.

But Dinah wasn't going after Lucian. She was going after Blue. Grabbing Blue's outstretched hands, she dragged her across the floor and flung her face-first onto the ladder that led down into the root cellar.

Blue grabbed on to the sides of the ladder, desperately trying to keep from sliding all the way down to the ground. Below her, Lucian cried out as the door to the root cellar slammed shut and locked with a sharp snick, leaving them in utter darkness.

FORTY

"BLUE?"

Lucian's voice floated out of the darkness at the far end of the root cellar, where he was carefully searching the shelves for the alluminae flax she'd harvested nearly a month ago from a riverbed north of the city.

"Yes?" She tried and failed to make her voice strong and steady. Panic raged within as she sat in the center of the root cellar, her back to one of the wooden chests Papa had left behind, her arms wrapped around her middle. If she held on tight, she could keep herself from falling apart at the seams. She wouldn't think about being trapped in the cellar once more in the dark. Wouldn't think about hours spent crying, screaming for help.

Wouldn't think about Mama.

She wanted to put distance between herself and the chests lined up behind her, but her legs refused to hold her, and when she tried to crawl, she crumpled to the floor. It was worse—so much worse—to struggle and fail than it was to just sit and hope the fear would settle.

Lucian had found her moments after Dinah threw her down into the cellar and locked the door. He'd called to her, listened to her frantic gasps for air, and patted the floor in the darkness until he'd reached her side.

His hands were cold, the bravado in his voice thin as glass, but he'd immediately realized that Blue was in trouble. He'd stayed with her, his arms wrapped around her shoulders, his voice trying so hard to sound calm as she struggled to breathe past the noose of panic that was closing about her neck. When she'd finally been able to speak, she'd told him where to find the alluminae. Being locked in the cellar was bad enough. Being locked in utter darkness was terrifying.

"Did you find it?" she asked, her teeth chattering as images from her nightmares spun through her thoughts.

Blood on the dirt floor.

Mama lying broken and still.

Silence as her breath left her body.

Blue's magic coiled in her hands, useless to bring Mama back.

"I think so," Lucian said. There was a small crash, and he swore. "Broke something."

"That's all right." Blue drew a deep breath and hugged herself tighter. "Just back away from it. I have all kinds of things down here. I don't want you accidentally exposed to something dangerous."

"Whatever I broke smells awful." His footsteps shuffled along the edge of the wall.

"Once you reach the shelf with the ceramic jars, turn toward the sound of my voice," Blue said.

She'd use the alluminae to give them some light. And then she'd figure a way out of the cellar. Surely she had something stored down here that could help. She tried racking her brain to find an answer, but her thoughts were hazy with panic, and it was all she could do not to relive her worst nightmare over and over again.

It didn't matter if she couldn't find a solution off the top of her head. Once she had light, she could see her inventory. Once she could see the inventory, she could see the possibilities. And once she could see possibilities, she could find a way out and warn Kellan and his family that Dinah was releasing the wraith and coming for them.

"I'm at the jars."

"All right, turn toward the middle of the room." Her voice was thready. She tried taking a slower breath, forcing herself to hold it for a quick moment before exhaling. "I'm here. Watch out for the chests. Move slowly."

She kept talking to him as he shuffled toward her, and then he was at her side, pressing a sheaf of alluminae into her hands. The long, graceful strands of flax were dry and soft. A thin cord tied the sheaf together in the middle. Blue swept her trembling fingers over the flax until she reached the small bundles of dried seedpods near the top of the sheaf. She squeezed the pods until they cracked open, releasing the pale glow of the alluminae seeds within. The seeds had a silvery-white sheen, like a candle made of starlight.

"This will give us hours of light," she said, her voice already steadier as the darkness crept back, taking its nightmares with it.

She could do this. She could survive inside the root cellar long enough to find a way out of it. She had to.

Quickly, she divided the sheaf into seven equal sections. Laying one of the smaller sheaves on the chest behind her to illuminate the center of the room and lead them back to the ladder, she gave five sheaves to Lucian, keeping one for herself. "Set one at each corner of the room so we can see the entire space and keep one for yourself so you can move around safely."

He did as she asked, and she slowly climbed to her feet, clutching her sheaf to her chest. Her knees shook, and her stomach pitched as the walls tried to close in on her. She forced herself to breathe evenly. To ignore the frantic cadence of her heartbeat.

Kellan, Nessa, and the queen needed her to think. To plan. She couldn't do that if she let her fear overwhelm her. Glancing at the shelves on the wall to her left, she mumbled the names and scientific properties of each item as she slowly shuffled toward it, her body still shaking like a leaf trapped in a windstorm.

"Bolla root: dried, not minced. Good for strengthening potions, protection from illness or harm, and longevity. Edible. Doesn't bond with syphur weed, korash acid, or mink's foot herb." She crept closer. "Huckleberry: dried and ground. Good for luck, protection, restful sleep, and dissolving bad potions. Doesn't bond with syphur weed, hembane, or chorra wood."

This was good. She could think about the ingredients on her shelves. Concentrate on how to combine them, on what to produce. She could fill her thoughts with these and nothing else, and she could survive being in the root cellar a little longer.

"Did you say something?" Lucian asked, his voice calmer now that there was light in all four corners of the room.

"Just looking at what I have on the shelves. Deciding what to use to get us out of here." And what to use to stop Dinah and the wraith before they hurt the royal family.

Panic tightened Blue's throat again, and she beat it back. She would destroy the wraith. She had to. She couldn't lose anyone else she loved.

As the soft light of the alluminae filled the room, Blue paced its length, cataloging her inventory, discarding options nearly as fast as she thought of them.

An ordinary protection spell wouldn't stop the wraith. The witch who'd become the wraith had fae in her blood, just like Blue. Spells that worked against the fae were far harder to produce, and Blue had little experience with them.

She paused before a shelf of carpa leaf, bergamot, and billy fern. Turning, she found Lucian balanced on a stack of wooden boxes as he reached for one of the old cauldrons that rested on a top shelf. "Careful," she said softly, so as not to startle him into falling.

He grunted in reply as his fingers found the edge of the cauldron and worked it toward him. When he finally pulled it free in a shower of dust, he coughed and climbed back down, his prize in his hands. "I don't know how you're going to make a fire so you can do your spells properly, but now at least you'll have a cauldron to use."

"Thank you," she said, giving him a small smile. "Lucian, how did Dinah catch you?"

He scowled. "I came here looking for you. Wanted to tell you that I'd heard about two other children gone missing. She invited me in. Said you were in the root cellar. Opened the door for me and said to be careful on the ladder as you were in the far end with your candle. Then she shoved me in and locked the door behind me. It's lucky I didn't fall and break my neck."

Blue swallowed hard at that image, blinking away the memory of Mama so she could focus on the boy standing in front of her. "She recognized the ingredients for the spell Mama used on the lock in the Wilds. That means she's studied either alchemy or witchery."

"Nobody studies witchery unless they've got some fae in them."

Blue nodded. It took a touch of fae in the blood to give one some magic. Which meant Dinah might have a bit of magic, just like Blue. Ordinary spells wouldn't work as well on her, but the same spell she did for the wraith would work on Dinah. Unfortunately, Blue was fresh out of ideas for anything that could stop a monster like that. A protection spell wouldn't be strong enough. A binding spell would require the monster's blood, and even if Blue could get close enough to the wraith to get some of its blood, she wouldn't have time to finish the potion before the wraith destroyed her.

That was the essential problem. Any spell used against the wraith would require Blue to get close enough to the creature to be its next victim. How had her mama done it? How had she come close enough to the monster to imprison it?

Blue lifted her hands and examined the blood that had dried on her palms. Her blood and Dinah's. The same combination that had bonded Dinah's blood to the volshkyn leaf in the kitchen.

That's how Mama had done it. She'd bonded something to the wraith using Blue's blood. Something that drove the wraith into the Wilds, where the lock was waiting to seal it away.

Maybe that's why Blue's magic had exploded when the wraith was near. She hadn't been reaching for the monster. She'd been reaching for her own blood. For the magic that was compelling her to finish destroying the creature.

That gave her food for thought. She'd felt no compulsion to touch the dancing fern leaf that had bonded with the walla berry juice. No need to touch the gate where her blood had bound the spell that locked the wraith away.

What had Mama bound to the wraith itself? Something to weaken it so they could get it into the Wilds in the first place? Something to make sure if it escaped, Blue would be able to help track it down and deal with it? Whatever it was, Blue wasn't going to ignore the magic that had ignited in her blood.

She had to trust that she held the key to destroying the monster. Now it was a matter of figuring out where the key was hidden. She turned to Lucian. "Help me gather a sample of everything that's stored in here."

"Everything?" His eyes widened.

"Everything. I need to make a potion to destroy the lock on the door, and I need to make a weapon to use against the wraith."

They pushed the wooden chests in the center of the floor together to make a long worktable. Blue barely thought about where she was standing. She was far too busy cataloging her ingredients and putting them into groups—those that would bond well together and those that didn't bond well with anything she currently had in stock. When it was organized, she rolled up her sleeves and got to work.

Hours passed. Blue's stomach rumbled, a reminder that dinnertime had come and gone. She fought back a yawn as Lucian curled up to sleep on a stack of empty burlap bags. Blue couldn't afford to fall asleep. Not when so many lives were at stake.

Blue's eyes were gritty with exhaustion, and her muscles were stiff and sore by the time she had a potion capable of melting the door's lock. She also had several other experiments resting in jars—bolla root and thresh with a dash of silver, carpa leaf and dancing fern with copper and fria stone, and a noxious-smelling stew of black moss, feringut, rose lead, and myrrh. All of them were decent weapons if she wanted to briefly paralyze the wraith or knock its power down a notch, but none of them would do what she needed.

None of them would kill the wraith.

"Is this ready?" Lucian held up the jar that contained the acid she'd made for the door lock.

"Put gloves on," she chided. "And then yes, go pour it on the lock. Once the door opens, leave it open, but don't go anywhere without me."

The alluminae was fading, which meant they'd been trapped in the cellar for a full night and most of the following day. The wraith might already be ravaging the city, but Blue thought Dinah wanted something different than to use the monster to destroy Falaise de la Mer. She hated the royal family. Blamed them for imprisoning the wraith and somehow ruining Dinah's life. Perhaps the fae in her blood had allowed her to use the wraith for her own ends. Perhaps she'd been a friend to the witch turned wraith. Perhaps she'd sacrificed too much to the wraith, but the creature had been imprisoned before it could uphold its end of the bargain with Dinah.

It didn't matter why Dinah hated the royal family. All that mattered was that she wanted revenge with every fiber of her being, and the betrothal ball tonight would be the perfect way to get it. All the royals, anyone of influence who was also involved in imprisoning the wraith, would be under the same roof. What better way to exact vengeance than to turn the wraith loose on them all while they danced in celebration of Kellan and his soon-to-be bride?

The idea of Kellan choosing a girl from one of the head families sent a pang though her heart, but she ignored it. She had a wraith to destroy. Her broken heart would have to wait.

How was she going to kill the monster?

She closed her eyes and thought through all her options. She'd tried every combination of compatible ingredients. Used her blood to alchemize them. They were solid potions, but if these were enough to kill the wraith, Mama would've already done it years ago.

She needed something that could dissolve the thing. Acid, maybe, though transporting that safely would be difficult and throwing it at the wraith was an imprecise delivery system. The wraith could dodge most of it. It could splash onto people around the creature. It could wound it, but not kill it, and then Blue would've only made it angry.

No, she needed to kill it from the inside out. A poison. Something strong enough to destroy a fae.

But she didn't have a poison strong enough to kill a fae. Unless . . .

Her eyes flew open, and she stared at the group of items she'd moved to the side because they weren't compatible with anything else.

Would they be compatible if she used her blood? There was only one way to find out. Pulling the jar of syphur weed and the satchel of mink's foot herb to the center of her makeshift workstation, she carefully shook out a pinch of each into a small bowl. She added a dash of yaeringlei oil to act as a conduit and then scratched open the wound on her hand so she could squeeze out a few drops of blood. The mixture immediately bubbled, smoke rising to sting Blue's eyes. Hastily, she backed away, lest she breathe any of the poison into her lungs, and waited for the bubbling to stop. When all was silent again, she crept forward and looked into the bowl.

The syphur weed and mink's foot had dissolved, turning the oil into a thick brown liquid that smelled like death itself.

There was no way to know if the amount of liquid in the bowl was enough to kill the wraith, but it was certainly enough to take down at least four horses. Maybe more. She'd used far more generous amounts of each ingredient for this potion than she ever had when using them separately to make a spray for farmers to use to keep bugs and vermin away from their crops.

It was the strongest poison she could create. Two lethal doses bonded together with the strength of her blood. Now she just had to figure out a delivery system.

"Blue, someone's in the house!" Lucian whispered from where he was balanced at the top of the ladder, the jar of acid poised over the doorknob. "I hear footsteps upstairs."

Quickly, Blue poured the contents of the bowl into her last empty jar, corked it, and hurried toward the ladder. She'd figure out the delivery system once they were clear of the house.

"Get us out of here," she said.

The acid sizzled against the doorknob, and the hot stench of melting iron filled the air. Soon, Lucian had the door open. The sounds of Halette and Jacinthe getting ready for the ball drifted down from upstairs as Blue and Lucian crept out of the root cellar. Blue grabbed the volshkyn leaf that had bonded with Dinah's blood from the floor, and they tiptoed out the front door and began running.

FORTY-ONE

MOONLIGHT BATHED THE landscape in silvery light as Dinah stalked over the marshland that led to the Wilds, triumph a wicked flame inside her bones.

She'd spent the day in the de la Cours' shop testing the spell's ingredients. Figuring out which ratios made the most sense. And figuring out a counterspell strong enough to destroy the lock as long as she used Blue's blood to bind the lock and the spell together. All those years studying to be a witch had paid off.

All this time, the answer to her problem had been standing right in front of her. She hadn't known Blue's family possessed magic, but now that she did, everything made sense.

Riva, that fickle witch, hadn't had enough power on her own to defeat the wraith. She'd needed someone with a different sort of magic. Someone who could create unbreakable bonds.

Someone like Blue.

But Blue's bonds weren't unbreakable. Not if Blue's blood was used against itself. Dinah had tried it out in the shop with extremely satisfactory results.

She kicked bones aside, sending a small corpse spinning down the hill as she approached the gate. The strands of silver, gold, and rose lead glittered in the moonlight, and Dinah's smile stretched wide and feral as the wraith's scream split the air.

Pulling the potion from her pocket, she carefully poured it over the lock. The metal sizzled and hissed, acrid smoke rising to sting Dinah's eyes.

Sixteen years of waiting and planning. Sixteen long, torturous years pretending to adore the royal family who'd ordered the wraith's destruction. Pretending to be satisfied with an ordinary life. With the fragile power that came from wealth and status. Power that could so easily disappear with a single wrong move.

The lock was melting, silver running into gold running into rose lead and bleeding down the iron bars of the gate. The wraith rushed forward, its scream turning from anguish to vicious anticipation as the iron cracked.

Dinah didn't want power that could disappear. She didn't want friendships with those who were afraid of magic. Afraid of strength and will and purpose.

She wanted to be limitless, and she was about to get her wish.

The gate shivered, its bars disintegrating into flakes that tumbled toward the forest floor like rivers of ash. The wraith fell silent, its arms reaching across the empty space where the gate had stood as the last of the iron dissolved and swirled into nothing. The ground shuddered, and a loud snapping sound echoed around the Wilds—a whiplash of magic that tore through the invisible cage that held the wraith back.

The creature rushed forward, colliding with Dinah, a shadow of terrible cold that clung to her skin and whispered against her bones. For one long instant, they held on to each other, the wraith's mouth gaping wide as if it might sink its fangs into the source of its freedom, but then Dinah whispered, "We have work to do."

Turning, Dinah walked out of the Wilds, across the marshland, and onto the road that led to Falaise de la Mer, the wraith floating silently beside her, while the bells along the road rang frantically. When they reached the crossroad that would lead them north toward the castle, set high on a distant hill and lit with fiery torches, the wraith turned toward it.

"Not yet," Dinah said as the hunger that had hollowed her spirit for so many years howled for the vengeance it craved. "Tonight, the royal family and everyone in the city will be there for the ball, and I have a very special betrothal gift I'd like to bring the prince."

The wraith hovered behind Dinah as they walked to the de la Cour farmhouse, moved silently across the property, and climbed down the steps carved into the side of the cliff. Before them, the Chrysós Sea was a vast, dark shadow sprinkled with starlight.

"Join me," Dinah said.

The wraith floated against Dinah's back as if hugging her from behind. Its black cape covered her, and its clawlike fingers rested on her own. Together, they walked into the sea.

The waves splashed against their knees, tugging at the cloak until it spread behind them like a pool of spilled ink. The vicious triumph burning in Dinah's bones carved its way into her heart as she waded out to her waist, her arms spread wide, the wraith wrapped around her limbs as if they were one.

"Let's see how the queen and her children like choosing

between death and losing a part of themselves."

Throwing her head back, she plunged their joined hands into the water and said, "By the power of blood, bone, and spirit, I command you to give up your dead."

The wraith opened its mouth and wailed, its magic unleashed in a tidal wave of unstoppable strength. The sound was a soft, haunting melody that grew, swelling into a scream of terrible power that shook the ground and struck the sea like a hammer.

The waters bubbled and churned, the currents shifting until they tore a path between the wraith and a distant point in the sea, just under the far horizon.

"Come to me," Dinah commanded.

The water at the horizon rushed forward along the path, carrying with it a skeletal shape that rode the wave like the figurehead on a boat. When it reached Dinah, the water stopped, swirling away from them in frothy eddies and leaving the skeleton standing silent and still before them.

Dinah and the wraith lifted their hands and touched the skeleton's breastbone.

"Take your form, draw your breath, and answer only to me," Dinah said.

The wraith exhaled, a long rush of blood-scented air that wafted over the skeleton, scouring its bones from head to toe.

For a long moment, nothing happened, but then the skeleton jerked forward, its movements spasmodic and uncontrolled as muscle, veins, blood, and skin spun into being over its bones. It knit together, one limb at a time, until finally the last piece of skin settled onto its face. Its dark eyes flew open, and Dinah was staring into the face of Queen Adelene's departed husband, King Talbot.

Dinah laughed, triumphant and wild, as the king turned to her. She smiled.

"Welcome back to the world, Your Majesty. Or should I say, the remnant of Your Majesty? Not that it matters. Let's get you cleaned up and dressed. You have a ball to attend."

"A . . . ball?" The remnant's voice was thick and uncertain.

"Don't worry, you won't have to dance."

"What will I have . . . to do?"

The wraith swirled around Dinah, wailing its victory while Dinah said softly, "You will kill your wife and your children."

FORTY-TWO

"WHERE ARE WE going?" Lucian asked as Blue turned toward the garden instead of the road.

"My grandmother's house."

"Why?" He kept pace easily with her, his long legs eating up the distance.

Blue clutched the jar of poison to her chest and prayed Dinah and the wraith weren't outside. "Because she can keep you safe."

And maybe she could help Blue figure out how to poison the wraith.

"What about you?" he asked.

"I'll be fine." Blue launched herself out of the garden and into the orchard.

She'd be fine, but she shouldn't be. Dinah was furious with Blue's family as well. She'd killed Papa to get control over the farmhouse and the shop so that she could find the spell. Once she had the spell, she ought to have killed Blue too.

Unless she thought she might need Blue alive because she wanted to perform other spells that would need a binding agent like Blue's blood. As Blue had just discovered, her blood could hold even the most incompatible substances together, and unless someone had a spell that also contained her blood, that bond couldn't be broken.

Her blood had been the key all along, and now that Dinah knew it, there was no way she was going to leave Blue alone. No, she'd use the wraith to kill everyone she hated, and then she'd keep Blue for the rest of her life, using her blood whenever she wanted.

Blue would rather die than watch those she loved be killed, knowing her own blood had been their undoing. She'd rather die than live the rest of her days as Dinah's slave, her blood destroying more and more lives.

She stumbled to a halt just inside the grove that led to Grand-mère's, her heart pounding in quick, sickening thuds.

She'd rather die.

The solution to her problem hit her, a wave of ice that prickled through her veins and settled into the pit of her stomach like a stone.

"What's wrong?" Lucian asked, pausing as he reached the steps to the cottage and realized Blue wasn't with him.

She stared at him without seeing him. Instead, she saw the hill full of small corpses. Ana's arms with two jagged-edged circles torn out, her skin pale as parchment. She saw the wraith coming for her, its gaping maw open wide, vicious teeth glistening as it wailed its insatiable hunger.

"Blue?" Grand-mère called from the porch.

Blue reached out, one hand grasping the trunk of a shirella tree while the hand that held the poison pressed hard against her fluttering heart.

The wraith would come for her if she got close enough to it. It had already tried at the gate. Whatever Mama had bonded to it with Blue's blood connected them. The firestorm of magic that had driven Blue to reach for the monster had also driven the monster to reach for her.

It would come for her. She just had to get close enough. And when it came, she'd be ready.

She couldn't throw the poison on it, or stab it with a poisoned knife, or hope that somehow she could wrestle the thing to the ground and pour the poison into its mouth. Especially when she wasn't sure if the poison was strong enough to kill a creature with fae in its blood.

But there was one sure way to kill it. One sure way to make certain the poison it drank bonded permanently with its own blood, organs, and tissue.

She'd put the poison in her own blood. Bond it to herself so that she became the weapon. And then she'd feed herself to the wraith. When it drank her poisoned blood, her magic would do the rest.

The wraith would be dead. The kingdom and those she loved would be safe.

The fact that she would also be dead sent a sharp ache through her. She let it hurt her, just for an instant. Let herself look down the years she'd no longer have and see all the possibilities. Love, family, memories made in the everyday, ordinary moments that threaded together to create the life she'd always wanted. Simple joys and endless experiments. Magic and moonlight and sleeping in late with Pepperell's heavy weight on her chest.

And then she put them away, sealed them shut in a corner of her mind, and turned to face Grand-mère, who stood close now, her eyes worried.

"What is it?" she asked her granddaughter, the heaviness of dread already wrapped around her words.

"Dinah got the spell and let the wraith out. She's going to kill the royal family and whoever else she wants to kill at the ball tonight, and then I think she plans to come for me and keep me a prisoner."

Grand-mère drew her wand. "Not on my watch, she won't."

Blue closed the distance between them and enfolded her grandmother in a tight hug. "I love you, Grand-mère."

The older woman's arms wrapped around Blue. "I love you too. Now stop looking like I'm going to let that snake in the grass and her pet wraith take my granddaughter. I might not have the kind of magic that can do more than some simple trans-figurations and object movement, but that's enough for me to send a knife into that Chauveau woman's heart."

Blue pulled back and smiled though she wanted to cry. "I hope you get your chance. Now, I need your help. I'm going to the ball and—"

"*We're* going to the ball," Grand-mère stated firmly. "I know you want to protect the royal family, but someone has to be watching out for you."

"I'll be fine." Blue found the words easy to say. A strange sort of calm descended, blanketing the sharp ache in her heart and draining her fear away.

She could see the path before her, every step illuminated as if she held a lantern in her hand.

She'd bond the poison to the blood that ran through her veins. Get dressed for the ball. Send Lucian and Grand-mère through the city to get as many street kids to safety as possible. Dance with Kellan. Let herself feel how much she loved him. Let him see it on her face. It wouldn't matter once she was gone, and it was one last memory she could hold close as she waited for Dinah and the wraith to make an appearance. As she threw herself at the monster and let it feast.

"You'll be fine because I'll be there to watch over you." Grand-mère's voice was sharp.

Blue smiled gently and held up the jar of poison. "I'll be fine because I used my blood to make a weapon capable of taking down the wraith."

There was no need to tell Grand-mère exactly how the weapon worked.

Before Grand-mère could argue further, Blue cast a quick glance at the sky. A crescent moon lit the night, and the stars swept the velvety surface like bits of white sapphire. Soon, the ball would begin. Blue didn't have much time.

"I need your help," she said. "Please trust that I know what I'm doing. I know what I'm capable of. There are people far more vulnerable than me who need your protection tonight."

Grand-mère studied her for a long moment, and then she pulled her once more into her arms, hugging her fiercely. When she let go, she said, "What do you need?"

"A ball gown, a carriage, and Mama's dancing slippers," Blue said.

Grand-mère's brows rose. "Is that all?"

Blue smiled. "A little transfiguration fun. You haven't done that for a while." Her smile slipped. "Unless you think giving me a grand ball gown, a carriage, a groomsman, and a pair of horses is too much for you."

Grand-mère scowled. "Don't be impertinent. Like you, I know exactly what I'm capable of."

"Then let's get started. I need to alter Mama's shoes a little. Will you bring them to me in the kitchen?"

While Grand-mère barked a list of things for Lucian to collect—a fat pumpkin she grew in the garden that bloomed year-round for her, regardless of when things were in season elsewhere, some mice from the attic, branches from a rynoir tree, and a bouquet of brilliant yellow roses—Blue hurried to the kitchen. She had to work fast before Grand-mère saw what she was doing and asked too many questions.

A quick slash of one of Grand-mère's cooking knives opened the cut on Blue's hand again. She uncorked the jar of poison, held it over her wound, and hesitated.

What if it didn't bond with her blood? What if her blood only worked if she was using it to bring together two different substances? There was no time to experiment. No time for caution and triple-checking. For alternate hypotheses and measured steps.

The kingdom needed a girl full of poison and reckless courage.

Holding her breath, Blue carefully poured the poison into her wound.

Instantly, she doubled over, the jar falling to the floor where it smashed into pieces. The poison was fire scouring her veins, blistering her from the inside out. It was heat and knives and agony. She fell to her knees, her dress tearing on shards of glass. The agony blazed through her, seizing her lungs, her throat, her mind.

She threw back her head, the muscles of her neck straining as she tried to unlock her jaw to release a scream.

She was dying. The poison was eating its way through her, and she'd never get a chance to tell Kellan she loved him or hug Grand-mère one more time or kill the wraith.

She had to kill the wraith.

"Please," she whispered, her voice a faint breath forced through lips stiff with pain.

A different fire ignited within her—a storm of magic that rolled through her like a thunderclap, gathering the agony that blazed in her veins and pulling it into the center of her chest, a ball of furious torment that tumbled and churned.

"Blue!" Grand-mère shouted, her voice a distant shadow behind the tremendous thunder of Blue's heart as her magic fought the poison for control.

Hands reached for her. Curses surrounded her as Grand-mère's shoes crunched through glass still stained brown with the poison's residue.

"What have you done?" Grand-mère cried, her wand raised and pointed at Blue, as if somehow she could transfigure the poison out of her body.

The storm in the center of Blue's chest grew, pressing hard against her bones until she thought they'd snap. And then the storm exploded outward, sending jagged bolts of magic and pain through Blue's veins. Her fingers ached. Her toes curled. And her hair stood on end.

When the blood in her veins settled, sluggish and swollen with poison, Blue drew in a shaky breath.

It was done. She'd set her feet on a course that couldn't be reversed. Her skin was cold as she grasped Grand-mère's outstretched hand and rose to her feet.

"My child." Grand-mère moved to hug her, and Blue stepped back.

"My hand is still bleeding," she said. "Don't touch me until I've bandaged it. I don't want you to be hurt."

"You put that poison in your blood, didn't you?" Grand-mère's tone was a slap, but tears shone in her eyes. "Made yourself a weapon because you're going to offer yourself to the wraith."

Blue carefully bandaged her hand and cleaned up all traces of the blood and poison that remained on the kitchen floor. "It's the only sure way to kill the monster."

Grand-mère abruptly left the room. Blue turned and found that she'd placed Mama's golden dancing slippers on the table. Taking the volshkyn leaf out of her pocket, she quickly wiped a bit of her blood from the towel she'd used to clean the floor onto the leaf, split it in two, and then bonded it to the inside arch of each shoe.

She was banking on the volshkyn's remarkable ability to be drawn to what had been bonded to it. It would help lead her to Dinah if for some reason Blue was wrong about Dinah showing up at the ball.

Grand-mère returned to the kitchen, her eyes swollen and red. Quietly, she said, "I'm proud of you, Bernadina de la Cour, and your parents would be too. You're brave and smart, and I'm counting on you to be both tonight." She moved closer, her fierce gaze pinning Blue in place. "You use that courage to lure the wraith and let it drink. And then you use that beautiful brain of yours to figure out a way to survive it. Promise me you'll try."

Blue swallowed hard against the rising lump in her throat. "I'll try."

Grand-mère nodded once, one tear spilling over onto her cheek, and then she said, "Then let's make you fit for a prince's ball."

Blue took the dancing slippers and walked with Grand-mère out onto the path that led from the cottage to the farmhouse. Pepperell rose from his bed on Grand-mère's porch to follow them, winding anxiously through his mistress's legs. Lucian stood beside a large pumpkin, a pile of medium-size rynoir branches, and a bouquet of gorgeous yellow roses. He held two squirming white mice in his hands.

Grand-mère turned. "First let's take the twists out of your hair." She waved her wand, and all of Blue's curls sprang free, lifting to form a halo around her face.

"Now for a dress." The wand pointed at the yellow roses, and Grand-mère muttered something under her breath. The flowers rose into the air, drifted over to Blue, and surrounded her. They began spinning, slow and stately at first, and then faster and faster, dancing around Blue until ribbons of petal-soft yellow flowed in streamers from the thorny rose stems to wrap around the dirty, ragged dress Blue was wearing. Grand-mère pointed her wand at the heavens and twirled it. Starlight fell from the sky in long, shimmering strands of silvery-white and spun around Blue.

When Grand-mère's wand dropped, Blue stood in a dress of golden-yellow silk that left her shoulders bare and hugged her tiny waist. The skirt bloomed outward, like an upside-down rose with delicate tiers of icy-silver-white lace tucked beneath each petal.

Grand-mère's wand held one more wisp of silver-white on its tip, and she aimed it at a pebble on the ground. The rock floated upward, bathed in starlight, and became a diamond hairpin that nestled in Blue's thick black curls above her left ear.

Blue slipped Mama's dancing slippers on and spun once. A laugh bubbled up, even though she felt like crying.

It was beautiful. Magical. It was a dress fit for a princess. And for a little while, Blue was going to pretend to be a princess instead of a girl full of poison and dark purpose.

"Now for a carriage." Grand-mère aimed her wand at the pumpkin and the pile of twigs. The pumpkin shuddered and then began expanding, doubling in size and then again and again until it was a full-size carriage. The twigs bent themselves into wheels and spokes, steps and harnesses, a coachman's seat and a carriage tongue. Grand-mère borrowed starlight again and bathed the pumpkin coach in it until it sparkled like a silver-white jewel.

"The mice!" she said.

Lucian plopped the mice down in front of the carriage, where they immediately started scampering away.

"Not so fast." Grand-mère aimed the wand, and the mice lifted off the ground, hanging suspended in midair. Soon, their tiny bodies rippled and then expanded. In an instant, they were two gorgeous white horses standing patiently in the carriage's traces, waiting to be hooked to the coach they would pull. "Lucian, be a good boy and get those horses laced in."

Lucian scrambled to obey, his eyes wide with wonder.

Grand-mère turned in a full circle, hunting for one more thing. "A coachman. Something careful and loyal."

Her eyes landed on Pepperell, and Blue held up her hand. "Don't change him, Grand-mère. I want to remember him just as he is."

Grand-mère's scowl could've dropped the wraith on the spot. "You'll have many more memories with him. You're going to use that brain of yours to survive. You promised."

"I promised I'd try," Blue said gently.

The older woman sniffed. "Clearly, I have more faith in your abilities than you do. I'm never wrong, my child."

Blue bent to pet Pepperell's fluffy head, and then yelped in surprise as he shuddered and spun into the air, coming back down in front of her, a tall, pudgy man with bushy gray eyebrows lowered over one glowing golden eye. A handsome coachman's uniform in red and gold and shiny black boots completed the look.

"Pepperell?" Blue asked, cautiously reaching out to touch his shoulder.

"Meow," he said.

"He still sounds like a cat." Blue looked at Grand-mère.

"Because he is a cat, my dear. But he'll look the part, the carriage will do the work to guide the horses, and I trust that Pepperell would protect you with his life if necessary."

"It won't be necessary," Blue whispered to Pepperell as his bushy gray beard twitched.

"Lucian, I need you to go into the city with Grand-mère and collect as many street kids as you can. Don't try to go to all nine quarters. Send runners. Get everyone into the shop. Grand-mère has a key." Blue turned to her grandmother. "There are ingredients for a powerful protection spell—"

"I know how to keep someone out of a building," Grand-mère said, her voice thick with tears, though she didn't let them fall. Gathering Blue close for one last hug, she said, "The enchantments will last about four hours, so you have until the midnight bell before everything turns back to the way it was. Remember, I'm proud of you, and I love you. Now go dance with a prince and kill yourself a wraith."

FORTY-THREE

THE NUMB CORNER of Kellan's heart had spread until he felt half-empty.

He'd stood for his valet, for his hairdresser, for his tailor, and for his mother. Every detail was perfectly in place, from his close-trimmed curls to his white dancing coat with its polished gold buttons and royal purple sash, to the tips of his shiny black boots.

He looked like the perfect prince. And tonight, he'd play the part of one by following the law of the land, regardless of the destruction it would wreak on his own heart. Tonight, he'd choose one of the head families' daughters for his betrothed, and all dreams of kissing Blue or telling her he loved her would have to die.

Nessa walked into his suite, her purple dress flowing in a pretty bell-shaped skirt, her tight curls brushed into an updo and secured with jewels so that she looked at least fifteen instead of twelve.

You look handsome. She smiled at him.

"Please. No one will even look twice at me once you walk into the room, little bird."

She rolled her eyes, though she looked shyly pleased. *Who are you going to choose?*

He sank a little further into the numbness and was spared from explaining once more his reasons for choosing Emmaline Perrin when their mother swept in, resplendent in a diamond-sprinkled purple dress with a headscarf of delicately woven gold. "It's time."

Kellan pressed one hand to his fluttering stomach and let the sudden punch of dread settle once more into his bones, where it had lived for the past two days since he'd seen Blue.

She wasn't coming tonight. She'd made that clear. And it was better that way. Better that he not see her, not dance with her, when he had a declaration to make for another girl. Because surely there was no way he could dance with Blue and not have the entire kingdom know that she was the girl who held his heart.

"Are you ready?" the queen asked him, her expression the same relentless expectation of perfect gamesmanship he'd seen since he was old enough to understand the precarious political situation he would have to navigate before his nineteenth birthday. He wished his friend Javan had responded to his invitation for the ball. Of all of his friends, the studious, duty-obsessed prince of Akram would've understood Kellan's dilemma best.

He straightened his spine, lifted his chin, and swallowed down his regret until his expression was as smooth and regal as hers. "Always."

Together, the three of them left the family's wing and descended the grand staircase. Carriages were already pulling up to the entrance, depositing their riders on the front steps, and then pulling away to park by the stables. Music poured out of the room at the far end of the hallway, and staff moved swiftly to take cloaks and offer drinks as the attendees greeted the royal family and then made their way to the ballroom.

Kellan lost track of how many variations of "Thank you for coming. So glad to see you" he'd said. How many probing questions he'd dodged and how many veiled threats he'd turned into flattery as members of the head families tried to figure out his intentions. Truly, he was far happier to greet the commoners in attendance. They smiled at him with unfettered excitement. Their words were simple and honest, and he found it easy to respond in kind.

Some of them worked up the courage to wish him well on his impending nuptials. Some worked up the courage to quietly ask him when someone was going to see to the crime in the Faure quarter or stop the extra taxation levied by brokers in the Evrard quarter. Other items were brought to his attention as well—a quick comment here, an overheard remark there—until Kellan began to gain a picture of a city whose leaders had spent far too much time over the past weeks and months competing for a betrothal instead of governing as they ought. If that was true in Falaise de la Mer, where the castle was perched on a hill and every head family was in residence to oversee things personally, how much truer was it for the surrounding cities across the kingdom?

Kellan filed it away to consider tomorrow in between meetings with head families to award them consolation contracts, diplomatic positions, and royal favor so that he could keep their loyalty even though he'd just given half the throne's power to a girl from another quarter. It was ridiculous that he'd have to even waste time doing that when the people of Balavata needed action taken. Perhaps the first order of business once he was crowned king would be to change the betrothal law so that an heir could marry anyone they chose, as long as that person wasn't from one of the head families. It would free the head families up to govern and cherish the power they did have, knowing there would be no opportunity to gain more. And it would give Kellan's children the freedom to choose a betrothed from a far larger group of people.

Maybe it wouldn't give Kellan a chance with Blue, but he could at least stem the tide of political gamesmanship and danger that marked Balavata's government.

"We should go in," his mother said. "The dances are about to start."

Kellan looked out over the drive. There were still wagons and carriages as far as the eye could see, but he supposed she was right. All the head families had already arrived, and for tonight's proceedings, that was all that mattered.

Disgusted with the entire thing, Kellan stayed an extra few moments to greet more commoners who walked up the front steps. When he could withstand the heat of his mother's glare no longer, he turned and escorted the queen and Nessa into the grand ballroom at the far end of the castle's main floor.

A page announced the royal family before they entered, and there was thunderous applause as Kellan and his family mounted the royal dais. His mother thanked everyone for being there, mentioned the various rooms that were open for refreshments or resting, and had the staff throw open the doors the led to the garden.

The cool evening breeze flowed in, and Kellan closed his eyes against the pang in his heart. He missed his father more tonight than ever. Missed the advice he'd never hear, the hugs he'd never receive, and the look of pride he hoped would've been in his father's eyes as he saw his son successfully manage the tricky betrothal process while still keeping Nessa and his mother alive despite those who wanted the throne at any cost.

The musicians struck up a soft, lilting melody for the first dance. It was time for Kellan to set the tone of the evening. Choose a girl from a head family for the first dance, spread his favor to a few others in between dances with commoners, and then make his official announcement. It was infuriating that nowhere in that list of tasks was there an expectation for him to ask the girl if being betrothed to him was what she really wanted. Another law he would change once he was king.

His eyes opened, and he froze.

Blue was entering the ballroom, her delicate golden-yellow gown flowing gracefully around her small body, her brown skin glowing luminously under the candlelit chandeliers.

"Kellan," his mother warned, but he wasn't listening.

One dance. That's all he would take. Just one before the rest of his life settled into stone.

He stepped down from the dais, moved through the crowd, and bowed in front of her. When he rose, he held out his hand and said, "Miss de la Cour, may I have this dance?"

"Yes." She smiled at him, her eyes sparkling with something bold and reckless. Something that felt like diving off a cliff in the dead of night with no idea what lay below.

She placed her hand in his, and he swept her onto the dance floor amid gasps and the occasional glare from members of the head families.

Kellan looked at Blue and drank in her beauty. Her dark brown eyes, dreamy and wild when she looked at him. Her hair rising in a nimbus of gorgeous black curls to frame her face. Her skin . . . cold.

He frowned and pulled her closer as they swept into the next measure of the dance. "Are you well?"

She smiled, the reckless light in her eyes daring him to do things he knew he'd soon have no right to do. "I'm well enough."

"You said you weren't coming."

"I changed my mind."

He sucked in a breath as she brushed against him before twirling out and back in. The pulse at the side of her neck was beating fast, a tiny bird fluttering beneath her skin. He wanted to press his lips to it. Wanted to feel the silk of her dress as he pulled her to him. Wanted to be so tangled up with her that he forgot the rest of the world.

For a few glorious moments, there was nothing but the feel of her hand in his, the movement of their bodies as they swayed to the dance, and the look in her eyes as she held his gaze. Then she said quietly, "I don't want to have any regrets."

His chest ached. "I don't either. I wish things were different. That the laws allowed—"

"I love you," she said, bold and clear, as if daring those around them to eavesdrop. "I love you, and I wish I'd said it sooner. I want you to remember me like this."

If she'd punched him in the gut, she couldn't have taken the air out of him faster. "Blue—"

"When you think of me, think of me like this," she said. Her lips parted as she looked up at him, and he had to fight the urge to lean in and kiss her. "Remember me dancing with you in a beautiful dress. Think of the way I kissed you and the way I looked when I said I love you."

His grip on her cold fingers tightened as they entered the last few moments of the dance. "It's not like I'm never going to see you again, Blue," he said softly. "It will be hard, but I'll still come to the shop. I'll still stop by the farmhouse with Nessa. Unless you don't want me to." The possibility sank into him, cutting deep. "Wait. Is this good-bye?"

She had every right to say yes. Every right to walk out of the ballroom and out of his life altogether. He had nothing more to offer her than his friendship, and they both knew that wasn't enough.

"It's me asking you to remember the truth," she said as she moved closer to him than the dance movements allowed.

He didn't care. Let them stop moving while the world twirled and spun around them. Let his mother and the head families glare at him, while the commoners wondered what he was doing.

This was his last chance to tell Blue what she meant to him. He wasn't going to waste it.

"Blue, I love you. You're my best friend. I don't want to lose any of that."

Her smile lit up the ballroom, reckless and wild, and he leaned closer.

"You'll never lose me," she said softly. "Not really. I'll always be the girl in the golden dress who loved you first. And whatever happens, I want you to promise that you won't swim out in the sea for me. You won't jump off a cliff into shallow water over me. You'll remember that I love you, and that everything I did was my choice, not yours. Promise me."

He met her gaze as time seemed to slow and then stop. "Why

are you talking like you're going to die?"

She let go of his hand and pressed her palm to his cheek. Her other hand stayed firmly against his shoulder. "Dinah knows the spell. By this time, I'm sure she's released the wraith. She plans to kill you and your family."

His gaze flew to the royal dais where his mother and sister sat. His mother gave him a look that would've dropped a lesser boy to his knees.

"Don't worry," Blue said, a tinge of sadness coating her words. "I'm not going to let that happen."

"We have to warn the guards. The castle needs to be locked down!" Kellan scanned the room for the closest guard, but all he could see were couples dancing.

"I already did that when I arrived." Blue turned his face to hers again. "Grand-mère and Lucian are gathering up the remaining street kids and keeping them safe in the shop. The guards have made sure no one is outside the castle. There's nothing to distract Dinah and the wraith from coming straight for you and your family. But she won't get to them, Kellan. I swear on my life. And if for some reason she doesn't come straight to the castle, I bonded her blood to some volshkyn leaf and attached it to my shoes. It will lead me to her."

Panic hit, hot and vicious. "I'll help you. What's the plan?"

Her expression was full of terrible gentleness and regret, and he pulled her closer.

"Whatever you have planned, I can help. You are not facing the wraith alone."

"Yes, I am," she said simply, and then wrapped her arms around him. "I'm the thing it really wants, and I'm the weapon that can destroy it."

He held on to her and struggled to breathe past the fear that was taking over. "You aren't making sense. If you have a spell ready, let me help you. I can distract it while you throw the potion or . . . how are you doing it? We can talk this through."

She pulled away and tipped her head back to look at him. "I'm killing it, Kellan. I'm ready."

"Not yet!" He grabbed for her as she stepped back, and she winced as he latched onto the hand that had been on his shoulder. He turned her palm over and found a bandage stuck to it. The faint outline of dried blood rested beneath the outermost layer of the bandage. "What did you do?"

"Don't touch that!" She jerked her hand away, her eyes bright with fear. "You can't touch my blood at all. No matter what happens. Don't touch my blood. Don't let anyone else touch it either."

He stared at her for a long moment while her words fell into place. Panic seared his thoughts.

"You were saying good-bye." He forced the words out. "You've done something to yourself so that the wraith comes for you."

"It was always going to come for me," she said, moving closer so that she was once more standing a mere breath away from him. The musicians started a new dance, but still Kellan and Blue stood in the center of the ballroom while the dancers swirled around them.

"I don't understand."

She pressed her uninjured hand to his cheek once more. "I'm bonded to it in some way. Mama must have used my blood in the spell that sent it to the Wilds as well as in the lock. It came for me at the gate, and it will come for me now."

"And you're ready to die." The words weighed as much as his entire kingdom.

The reckless light was back in her eyes, but her expression was serene. "I'm poison, Kellan."

"You are not poison. You're the kindest, smartest, most incredible girl I've ever known."

She smiled a little. "Thank you. But I mean I'm literally made of poison. I made the most lethal potion I could and then poured it into my bloodstream so it could bond with my blood. When the wraith drinks from me, my blood will make sure the poison bonds with the wraith. I'll kill the monster, Kellan, and you and your family will be safe."

The room tilted, and he hung on to her to keep his feet. "I can't . . . There has to be another way."

She let her hand slide slowly from his cheek to his shoulder, and then she stepped back. "Remember me like this. The girl in the yellow dress who loved you first."

And then a ripple of unease ran through the crowd, starting at the door that led to the entrance hall and expanding until the dancers went still and the musicians fell silent. Someone screamed, and then the queen was on her feet, her dark eyes blazing with fear, her hands clutching the front of her dress as she stared at the doorway.

Kellan turned and the foundation beneath his feet cracked and slid away.

His father stood in the doorway, his eyes locked on his son, a sword in his hand.

FORTY-FOUR

KELLAN LUNGED IN front of Blue as the thing that used to be his father moved across the crowded ballroom toward them, his gait oddly disjointed but impossibly fast. The sword he held gleamed beneath the chandeliers. People screamed and ran off the dance floor, leaving Kellan, Blue, and the team of guards who were rushing to defend their prince.

This was madness. His father couldn't be alive. Couldn't be striding toward him with a weapon in his hand. It was impossible.

It was also true.

The air felt too thick to breathe as Kellan watched the king swing his sword like a vicious pendulum, slicing into those who would try to stop him. Two of the guards went down, blood pouring from their wounds.

This was his father. His *father*. Kellan had wished for so long to have more time with the king that for a terrible moment, he thought he'd caused this. He'd dared the sea one too many times to exchange his father's life for his, and now here was his wish, driving his sword into the side of the third guard, and then dragging it free, his eyes never leaving Kellan's.

Did he want vengeance? Did he, like Kellan, hold his son responsible for cutting his life short eleven years ago? Kellan's hand, already curled around the hilt of his dress sword to pull it free, hesitated as more guards sprinted across the dance floor toward the king.

"Kellan, get out of the way!" Blue rushed in front of him, shielding him with her body as the king reached them.

The king's sword swung toward her, and the paralysis that had rooted Kellan to the floor broke. Lunging forward, he pushed Blue to the side as he raised his own sword. His blade slammed into his father's, a shriek of metal against metal, and held.

Kellan planted his feet and put all his strength into pushing against his father's sword. They stood face-to-face, swords crossed above their heads, and the numb corner of Kellan's heart blazed to life with unbearable agony.

"Father," he said softly. "Please, put down your sword."

The king's expression was slack, his brown eyes flat and empty. He pushed harder on his weapon. Behind him, the guards closed in.

"Talbot, *stop*!" The queen's voice split the air, filled with desperation and grief.

The king's body jerked, and his head slowly pivoted until he was staring at the royal dais. The queen stood, body trembling, her hands clutched together in front of her chest, as if praying. Nessa was beside her, her eyes huge as she stared at the man who'd been her father but who'd died before she could make any memories with him.

The guards reached the king, and the queen flinched as two of them drove their blades into the back of his knees to incapacitate him. A third went for the king's sword hand. The weapons struck their target, biting deep. Thick black sludge that smelled of sea brine and decay oozed out of the wounds, but the king didn't fall. Didn't lose his grip on his sword. Didn't waver.

In horror, Kellan watched the wounds knit back together as if an invisible thread had been pulled. If they couldn't disarm him or incapacitate him, how were they going to stop him?

The king was still staring at the queen. At Nessa, who'd wrapped her arms around herself and edged to the back of the dais.

"Look at me, father," Kellan said firmly as grief opened wide and hollow within him.

If the king couldn't be disarmed or stopped, there was only one solution. He was going to have to figure out how to kill his father. The thought was a cold, creeping frost settling over his bones.

"Look at me," he said again, his voice shaking.

"Dinah used the wraith to do this," Blue said beside him. "This isn't really your father. It's what little was left of him—the memories in his bones that the wraith used to re-create him." Her small hand brushed against his back, a comforting touch that said she knew he was in agony. "If any part of him remains here, he's trapped behind the control the wraith has on him."

Kellan swallowed hard as his father's face swung toward him again. He kept his sword up, kept pressing back against the blow the king wanted to deliver, as the guards tried again to bring his father down. One sword to the stomach. One to his chest. One through his neck.

Black goo oozing. The sickening smell of brine and decay. His wounds knitting back together effortlessly.

And still his father stood, empty eyes staring at his son, his sword pushing, pushing, pushing, trying hard to land a killing blow on the prince.

"Call off the guards," Blue said softly. "If he turns away from you, he might kill them. They can't stop magic with a sword."

"Stand down," Kellan said, his gaze locked on his father. Was there a flicker of awareness in the king's eyes? A shred of the man who'd loved his family and his kingdom so well? "Father? Can you hear me?"

As the guards backed away, their swords still raised, Blue crept away from Kellan's side, and slowly circled the king, studying him intently.

"Be careful," Kellan breathed as she frowned and moved closer to the king.

"Oh yes, do be careful." Dinah Chauveau walked through the open door the guards had used to enter. A tall, knife-thin figure in a tattered black shroud hovered just behind her, the gaping black pits where its eyes should be focused on Blue. "We wouldn't want anyone to be hurt. Well, anyone besides the royal family. The king has strict orders not to let his wife and children survive the night."

"No." Kellan pushed his sword harder against his father as panic crashed through him.

He wasn't ready for this. Would never be ready for this. Blue was going to sacrifice herself to kill the wraith, and then he would have to kill the remnant of his father. What would be left of him when it was over?

"I see it," Blue whispered, her face close to the king's. "A thread where his cheek meets his right ear. It's nearly translucent. That's the magic that's holding him together."

"Isn't this lovely?" Dinah's voice vibrated with rage. "All the people who ruined my life gathered together under the same roof. Well, everyone except for my dear little sister, but I'll deal with her shortly."

"What is the meaning of this?" the queen demanded, her regal expression back in place, though her body still trembled, and her eyes kept darting to the king. "How dare you free that creature and bring it here?"

"How dare *you*?" Dinah stalked toward the dais, the wraith trailing behind her, a soft, keening sound escaping its mouth. "You and Talbot, the royal council, the de la Cours, and my sister all plotting together behind my back."

The queen's brows collided. "If you have a sister, it's the first I've heard of it. Nobody plotted anything against you. If you were using the wraith sixteen years ago to bargain for power for yourself, then I'm glad we took it away from you."

"Are you?" Dinah's smile sent a shudder over Kellan's skin as he leaned against the force of his father's weight. His palms were getting clammy, his grip starting to slip.

"Father," he whispered, hoping the flicker of life he saw in the king's dull eyes was real. Terrified that if it was, that meant he truly would be killing his father all over again.

The queen's spine grew ramrod straight, and she glared at Dinah. "The wraith is an abomination who feeds on the blood of children to gain its power. It deserved to be imprisoned—"

"Actually, it deserved to be destroyed," Blue said, the wild, reckless light back in her eyes as she left the king's side and walked toward the wraith. The creature jerked its face toward hers and lifted its bony nose as if trying to identify Blue by scent.

Kellan could barely breathe. She was going to die, and there was nothing he could do about it. "Father, please. Lower your sword."

The queen met Blue's eyes for a long moment, and whatever she saw there had her lifting her chin and staring Dinah down. "Yes, the wraith deserved to be destroyed."

"You can't destroy the wraith," Dinah mocked. "You can't even destroy the remnant we dragged out of the sea to hunt you down and kill you. I'm going to enjoy watching you beg for your life, Adelene. I know I begged for mine."

"You've never begged for anything in all the years I've known you, but now you will have that chance." The queen's voice filled the room. "Dinah Chauveau, I charge you with treason against the crown. You are hereby sentenced to death. Guards!"

Dinah threw her arms out, and the wraith spun into the air. Its mouth opened wide, and it screamed, an undulating howl that swelled to fill the room, climbing in volume and pitch until Kellan thought he would burst from the power of it. The floor shuddered, sending several people to their knees, and a spider web of cracks spread along the walls. People screamed and sobbed, grabbing on to those around them for support.

"You can't kill me." Dinah laughed, cruel and feral. "You tried once before, and I almost wish you'd succeeded. At least I would have been dead instead of condemned to live without my heart."

Blue moved closer to the wraith, candlelight dancing on the bare skin of her arms as she raised them up like an offering.

"Blue." Kellan whispered her name, a broken prayer that sounded too much like good-bye.

"Blue." His father repeated the name, still watching him, though Kellan was sure now that the flicker in his father's flat expression was truly him.

"Father." Kellan had to swallow past the grief that was choking him. Grief for the time he'd lost with his father and for what was left of the man he'd loved. For what he had to do to break the wraith's hold on the king. And for Blue, who was now standing five lengths from the wraith. "Please put down your sword. I don't want to have to kill you, but I can't let you get past me, or you'll kill your wife and daughter."

"Arrest her!" the queen shouted.

Guards converged on Dinah, and Blue ran for the wraith. Kellan shoved against his father's sword and felt it drop a fraction.

The wraith screamed, and the guards stumbled, blood leaking from their ears and noses. Dinah laughed. "How does it feel to be helpless now, Adelene? I'm going to take your children. Your kingdom. And your life. And there's nothing you can do to stop me."

"Don't forget about me," Blue said, and Kellan's heart ached at the fierce courage on her face as she approached the wraith, her arms still raised. "Don't forget that my mother is the one who locked the wraith away in the first place."

Dinah swung to face Blue, her lips peeling away from her teeth in a snarl. She reached up to snap a chain from around her neck. "I couldn't possibly forget you. You're the key to fixing everything." She held up the chain. A small vial dangled from the silver links, and within that vial rested a single drop of blood.

"Father, lower your sword now, or the girl I love is going to die." Kellan met his father's gaze and begged him to be there. To fight past the wraith's magic. Kellan didn't know what Dinah planned to do with that drop of Blue's blood, but it wasn't good. And it wasn't something Blue had planned for when she'd turned her body into poison.

The king's sword lowered another notch.

"You've already won," Blue said calmly. "You figured out the spell. You set the wraith free. You don't need to kill anyone in this room, Dinah. You already got what you wanted."

The wraith trembled at the sound of Blue's voice and jerked toward her. Thrusting its face close to her, it opened its mouth, exposing a double circle of tiny sharp fangs.

"You know nothing about what I want." Dinah uncorked the vial and tilted it until the drop of blood rolled onto her fingertip. "What I want is to hunt down everyone who hunted me. What I want is to drink the blood of my enemies' children. What I want is to tear my dear, sweet sister in two the way she divided me sixteen years ago. And now, thanks to you, I get to have it all."

The queen blanched, and Blue froze, her eyes wide as the wraith whirled to face Dinah.

"No!" Blue lunged for the wraith, tearing at its shroud as it lifted its arms to meet Dinah's outstretched hands. The drop of blood on Dinah's finger disappeared beneath the wraith's bony limb, and for an instant, nothing happened. But then Dinah threw back her head, the cords of her neck standing out as she screamed in pain. The wraith shivered, its hand sizzling where it met Dinah's, and then the two collided against each other with a thunderclap of power that reverberated throughout the ballroom. Dinah and the wraith fell on the floor in a heap, the wraith's dark shroud settling over them like a tattered blanket.

Blue's frantic gaze found Kellan's. Behind her, the shroud shuddered, and then a single creature rose to its feet. It was

Dinah, but not. The same dark hair, same sharp bones and pale skin. But her eyes were entirely black. Her fingers were long, skeletal things. And when she smiled, her teeth were double rows of fangs.

Kellan shuddered, horror crawling up the back of his throat like sickness. Dinah and Marielle the witch were one and the same.

"Look out!" he yelled as Dinah turned toward Blue.

Blue pivoted in time for Dinah's fist to send her crashing to the floor. One of her dancing slippers flew off her foot and sailed under the dais.

Dinah laughed, a powerful swell of sound that grew and grew until it was a creature of teeth and fury battering those around it. Dust fell from the cracks in the walls, and the floor buckled. She threw her arms out, and magic swept the room in a tidal wave of force and fury. The windows shattered, glass exploding out onto the castle grounds. Every person in the room was knocked screaming to the floor, including the king.

Kellan landed beside his father. The king's sword clattered to the ground, and the prince kicked it out of reach.

"Kill," the king muttered.

"No. Father, please. It's Kellan. It's your son." Kellan wrestled with his father as the king struggled to reach the sword. "You taught me how to swim, remember? You showed me how to eat a shirella in three bites, how to scale a wall, how to make Mother laugh. We used to picnic every weekend with the de la Cours. Please, remember. *Remember*."

He brought his face close to his father's as Dinah grabbed Blue and hauled her toward the dais. "You love us. You love me. You loved me so much you gave your life for mine."

Kellan's throat closed over the words, and he dug his fingers into the king's tunic to keep him from reaching the sword while Blue turned to look at him one last time, her expression peaceful, though there was pain in her eyes.

She was saying good-bye, and there was still so much he had to tell her. So much he wanted to know.

"Swimming," his father whispered. The hand that had been reaching for his sword stopped.

Kellan looked into the king's eyes and found a glimmer of his father staring back.

"Kellan?"

"Yes." Kellan pressed his forehead to his father's for a moment. "Please let me go help Blue. I need to know that you won't go after Nessa or Mother."

"Can't."

Kellan pulled back to look at his father, his heart breaking at the torment on the king's face.

"Controlled." The king's jaw clenched. "Can't fight it. Kill me, son. I don't want to hurt you."

"I can't kill you again." The words ripped their way out of him, carrying the unbearable weight of years of grief and guilt.

"This is going to be fun, Adelene." Dinah jerked Blue to her feet and wrapped her too-long fingers around Blue's shoulders as they stood in front of the queen. "The king will kill you and your children. I'll take the throne. And Blue here will be at my beck and call. Her blood will bond anything I want. There's no spell, no potion off-limits to me now. As much as I'd love to stay and see your deaths with my own eyes, my sister is still an accomplished witch, and she'll have ways of knowing about this if I stay too long."

"Dinah—"

"I think you should start calling me by my real name." Dinah's smile stretched wide and triumphant. "Marielle, blood wraith of Balavata. Come along, Blue. You're going to help me kill my sister."

"No!" Kellan shouted as Marielle wrapped one hand around Blue's arm and flung the other one out, sending a gust of power to knock any resistance out of her way.

Marielle dragged Blue toward the exit, pausing once to look at the king. "Kill them all," she said, slamming a wave of magic into the king with a casual flick of her hand.

"Blue!" Kellan yelled, but it was too late. Marielle had already dragged Blue out of the ballroom.

"I chose," the king whispered, his sword hand clenching into a fist. "Chose to save you."

Kellan met his eyes and found love.

"Forgiven." The king's sword hand opened and strained toward the weapon. The love in his eyes dimmed to something dark and empty once more.

Kellan slid his hand over his father's cheek as tears filled his eyes. "I love you," he said quietly as his fingers found the thread right where Blue had said it would be. His chest tightened, grief pouring through him, and he gently pulled on it. The king shuddered, eyes rolling wildly in his head, and then as the thread came free, his body fell apart. Skin separated, muscle collapsed, and the black ooze that was his blood dried into brittle flakes until everything that bound him together disintegrated into dust.

Shaking, Kellan climbed to his feet and faced his mother, who was staring aghast at the dust that had been the body of the king. "Where is she going?"

His mother shook her head. "I don't—"

"The witch! The other one. Where does she live? We have to get to Blue." Kellan sheathed his sword and stalked toward the dais.

"It's been sixteen years, Kellan. I don't know. I thought Riva had left the kingdom. If she lives nearby, then she's kept that well hidden."

A maid rushed into the ballroom, her face pale with fright. "Your Majesty! I couldn't stop her. I tried, I swear, but—"

"No one could stop the wraith," the queen said, her eyes still on Kellan.

"Not the wraith, Your Majesty. The princess."

The room tilted, and there was a ringing in Kellan's ears as he rounded on the maid. "What about the princess?"

"She followed the wraith, Your Majesty. She was signing so fast, I'm not sure I understood her, but I think she wanted to save her friend."

"Kellan." The queen collapsed into her seat, her body shaking.

"I'll find her. I'll protect her." Somehow. If he had to turn over every rock in the kingdom, he was going to find Nessa and Blue before it was too late for either of them. A flash of gold caught his eye from beneath the dais, and he crouched to pull out one of Blue's dancing slippers. A small, diamond-shaped leaf was adhered to the underside of the arch.

Kellan smiled grimly. The volshkyn leaf Blue had bonded to Dinah's blood. She'd said it would lead to Dinah. He'd use the shoe to find the wraith, and in doing so, he'd find his sister and the girl he loved.

FORTY-FIVE

BLUE WAS IN deep trouble.

She was full of poison. A prisoner of Marielle's, being dragged out of the city. There was no one to help her. No weapon she could use besides her own body, and the wraith no longer wanted to consume her.

Blue stumbled along behind Marielle in her one surviving dancing slipper, her skin bruising beneath the wraith's relentless grasp. They'd left the city by the western gate and turned into an orchard after the city was already lost to view. The orchard ended in a tangle of overgrown rosebushes, fennel, and hazel trees. Blue stumbled again, and her remaining shoe came off. Marielle never hesitated. She tightened her grip on Blue and pulled her forward. Blue's skirt caught on a rosebush and tore as they plunged through the trees.

How was she going to stop the wraith if it refused to drink her poisoned blood?

And how long could Blue survive the poison that was bonded

to her? Already, her skin was cold, her heartbeat slowing. The moment the wraith cut Blue's finger and tried to use the blood for a spell, she'd know it was tainted. The poison would bond with the spell, changing it, ruining it, and giving Blue's secret away.

Somehow, she had to make the wraith want to bite her before it was too late.

Starlight barely illuminated the landscape, but the wraith never hesitated. Pulling Blue through a slim opening between hazel trees, she pivoted left and plunged through what looked like an impenetrable wall of greenery.

Blue tripped as they broke through the greenery and into a small clearing. The wraith dragged her back onto her feet and through a garden until they reached a tiny cottage that listed to the right. Two of the porch steps were caved in, and Blue had to scramble to keep from falling again as Marielle's long strides ate up the distance between the steps and the front door.

The wraith raised a hand as if to knock, and then flattened her palm on the door instead. Throwing her head back, she shrieked, an unearthly howl that reverberated throughout the clearing. The door blew inward off its hinges, colliding with a short, well-rounded woman and sending her against the far wall. The woman slid to the floor, her hand clutching a hazel-wood wand, and then scrambled to her feet as the wraith entered, Blue by her side.

"Marielle!" the woman said. "What have you done?"

"I've come to collect what you owe me." The wraith's voice shivered with fury and power.

"I owe you nothing." The woman raised her wand. "Now leave before I have to kill you."

Marielle laughed. "You had your chance to kill me, Riva. You failed."

Sparks lit the woman's eyes, and she took a step forward. "I wasn't trying to kill you, Marielle. I was trying to save you."

The wraith snarled. "You split me in two. Do you know what it's like to feel like you've been gutted? To have your heart, your power, and your magic imprisoned while you are forced to carve out a new life for yourself as an ordinary human?"

"If I hadn't split you in two, you'd be dead now." Riva raised her wand and took another step forward. "You'd have starved out there in the Wilds. Gone mad with hunger until you withered away to nothing. I thought if I separated you from your magic, you could have the best of both worlds. The throne would stop hunting you, believing you to be caged, and you could start over without the temptation to do such wicked things."

A sound scraped the porch behind them, and Blue glanced over her shoulder at the still-open front door. Her stomach plummeted when Nessa crept up the porch steps, her finger pressed to her lips in a plea for Blue's silence.

The wraith needed Blue alive. She didn't need Nessa. The instant she realized the princess had followed them, she was going to kill her.

I'm going to make some noise to surprise the wraith into letting go of you. Be ready to run. Nessa's eyes were wide with fear and resolute courage.

Blue shook her head slightly, trying to convey with her expression that Nessa should get out of there before the wraith realized the princess she wanted dead was standing on the porch.

Nessa's jaw set stubbornly, and Blue's stomach dropped. The princess was going to do what she planned, and Blue couldn't stop her. Couldn't stop the wraith from taking her, either. All she could do was hope to grab the wraith's attention for herself while she figured out how to make it want to bite her.

I'll find something to throw at it, and then we'll both run.

Neither of them could outrun the wraith, and Blue was the only one Marielle wanted to keep alive. Nessa crept past the open doorway, searching the far end of the porch for something to use against the wraith, and Blue looked at the women, who were still shouting at each other. She had no plan, no list of possibilities to try, and no time to do anything but improvise.

Before either sister could be distracted from their argument by the sound of Nessa on the porch, Blue took a step toward Riva, yanking on the wraith's arm like she wanted her freedom. The women's eyes snapped to hers, and Blue started talking as fast as she could.

"Dinah . . . I mean, Marielle has been taking street kids from Falaise de la Mer and feeding them to the wraith for years. Did you know about that? Was that an acceptable cost to saving your sister from the consequences of her actions?"

Riva looked stricken. "I wondered, but there was no proof—"

"There was plenty of proof if you'd simply gone to the Wilds instead of hiding away here in your cottage while she continued to hurt innocents." Blue's voice rose. "You knew she was still in the city. You knew she was wicked—"

"I cut the wicked part out of her!" Riva cried, her cheeks flushing.

"There is no part of her that isn't wicked!" Blue lunged toward Riva, but the wraith's grip held her back. "She killed my papa. My friend Ana. Countless children. I stepped on their bones! I saw the carnage. And then she pulled the king's body from the sea and brought him back to life just enough to send him to the castle to kill his children. And all of that happened because you decided to separate part of her from her magic instead of letting her be caged like she deserved."

"This is charming. It really is." Marielle moved toward Riva. "I do love seeing someone hate you nearly as much as I do, sister dear. But I'm afraid I have people to kill and a throne to take, so it's time for you to go ahead and die."

Riva's wand swished, and a jet of pale yellow light flashed from its tip. Marielle laughed as flames caught on her cloak and spread. With a wave of her hand, the flames coiled themselves around her arm, a snake of fire with its head pointed at Riva.

"Blue, a drop of blood if you please." The wraith's fingers curled into claws around Blue's arm. "I think we'll see what happens when we bond fire to a witch."

Blue laughed, a little forced, a little desperate, her mind racing to come up with a way to keep Marielle from using her blood. "I thought you were the invincible, all-powerful blood wraith. And yet you can't even kill a harmless little witch without my help."

The wraith's black eyes turned toward Blue, and it gnashed its teeth at her. "I can kill anyone without help. Including every single little street brat you hold so dear. Shall I start with them next? Or would you rather I make a visit to your grandmother's cottage first?"

Movement flashed out of the corner of Blue's eye, and she turned just as Riva collided with her, breaking the wraith's hold on her. The witch stood between Blue and her sister, her wand raised, her voice trembling as she said, "Run, child."

Another pale light shot from the wand and exploded into a hail of spiders that crawled over the wraith's skin and poured down her nose, ears, and mouth. The wraith threw the fire snake at Riva as it staggered back, choking on spiders.

The fire hit Riva, wrapped around her, and ate into her skin. Blue whirled and ran onto the porch, where she'd last seen Nessa, but the weathered gray boards were empty. Frantically, Blue scanned the garden, but it was silent and still. She turned back to the cottage as Riva doused herself with a water pitcher. The wraith stood tall, her skin shuddering as she opened her mouth and wailed, a terrible gust of air that flew out of her, filled with spiders and magic.

Blue was thrown off the porch and onto a bed of lavender. Scrambling to her feet, she hissed, "Nessa? Nessa!"

The garden was silent.

"I should have just let you die!" Riva's voice rose.

Blue crept up the steps again, her heart in her throat as she came to the doorway. Riva crouched, her back to the door, her skin seared and her hair smoking. Her trembling hand clutched her wand. Marielle faced her, both hands raised, magic shimmering between her outstretched palms like a translucent storm of power. And behind Marielle, a narrow wooden chair clutched in her hands, was Nessa.

"That's always been your problem, sister. You could never stomach doing what needed to be done." Marielle locked eyes with her sister.

Riva muttered something, and the tip of her wand glowed.

Blue rushed through the door, aiming for the wraith, as Nessa swung the chair over her head like an ax, slamming it into Marielle's back.

A spell erupted from the wand and struck Marielle as she whirled to face Nessa. Thorny vines spread rapidly along

Marielle's back, wrapped around her body, and sank barbs into her skin. The chair landed on the floor in pieces.

And Marielle, her palms still cradling the storm of magic, slammed her hands together.

The storm exploded outward—a silvery-clear pulse of magic that tore through the cottage, blew out the windows, and sent Blue hurtling through the door.

She landed on her back in the same bed of lavender, and all the air left her body. Frantically, she tried to ease the fist that had wrapped around her lungs as the cottage creaked and tilted, cracks running along its walls. She had to get up. Get to Nessa.

A thin wheeze of air flowed into Blue's lungs, and she struggled to her feet. Dread was a shroud of stone wrapped around her as she mounted the steps once more and saw Nessa held tightly in the wraith's grasp while Riva lay in an awkwardly crumpled heap on the floor.

"You're supposed to be dead." The wraith spat the words at Nessa, its black eyes blazing with fury.

So are you. Nessa was bleeding from her ears, and there were bruises blooming on her face, but she was alive, and Blue had to keep her that way.

A thud sounded behind Blue, and distantly she thought she heard Kellan's voice shouting, but all her attention was focused on Nessa. The princess squirmed in the wraith's grasp, clawing at the hands that held her, terror in her eyes.

Blue ran into the cottage.

The wraith opened its mouth wide, double rows of jagged teeth gleaming, and Nessa screamed, a high, thin wail that tapered off abruptly as the wraith sank its teeth into her shoulder.

"No!" Blue leaped over Riva's body and threw herself at the

wraith. It was like throwing herself at a boulder.

Desperately, she cast around for something to use as a weapon. The floor was scattered with debris. Books, parchment, jars of herbs, Riva's wand, and the broken bits of the chair Nessa had used against Marielle.

Only one of those had any chance of being the kind of weapon Blue needed.

Blue snatched up the wand and waved it at the wraith.

Nothing happened.

Nessa's body twitched, and she moaned as the wraith continued feeding.

Panic blazed through Blue, but she forced herself to think. A wand concentrated magical power. Blue's power told her what wanted harvesting. What to combine. And bonded those things together. She had to think about what she wanted to harvest. What she wanted to combine. She had to will those things to bond.

She drew in a deep breath and raised the wand as Kellan burst into the cottage. He brushed past her as he attacked the wraith, desperately trying to wrench his sister from the monster's grasp.

Blue made herself look at nothing but the wraith. Think of nothing but the wraith. The wraith and Blue.

Harvest the wraith. Combine it with my blood. Bond us together.

She aimed the wand at the wraith and held fast to what she wanted.

Her magic ignited, a swirling firestorm of power and hunger aimed straight at Marielle.

"Kellan, get back." Her voice, full of magic, echoed throughout the cottage, shaking its walls.

The wand shivered eagerly in her fingers.

He stumbled back, one hand still on Nessa, his eyes beseeching Blue to save his sister.

She wasn't going to let him down.

The storm churned through her veins, boiled in her blood, and then exploded out of the wand in a stream of brilliant light. The light struck the wraith, wrapped around its chest, and sank into its body.

Marielle dropped Nessa and came for Blue.

Blue opened her arms, her skin swelling with the poisonous blood that flowed in her veins. The wraith collided with her, mouth gaping wide. There was a flash of bright, burning pain as it sank its teeth into her neck, an instant of seeing the horror on Kellan's face, and then there was simply nothing.

FORTY-SIX

KELLAN WAS DESPERATE.

The wraith had Blue pinned to the floor, its vicious fangs sunk deep into the side of her neck. Every pull, every swallow of blood sent a tremor through her. Her eyes were closed, and she looked weaker by the second.

Nessa was huddled beside him, blood slowly dripping down her shoulder from the wraith's bite mark. She shivered as she stared at Blue.

Save her.

"I have to save you first, or she'll never forgive me," he said in a voice that broke at the end.

Pulling his coat from his shoulders, he wrapped Nessa in its warmth and scooped her up. Her hands moved furiously.

Put me down and save her. It's killing her.

"And she's killing it. She bonded a powerful poison to her blood as a trap for the wraith. We have to trust that she knows what she's doing." Please, please let Blue know what she was doing. Otherwise, he'd just condemned her to a pointless death, and he'd never be able to live with himself.

If you won't save her, I will.

Kellan's arms tightened around his sister, and he hung on for a moment as he pressed a kiss into her hair. "You already did. You followed her, and I followed you."

Actually, the enchanted dancing slipper had done the following. It had pulled him through the city streets, out of the western gate, and down the lane until he'd reached an orchard in time to hear the thunderclap of the wraith's magic as it half destroyed the cottage. But he didn't say any of that to Nessa. Not when he needed her to believe her job was done so that she'd stay clear of the wraith.

Settling her on the porch, his coat securely wrapped around her, he said, "Stay here, Nes. I can't concentrate on helping Blue if I have to worry about you too."

She nodded once, tears shining in her eyes, and then he raced back into the cottage and fell to his knees beside Blue.

The wraith was still drinking, its clawlike fingers tangled in Blue's golden dress, its tattered black cloak spread out behind it.

Kellan drew his sword.

How much poison did it need to drink before the venom took hold? How much blood could Blue afford to lose? How long before trusting Blue turned into simply letting her die when he might have saved her?

Another swallow. Another tremor through Blue, this one much weaker than the last. A tiny gasp of air as Blue's chest started to rise and fall faster and faster.

She was dying, and the wraith was still drinking. The numb

corner of his heart shattered into brilliant splinters of pain.

Maybe she'd weakened it. Maybe as the poison bonded with the wraith's blood, it would die slowly. Kellan no longer cared. The time for waiting was over.

He stood, aimed his sword at the back of the wraith's neck, and drove the blade down as hard as he could. The sword struck a shimmering, translucent barrier and bounced back, throwing Kellan to the floor.

It wasn't the wraith's magic. He'd experienced that firsthand in the ballroom. No, this was Blue's doing. She hadn't just used her blood to poison the wraith, she'd used her magic to bind the wraith itself to her until the poison did its job.

Slowly, he crawled back to her side, grief swelling in his throat.

There was nothing he could do to save her. She'd sacrificed herself for the kingdom. For Nessa.

For him.

She'd known all along that this might be the outcome. She'd spent their entire dance trying to tell him good-bye. She wanted to be remembered as the girl in the yellow dress who'd loved him first.

Kellan didn't want memories. He wanted Blue.

The wraith shuddered—a quick, jerky movement that pulled its mouth free of Blue. Kellan shoved it, and it fell to the floor. Swallowing hard at the gaping wound in Blue's neck, he tore off his shirt and pressed it against the bleeding.

"Don't touch . . . poison." Blue's voice was a faint whisper.

"Shh," he said, his voice desperate as he swept a shaking hand over her face. "Stop worrying about me. Save your strength."

The wraith was on all fours, fingers dug into the wooden

floor like claws, mouth hanging open while blood dripped from her fangs. Her black eyes were wild as a guttural, choking sound escaped her throat.

"What have you done?" she rasped as her back arched, and lesions split her skin, leaking blood and puss.

Kellan whipped his head toward the wraith and snarled, "She killed you. She figured out how to do the one thing no one else could do, and she killed you."

The wraith gnashed her teeth as foam rose from her throat to spill out of her mouth. A howl of rage and agony tore through her as she convulsed. Kellan curled over Blue, shielding her body with his as the last of the wraith's magic slammed into them, a hundred shards of power trying to rip them to pieces. He hung on, his breath coming in quick, hard pants as he absorbed the brunt of the attack.

The cottage shook, its walls groaning as debris danced across the trembling floor. And then the wraith collapsed and went still.

"You did it," he whispered against Blue's ear. "You killed the wraith."

Blue was silent.

He pulled back and looked at her. Her eyes were closed, her lips pale, and her breath was shallow. "You can beat this," he said. "Come on, Blue. You're the strongest person I know. You can survive."

He was lying. He could see it in the weakness of her body, the graying pallor of her skin. She couldn't survive the poison in her blood and the drain of losing so much of that blood to the wraith. He didn't know how to help her, but he knew someone who might.

"I'm taking you to Grand-mère. Stay with me, Blue. Just hold on long enough for me to get to her."

He bent to gather Blue in his arms, and then Nessa was there. Pushing him aside, her hands full of herbs, roots, and dried leaves, she crouched beside Blue. Setting her things down, she signed rapidly. *Move your shirt. We have to draw the poison out of her blood.*

"I'm taking her to Grand-mère's."

There's no time! I know how to make a tincture that will combat poison.

"Nes, she bound it to her blood with magic. It's not coming out." He bent to gather Blue in his arms, but Nessa threw out her hands to stop him.

Then we bond a healing potion to her blood instead.

Kellan paused, a faint hope stirring in his heart. "You know how to do that?"

I know how to make a healing potion. Blue taught me. Usually you have to let it steep and then cure it for forty-eight hours, but we'll figure out another—

"Use her blood. It bonds things. Just . . . here." He pulled his shirt from her neck, wincing at the amount of bright crimson blood that was soaked into the fabric. "Make your potion on my shirt. Her blood will touch all of it. That should bring the ingredients together faster, and then you can put it directly into her wound."

Nessa didn't hesitate. Quickly and competently, she sorted through the items she'd gathered, placing a pinch of this, a leaf of that, and a dusting of something that looked like gold on Kellan's shirt. When she was done, she uncorked a jar of oil and poured that over the pile of herbs and leaves. Then she gathered the unstained edges of the shirt, covered her hands with the fabric, and pressed them into the ingredients so that the excess blood in the shirt rose up to meet the mixture.

"What if the poison in her blood alters the potion?" Kellan asked, his stomach in knots.

Nessa raised one brow without looking away from her task.

"You're right. What choice do we have?"

The shirt began to sizzle, and steam that smelled of wintermint, herbs, and blood rose from it. Nessa unfolded the shirt and lifted it to Blue's neck. Kellan reached over to steady her hands, and together they poured the potion into the wound.

"How will we know if it's working?"

We wait and see. Nessa squeezed her brother's hand and then let go. *You love Blue, don't you?*

"Yes."

You should choose her.

An ache spread through Kellan's chest. "I wish I could, little bird."

Well, you're going to be the king.

"That doesn't make me above the law."

Maybe the law should take into account the fact that Blue sacrificed herself to save the entire kingdom.

Before Kellan could answer, Blue sucked in a deep gasp of air, and her eyes flew open. Her back arched, and her hands curled into fists as she cried out in agony.

"We're here." Kellan wrapped his arms around her and pulled her to his chest, holding on as pain racked her body. "We're right here. You're going to be all right."

For a long moment, she seemed determined to prove him a liar. She shook, her skin cold and clammy, her eyes wild and unseeing. But then she whispered, "The wand."

Nessa snatched the hazel-wood wand off the floor and shoved it into Blue's hand. Blue closed her eyes, and then the tip of the wand began to glow. She tried to point it at her neck, but her arms trembled too badly. He wrapped his hand around hers and helped guide the tip of the wand until it hovered just above the wound.

"Something. Contain," she said through gritted teeth.

"Nessa, a jar," Kellan said.

Nessa grabbed the jar that held the oil, dumped its contents onto the floor, and then put its mouth just below the tip of the wand. Blue clenched her jaw and threw her head back as a stream of green-black liquid gathered at her wound and then rose, arcing from Blue's blood to the mouth of the jar in a graceful stream. When the last of it was inside the jar, Nessa capped it with steady fingers, and Blue slumped against Kellan's chest.

"Thank you," she whispered. "Both of you."

Kellan closed his eyes and pulled her as close as he could while his grief and fear settled into the realization that she had survived. He didn't have to say good-bye. Didn't have to live the rest of his days with nothing but memories and missing her.

Instead, he could spend the rest of his days loving her.

She sighed and snuggled closer, her breath growing soft and even as sleep took her.

Laws be hanged. Nessa was right. There had to be a way to honor the girl who'd sacrificed herself for the kingdom. A way to make her eligible for the betrothal without causing a war between the throne and the head families. There had to be a loophole, and he was going to find it.

Voices filled the garden, and then guards were charging

inside the cottage, their queen right behind them. She carried one of Blue's dancing slippers in her hand. Her eyes scraped over the cottage and landed on her children. With a cry of relief, she rushed to them and fell to the floor beside Kellan. Gathering Nessa onto her lap, she kept one arm around her daughter and wrapped the other around her son.

"How is Blue?" Her voice was husky with tears, her eyes swollen and red-rimmed.

"She'll be all right, thanks to Nessa," Kellan said softly. "Blue killed the wraith."

"I see that. I hope that creature suffered." The queen sounded vicious.

"She did." Kellan stroked a hand down Blue's back, grateful to feel warmth seeping into her skin as the healing potion did its work.

"How did Blue manage it? Valeraine couldn't figure out a potion strong enough to take the wraith down," the queen said.

His voice shook as he said, "She used the magic in her blood to bond two incompatible poisons so she could create the most venomous potion she could think of, and then she put it in her own bloodstream so that when she convinced Marielle to drink from her, her blood would bond the poison to the wraith."

"Brave girl." The queen let go of Kellan to rest her hand on Blue's head. "Sweet, smart, impossibly brave girl."

"I'm going to marry her," Kellan blurted.

Nessa grinned and bounced in her mother's lap.

He'd expected resistance. An argument. A reminder of everything that was at stake with the head families. Instead, the queen smiled.

"With the wraith dead, killed by magic used for good instead of evil, you could lift the ban and invoke a betrothal by trial," she said.

He blinked. A betrothal by trial was only used during betrothal periods when an heir felt unable to choose between qualified members of head families or in the very rare instances when there were no members who were of age. The heir set up a test, and the person who passed it gained the honor.

"I think Blue has been tested enough," he said slowly, while his mind raced. What could he set up that only Blue could pass?

Too bad the test wasn't who could kill the wraith. Nessa raised a brow at their mother, a clear challenge.

Kellan frowned, his gaze drifting around the cottage while he considered his options. When his eyes landed on the golden dancing slipper his mother had used to follow them to the cottage, he smiled.

"Nes, you're brilliant. It's only right that the throne honor the person who destroyed the biggest threat to our kingdom. And that person is the one whose foot fits into that golden slipper."

I hate to point out the obvious, but plenty of girls could fit into that shoe.

His smile widened. "Not when Blue's grandmother gets done with it."

FORTY-SEVEN

IT HAD BEEN three days since Blue had killed the wraith and then survived with the help of Nessa and Kellan. She'd spent those days in Grand-mère's house drinking healing teas, eating too much, and sleeping with Pepperell's suffocating weight planted firmly on her chest. Most of the time when she awoke, she found Kellan, Nessa, or both sitting just outside her room.

Nessa wanted to tell her all about her role in helping save Blue and wanted to know when Blue could teach her how to use a wand. She was devastated to learn that wands only worked for those with magic in their blood.

Kellan wanted to hold her. Walk with her in the orchard in companionable silence. Or haltingly describe how he'd felt when he thought she was dying.

The Chauveau girls had moved back to their quarter and were staying with an uncle and his sons. The royal magistrate was trying to determine who could claim ownership of the

Chauveau empire now that both Dinah and her creditor were dead. According to Grand-mère, the queen had her hands full sorting through that mess along with managing the blood debt the Roche family owed for Martin's crime of murdering Marisol Evrard and Genevieve Gaillard.

On the third day, Kellan showed up for breakfast, ate enough to feed at least five horses, and then leaned across Grand-mère's table and winked at Blue. "Time to get ready. I assume Grand-mère can make you another fancy dress?"

Blue frowned. "Ready for what?"

"My betrothal announcement. I didn't want to do another ball, obviously, so I called a special assembly. Every girl of eligible age in the city is required to be there."

"I . . . Every girl?" Her frown slid into a suspicious scowl.

"Every single one." He grinned.

Her eyes narrowed. "I don't think I'm feeling up to going anywhere."

He crooked one of his brows. "You were just telling me you wanted to go for a swim."

"A swim doesn't require a fancy dress and pretending."

"Oh? And what would you be pretending?"

"To enjoy myself." She looked down at her hands. Didn't he realize that she couldn't stand to see the boy she loved choose someone else?

His voice gentled. "Blue?"

Slowly she raised her eyes to his.

"Do you trust me?" he asked quietly.

"Yes."

He left his seat and crouched in front of her. "Do you know

how much I love you? How I'd rather die than hurt you?"

"Yes." She breathed the word as he framed her face and pulled her mouth to his.

His kiss was as gentle as his words, and she leaned into him until he pulled away and pressed his forehead to hers instead. "Then please believe me when I say that of everyone in the kingdom, you are the one person I desperately need to be present for the announcement today."

He kissed her again, and then Grand-mère cleared her throat sharply from the doorway.

"That'll be about enough of that foolishness in my kitchen. Get yourself to the castle, Kellan. And don't forget this." She shoved an object wrapped in cloth into his arms as he stood. "You've got four hours."

He nodded. "The announcement begins in one hour. Please don't be late."

"Faster you leave, faster I can magic up something fancy for Blue to wear."

And then Kellan was gone, and Blue was staring at her grandmother while Kellan's words echoed in her head.

"Why does he need me to be there today?" she asked.

"Let's get some flowers for the dress. Rynoir blooms, I think." She managed to sound both excited and smug.

"Grand-mère, why does he need me?" Blue's voice was sharp, as hope, painful and tender, bloomed. "He can't choose me."

"Can't he now?"

"No. It's the law."

"Well, I'm sure you know every little detail and possible loophole in all of Balavata's laws, so perhaps we'll just forget the dress after all." Grand-mère turned away, and Blue shot out of her chair.

"No, wait. What loophole?"

"Get yourself to the castle and find out."

An hour later, Blue stood in the grand receiving hall at the castle, surrounded by a crowd of girls her age, their parents or guardians in tow. The queen sat on a throne at the far end of the hall, dressed in regal red. Kellan stood at her side in his own formal attire. Nessa stood beside him, her face wreathed in smiles as she gazed out at the crowd.

Kellan held a flat red velvet pillow in his hands, one of Blue's dancing slippers balanced in its center. Blue caught her breath and raised her eyes to his face.

He was watching her, a shy, hopeful smile tugging at his lips. When he saw that he had her full attention, he winked.

Heat flushed her skin, and the fizzy feeling she got whenever she was with him exploded through her veins.

"Welcome!" The queen's voice filled the room, and the crowd went silent. "We are here for three reasons. First, to confirm the rumors that the dreaded blood wraith is dead, and our kingdom is free of the fear that she will haunt our streets."

Cheers rose from the crowd, and a few people close to Blue leaned in to whisper their gratitude. It was clear that the rumors of the wraith's death had also included quite a few stories of Blue's involvement in it all.

Kellan's smile widened.

"Second, we are here to confer upon Princess Vanessa the Royal Heart honor, a title usually reserved for heroes within our army who distinguish themselves in battle. In this case, Princess

Vanessa went into battle on her own, determined to follow the wraith, rescue her friend, and destroy the monster who has caused our kingdom so much pain. She was hurt in her battle, but she persevered and, in the end, saved the life of the person who managed to kill the wraith."

Nessa's mouth dropped open, and she signed rapidly as her mother nodded for the guard closest to her to present the large purple iron heart pendant to the princess. The queen smiled. "The princess thanks her kingdom for this honor and assures us she'd do it again, but that she's really glad she won't have to."

The crowd clapped enthusiastically for Nessa, who grinned as she fastened the pendant around her neck.

The queen continued, "Finally, we are here to complete the betrothal announcement that was interrupted at my son's ball three nights ago. Due to the unprecedented event of the wraith's appearance and subsequent defeat at the hands of a marriage-eligible girl in our kingdom, the throne is invoking a betrothal by trial."

An audible gasp swept the room, and several members of the head families looked furious. Someone sidled up to Blue and said softly, "You belong together, you know. Anyone with eyes can see it."

Blue turned to see one of Gen Gaillard's cousins. Julia or Janelle. Blue could never tell the twins apart. Her hair was swept to the side, her golden skin glowing against her blue gown, though her eyes look red-rimmed and exhausted. "Thank you," Blue said.

"No, thank *you*. What you did was incredibly selfless and brave. You'll make an amazing queen."

Queen.

Blue's heart thudded against her chest as she raised her eyes to Kellan's again. How was she supposed to be a queen? She knew nothing about ruling. Nothing about playing political games or flattering people. Her hands shook as she pressed them together. She would be a disaster.

Kellan stepped forward, the dancing slipper held in front of him. "This betrothal trial recognizes that a queen should be courageous, intelligent, selfless, and willing to do whatever it takes to protect the people in her kingdom."

Blue's nerves settled as he held her gaze, his eyes soft.

"The dancing slipper I hold was worn by the person who defeated the blood wraith at great personal sacrifice. She lost the shoe outside the witch's cottage the night of the ball. The betrothal trial states that I will only marry the girl whose foot fits this slipper."

Blue's brow rose. Any number of girls could fit that slipper.

Kellan sent her a look that clearly told her to trust him as parents rushed to line their daughters up ahead of their competition. Blue watched in bemusement as girl after girl stepped up to Kellan and tried to put her foot inside the shoe.

For one, the slipper lengthened until her foot slid right out as she tried to take a step. For another, it shrank until she could barely wedge her toes inside. Every girl in the kingdom stepped up to try on the slipper, and every girl failed to fit her foot inside the shoe.

When Blue was the last girl left, she stepped up to Kellan, the fizzy feeling in her veins sparkling like sunlight on water as he knelt before her and offered her the slipper. She rested one hand on his shoulder for balance and slid her foot into the shoe.

It fit perfectly.

The crowd erupted, but Blue didn't see anything but Kellan. Looking up at her, he said, "Blue de la Cour, this betrothal trial recognizes you as the bravest, smartest, most selfless person in the kingdom. You are the rightful next queen. Would you do me the honor of accepting my proposal?"

She leaned down, her lips a breath away from his, and said, "Yes."

He rose to his feet, pulled her into his arms, and kissed her. And then there was nothing but the taste of his lips, the heat of his skin, and the steady beat of his heart.

EPILOGUE

IF BLUE HAD to make one more decision—seven-tiered cake or eight? rose centerpieces or finola blooms? candles or antique lanterns?—she was going to scream. Add to that regular sessions with a tutor to train Blue on royal etiquette in Balavata and the other nine kingdoms, political maneuvering within Balavata's system of government, and all the many, many duties of a queen, and nearly every hour of her days was spoken for.

Those that weren't taken up with wedding planning and queen training were devoted to meeting with various heads of the royal staff, brunches with the head families, observing council meetings, and dress fittings with the royal seamstress since Grand-mere's magic dresses only lasted four hours and apparently Blue's wedding was going to be an all-day affair.

What she wouldn't give for one hour in her storeroom chopping up bolla root and experimenting with snake venom. Or a trip to her farmhouse just to sit in the garden and let the plants tell her which ones needed harvesting.

She closed the door to her suite of rooms in the castle's family wing and eyed Pepperell, who had taken to royal life like he'd been born to it. Her cat was sprawled on the fluffy red pillow the royal seamstress had made especially for him, a dish of cream and another dish of minced fish sitting close by.

"You're spoiled rotten," Blue said as she scratched his head and then opened the doors that led out to her balcony. He gave her a regal look as if to say, "I'm only getting what I deserve."

She stepped onto her balcony and leaned against the balustrade. The sky was a velvet black dusted with stars, and the warmth of late summer brushed against her skin like an invitation. She could smell the faint hint of salt in the air, though she was too far north to hear the sea.

How long had it been since she'd had a swim in the crisp, golden water? Two months ago, when she and Kellan had taken Nessa there for a picnic? Before the wedding loomed and every second of Blue's life was relegated to training her how to be a queen.

Longing was an ache in her chest that wouldn't be satisfied with anything the castle had to offer.

She needed her farmhouse. Her garden and her sea. A few precious hours when she was just Blue, not Bernadina de la Cour, future queen. Surely there was a safe way off the castle grounds. Stars knew, Kellan had accomplished the same feat more times than she could possibly count.

Her mind made up, she returned to her room and changed into dark gardening pants and a dark shirt. Pulling on a pair of sensible boots, she doused the candles in her room, crept out onto the balcony, and began climbing along the silver trim that lined the castle like metallic frosting.